I0740600

Samuel T. Livermore

A History of Block Island from its Discovery
in 1514, to the present time, 1876

ISBN/EAN: 9783337368357

Printed in Europe, USA, Canada, Australia, Japan

Cover: Foto ©Andreas Hilbeck / pixelio.de

More available books at **www.hansebooks.com**

A

HISTORY

OF

BLOCK ISLAND

FROM

ITS DISCOVERY, IN 1514,

TO

THE PRESENT TIME, 1876,

BY

REV. S. T. LIVERMORE, A. M.

"Knowledges are as Pyramids, whereof History is the Basis." — BACON.

HARTFORD, CONN

THE CASE, LOCKWOOD & BRAINARD CO.

1877.

Samuel T. Livermore

A History of Block Island from its Discovery

in 1514, to the present time, 1876

DEDICATION.

———

This volume, commenced as a Centennial Offering, by appointment of the Town Council of Block Island, in June, 1876, is respectfully

DEDICATED

To the Memory of

The Early Settlers of the Island;

to that of

Their Departed Posterity,

and to

The Inhabitants now Living,

by

THE AUTHOR.

PREFACE.

If any object to the title of this book on the ground of its containing the *facts* of history rather than history itself, our apology is that history is believed to be *in* the facts here presented, and that it will be better understood by those of limited culture than it would be if presented in the language of those who would fuse the facts into the philosophy of history. These facts have been gathered up hastily, and many of them snatched from the verge of oblivion, amid pressing duties of another character. They are here compiled for the pleasure and benefit of present readers, and for the use of some future historian who may pass them through his mental crucible, and bring out the golden current to the satisfaction of those who make the nice distinction between history and the facts of history. But in the meantime, let not the mint despise the mineral or the miner.

As for style, the writer has aimed at one point, and endeavored to shun another. Though in doing the first he has sacrificed the ornate for the naked, this has been done with the conviction expressed by Bacon, thus : "This nakedness as once that of the body is the companion of innocence and simplicity." In doing the second he has hoped to shun what the same great philosopher calls " the first distemper of learning, when men study words and not matter." Therefore those who read this book simply for the ornaments of language will be disappointed. Those who look for the waymarks of time on the extraordinary island here represented will be rewarded according to their own estimate of the facts herein presented. Part of these facts may seem trivial to some, while to others they may be valuable. There was some wisdom in the cock that disregarded the diamonds, but greedily picked up the barley corns. Others picked up the jewels. Another has well said : "Without a detail of the most trifling facts in the early history of New England it will be impossible to understand the nature of their present religious and political establishments." So, future generations will need a minute detail of our present condition.

In so small a work as this, covering a period of more than two centuries, nothing can be elaborate. And yet it is hoped there may be found here a sufficient concatenation of incidents and events to entitle this book to the character of a history rather than to that of mere chronicles. In the biographical sketches the writer has sought chiefly the weal of the Islanders, hoping to awaken in them a deeper interest in their genealogical records. He has also endeavored to give some outlines of the various classes of characters—or at least a specimen of each class. Perhaps good may thus result from enabling some to see themselves as others see them.

In these sketches are elements of history. Each generation, in a measure, transmits itself to posterity, and the people of to-day repeat the words, the acts, the feelings, habits, and manners of those who lived centuries ago.

The writer's sources of information have been obscure, remote, and various. A colony so isolated from the main land, without printing press, with no mails for one hundred and seventy years, with a very meager written record of its own, has remained more than two centuries without a published history, while many very erroneous accounts of the Island, written by visitors, have been sent abroad. Dependent upon tradition, to a great extent, the Islanders have perpetuated legends that have come down to the pres-

ent grotesque with fiction and superstition. A few of them
are here presented. from only one of which—the *Palatine*,
has it seemed necessary to lift the lion skin. The task of
gathering isolated fragments here and there upon the
main land, and of classifying them with others found upon
the Island. has been laborious and perplexing. Without
ready access to public libraries, while on the Island. the
writer has been favored with assistance from others. He
acknowledges his indebtedness to the courteous Librarian
of the Massachusetts Historical Society ; to the Boston
Public Library; to Mr. James Hammond of the Redwood
Library at Newport ; to Mr. Charles H. Dennison of San
Francisco ; to Mr. Ambrose N. Rose, Town Clerk of
Block Island ; to Hon. Nicholas Ball. of the same place ;
to the aged Islanders, and to others.

Errors, doubtless, will be discovered in this work, and
for them the writer offers no apology, but simply asks for
their discovery and correction, and that while the dross is
condemned the genuine metal may be accepted at its true
value. All information of its errors will be thankfully
received by the author, and while asking no praise, and
expecting no emoluments for his labor. he hopes to escape
unmitigated censure from the professional critic for the
presumption of making this humble offering to the public.

S. T. LIVERMORE.

Bridgewater, Mass., March 22, 1877.

BLOCK ISLAND.

DISCOVERY.

When Block Island was first *seen* by civilized navigators is only a matter of conjecture. When it was first inhabited by Indians will probably ever remain a mystery. The first account of it which we find was given in 1524, more than three and a half centuries ago. Its shores were then cursorily examined by the French navigator, Verrazzano, who gave a report of it to Francis I., king of France. He described its location as being about fifty leagues east from New York harbor, and as about three leagues from the main-land, and represented its form as similar to a triangle. He says, "It was full of hills, covered with trees, well-peopled, for we saw fires all along the coast." Evidently none of his crew landed to gain any knowledge of the inhabitants.

In 1614, ninety years after the French navigator passed its shores, the Dutch explorer and trader, Adrian Block, having been detained through the winter on Manhattan Island by the burning of his vessel and cargo of furs, built there a new one—a yacht, which he named the *Unrest*, of sixteen tons burthen, and with it explored the coasts of Long Island Sound, and from the fact of his giving his name to this Island it is more than probable that he landed on its shores, and from some particular liking gave it his own name. Those who admit this inference to be sufficient evidence of his visit here will accord to the *Unrest* the honor of being the first vessel anchored within the waters of this Island, as a visitor, and to

Adrian Block and his crew the distinction of being the first civilized men ever known to have come upon its soil.

In 1636, twenty-two years after Block's discovery, a trader from Boston, by the name of John Oldham—accustomed to traffic with the Indians, came to this Island with a small sailing vessel to trade with the Manisseans who "came into his boat, and having got a full view of commodities which gave them good content, consulted how they might destroy him and his company, to the end they might clothe their bloody flesh with his lawful garments." Their murder of Captain Oldham thoroughly advertised the Island in Boston, and doubtless gave to many in New England their first knowledge of its existence. The expedition which Massachusetts sent to the Island under the command of Col. John Endicott to punish the Indians here accomplished not only that object, but made a more thorough exploration of the Island than ever made before, and also established a claim to it by right of conquest. It was now considered fully discovered and explored, and its large and fertile plantations just disburdened of great crops of corn by the Indians, with heavily timbered forests, and splendid fishing-grounds, made it an inviting home for the pioneer settlers of the colonies.

ITS NAMES.

But few parts of the world, during the same period, can boast of more names than Block Island, and were we to predict which one of them would remain the longest we should say that its first name will be its last one to be spoken and written.

Manisses, was the first one known by the Indians who were its occupants when settled by the English. This name, according to the best interpretation we have, had a religious as well as a local signification, meaning the "Little God," or the "Little God's Island," having reference, probably, to its sachem, whom tradition represented as subordinate to the great Narragansett sachem on the main-land, and distinguishing him thus for his valor. Whittier, in his poem entitled "The Palatine," had good reason for choosing this euphonic, aboriginal name as the most poetic and desirable.

Claudia, comes next on the list. This name was given by Verrazzano, in 1524, in honor of the mother of King Francis I. It did not adhere, however, and after a trial of a century, being of no special honor to that worthy mother, one more substantial and enduring became its successor.

"*Adrian's Eyland*," soon after 1614, was the name put down upon the Dutch maps, and this was the name most familiar to those then sailing past its shores on trading expeditions to and from Manhattan. This name had the advantage of euphony and historic association with distinguished persons and places of antiquity.

Block Island, virtually the same as the one last-mentioned, was destined to be the name in 1876, and how long after none can say, by which the place was to be known most familiarly to the public. It was made so by the early settlers of the colonies, and whether intended or not, there was a prophecy in the name that was ominous to sailors, for upon its shores a multitude of fair vessels have fatally stumbled.

New Shoreham, in 1672, when the Island received its town charter from the Rhode Island Assembly, was made an antecedent, or prefix of the name Block Island. In that charter, the name of the incorporation is repeatedly given as "New Shoreham, otherwise Block Island." Whether the Islanders asked for this lumbersome name or not we cannot say. To some, at least, it is now suggestive of shores and blocks. The inhabitants, as is evident from their records, considered the name too heavy, and frequently wrote it simply *Shoreham*, or "*Shorum*." The long word—"otherwise," to connect the old and new names in the charter, they reduced to *alias*, and sometimes wrote it "*ales.*"

The reason for adopting the new name, in 1672, instead of being as newspaper correspondents have conjectured, is plainly stated in the charter, the authors of which were, perhaps, the committee consisting of Roger Williams, Thomas Olney, and Joseph Torrey, appointed in 1664 by the General Assembly "to draw up their thoughts to commit to the farther approbation or correcting, as commissionating them [Block Islanders] in point of preservation of his Majesty's peace there." The section alluded to in said charter reads as follows:

"And furthermore be it enacted, that the said town of Block Island, at the request and for the reasons by the inhabitants showed, and *as signs of our unity and likeness to many parts of our native country*, the said Block Island shall be called New Shoreham, otherwise Block Island." The shores of the New World were here associated with those of the Old, and the final syllable, *ham*, signifying a house, or farm, or village, had reference to "many parts" of England whose names terminate with a *ham*. There is also a New Shoreham in Sussex Co., Eng., on the Adur River, three miles from its entrance into the English Channel.

By popular consent the *New Shoreham* part of the name is now generally omitted, and Block Island is deemed sufficient, and thus the first step is taken in going back to the name *Manisses*. In the early part of the 18th century the Island was known to some extent in Massachusetts by the name of "*Ministerial Lands*," from the appropriation of a part of it for the support of a minister.

POSSESSION.

The first possession of the Island of which we have any account was that maintained by the Narragansett Indians. How long they had held it before Captain Oldham's trading expedition there in 1636, we are not informed. Judging, however, from the strength of the Narragansett tribe, they may be supposed to have owned it for centuries. It naturally belonged to them. from its location, as it now belongs to Rhode Island. lying. as it does, directly south of the middle of the southern boundary of said state, and twelve miles distant.

From the Indians it passed into the possession of Massachusetts soon after the death of Captain Oldham, in 1636. It was acquired by the conquest of Colonel Endicott to punish the natives. Its transfer to that colony was acknowledged by Miantinomo, the great sachem of the Narragansetts, to Governor Vane, in 1637, and was stated then to be "by right of conquest." This transfer and possession were acknowledged by its former possessors as, in "January, 1638, the Indians of Block Island sent three men, with ten fathoms of wampum for part of their tribute," to the Massachusetts Colony.

In 1637, Gov. Winthrop said : "Miantinomo, the Narragansett sachem, came to Boston. The governor, deputy, and treasurer treated with him, and they parted upon fair terms. He acknowledged that all the Pequod country and Block Island were ours, and promised that he would not meddle with them but by our leave."

In a letter from Roger Williams to Gov. Winthrop in 1637, the former stated that the sachems of the Narragansetts had left the Block Island Indians to the governor, at the time of Mr. Oldham's death, and "so have done since ;" that said sachems had sought the head of Audsah, the murderer of Oldham ; that the Block Island Indians had obligated themselves to pay to the Governor of Massachusetts 100 fathoms of beads annually, and that they were wholly said governor's subjects.

In 1658, the possession of Block Island was transferred from said colony to private individuals. The following account of this transfer is found in the Eccl. Hist. of New England : "1672, Nov. 3d, Block Island, granted in 1658, by Massachusetts, to John Endicott, Richard Bellingham, Daniel Dennison, and William Hawthorne, is now incorporated by the R. I. Assembly under the name of New Shoreham" (Vol. II. 549). That state having received this Island from the Indians in consideration of the damage they had done in the Oldham affair, had acquired a genuine title, and accordingly transferred it to these gentlemen. Soon they transferred its possession again, an account of which we obtain from a most authentic source, the old town records of Block Island, entitled,—

"NEW SHOREHAM TOWNE BOOKE MADE IN THE YEARE 1675."

This book contains a copy of the original compact of the first settlers of Block Island. This copy was taken by the town clerk, in 1695, from the "old book of Records," of the existence of which we can gain no information.

In 1660, the last transfer of Block Island, as a whole, was made by Messrs. Endicott, Bellingham, Dennison, and Hawthorne, selling the same to a company of sixteen men, most of · whom constituted its first settlers. The compact, purchase, and settlement were mainly as follows :—

"RECORD OF THE PURCHASING AND SETTLEMENT OF BLOCK ISLAND."

" *Memorandum in the year of our Lord 1660 ; as followeth :*—

"Mr. John Alcock, physician in the town of Roxbury, in the Colony of Massachusetts, being connected with Mr.

Thomas Faxun, Peter George, Thomas Terry, Richard
Ellis, Samuel Dering, Simon Ray, all of Braintree, with
sundry persons belonging to other towns :

"Mr. John Alcock acquainting them of an island that
was to be sold, namely, Block Island, which might make
a situation for about sixteen families, and also declaring
the price to be four hundred pounds, and that if they
would be concerned with him proportionably towards the
erecting a plantation on Block Island, he the aforesaid
John Alcock would then proceed in the purchase thereof,
granting him for his trouble and pains five pounds for a
sixteenth part, or twenty-five acres of land as an equivalent, and to be at equal proportion at payment for said
purchase in manner and form as followeth :

"Twenty-five pounds to be paid for every sixteenth part,
the remainder of the payment for to be paid in country
pay, such as the country afforded, and accordingly timely
notice was given unto all those that might think convenient
for to be concerned with the erecting the concerns aforesaid for to make their personal appearance at the house of
Mr. John Alcock, August the seventeenth 1660, then and
there to confer about the premises above mentioned, and
accordingly was forthwith attended by those hereunto
subscribed :

"Mr. John Alcock, M. D.	Simon Ray,
Thomas Faxon,	Felix Wharton,
Peter George,	Hew Williams.
Thomas Terry,	John Gluffer,
Richard Ellis.	Edward Vorse,
Samuel Dering,	John Rathbone.

"And according to the forementioned premises forthwith
agreed with Mr. John Alcock for the payment of said
Island proportionably as above mentioned, and also a consultation which way for to proceed concerning the erecting

a plantation on the ·aforesaid Block Island considering the remoteness thereof both by land and sea and could not be settled without great charge, whereupon some of our company began for to decline; still the remainder proceeded in the management thereof as voted all and every person that was concerned with land on Block Island should bear their equal proportion of all charges belonging unto the settlement thereof :

" Whereupon, for the premising and settlement of Block Island it was agreed upon that whose names here subscribed, Mr. John Alcock, Felix Wharton, Hew Williams, Thomas Terry, Samuel Dering, Simon Ray, all of them agreeing forthwith for to build a barque for the transporting of cattle to said Island for the settlement thereof, Thomas Terry, Samuel Dering, Simon Ray procuring the hull for to be built; Mr. John Alcock, Felix Wharton, Hew Williams for to provide the sails and rigging, and so accordingly proceeded in the management thereof. Further, for the better and quicker transporting of passengers, considering that there was no harbor, Samuel Dering, Simon Ray built a shallop upon their own cost and charge for the promoting and settling of said Island, and by the end of the year 1660 the barque and shallop were finished for the same purpose before mentioned, and William Rose, first Master of the barque for the employment that the barque was built for; and William Edwards, and Samuel Staples undertaking to sail the shallop around the Cape, and for to meet the passengers at Taunton there to take them in and sail for Block Island.

"In the year 1661 the barque set sail from Braintree, in the beginning of April, for Block Island. The shallop received its passengers at Taunton, namely :

" Thomas Terry,	Duncan Williamson,
Samuel Dering,	John Rathbone,

Simon Ray,	Edward Vorse,
Wm. Tosh,	Nicholas White,
Thormut Rose,	William Billings,
Wm. Barker,	⤙ Trustaram Dodge, ⤙
David Kimball,	John Ackurs,
Wm. Cahoone,	[Thomas Faxun had pre-ceded with the surveyor.]

"MEMORANDUM IN THE YEAR OF OUR LORD 1661.

"*Further Settlement of the Plantation Block Island.*

"Notice was given unto all the proprietors for to assemble themselves at the house of Felix Wharton, in Boston, the first Tuesday in September 1661, there to consult and agree upon some able knowing man to survey the Island that every purchaser might have his proportion that he or they might improve it to the best advantage they could, Mr. John Alcock propounding unto the assembly there met of a man that he knew for to be an able proved surveyor, one Mr. [Peter] Noyse of Sudbury, forthwith the assembly accepted of Mr. Alcock's proposal, and forthwith it was voted that Mr. Noyse, Mr. Faxun, an able knowing man, that they should go to Block Island and by lot divide unto every man concerned his due proportion as near as they could ; and so accordingly they did proceed in the managing thereof according unto directions of the purchasers and proprietors of said Island that took it into consideration at the time of this assembly and agreed upon that there should a quantity or portion of land be laid out for the help and maintainance of a minister and so continue forever, and accordingly Block Island was surveyed and lotted out proportionally unto the purchasers by Mr. Noyse and by Mr. Faxun, as doth appear by the surveyor's works in the plot and draught of said Island measured and bounded unto every purchaser according to proportion by lot as followeth :

2*

"The North Part of the Island as by Lot.

"Mr. Richard Billings,	-	- First Lot.
Mr. Samuel Dearing, -	-	- 2 "
Nathaniel Wingley, Tormot Rose,	-	3 "
Edward Vorse, John Rathbone,	-	4 "
Thomas Faxon (2 lots),	-	- 5 & 6 "
Richard Ellis, -	-	- 7 "
Felix Wharton,	-	- 8 "
John Glover, -	-	- 9 "
Thomas Terry,	-	10 & 11 "
James Sands, -	-	- 12 "
Hew Williams,	-	- 13 "
John Alcock, -	-	- 14 "
Minister's Land,	-	- 15 "
Peter George, -	-	- 16
Simon Ray, -	-	- 17 "

"The Western Part of the Island as by lot Divided:

"Mr. Thomas Faxon, -	-	- 1 & 2 Lots.
Nathaniel Wingley, Tormot Rose,	-	3 "
Thomas Terry,	-	- 4 & 5 "
Felix Wharton,	-	- 6 "
John Alcock, Physician,	-	- 7 "
P. George and S. Ray,	-	- 8 & 9 "

" South East Part of the Island.

"John Rathbone and Edward Vorse, -	10 Lot.
Richard Billings,	-	- 11 "
Richard Ellis, -	-	- 12 "
Hew Williams the thirteenth,	-	13 "
John Glover and James Sands,	14 & 15 "
Samuel Dering,	-	- 16 "

"The other small divisions by lot divided unto every purchaser by proportion.

"The above written on both sides, being a true copy extracted out of the old book of records of memorandum for the first settling of Block Island, by me,

November this 29th 1695

Pr NATH¹ MOTT
Town Recorder."

The above memoranda are here given verbatim, but not in all cases *literatim*; the spelling is almost too antique to be intelligible. From the foregoing record it is seen that several of the purchasers in the compact were not among the very first settlers. It seems, too, that after the company of sixteen bought the Island in 1660. they built their transporting vessels in the fall and winter of 1660–1 ; sailed from Braintree "in the beginning of April" 1661, as Braintree then was bounded on the north by Neponset River and Massachusetts Bay ; and in September of 1661 sent forward Messrs. Noyes and Faxun to survey and apportion the Island ; and it is probable the company did not embark from Taunton before the spring of 1662. The proprietors were all notified to meet in Boston in September, 1661. There they appointed their surveyor, who was needed to apportion the Island before the settlers moved there, that each might know where to locate. After his appointment, the time necessary for his journey, and for his complicated task would necessarily delay the settling party at their old homes, or at Taunton, into the winter of 1661, and hence they probably moved in the spring of 1662, and then by their possession and improvement of the land established the titles which have descended to succeeding generations.

From Taunton it is supposed they sailed down the Taunton River, into Narragansett Bay, followed the coast down to Point Judith, and thence crossed to Block Island, landing at Cow Cove, as then quite a bay was there and as it is supposed the first cow ever upon the Island there swam ashore, greatly to the amusement of the native spectators.

THE ISLAND.

LOCATION.

It is located directly south of the central part of Rhode Island, twelve miles from the main-land. It is southwest from Newport about thirty miles, and about eighteen miles north of east from Montauk, the east end of Long Island. According to the Coast Survey, its position is: latitude 41° 08′ North, longitude, 71° 33′ West, and it lies so far out in the sea that in summer its surface is cooled by the most refreshing breezes, and in winter its hills are swept by fearful gales, and its shores are wreathed with the white foam of assaulting billows. It is about eight miles long, and three miles wide, longest N. W. and S. E.

> " Circled by waters that never freeze,
> Beaten by billows and swept by breeze,
> Lieth the Island of Manisses."

SURFACE AND SOIL.

The little pilgrim band of settlers came prepared for hardships, evidently putting in practice Bacon's maxim that,—"In counsel it is good to see dangers, and in execution not to see them except they be very great." The exception, however, they seem to have disregarded. There is reason for believing that on their arrival at the Island, after a scrutinizing glance at the features of the natives, they looked with unusual surprise upon the singular surface that many years before had drawn from the passing voyager the remark to his king : "It was full of hills." It is doubtful whether a more uneven surface on the earth can be pointed out than that of Block Island. The steep sides of a high mountain may be inclined planes of an even surface, but here we have neither even hill-sides, nor level plains. No person ever saw the surface of the ocean more uneven than is the land of Block Island, excepting those who witnessed the flood in the days of Noah. It is necessary to resort to the imagination to give an adequate view of this extraordinary unevenness which puts this Island among the natural curiosities to the observer.

Imagine, then, several tidal waves moving in nearly the same direction—from west to east, each rising about one hundred and fifty feet above the level of the sea, and their bases nearly touching each other ; and on the tops, sides, and intervals of these, "chop-waves" in every conceivable shape and position covering completely the tidal waves ; and when the reader has done this he has an outline of the view under the observer's eye who stands in a good light upon Beacon Hill.

Another peculiarity of the surface found by the first settlers has almost entirely disappeared. When they landed on the Island it must have been difficult in some places to have stepped amiss of a stone. A glance at the walls now standing are evidence enough that before they were built the surface of the ground was wellnigh paved with small bowlders. It is no exaggeration to say that more than three hundred miles of stone-wall now constitute the fences of Block Island. From this fact one may infer how stony the ground was in its natural condition. These stones are all so nearly round as to present the appearance caused by the action of glaciers or of the ocean. While they so frequently disturbed the plow and the hoe of the pioneers, few, perhaps, thought of their great value in future ages to fence the fields after the primitive forests had disappeared.

A heavy growth of timber clothed much of the surface of the Island at the time of its settlement. One would hardly think this possible while looking upon its present nakedness. But for sixty years after the settlers came they had an abundance of timber for building their houses and barns, and their fences, and for their fuel. In 1689, when our vessels and the French privateers had an engagement near the Island, Rev. Samuel Niles, a witness on the land, says the artillery echoed loudly from the woods. Those acquainted with forests and echoes know that the latter come from the former only when the trees are large and standing near each other. Oak, hickory, elm, ash, cedar, and pine were abundant. But as the term "firing," then used for the word "fuel," is still common among the islanders, so the notion then that the products of the soil were more desirable than the timber, still continues. So long has the destitution of native timber here existed that when the writer came upon the Island in 1874, not an inhabitant knew where, or when the forest trees were standing. Their existence is demonstrable from incidental fragments of history.

As the timber disappeared, the necessity of making walls for fences secured the clearing of the fields until they became smooth and beautiful, inviting to the plow and the mower. The industrious farmers have also filled many a slough with the thousands of cart-loads of small cobble stones. No ledges meet the eye. None have yet been discovered on the Island. There are bowlders, however, large enough to be blasted for walls, and to be split for the stone-cutter.

The settlers found perhaps a better soil than they left in Massachusetts. The inexhaustible stores of peat in the little swamps of the Island are evidence of the fertility of the soil which produced those stores composed of leaves, bark, nuts, roots, and decayed wood, all of which were washed down the little steep hills into the little deep valleys at their feet. The northerly part of the Island was distinguished for its great crops of Indian corn long before the settlers came in 1662. In 1636. Col. Endicott found and destroyed there immense stores of corn, and the settlers gave to that part the name "Corn Neck," having reference to the great products of that cereal. The soil is not, and possibly never has been suitable for raising wheat. It has no lime apparently. Its stones are granite with hardly an exception. Its basis is sand and gravel, with a few spots of valuable clay. The sand is impregnated with iron, and in some localities the black iron sand predominates. There are acres of it along the bathing-beach. Rye, barley, oats, and potatoes have been the principal products of the soil, which everywhere has alluvial appearances, is quick, and excellent for producing garden vegetables and luxuries, for the culture and enjoyment of which the Islanders have never attained to more than a negative distinction.

The distribution of water over the Island not only adds to its extraordinary beauty, but also supplies the farms with exhaustless pools, ponds, and moisture. It is doubtful whether another part of the continent has, on so small a surface, so many unfailing deposits of water. They are spoken of in detail under the subject of Ponds, in this volume. Their water is not the most wholesome, for it is almost invariably impregnated more or less with peat or iron, or both, from both or either of which but few springs and wells on the Island are free. Cistern water is the better and more common for domestic purposes.

RESOURCES OF BLOCK ISLAND.

PEAT AND TIMBER.

The most important of the Island's resources may be distinguished as *Peat, Sea-weed,* and *Fish.* This classification, at first, may cause a smile with some, but not with those who for years have been studiously seeking an answer to the question,— *What has kept Block Island from barrenness and depopulation?* One hundred and fifty years ago the inhabitants looked upon this question with alarm. A town meeting was then called for its consideration. Wood was the only article then used here for fuel ; but that was rapidly diminishing. In the preamble of that meeting it was said that there was "great scarcity of timber and fencing stuff and many people hath not enough for firing and fencing, and the main land being so far off from this place, so that if we do not endeavor to preserve our timber and fencing stuff *the inhabitants must be forced to depart the Island.*" Their fences could be made of stone and ditches, and the timber for building could be brought from the main-land, but to bring to the Island all of its fuel was too much, and the sense of the town *then* was that before this would be done the Island would be depopulated. What, then, prevented this depopulation when the *wood* of the Island was exhausted? That little, humble word, *Peat,* furnishes the answer, and for one hundred years it kept the growing population comfortable, cooking their food and warming their cottages, in which some of the hardiest, most active and distinguished persons of the country were born and reared. Yes, it was a wise pro-

vision of Providence that put so many deep pockets into
the surface of this Island and filled them so full of fuel.
Without it men would have come here in boats in the
fishing season, but not to remain with their wives and
children. Then let poets sing as they may of this kind
of fuel. of

> "Old wives spinning their webs of tow,
>   Or rocking weirdly to and fro
> In and out of the *peat's* dull glow,"

a glance at the Island to-day is proof enough that
spinning and rocking were not *all* they did by those humble firesides. Nor has the day yet dawned when their
descendants can dispense entirely with this kind of fuel.
To a considerable extent it is still used by the poorer families, and to some extent in nearly all. Indeed. it is within
the memory of many of the inhabitants that a ton of
Franklin coal here was not worth a pound of tobacco, for
an Islander, in 1846, took that quantity in his boat, where
it had been thrown from a wreck upon the shore, and
carried it to Providence and there sold it for a pound of
said stuff. Peat had been the common fuel, and was adequate until something better could be substituted. It did
good service, for without it the Island long since would
have been nearly, if not quite, destitute of families, especially in winters, and a few fishing shanties would have
occupied the shores, instead of the many comfortable
homesteads and popular hotels now existing.

There are some interesting facts concerning the *fuel* of
Block Island. One of them is, that the inhabitants, in
1875, had lost the knowledge, to a great extent. of the
use that their ancestors had made of the native timber.
After a residence among them of more than a year the
best information which the writer could obtain from them
on the subject was only traditional that timber once grew

upon the Island, corroborated by reference to the peat deposits, and that said timber was used by the early settlers for building purposes. A thorough searching, however, of some of the old and almost illegible records has brought to light the fact that when the Island was settled, heavy forest timber was abundant here, and supplied the people with wood for fuel and timber for buildings and fences. In an inventory of Robert Guthrig's estate, in 1692, mention was made of "forty-two acres *in the west woods*, at 20 shillings per acre."

Rev. Samuel Niles, in his history of the *Indian and French Wars*, says he was on Block Island during a naval engagement between the French and English near the Island about the year 1690, and that "In this action the continued fire was so sharp and violent, that the *echo in the* WOODS made a noise as though the limbs of the trees were rent and tore off from their bodies." Such an echo could be only in a dense forest of large trees.

In 1714 the town enacted "That no manner of persons whatever cut any timber, trees, or poles on any man's land without his leave, and if any person do he shall pay the sum of five shillings for every tree or pole so cut."

In 1721, the venerable Simon Ray, always seeking the welfare of his fellow-citizens, secured the following enactment from the freeholders at a town meeting :

" Whereas this town of New Shoreham, being settled sixty years, by which long continuance of the inhabitants thereof hath occasioned great scarcity of timber and fencing stuff, and many people hath not enough for firing and fencing, and the main-land being so far off from this place, so that if we do not endeavor to preserve our timber and fencing stuff the inhabitants must be forced to depart the Island :

"Therefore it is enacted by the freemen of the town above said that an upright fence shall not be above four feet high from the ground to the top thereof, and if it be hedge and ditch, or stone ditch, or stone wall, it shall be in the same proportion according to the town viewers, and no persons whatsoever shall be constrained to make any fence against his neighbors higher than the above said, and if any cattle, sheep, or horses break through or over such fence they shall be counted unruly, and where the trespass is made the damaged person shall have his damage, any clause, act, or acts to the contrary notwithstanding, in this town above named."

This act was voted upon by each freeman making a dot with a pen under the word "Pro," or "Con," those under "Pro" being seventeen, and those under "Con," being four, twenty-one in all. In the surveys of land also mention was made of a "hickory tree," of a "black oak," and of a "cedar." In the peat deposits roots and trunks of large trees are frequently discovered. The kinds of timber most common here were oak, elm, pine, hickory, ash, and cedar, with a thick growth of alders, in swampy places, which were small and numerous.

That peat was not burned here until after the year 1721 is quite certain, for then its value was not understood, as may be seen from the fact that without timber the inhabitants supposed they would be obliged to leave the Island. There were stones in abundance for fencing, and for houses, and Capt. James Sands had a stone house. But the absence of fuel was sufficient to compel a depopulation, a thing which the people would not have feared if they had known the use of peat as now understood.

Peat as the common fuel of the Island became so about the year 1750. Who introduced its use we cannot ascertain. For about one hundred years it was the only fuel, except as small supplies were had, for a few families, from wrecks, and from boats bringing wood from the main-land. The quality of the peat was found to be excellent, making, when properly dried, a very hot fire. Much of it has lost its woody appearance, and looks more like dark mud than like fuel, and it burns with an intensity which indicates, in some instances, the presence of petroleum. Around its dim light in old-fashioned fireplaces several generations were warmed and fed for a hundred winters, contented with their lot, and little dreaming of the better time coming, when cargoes of coal should be landed in a national harbor on Block Island, when stoves should supersede the fire-place, and kerosene and gas the dull light of peat and candles.

It was well distributed among the inhabitants, many families owning shares in the same beds, and this ownership has been transmitted down from generation to generation until now. The beds are also numerous, and in every part of the Island. Some cover several acres, and others are much smaller. Some are shallow, and others are deep, and most of them were formed by vegetable matter, leaves, bark, nuts, grass, ferns, decayed wood, etc., that for ages had been washed down the surrounding steep little hill-sides. Thus peat beds were deposited upon some of the highest parts of the Island, as upon Clay Head, and the supply was ample, if not exhaustless.

The present quantity of peat on the Island cannot be estimated easily. Those best prepared to judge readily, admit that if the present population, eleven hundred and fifty, were to remain uniform for a hundred years, with no other fuel than the peat which they now have, their supply would be abundant. Three beds of considerable known size, that may be very much larger than known to be, one on the east side of the Island, and two on the west, extend a considerable distance from the shore into the ocean. It is stated by Mr. Anderson Dickens, a gentleman of careful observation and truthful estimate, that at low tide, on the west side, he has traced one bed from high-water mark one quarter of a mile out into the sea and there brought away peat that burned well after it was dried. Similar observations warrant the above estimation of the one hundred years' supply. It is still used to a considerable extent, and where it is used the passer-by is generally informed by its peculiar odor.

Tug is its more common name among the Islanders, a name applied to it more than a century ago, and refers to the hard work of getting it from the bed. There it is very wet and heavy. Sometimes it lies so deep as to require much effort to throw it out with shovels. It is then carted away in the consistency of mud, and dumped upon smooth ground where it is made into balls, about six inches in diameter, with naked hands, and these balls are dropped side by side upon the sward, flattening out considerably next to the ground, and there are left to dry for one, two, or three weeks, and then they are stacked up in little pyramids about three feet high until thoroughly dried, when they are drawn in carts to the *tug-house*. A fire made from it needs to be frequently replenished. Its value, in equal quantity with hard wood, is some less than the latter. Peat dug in 1875, on the Island, 544 cords.

During the past few years many cords of wood have been brought from Long Island, and sold for about the same as it costs upon the main-land.

Hard coal, as fuel upon Block Island, was introduced about the year 1846. Previous to that it was valueless here because there were no stoves in which it could be burned. A cargo of it thrown from a wreck was lying then in Cow Cove. Jonathan Ball, going to Providence, took a ton of it in his boat, and on his arrival sold it to a Mr. Lloyd for one pound of tobacco, as previously stated. When first introduced some had great fears of its burning up their stoves. Now it is used quite extensively in nearly every family. About three hundred tons are con-

3*

sumed annually, and it is shipped to the Island directly. A soft species has been lately discovered on the Island, near the harbor.

SEA-WEED.

Sea-weed has been another indispensable resource of Block Island. Its soil in the outset was fertile, but its fertility soon would be exhausted unless duly replenished. As long ago as 1779 it was a serious question with far- mers how they should maintain the productiveness of their land. Even during the Revolution, when communi- cation between the Island and the main was almost anni- hilated, and so many articles from the main were needed here, the little boat that brought back other necessaries brought also "a quantity of ashes," and these were doubt- less intended for the soil, but were quite inadequate. That the use of sea-weed as a fertilizer was common anciently is evident from the antiquity of the claims established along the beach. The tenacity with which these claims are now held by the Islanders indicates their value. Without the grasses torn from the rocks along the shore, and from the meadows on the bottom of the sea—torn loose and driven upon the shores during the storms of autumn, winter, and spring, the farms of Block Island, long ago, would have become utterly barren. This is easily demonstrated by the sterile condition of those fields too common here that might never repay the cost of making them fertile. The same is also proved by the productiveness of the many fields where the sea com- pensates for the exhaustion of the ample harvest.

The shores of the Island are minutely divided into claims, where each man gathers this invaluable fertilizer. In the midst of storms, and immediately after them, men and boys may be seen with forks and rakes gathering it on the beach, not waiting always for it to land, lest the receding tide or change of wind might bear it away beyond their reach. While it is attainable it is either put into piles on the shore, above the tide, and subsequently carted to the farm, or it is put directly into the vehicle and spread upon the field, or put into large heaps of compost near the fields for which it is intended. In the latter case it is usually composted with soil, muck, and fish offal, lying from fall until spring, and frequently it is put into barn-yards, and into pig-yards until it is decomposed, or nearly so.

Sea-weed is used in various ways. On arable lands it is either spread over the field and then plowed under, or it is put into the hill by the planter, who uses it freely for corn, potatoes, beans, and garden vegetables. For grass, its most profitable use seems to be that of covering the meadow completely in autumn. Two important things are thus accomplished—protecting the grass-roots, in the absence of snow, from the frosts, winds, and sun in winter, and at the same time nourishing the soil by the salt in the sea-weed, and by the decomposition of the latter. Thus beautiful crops of the best qualities of grass are produced, the soil kept from sterility, and the Island saved from an otherwise inevitable depopulation.

The quantity of sea-weed used upon the Island is immense. The annual gathering begins in October and continues, at intervals, until April. The portions of the beach owned by the town exhibit the greatest industry. There the weed is common property, and those who are there first in the morning, latest at night, and wade into the surf the deepest, are generally most profited, excepting those who thus secure a crop of pains called *rheumatic.* This kind of industry, common and private, on public and individual beaches, secures an annual value that could not be bought of the Islanders for twenty thousand dollars, nor could they get an equal quantity of fertilizers from abroad for fifty thousand dollars. Its quantity, as reported by the last census, was six thousand cords, gathered on the shores of Block Island in the year 1875. This quantity is equal to over ten thousand single team loads, and each load is worth more than two dollars. Hence, this resource of the Island, during the period of twenty-five years, amounts to the handsome sum, or its equivalent, of half a million of dollars.

That sea-weed is an indispensable resource here is demonstrated thus: Without it the Island would become sterile; without a productive soil here the population could not be supported, since for that the fisheries are inadequate, and neither manufacturing nor commerce here exists. But the Islander rejoices in the abundance of the sea which supplies him with fish as well as with vegetation.

BLOCK ISLAND FISHERIES.

The natives, centuries ago, were greatly dependent upon the fisheries of the Island for their support. To what degree they subsisted upon fish we have no means of knowing. The only relics of their implements for fishing with which the present Islanders have any knowledge, are the stone sinkers used on the fish-lines of the Indians. These were round pebbles weighing from half a pound to two pounds, taken from the beach. They were fastened to the lines by having a groove cut around them into which the line was sunk and tied. Their size and weight are good evidence of the depth of water in which they were used, and this depth indicates the size and kind of fish caught by the Manisseans. Their wampum strings were evidence that they did not fish with "grape vines" for lines, as some have supposed. For hooks they may have used a sharp, slender tooth fastened to a bone, or to a slim stone for a shank, as did the ancient natives of the Sandwich Islands. That the Indians caught fish in 1675 may be inferred from the fact that then Peter George's Negro, Wrathy, was made the more wrathy by being whipped with twelve lashes for "staling fish from Steven, the Endian."

The fisheries of Block Island were doubtless considered as one of its unfailing resources by the first and early settlers, and as such the fisheries have proved to be for more than two centuries. And at the present time, with all the modern improvements of agriculture, and with the increasing income from summer visitors, and all other resources, there is good reason for believing that were it not for the fisheries here the population would soon be more than decimated, and by the absence caused by this decimation the remaining portion would be greatly reduced in property and numbers within a few years. Indeed, the amusement of fishing, and the luxury of eating the fish direct from the salt water is a great attraction to said visitors, and this also must be included in the value of Block Island fisheries.

The fishing business here was carried on in its seasons a hundred and seventy-five years ago. In 1702 the following town record was made which is instructive in several points, not the least of which is the law and order then maintained here. We quote it entire for various reasons.

"Apr. 14th, 1702. Then Capt. John Merritt brought before us one John Meeker for being a delinquent for absenting himself from out of said Merritt's employment, being his servant for the fishing season for forty shillings pr. month with six pounds of bread and six pounds of pork a week, the which considerations the said Meeker did promise to his faithful service till the middle of June or thereabouts, as by witness on oath doth appear before us. We therefore determine and give our judgment that the said Meeker shall perform the said conditions as above said. The forty shillings pr. month is to be paid current money of this Colony with cost of court, which is one shilling for the constable's fees, and two shillings for other charges which said Meeker is to pay."

"Given under our hands,   .

Simon Ray, Sen. Warden,
Edward Ball, Dep. Warden."

In the same year, 1702, the fishing business was carried on here somewhat extensively, as indicated by the fact that then the town sold six barrels of "oyle for ammunition." Even earlier than this the town engaged Robert Carr, in 1695, and afterward Robert Carr, Jun., to be "forward in making a harbor and promoting the *fishing trade.*" The chief argument for a harbor then, and has been ever since, was for the benefit of the Block Island fisheries. As far back as 1670, the first legislative act for constructing a harbor here, mentions no other reason for so doing than the "incouradging *fishing designes.*" The old pier then built, after fifty years service, had got the fishing business well established, and in a legislative act in 1723, to aid in building a new pier, the General Assembly, as a reason for said act, said,—"For the want of a pier at said Island, for the encouragement of the navigation of this Colony, *especially the fishery,* which is begun to be carried on successfully, &c."

The value of these fisheries is also indicated by the white oak poles, now standing at the Harbor, put there for the convenience of the boats of fishermen. They were a substitute for the old and the new piers which had been destroyed by a storm, and as such they served until the construction of the present national harbor, inadequate as they were, leaving a necessity on the fishermen of turning out at midnight in a cold storm to yoke

their oxen, go to the harbor, and haul their boats up the
bank for safety.   But even for this the fishing business
paid, as neither then. nor now, have other resources been
adequate to the needs of the population sustained on the
Island.   Nor have the hard earnings of the industrious
inhabitants been squandered abroad for unnecessary luxuries at home.   It is within the memory of even the
younger portion of the Islanders that two partners in a
fishing boat, after selling their fish at some port on the
main, have brought home a barrel of flour, placed it upon
a sheet, found the middle from chime to chime, and
"sawed it in two."

The seasons for the principal fishing are fall and spring.
In the fall of the year, especially in November, the inesti-
mable droves of cod-fish travel southerly, and, by the
uniformity of their movements, evidently well understand
the "paths of the seas." If diverted from their paths,
and likely to be overtaken by a storm in too shallow
water, they are sagacious enough to swallow smooth pebbles for more ballast, or to enable them to sink deep to
prevent the storm from driving them ashore.   From this
fact their captors have sometimes been warned of their
own dangers, which are neither few nor small.   To find
the paths most frequented by these deep sea passengers is
one of their means of success, and when they do not "strike
them" in one path, they know where to try them in another.   These paths lie all around the Island which has
been to millions of fish as it has been to multitudes of
vessels—a block in the ocean, on which many have been
wrecked.   In the autumn fishing. the cod come much
nearer than in spring, and this is a great favor to the
Islanders, as they have less distance to go in the short
days, and are less exposed to the dangers of the sea in
returning, as they are obliged, at times. to come into harbor quickly for shelter from a sudden storm.   They fish

with hand lines, in water from ten to twenty fathoms deep. The salt water is so softening to the skin, and the weight of the cod is so great that cots or gloves are necessary to protect the hands. The deep grooves cut by the lines in the oak "gunnels" of the old boats indicate the amount of "hauling," and the value of the business. One old fisherman was heard to say of his boat, then about thirty years old,—"That old craft has had fish enough in her to sink her with specie," and he was not wide of the truth. "High-hook," is the term that distinguishes the best fisherman for a day or longer. " Who is high-hook to-day ?" is a common inquiry after thirty or forty boats have landed at the harbor.

After the fall fishing, when winter has set in, there are a few smacksmen who continue through the cold weather. Their vessels have decks, cabins, fires, berths, and cooking conveniences. In their center is a " well "—a place open from top to bottom, admitting sea water equal in depth to the draught of the vessel, and in this water, fish are kept alive by fresh water coming in at the bottom, and thus 1,000 to 1,500 at a time are taken away to market. They are caught, to a considerable extent, by " trawls."

The spring fishing is much like that in autumn, except in the distance from the Island. Then the "paths of the sea " most frequented lie at distances of five, ten, and twenty miles. Then the fish are moving northerly, and for some reason, perhaps from the course they get from the southerly shore of Long Island, they shun Block Island more than in the fall. They also seem to be more numerous in spring, probably because their "paths " are narrower. These are generally called "banks " by the fishermen, and indicate the best localities for fishing. Many more are caught, too, in the spring season, which begins about the first of April and continues until June. During this season the congenial weather, the distance of the sail, the number in the business, the early starting in the morning, the strife for the honors of being "high-hook," the rapid footsteps along the streets from two o'clock until four in the morning, the rattle of sails hoisting in the harbor, and the sailor phrases of the fishermen, make up a scene of life and beauty to which the landsmen and even summer visitors are strangers.

> "When boats to their morning fishing go,
> And, held to the wind and slanting low,
> Whitening and darkening the small sails show."

It is a charming scene in the month of May, to view from an elevated point on the land, from thirty to fifty small sails, as a long, narrow cloud skirts the eastern horizon, under which the red sun begins to show his brow just rising out of the sea, and towards which the vessels are gently moving, stretching from the last ones rounding the breakwater to those apparently sailing into the face of the sun, while the stillness of nature is broken only by the dull music of waves along the shore. Far different is the scene in the afternoon, when one of the same boats after another straggles in, with wet and wearied fishermen, with ballast of tons of stones thrown overboard to give place for the hungry, and hunger-stopping cod-fish— such as Cooper's Leatherstocking would call "*sock-dolli-gers*," and when the task of dressing about forty cart-loads is progressing. The rapidity with which this work is done, until the fish in the boat are the fish in the pickle, is worthy of observation. The process, where two or three parties are concerned in the boat, is this :

The fish are thrown upon the shore; if one owns the boat, and another is his partner in fishing, the fish are divided into three equal parts; one man then turns his face from the fish, while the other man points to one pile and says, "Whose is that?" the other answers, as he

4

chooses ; and the same is done to one of the other piles, leaving the third share as due to the boat, or its owner. This division is made quickly, and the answers from the man who turns his face from the divided fish are final. Then begins the work of dressing, carrying to the fish-house, and salting. In the meantime farmers are there with carts and oxen to get the offal to fertilize their fields. About the middle of the afternoon some one by general consent is proclaimed "high-hook," and squads of tired men are seen propelling their heavy feet homeward to report the success of the day, to eat a fisherman's meal well prepared, and to go to bed, sometimes, with the sun, and to rise again several hours the earlier. Occasionally their day's work is much more brief, and less profitable, as when a sudden storm comes down like a hawk upon a brood of chickens. Then a speedy return to the harbor begins, in some instances between the casting of the anchor on the fishing ground and the dropping of a hook into the water, or even before the casting of the anchor. Many anxious eyes have watched them thus returning over a sea suddenly thrown into fury by a storm that came from afar with fearful velocity. The casualties, however, have been almost miraculously few.

The quantity caught in the spring is considerably larger than that secured in the fall, but the income from the one season is about the same as that from the other, for in spring more are spoiled in drying, by being sun-burned, and in the fall the profits of dog-fishing, previous to that for cod, yields a considerable income from the oil, and the carcasses of the dog-fish used for the fields, a use that might be made more profitable, if instead of leaving them scattered upon the meadows, to waste their best fertilizing qualities in the air, making it offensive and unhealthy, the farmers would save that waste by putting said fish into a heap of compost. If any doubt this let them remember that the smell alluded to is nothing but fish manure *in the air*, from which place they do not get it back again.

The summer fishing of Block Island with hooks, though not to be compared with that of fall or spring, is considerable. It is carried on principally by a few who supply the hotels, boarding-houses, and families of the Island, and occasionally send away a quantity packed in ice. They catch blue-fish, or "horse mackerel," as they are called, mostly. They are in greatest demand by the thousands of visitors.

Pound-fishing, is a new branch of the business at Block Island. It was commenced in 1867 by a company of Islanders whose success was sufficient to lead to the construction of a second pound in 1868. Two more were set in 1874. The first company has been dissolved, and the other three remain. They are in operation during the summer, and begin soon after the spring storms, and are taken up before the rough seas of the fall destroy their seines and carry away their spiles. The following description of one will apply to all.

Pound No. 3 was established in 1874, and was constructed thus : A straight line of spiles, oak, twenty-five feet apart, is run from the shore, at right angles with the beach, 1,800 feet, driven down firmly by a spile-driver. From the shore end to the other the bottom descends gradually until at the latter the water is thirty feet deep. This long line of spiles may be considered as fence-posts rising about ten feet above the water. To these posts is fastened with ropes and cords a fence of cotton netting, rising from the bottom of the sea several feet above the surface of the water. This netting is made the same as a seine, and is made in pieces fifty-six feet long by fifty-four feet in width, and is fitted to the depth of water. This line of spiles and netting is called the *leader*.

The sea or deeper end of the leader terminates in that

division of the pound called the *heart*, so called on account of its form, which is constructed of spiles and seine the same as the leader.

Imagine, now, a thousand fish, some shad, some scup, some cod, and other kinds coasting along the Island until they come to the "leader," from both directions. As they cannot safely come ashore to go around that fence, they swim along the leader intending to go around the deep water end ; but when they have gone around that end they find their noses running against the fence of the "heart," and they go from side to side in that and still keep the notion of going into still deeper water, sailor-like, until they escape from the opening seven feet wide, at the little end of the heart, into the *Pound* proper. Here they are as secure as stray cattle locked in a pound upon the land, and in water forty feet deep.

This pound is made of spiles and twine as was the leader. It is fifty by fifty-six feet square, and its bottom is covered with the same netting that forms its sides. Should a few fish chance to pass out of it through the mouth of the heart they are quite certain to be led back again by the deceitful meshes of this structure. The sides of the pound are so arranged that they can be raised, and thus the fish in it may all be turned over to one side, and there scooped out with wire baskets, and transferred to the smack adjacent that takes its cargo quickly to New York, and then brings back a smaller cargo of money to the fishermen who are very faithful pound-keepers.

On one side of the pound are two *cars*, each adjacent to the pound, and twenty-eight feet by twenty-five, and of the same depth as the pound, and constructed of the same materials. They are used for keeping a surplus of fish that might accumulate, by transferring them to it from the pound.

The term pound, in general, means all its parts, namely,

the leader, the heart, the pound proper, and the cars. The spiles are from twelve to fifty feet in length, and 130 are used. The whole cost of this pound was $2,500.

The spiles and netting are all put down each spring, and taken up at the close of the summer fishing. The smack that carries the fish to New York has one-half the income of the pound. What that is we learn best from the thriving appearances of the pound fishermen, and yet they well earn their money in cost, risk, and labor. The pounds are all on the west shore of the Island, and well pay the visitors to them for their trouble, as the gentlemanly fishermen row the strangers out into their large and lucrative "heart," so deceitful to the ocean "aristocracy."

The superiority of the Block Island cod-fish is well known. This is owing to the advantages for curing them at the fishermen's homes. They are dried there immediately after they are sufficiently pickled, and as soon as possible taken to market with a freshness that has no reference to salt, and which cannot be preserved by remoter fisheries, or even by fishermen who have no flakes upon the Island.

The drying process, especially in spring, is very critical. Many a quintal has been lost by an hour's neglect in too bright a sun unaccompanied by a cooling breeze. To many of the very respectable women of Block Island the public are indebted for much of the fine flavor of their fish preserved by the nice process of drying while the men are away in their boats.

The value of the Block Island fisheries to the inhabitants of the Island, if we estimated them with reference to the quantity exported, to what is consumed on the Island, and in reference to fertilizing uses, or in other words, if we estimate them by the sum necessary to buy out all the annual benefits of them to the Islanders, may

4*

safely be said to be not far from an annual sum of $75,000.

This estimate includes all the income which the fisheries secure through visitors, through exportation, home consumption, and fertilization, and without this income the Island would be depopulated well nigh, if not quite to the ruin of good society. Therefore we conclude this article on the Resources of the Island with the conviction that for one hundred years *peat was an indispensable resource* to the inhabitants, and that *sea-weed*, and *the fisheries* now are each a *sine qua non*.

Whales, for many years, have frequently been seen about Block Island. They are considered dangerous to the fishermen, and of but little value, on account of their being the *hump-backed* species, and about as useless for oil as a camel for food. The columns of white water thrown into the air, and seen from the Island, tell plainly who are there.

The whales and the fishermen have a similar fear of each other. The latter avoid the presence of the former, and *vice versa*. On one occasion a father and son were in their boat; the former in the bow, the latter in the stern, just a few yards back of which a whale was seen, head towards them, and able to sink them instantly. The son took a ballast stone to throw at him; but the father forbade him. The whale gave a beautiful comment on Gen. ix, 2, where it is said: "The fear of you and the dread of you shall be upon every beast of the earth, and upon every fowl of the air, upon all that moveth upon the earth, and upon *all the fishes of the sea*." He saw the fishermen, feared them, and sank into the deep.

Sea Moss. The gathering of this along the shores of Block Island has become a source of considerable revenue. The moss is the same as that generally known as "Irish moss," and is secured during the months of summer.

The first one known to have gathered it for the market here was a Mr. James West, who was not a native of the Island. He introduced the business about the year 1850, and instructed the Islanders in the process of drying and bleaching. He died in April 1875.

The moss grows upon the rocks below high water mark, and also below the low water mark. At low tide the women and children avail themselves of the most favorable opportunity for picking it from the rocks, or bowlders, and they even venture into the water waist deep at low tide in warm weather to secure it, enjoying the bath with the lady bathers on the east beach, and also the pleasure of accumulating a means of subsistence.

The moss is all of one quality when taken from the sea. It is then designated as *black moss*, and when this is dried it is sold at the Island stores for two cents a pound, and the merchants pack it in barrels and sell it for three cents a pound in the cities. Another quality is given to this moss by the slow and patient process of bleaching. This is done by keeping the moss in the sun, where it is moistened and dried until it loses its color, and becomes *white moss*. This brings a much larger price than the other, and is more profitable to the producer. It sells in barter at the stores for seven cents a pound, is there packed in barrels, and sold to city druggists for eight cents a pound. It is brought in bags of five to thirty pounds each to the stores by the women and children. The quantity of Block Island sea moss thus accumulated annually aggregates to more than ten tons, and this, as one of the minor resources, secures an income of over a thousand dollars to the Island. But little of the moss is used by the inhabitants. Mr. Lorenzo Littlefield is by far the most extensive dealer in this commodity.

THE BLOCK ISLAND BOATS.

These are so unlike others that they attract much attention. They have keels, at an angle of forty-five degrees with which rise the stern and stem posts, with "lapstreak" sides of cedar, with bows and sterns nearly alike, open, with two masts and narrow, tapering sails, of one to four tons burthen, sitting deep in the water, and unequaled for safety in the hands of the Islanders. While their number has averaged over forty during the last fifty years, not a life of an Islander has been lost on account of the sea unworthiness of the boats. They have been known to sail into the winds in storms that would quickly swamp larger vessels that should attempt to follow them. The masts are mere poles without shrouds and jib-stays, and by their elasticity adapt themselves to the force of the wind. While visiting the ports along the Rhode Island and Connecticut coasts and rivers they are quickly distinguished by their peculiarities, and are sometimes called *double enders* from Block Island. Where, and how their model originated it is not easy to ascertain. It is doubtful whether they will ever be superseded while the Island continues. They correspond materially to the boats anciently called *pinnaces* in New England. Cobble stones are used for ballast, and shifted from side to side when necessary. Prof. Baird, of the Smithsonian Institute, exhibited a model of a Block Island boat at the Centennial, made and rigged by his order.

THE MAILS.

No part of the United States, probably, has suffered more inconvenience from a want of mails than Block Island. For one hundred and seventy years it had none at all. Its correspondence was through offices on the main, principally at Newport.

The first mail to Block Island was established in Dec.

1832. Capt. Samuel W. Rose was contractor and carrier of it four years, at $416 a year, leaving the Island Wednesday morning at 8 o'clock, and Newport the next day at the same hour, wind and weather permitting. This was done in a "middling sized open sail boat."

In 1857 a writer said :—"The arrival of the mail is an event of special interest in a community thus situated, and its contents are called out and taken by those assembled around, either for themselves or neighbors, without delay." This custom continued up to the year 1876. Suitable P. O. boxes are now provided for individuals.

Previous to 1869 the mail was carried for many years by Capt. Wm. Rose, the last year of whose contract, on account of his death, it was carried by his son, John E. Rose, now known as the enterprising Capt. John E. Rose, of the fine packet, Nathan H. Dixon.

Capt. John E. Rose, in 1869, but recently arrived at his majority, contracted for the carrying of the mail during the next term of four years. In bidding for that contract he showed a "grit" worthy of better pay. A competitor and he ran their bids down to the sum of *one cent a year*, and the mail between Block Island and Newport was therefore carried four years for *four cents*, and Capt. John E. Rose says he has received only *one cent* of that pay yet, and that the one cent was paid him by a man in Providence who wanted to buy distinction by paying from his own pocket the whole expense of carrying the Block Island mail one year. The Captain's enterprise and perseverance have put him handsomely and domestically beyond the need of the three cents still due to him from the United States.

During the last four years the mail has been carried to Newport tri-weekly most of the time in the Henry B. Anthony, a staunch packet commanded by Capt. Addison Rose who has distinguished himself by being *on time*, by dangers braved, and by great skill in managing his schooner. Some will remember him for laying his marine troubles to some "Jonah aboard."

The first postmaster of Block Island was Wm. L. Wright, and his office was his bed-room.

The following, furnished by the Postmaster-General, is inserted here for reference, as to postmasters and appointment:

Wm. L. Wright,	appointed 13th Dec.,	1832.
Samuel Dunn,	" 26th July,	1837.
Alfred Card,	" 12th June,	1841.
George Rose.	" 23d Sept.,	1845.
Rev. Charles C. Lewis,	" 17th Apr.,	1852.
Rev. Elijah Maccomber,	" 17th May,	1855.
Samuel J. Osgood,	" 4th Aug.,	1860.
Wm. L. Milikin,	" 5th June,	1861.

The last one named is the present incumbent, in January, 1877.

In addition to the great improvement of the "Anthony," with her ample deck, hold, and neat cabin, and courteous crew and captain, over the open boats in which the mail had been carried previously, the recent proposals for a new contract contemplate the carrying of a daily mail in a steamer from Block Island to Newport, from the first of June, 1877, to Sept. 30th, and from October first to May 31st tri-weekly, leaving Newport at 8 A. M., and Block Island at 8 A. M., at all seasons. This arrangement will be a great accommodation to the public in visiting the Island in summer, and also to the Islanders in communicating with other places. Indeed, the increasing popularity of Block Island as a summer resort, and the rapidly increasing multitude who seek its luxuries demand enlarged facilities for communication. Business men in these times cannot remain quietly long at any place with-

out a daily paper fresh from the press, and frequent reports as to the run of their business. To the great advantages to the public, and to the Island, derived from the
Government Harbor here should be added, and -probably
will be, at no distant day, a signal station, by which hourly
information from all parts of the country could be obtained, and great benefit conferred upon commerce. After
that is done those upon the Island will talk no more
of "going to America," for they will be in it, and not
farther from Newport, communicatively, than they would
be in Europe.

About the year 1851 a long and severe storm occurred,
at the time of an election, and for want of communication with Block Island, the State of Rhode Island was
unable to get returns from New Shoreham, *alias* Block
Island, and thus the decision of the election was kept back
about twenty-one days. the storm lasting that time.

BLOCK ISLAND INDIANS,

OR

THE MANISSEANS.

It is impossible to give as full an account of them as is desirable. As they did not differ, however, from other Indians, materially, what is known of other aborigines may be taken, for the most part, as a knowledge of those of Block Island. The few scattered fragments of information here put together have been gathered from various sources, but in all cases are authentic. If it should seem to any that these Indians were more mild and peaceful than those on the main-land, since they committed less violence upon the early settlers, and that too while they were so greatly in the majority that they could have massacred every white person any day, during a considerable period of years, such should consider the restraining influences which compelled these Indians to be peaceful.

Twenty-five years before the sixteen families came to Block Island a terrible lesson was taught the Manisseans by the white people of Massachusetts for the killing of Captain Oldham, a trader here. Then they learned, as never before, the superiority of white men, as a few with fire-arms overpowered the whole Island, armed with bows and arrows. Endicott's slaughter of their warriors, destruction of their year's harvest of corn, burning of their mats and wigwams, and the very daring of the settlers, struck a terror to the natives of the Island.

Moreover, at this time, Ninicraft, the Narragansett

chief of the Manisseans, was closely flanked by two formidable powers. On the one side were the fierce Pequots, "a powerful nation that had, by their conquests and cruelties, struck terror to all the nations of Indians round about them." They had formed alliances sufficient to resolve to exterminate the English. Ninicraft, a nearer neighbor to the English, knew the power of the English better than did the Pequots. He dared not become an ally of Sassacus, the great Pequot Sachem, said to be "a god that nobody could kill," for two reasons, viz.: the fear of subjugation to the Pequots, and the danger of destruction from the English. He became an ally to the latter against the former, and when he had seen the powerful Pequots humbled by the slaughter of one thousand warriors before a handful of Englishmen who lost but two lives in the battle led on by Captain Mason, he well knew what consequences to expect from any hostilities of his men upon Block Island. It was not, therefore, a lack of hostile feelings and savage ferocity that restrained the Manisseans from destroying the early settlers, but self interest and the force of circumstances. And yet, enough of their nature was exhibited at times to cause great alarms in the little insular colony.

The first information which we gain of these Indians is obtained from the French navigator, Verrazzano, in his report to Francis I, king of France, in 1524. In speaking of Block Island he said : "It was full of hilles, covered with trees, well peopled, for we saw *fires all along the coaste.*" He probably sailed along the west shore, between the Island and Montauk, as he was bound north along the coast from the Carolinas. From the west side he rounded Sandy Point, and thus obtained a view of the northerly and easterly shores of the Island, enabling him to judge of its size and population without landing. A little effort of the imagination furnishes a view of the

Island then, three hundred and fifty years ago, when the aboriginal lords of the soil, never disturbed by the face of a white man, with their squaws and papooses, sat around their summer evening fires, eating their succotash, hominy, clams, fish, and wild game, braiding mats and baskets, and repeating the traditions of their fore-fathers, or in their wild war-dances, with painted faces, with demon yells and grimaces and horrid threats, cele-brating their victories over invaders from the Mohegans of Montauk, or the Pequots from the main-land.

Of their personal appearance no better description can be given, perhaps, than that which is furnished of their neighbors by Mr. P. Vincent, in his account of the Pequot war. He says : "Only art and grace have given us that perfection which they want, but may perhaps be as ca-pable thereof as we. They are of person straight and tall, of limbs big and strong, seldom seem violent or extreme in any passion. Naked they go, except a skin about their waist, and sometimes a mantle about their shoulders. Armed they are with bows and arrows, clubs, javelins, etc."

OLDHAM'S MURDER.

The second assault upon the English by the Indians in New England, was made by the Manisseans in the year 1636. Mr. Niles, born upon Block Island, in 1674, in his youth conversed freely with the old natives, as well as read and conversed with the best informed on the main-land concerning the Indians. He, in the main, is good authority. This assault, he says, was made upon Captain Oldham, a trader from Boston, whom the Indians killed, "with all his company, how many is uncertain. He went thither on a friendly trading voyage with the natives there ; but, as it was said, they fell into an unhappy quarrel which issued in the abovesaid slaughter." Mr. Niles, probably, got his information principally from the

Islanders, for of this assault, and of Captain Endicott's expedition to punish the offenders, he says: "We have no particular account." He had not read the history of said expedition written by one of Endicott's officers, Captain Underhill, who says : "The cause of our war against the Block Islanders was for taking away the life of one Master John Oldham, who made it his common course to trade among the Indians. He coming to Block Island to drive trade with them, the Islanders came into his boat, and having got a full view of commodities which gave them full content, consulted how they might destroy him and his company, to the end they might clothe their bloody flesh with his lawful garments. The Indians having laid the plot, into the boat they came to trade, as they pretended ; watching their opportunities, knocked him on the head, and martyred him most barbarously, to the great grief of his poor distressed servants which by the providence of God were saved." Niles says he was killed *with all his company.* Underhill says the Indians "consulted how they might destroy him *and his company,*" and to this adds that Mr. Oldham's *poor distressed servants were saved.* As Niles had a personal acquaintance with natives who were doubtless eye-witnesses of the tragedy, his statement that Oldham "with *all his company*" was killed seems to be the more reliable. A different version is given elsewhere.

The principal points of the retribution from Massachusetts for the killing of Captain Oldham are contained in the following extracts from Captain Underhill's account of the expedition against the Manisseans.

"This Island lying in the roadway to Lord Sey and the Lord Brooke's plantation, a certain seaman called John Gallup, master of the small navigation standing along to the Mathethusis Bay, and seeing a boat under sail close aboard the Island, and perceiving the sails to be

unskillfully managed, bred in him a jealousy whether that
the Island Indians had not boldly taken the life of our
countryman and made themselves masters of their goods.
Suspecting this, he bore up to them, and approaching
near them was confirmed that his jealousy was just. Seeing Indians in the boat, and knowing her to be the vessel
of Master Oldham, and not seeing him there, gave fire
upon them and slew some ; others leaped overboard,
besides two of the number which he preserved alive and
brought to the Bay.

THEIR SUBJUGATION.

The blood of the innocent called for vengeance. God
stirred up the heart of the honored Governor, Master
Henry Vane, and the rest of the worthy magistrates to
send forth a hundred well-appointed soldiers, under the
conduct of Captain John Endicott, and in company with
him that had command, Capt. John Underhill, Capt.
Nathan Turner, Capt. Wm. Jenningson, besides other
inferior officers."

Here it may be well to remark that these officers and
soldiers seem to have protected themselves against the
arrows of the enemy by wearing helmets, thick, stiff
collars, and breastplates. Captain Underhill breaks the
thread of his narrative to express his obligation to his
wife for inducing him to take his helmet contrary to his
intention. He says : "Let no man despise advice and
counsel of his wife, though she be a woman."

"Coming to an anchor before the Island, we espied an
Indian walking by the shore in a desolate manner, as
though he had received intelligence of our coming.
[Probably on the bathing-beach.] Which Indian gave
just ground to some to conclude that the body of the
people had deserted the Island. But some knowing them
to be a warlike nation, a people that spend most of their

timo in the study of warlike policy, were not persuaded
that they would upon so slender terms forsake the Island,
but rather suspected they might lie behind a bank [the
present sand-hills, then a continuous bank], much like the
form of a barricado. Myself with others rode with a
shallop, made towards the shore, having in the boat a
dozen armed soldiers. Drawing near to the place of landing, the number that rose from behind the barricado were
between fifty or sixty able fighting-men, men as straight
as arrows, very tall, and of active bodies, having their
arrows notched. They drew near to the water's side, and
let fly at the soldiers, as though they had meant to have
made an end of us all in a moment. They shot a young
gentleman in the neck through a collar, for stiffness as if
it had been an oaken board, and entered his flesh a good
depth. Myself received an arrow through my coat-sleeve,
a second against my helmet on the forehead ; so as if
God in his providence had not moved the heart of my
wife to persuade me to carry it along with me I had been
slain." [The Captain did not seem to consider that the
hearts and arrows of the Indians were as easily "moved"
as the heart of his wife.]

"The arrows flying thick about us, we made haste to
the shore ; but the surf of the sea being great hindered
us, so as we could scarce discharge a musket, but were
forced to make haste to land. Drawing near the shore
through the strength of wind, and the hollowness of the
sea, we durst not venture to run ashore, but were forced
to wade up to the middle ; but having once got up off our
legs, we gave fire upon them. They finding our bullets
to outreach their arrows, fled before us. In the meanwhile Colonel Endicott made to the shore, and some of
this number also repulsed him at his landing, but hurt
none. We thought they would stand it out with us, but
they perceiving that we were in earnest, fled , and left

5*

their wigwams, or houses, and provision to the use of our soldiers. Having set forth our sentinels, and laid out our pardues, we betook ourselves to the guard, expecting hourly they would fall upon us, but they observed the old rule, 'T"is good sleeping in a whole skin,' and left us free from an alarm.

"The next day we set upon our march, the Indians being retired into swamps, so as we could not find them. We burnt and spoiled both houses and corn in great abundance, but they kept themselves in obscurity. Captain Turner stepping aside to a swamp met with some few Indians, and charged upon them, changing some few bullets for arrows. Himself received a shot upon the breast of his corselet, as if it had been pushed with a pike, and if he had not had it on he had lost his life.

"A pretty passage worthy of observation. We had an Indian with us that was an interpreter ; being in English clothes, and a gun in his hand, was spied by the Islanders, which called out to him : 'What are you, an Indian or an Englishman ?' 'Come hither,' said he, 'and I will tell you.' He pulls up his cock and let fly at one of them, and without question was the death of him.

"Having spent that day in burning and spoiling the Island, we took up the quarter for that night. About midnight myself went out with ten men about two miles from our quarter, and discovered the most eminent plantation they had on the Island, where was much corn, many wigwams, and great heaps of mats; but fearing lest we should make an alarm by setting fire on them, we left them as we found them, and peaceably departed to our quarter ; and the next morning with forty men, marched up to the same plantation, burnt their houses, cut down their corn, destroyed some of their dogs instead of men, which they left in their wigwams.

"Passing on towards the water's side to embark our

soldiers, we met with several famous wigwams, with great heaps of pleasant corn ready shelled, but not able to bring it away, we did throw their mats upon it, and set fire and burnt it. Many well-wrought mats our soldiers brought from thence, and several delightful baskets. We being divided into two parts, the rest of the body met with no less, I suppose, than ourselves did. The Indians playing least in sight, we spent our time, and could no more advantage ourselves than we had already done, and having slain some fourteen, and maimed others, we embarked ourselves, and set sail for Seasbrooke fort."

There are local reasons for believing the above spoils were made upon the northerly part of the Island, as that was distinguished, in the early days of the first settlers, for its great products of corn, and then was known by the name of the "Corne Neck." It is now called The Neck. The Indians probably fled to the southerly and westerly parts of the Island. They were not conquered, but only punished by Endicott's expedition, until a second attack made by Israel Stoughton, in consequence of which the foundation was laid for Massachusetts to claim the Island by right of conquest, and accordingly its chief, Miantinomo, was induced to acknowledge the claim.

The *habits* of the Manisseans may be gathered from Capt. Underhill's account. Their abundance of corn, and numerous, comfortable wigwams indicated their industry. Their "well-wrought mats," and their "delightful baskets," evinced their skill, as did also their powerful bows and fatal arrows. Their hostile manœuvers were evidence of their practice in the tactics of war. Had they succeeded in drawing the English after them to some portions of the Island, as they once entrapped the Mohegans, Capt. Underhill and Col. Endicott might not have returned to their boats so cheerfully. Of their warlike habits Mr. Niles gives us the following account:

WARS AMONG THEMSELVES.

"They were perpetually engaged in wars one with another, long before the English settled on Block Island, and perhaps before any English settlements were made in this land, according to the Indians' relation, as some of the old men among them informed me when I was young."

"The Indians on this Island had war with the Mohegan Indians, although the Island lies in the ocean and open seas, four leagues from the nearest main-land, and much farther distant from any Island, and from the nearest place of landing to the Mohegan country forty miles, I suppose at least, through a hideous wilderness, as it then was, besides the difficulty of two large rivers. To prosecute their designed hostilities each party furnished themselves with a large fleet of canoes, furnished with bows and arrows.

"It happened at the same time the Mohegans were coming here in their fleet to invade the Block Islanders, they were going with their fleet to make spoil on the Mohegans. Both being on the seas, it being in the night and moonshine, and by the advantage of it the Block Islanders discovered the Mohegans, but they saw not the Islanders. Upon which these turned back to their own shore, and hauled their canoes out of sight, and waylaid their enemies until they landed, and marched up in the Island, and then stove all their [the Mohegans'] canoes, and drove them to the opposite part of the Island, where, I suppose, the cliffs next the sea are near, if not more than two hundred feet high, and in a manner perpendicular, or rather near the top hanging over, and at the bottom near the sea-shore very full of rocks. [Near the new light-house.] They could escape no farther. Here these poor creatures were confined, having nothing over them but the heavens to shelter or cover them, no food to support them, no water to quench their thirst. Thus they were kept destitute of every comfort of life, until they all pined away and perished in a most miserable manner, without any compassion in the least degree shown to them. They had indeed by some means dug a trench around them toward the land to defend them from the arrows of their enemies, which I have seen, and it is called the Mohegan Fort to this day." [1760.]

That fort, probably, has long since sloughed off into the sea by the action of frosts and rains upon the bluffs for more than a century. All personal knowledge of it has also faded away from the Islanders.

Of the Block Island Indians after the immigration of the English we have but a few outlines, bold indeed at first, but gradually fading to almost invisibility. In 1662 their warriors numbered about three hundred. The shores of the Great Pond were evidently the most thickly settled by the Indians. About it Roger Williams discovered the wigwams of several petty sachems. Thither they resorted for fish, clams, oysters, and scallops, as large deposits of shells now occasionally opened testify. We can easily imagine their lordly bearing, as several of these chiefs looked upon the vessel of Oldham anchored upon their shores, and as they laid the plot to seize his goods and take his life. The ringleader's name was *Audsah*, and he struck the fatal blows—fatal not only to Mr. Oldham, but also to the Indian life on Block Island. The fatal seed he then planted yielded him and his fellow-Islanders a fearful harvest. *Audsah*, like Cain, became a fugitive, was hunted from tribe to tribe, and at one time was sheltered on the main by one Wequashcuck, a petty sachem. They had a fort on Fort Island, a description of them there, and their declining to fight the seventeen Englishmen is given in the sketch of *Thomas Terry*. At that time, Mr. Niles says, "Their arrows were pointed with hard stones somewhat resembling flint. They had hatchets and axes of stone, with a round head wrought curiously, standing considerably above a groove ·made round it, to hold the handle of the axe or hatchet, which was bent in the middle and brought the extreme parts and bound them fast together, which were their handles to hold by and do execution with these, their weapons of war." This description corresponds with the shape of a stone axe found many years ago on Mr. John Ball's land, by his father, Isaiah Ball, and presented by the former to the writer.

The "dogs" of Block Island belonging to the Manisseans before the English came have their descendants here still, it is believed. They are not numerous, but peculiar, differing materially from all the species which we have noticed on the main-land, both in figure and disposition. They are below a medium size, with short legs but powerful, broad breasts, heavy quarters, massive head unlike the bull dog, the terrier, the hound, the mastiff, but resembling mostly the last ; with a fierce disposition that in some makes but little distinction between friend and foe. In Jan., 1719, by an act of the town, the Indians were not allowed to keep dogs.

In 1860, a visitor on the Island wrote : "There are not one-fourth as many sheep here as there ought to be, and as there *would* be, if it were not for that crying nuisance, the multiplicity of dogs. The farmers dare not risk the dangers from canine depredations which, at the present time, are full as great as when wolves howled over the ancient hills of the Island." Query : Did the Island ever have wolves ? The dogs then were very numerous, and wanted a change from fish diet. They also killed geese, a large flock in one instance, and buried them, as a future supply of fresh meat. The dogs now are more civilized. perhaps better fed.

HOT-HOUSES.

The Hot-Houses, or Russian Baths, were an institution of the aboriginal Block Islanders. Mr. Niles has left us the following description of them.

"They were made as a vault, partly under ground, and in the form of a large oven, where two or three persons might on occasion sit together, and it was placed near some depth of water; and their method was to heat some stones very hot in the fire, and put them into the hot-house, and when the person was in, to shut it close up, with only so much air as was necessary for respiration, or that they within might freely draw their breath. And being thus closely pent up, the heat of the stones occasioned them to sweat in a prodigious manner, streaming as it were from every part of the body; and when they had continued there as long as they could well endure it, their method was to rush out and plunge themselves into the water. By this means they pretend a cure of all pains and numbness in their joints, and many other maladies."

At one time, while Ninicraft, chief of the Narragansetts, was on the Island visiting his subjects, a quarrel arose between a few settlers and a few Indians, and fists and clubs were playing pretty lively, until the chief was called out of one of these hot-houses by a runner, and hastened to the turmoil and stopped it by rushing among them with a red coat in his hand, crying—"King Charles! King Charles!"

But one spot is now known to exhibit any of the remains of those hot-houses. It has been filled up so nearly that but a slight indentation in the ground remains, and may be seen at the south end of the Great Pond, in the bank near the water, and on the west side of a stone-wall that runs nearly in a line from Mr. Simon Ball's house to the pond.

ENSLAVED.

The relation of the Indians to the settlers on the Island soon became that of slaves to masters, as seen in the case of Thomas Terry, in 1669, soliciting aid from Governor Lovelace, of New York, and from the governor of Rhode Island, in recapturing six of his Indian slaves. The same relation is demonstrated, too, by the town records, as in the following instances.

In October, 1675, the town council of Block Island made a law "That no Indian whatsoever shall keep any gun in his custody, but shall be brought to his master's house, in whose ground he lives, every night, and give notice to his master, and return the gun again the night of the same day hereafter, or forfeit his gun." In 1680 an ordinance was passed prohibiting the sale of rum to an Indian.

In 1690, *Trugo*, an Indian, was sold into bondage, by his brothers and sisters, to Joshua Raymond for a term of thirteen years for thirteen gallons of rum and four cloth coats, the rum to be paid in annual installments of one gallon each. Trugo was to have his board and clothing, and two suits of apparel at the expiration of his bondage.

In 1693, several Indians were arrested and fined for sheep-stealing, and from the record we see the existence of slavery. It seems very strange that the fines were no heavier.

"*Harry.*—Old Ned's son,	0	5	0
Samson, Thomas Mitchell's man,	0	1	0
Jeffrey, Joshua Raymond's man,	0	1	0
Big George, Mr. Sands' servant, Ned's son,	0	5	0 "

Judging from the fines we must conclude that "Old Ned's" sons were five times as guilty as the others were. They were all arrested on suspicion. and circumstantial evidence was so close as to extort their confession.

It is evident from the following law of the Island enacted in 1709, that both Indian and Negro slaves were troublesome. It reads thus : "No Indian nor Negro cervants shall walk abroad After nine A Clock at night without his master or mistries leave, and if said servants or slaves shall be found or taken from home after nine A Clock at night by the Constable or any freeholder of s^d Town and brought to the Wardens or Warden shall be taken and stript and receive ten laches on his or hurs naked back."

From this we learn that Indian and Negro slaves were treated alike, to some extent, on the Island It should be borne in mind, too, that this stringency was at a time when slavery was popular, and slave-ships were frequently seen in the American waters. This act was in harmony also with another promulgated by the state of Rhode Island in 1667, viz.: "That if in Rhode Island, or in any other towns. any Indian shall be taken walking in the night-time, he shall be seized by the watch and kept in custody till morning. and brought before some magistrate, which said magistrate shall deal with him according to his discretion, and the demerit of the said person so offending."

The Block Island Indians were protected by many acts of humanity on the part of the early settlers. Some had lands under their own management, as seen in the petition of Simon Ray to the town in behalf of the heirs of Penewess, a petty chief, who died and left land on the Island from which "his countrymen" were entitled to rent. This protection was evinced by the following act :

"At a quartur Cort held for the town of New Shoreham at the hewes of mr. Robert Gutterig the second tewseday In July 1675 It dead evidently apere that mr. gorges [George's] negro rathy [Wrathy] and John drummers sone [Drummer's son] was gilty of staling fish from

Steven the Indian for the which wee ordur each of them to be whiped with 12 stripes or pay 6 shelens In mony or the true valu and that s^d rathe [Wrathy] is not hereafter. to be absent from his masters hews after sun set without leave from his s^d mastur on penalty of the acoused [accused] being whiped with 12 lashes."

The Indians, as well as the English, were protected against the evil of intemperance. That there were unprincipled men who would sell them rum, regardless of consequences, is seen in the stratagem of Thomas Terry in destroying their supply furnished by a Mr. Arnold, a trader on Block Island. This Arnold, like others, probably drank like the Indians and brought on a fatal attack of delirium tremens, or the *"horrors."* The record of him is this :—"Samuel Arnold, one of his Majesty's subjects being sick and outt of frame, not being in his right sences, Departed his house. [In the night.] The next morning Sarch was made for him and was found dead." The jury of inquest on Mr. Arnold's body gave the following verdict:

" The Jury being sollemly Ingaged came into the wood whare the s^d Sam'l arnall's corps Lay and haveing strictly vewed s^d corps do unonnimasly agree that he being griped with the pains of death ran from his house, being out of his sences, to this wood, and Dyed a natural death."

As a protection against Indian intemperance the town enacted, in 1692, the following:

"Voted that if any person shall sell any rum, wine, cider, or any strong drink to Indian or Indians upon the Lord's day, being the first day of the week, for any strong drink as aforesaid sold at such time, or delivered to any Indian upon barter or otherwise whereby to be a means to cause said Indian to be drunk on the Lord's day, every such inhabitant so doing shall pay into the public stock in money or equivalent in current specie the sum of forty shillings to be paid forthwith upon conviction."

In June, 1693, Capt. William Hancock, for violating the above ordinance by selling rum to an Indian on the Sabbath, was fined twenty shillings. During this year an Indian boy was thrown from a cart and killed. In the Coroner's report it is said :—"The cart-wheel came against a stump, and suddenly overturned the Ingen lad."

DISAPPEARING.

The disappearing of the Indians from Block Island was rapid and easily explained. Up to the year 1700 they numbered about 300. As these were mentioned by Niles in contrast with the sixteen men and a boy who challenged them to an open field-fight, it may be inferred that they were *men*, warriors. If this inference be correct, then we may put down their original number, at the time of settlement by the English in 1662, to be nearly 1000, including the women and children. From a "Memorandum of Block Island, or Manisses, A. D. 1762, by Dr. Stiles," we learn to how small a number they had dwindled during the first century of occupancy of the Island by the English. He says that in 1756 there were "few Indians, but no wigwams." From the same volume in which this statement is contained we learn that in 1774 the Indians of Block Island were reduced to fifty-one.

Their disappearance from the Island may be attributed mainly to three causes : *first*, the loss of their lands ; *secondly*, their subjugation to slavery, and *thirdly*, the need of them by Ninicraft, their chief, on the main-land. As instances of their running away it is sufficient to refer to the six who left Mr. Thomas Terry ; to *Chagum*, after whom Chagum Pond is supposed to have been named, who ran away with a canoe, was recaptured, and re-enslaved. (See Chagum Pond.) That they were not exterminated by wars is certain, for we have no account of any killing of Indians on Block Island after Col. Endicott's expedition against the Manisseans in 1636. A single remnant of the old aboriginal stock is living on the Island.

CHURCH FAMILY.

Peter Church, a full-blood Indian, fought for the English, in the old French War, on the main-land, and afterwards returned to his native Island where he spent some years before his death. His grave is in the colored burial ground.

Mary Church, daughter of Peter, was born upon Block Island, and worked in different families. She had three sons, and three daughters whose names were Hearty N. Church, Sally, and Thankful. The sons' names were Titus, Solomon, and Isaac. All are dead except Isaac. They left children, now widely scattered. Two of them, very respectable half-breeds, females, from Stonington, visited the Island in the summer of 1876.

Aaron Church, son of the above-named Titus, from his connection with the pirate Gibbs, has left a reputation that indicates his descent from the murderers of Capt. Oldham. In the year 1830 he shipped on board the brig *Vineyard*, early in November, at New Orleans, for Philadelphia. William Thornby was captain, and William Roberts, mate. After the vessel had been several days at sea Charles Gibbs, Thomas J. Wansley, and Aaron Church —desperate characters, especially the first-named, entered into a conspiracy to capture the vessel, which contained a cargo of sugar, molasses, and also $54,000 in specie. On the 23d of Nov. they executed their piratical purpose, in the night, by killing Captain Thornby and his mate, William Roberts, with a "pump-break," and threw their bodies overboard. Others of the crew, to save their lives, became feigned accessories, until they reached the shore and could expose the pirates with safety. Wansley was the steward, and a negro. Church was part Indian, and Gibbs, a native of Rhode Island, was a notorious villain, who probably led his accomplices into this their last crime.

When about fifteen miles from Long Island, having divided the money, which belonged to Stephen Girard, Gibbs took the long boat, and Church the jolly boat, sharing the money between them. One Atwell was with Church. Gibbs landed on Long Island, was arrested, tried, and with Wansley executed in New York April 22, 1831. Church started, it is said, for Block Island, with sails set in his jolly boat, in a rough sea, and was foundered, and drowned with his companions in sight of Gibbs and Wansley who "saw them clinging to the masts." Thus the pirate Aaron Church went down with his ill-gotten gain.

Isaac Church, the uncle of Aaron, is still living, at the age of eighty-eight, as he informs the writer. He can give but little information of his ancestry—does not know who was his father, but remembers well his mother who was more easily identfied. If his father were not an Indian his mother was surely a full-breed, and *vice versa*, for his hair and features are thoroughly Manissean. As he is older than the rest of the Islanders it is useless to question them about his parentage. They all, however, speak well of " Uncle Isaac Church," and his comfortable home is proof of his temperance and industry in former days. He has obtained distinction in a peculiar way that will long be remembered, viz. : *Attendance at funerals.* It is a common remark that " he has been to more funerals than any other person on the Island," and that "he goes to all funerals." It is easy to predict that many will be at his, and that many a tender recollection of " Uncle Isaac " will be cherished, by the children now living, who in maturer years will speak of him as the last and worthy

6*

representative of the ancient Manissean lords of the soil, who will soon be known only in history.

The descendants of Isaac Church are too far removed from aboriginal blood to be classed with Indians.

THEIR RELIGION.

Of the religion of the Block Island Indians no information of much account is attainable. That the natives of New England generally had some notions of a superhuman Being is well understood. The Pequots evinced this when they regarded their Chief Sassacus as "a god that nobody could kill," extolling him as superhuman because of his supposed immortality. Whatever he may have been, back of him in the minds of his warriors we see the fundamental notion of religion—the notion of supremacy. That notion was in the minds of the Manisseans, and they have left a record of it in the beautiful name of their Island. For it is said by very good authority that "Manisses," when interpreted, means, "The Little God," or the "Island of the Little God." This perhaps, had reference to some ancient petty sachem, while the great sachem of the Narragansetts was near Westerly, R. I., as Mr. Niles says he there viewed "the remains of Ninicraft's fort." But all is gone but the fame of their fierceness.

It is with feelings shaded with sadness that we take leave of this subject, as we look out upon the hundreds of little hills reflected from intervening waters, where the arrows of the Red men secured food from the innumerable fowls that rested here in their fall and spring journeys south and north, where the lights of their wigwams cheered the lonely voyager—lights around which were told the strange legends of antiquity and the war-songs of victory were wildly chanted, and young men and maidens courted, and where even savage hearts quailed, as the howling of the tempest and the crashing thunders commingled with "the sound of many waters," while the darkness of night at intervals was banished by the lightnings which for an instant lighted up the green hills, their great and little mirrors of water, and the foaming sea around, all preaching to the Indian of the Great Spirit as directly, perhaps, as did the prophet to the more civilized when he said : " Will ye not tremble at my presence,

> " Which have placed the sand for the bound of the sea
> By a perpetual decree, that it cannot pass it ;
> And though the waters thereof toss themselves, yet can they not
> prevail ;
> Though they roar, yet can they not pass over it ? "
>
> JER. v, 22.

So He has set bounds to nations as well as to individuals, and instead of boasting of a superiority over the savage tribes, the last of which are fading away, it is well to remember the old and demonstrated saying: " We all do fade as a leaf."

The " life and immortality bought to light " to us, were darkly seen by the Manisseans, as shown by their mode of burial. One of many instances may here suffice. On the farm now owned by Mr. Simon Ball, at the south end of the Great Pond, a few years ago there was a small land-slide which left standing in the bank in full view an Indian skeleton, very large, with a rude earthen jar at his feet well packed with scallop shells. From their known custom of burying eatables with the dead to supply them with food on their journey to another world, it is evident that this earthen pot of shell-fish was there buried with the Indian in a walking posture for the same purpose. By this custom they have left good proof of their belief in a future life. About all, therefore, that can be attributed to them of a religious character is : 1. A belief in the existence and power of the Great Spirit. 2. A belief in a conscious future state ; and 3. Their dim view of the soul's immortality.

Indian Head Neck, the old Indian burial-ground, has disclosed many human bones, and many shells which indicate the religious rite of burying food with the dead. In contrast with these, two heads of Indians, for some crime, were anciently placed upon the tops of stakes in said burial-ground, and from that circumstance the first settlers named that narrow bluff Indian Head Neck.

BLOCK ISLAND HOSTILITIES.

Although no distinguished battles have been fought either on, or near Block Island, yet it has always shared in the great national hostilities in which our country from time to time has been involved. Of conflicts here between the Indians our knowledge is only traditionary. This knowledge. however, is sufficient to leave the conviction that from "time out of mind," this Island was a bone of contention between neighboring tribes upon the main-land. As it lies nearest to the territory occupied by the Narragansetts it naturally came under the rule of their Chiefs, Ninicraft, Miantinomo, Canonicus, and other more remote sachems in past ages. Still, it was within reach of the eagle-eyed Sassacus and his warlike Pequots, and even the more distant Mohegans beyond the Connecticut river coveted the fertile plantations and productive fishing grounds of Manisses. Tradition points to their savage fleet of bark canoes launched beyond "two large rivers," and made to skim over the briny deep by the force of paddles flashing in the moonlight until they were silently dipped at midnight along the Island's shores at Cooneymus, or at Grace's Cove. It tells us too of the Mohegan dashes from Montauk, their shortest distance to row to Manisses. The Mohegan Bluffs will ever remain as a monument of the Narragansetts' victory over the Mohegans, and the friendship of Ninicraft their chief with the English will also immortalize his strategy in maintaining his grounds against the more warlike Pequots. Had he not done this the fate, too, of the little colony of sixteen

families, far from the main-land, might have been very
different from what it was ; for then Sassacus might have
weakened the Narragansetts, captured Manisses, and with
his fierce Pequots annihilated the little colony.   But Ninicraft's alliance with the English kept his Block Island
subjects from hostilities with the early settlers, and also
from feuds among themselves which are said to have
arisen previously between the Indians of the west side
and those of the east side of the Island.

WITH THE INDIANS.

The first act of hostility on Block Island in which white
men participated was the killing of Capt. John Oldham
by the Indians in 1636, an account of which is given in
the article on *Indians.*

The second act of hostility was that of Col. John Endicott in 1636, in his expedition to "do justice unto the
Indians for the murder of Mr. Oldham," and to take possession of their Island.   His officers were Capt. John
Underhill, Capt. Nathaniel Turner, Ensigns Jennison and
Davenport.   He had ninety soldiers.   Winthrop says,—
"They were embarked in three pinnaces, and carried two
shallops and two Indians with them.   They had commission to put to death the men of Block Island, but to spare
the women and children, and to bring them [men] away,
and to take possession of the Island."   (See article on
Indians.)

This commission was not to kill *all* "the men," but rather
to kill *only* men, and not women and children, and Endicott acted accordingly, killing only a sufficient number for
a severe retribution and for the capture of the Island.
Had the commission meant *all*, it would have said so, and
Endicott would have obeyed.

The Court and Council of Massachusetts sent out this
expedition to Block Island on the 25th of Sept., 1636.   It

is probable that Endicott, on his way to the Island, conferred with the Chief of the Narragansetts, Miantinomo,
and perhaps with the Pequots, for one of his soldiers
wrote back to a friend as follows :

"We are now in readiness for Block Island, only we
wait for a fair wind. We are informed of many Indians
there, so we expect the toughest work we have had yet."
"2d day of the 6th week of our warfare.

ISRAEL STOUGHTON."

In Winthrop's History of New England it is said :
"They arrived at Block Island the last of August. The
wind blowing hard at N. E., there went so great a surf
as they had much to do to land ; and about forty Indians
were ready upon the shore to entertain them with their
arrows which they shot off at our men ; but being armed
with corslets they had no hurt, only one was lightly hurt
upon his neck, and another near his foot. So soon as one
man leaped on shore, they all fled. The Island is about
ten miles long, and four broad, full of small hills, and all
overgrown with brush-wood of oak,—no good timber on
it.—so as they could not march but in one file and in the
narrow paths. There were two plantations, three miles
in sunder, and about sixty wigwams,—some very large
and fair,—and about two hundred acres of corn, some
gathered and laid on heaps, and the rest standing. When
they had spent two days searching the Island, and could
not find the Indians, they burnt their wigwams and all
their mats, and some corn, and staved seven canoes, and
departed. They could not tell what men they killed, but
some were wounded and carried away by their fellows."

Endicott did not very thoroughly search the Island, or
he would have found the Indians, and the heavy timber
then standing, abundant in 1662.

The full punishment and subjugation of the Manissean

were not completed by Col. Endicott until a second land-ing, in 1637, by the above-named Stoughton, of whom Winthrop (then governor of Mass.) says : " Mr. Stough-ton sailed with some of his company from Pequod to Block Island. They came hither in the night, yet were discovered, and our men having killed one or two of them, and burnt some of their wigwams, etc., they came to parley, and, submitting themselves to become tributa-ries in one hundred fathom wampum peague [beads] and to deliver any that should be found to have any hand in Mr. Oldham's death, they were all received and no more harm done them."

This conclusion of the Oldham hostilities clearly shows how unjust a reflection has been cast upon Massachusetts by those who have construed Endicott's commission to mean that "the whole male population of the Island must be exterminated," and that "the women and children were to be brought off as captives." (*Narragansett Weekly*, for Aug. 30, 1860. Also foot note "4." of Winthrop, I, p. 229.) By misconstruction the language of said commis·sion which meant *gentleness*, in killing *only men*, and only enough to subdue the Island, and to bring some away as hostages, wholly sparing the women and children, has been made to mean *cruelty*, with much injustice to Gov. Vane and his Council, and "the rest of the magistrates and ministers," all of whom were together at the special session to consider the course to be taken in the case of the death of Mr. Oldham. They could not have been ignorant of the great number of Indians on the Island, and of the impossibility of exporting in Endicott's little vessels the women and children, for Roger Williams was then in constant communication with the great chiefs of the Island and with the Massachusetts authorities. More-over, Endicott's commission required him to proceed direct from Block Island "to the Pequods," to make war, if necessary with them; but how could he do this with his vessels loaded down with the women and children of said Island? No. Endicott's commission simply meant,—kill *men*, but spare women and children; capture the Island; bring away a few natives as hostages, and kill only as many men as necessary to accomplish this end; "thence go to the Pequods, &c.," and he complied with this commission.

The hostile feelings of the Block Island Indians towards the white settlers were latent rather than manifest, as in other parts of the colonies. On one or two occasions they were on the verge of an outbreak, as in the squabble between a few of them and a few settlers, and at the time the Indians assembled on Fort Island for a pitched battle, as related in the biographical sketches of James Sands, and of Thomas Terry.

That the Indians of Block Island were very dangerous in the estimation of the settlers is evident from the acts passed at various times to keep them from violence. For there were traders then, as now, who, regardless of the peace and interests of society, for "filthy lucre," endangered the lives of all by selling to the natives fire-arms and *fire-water*. In 1675, the vigilance of the citizens required the disarming of every Indian at sundown. Their guns were then delivered up to their masters, and returned to them in the morning. They were about twenty times as numerous as the English. In 1675, too, a "squadron" of soldiers for self defense, was maintained by the Islanders. It was kept up by each citizen serving in rotation. The house of Robert Gutterig was their rendezvous. There they met, according to their turns, before the sun was an hour high, upon failure of which each delinquent was obliged to pay the penalty of "five shillings, and that to be kept in the hands of the treasurer for a common stock for ammunition." There was one excuse, however, then, the force of which is felt even now. In case the easterly wind blew strongly, accompanied by rain or snow, the soldier was excused from leaving home and repairing to the garrison that day, unless it cleared up before twelve o'clock. Flint locks and wet powder were then common, the latter in rainy weather. At this time, so far as we can learn, there was no protection from the main-land for the infant colony. The nearest intimation of it is the fact that in May, 1664, Messrs. James Sands and Joseph Kent petitioned the General Assembly, and in response Roger Williams, Thomas Olney, and Joseph Torrey were appointed a committee to consider said petition and report on it in reference to the "preservation of His Majesty's peace there," on Block Island.

In this perilous time, 1676, the Islanders passed the following ordinance, viz.: " Voted that every male from the age of sixteen years old and upwards, shall provide himself with a sufficient fire-lock gun and two pounds of powder and four pounds of shot and lead at or before the last of March next ensuing, upon the penalty of twenty shillings for such neglect." At the same time the sale of strong drink in smaller quantities than a gallon was prohibited under the penalty of twenty shillings, except where license was given. Rum then, as now, fired the savage feelings, which threatened the extermination of the little colony of Islanders, and up to the year 1693 we find stringent laws enforced to restrain unprincipled venders on the Lord's day, fining them forty shillings for selling to an Indian, "rum, wine, cider, or any strong drink " to make him intoxicated. About this time King Philip's war was in progress, and other sachems were plotting the extermination of the New England colonies. The Islanders, therefore, must have been more or less than human, if they were not filled with alarm by the rumors of white men, women, and children on the main slaughtered, and tortured to death by savages, while the same uncivilized spirits, far outnumbering themselves, were lurking day and night about their scattered homes. It was then that the wisdom of the high-toned civilian, James Sands; the calm, religious faith of the pious Simon Ray; and the heroism of the fearless Thomas Terry were frequently taxed to their utmost and combined in councils of defense and even offense. It was then that the cottages and wigwams of Block Island were filled with anxious minds plotting, talking, and dreaming of bloodshed. It was then that a clear insight into the weakness accompanying the Red Man's consciousness of his inferiority, and a rational view of the comparative dangers of timidity and defiance on the part of the few settlers, that the latter, commending themselves to the God of their Pilgrim fathers, put their wives and children into a feeble garrison, and challenged their hostile neighbors to face them on the field of battle. To no scene of sublimer faith and heroism can the historian point than was exhibited on Block Island when, at Fort Island, the little band of sixteen men and a boy marched to the music of a single drum beaten for dear life by Mr. Kent, until they faced the frowning fort of twenty times their number, standing there within gunshot of the enemy armed with guns, bows and arrows, clubs and scalping knives. Was a braver challenge ever given ? A little handful of less than tens virtually saying to hundreds, "We stand within the reach of your savage weapons—strike the first blow if you dare, and we will send you all to—to the hunting grounds of your dead men."

The victory thus won was so complete, without the discharge of a gun or an arrow that from that day to the present, when but one Indian remains (Uncle Isaac Church), an unbroken friendship has continued between the Manisseans and their successors, a remembrance of which is a rich legacy to the rising generations.

WITH THE FRENCH.

War between France and England in 1690 greatly disturbed the peace of the colonies, no part of which, perhaps, was more exposed to the depredations of the former than was Block Island. In the month of March of that year the opening conflict was "proclaimed by beat of drum" in the streets of Newport, and not long after the notes of war vibrated across the waters to this Island and caused many a tearful cheek, and deep anxiety in the hearts of the bravest. In May, 1690, came a tax of seventeen pounds and ten shillings to be collected of the Islanders "for the support of their Majesty's interest against the French and Indian enemies." Thus after thirty years of perils at home, they saw the distant war-cloud gathering and from its border saw its first few hail stones striking on their shores. A merciless enemy was coming on the wind—one that purposed, with an infidelity unbecoming a savage, to exhaust his own resources of cruelty, and with these combine the fierceness of the Indians. In no direction from their shores could the Islanders look for protection, except upward. The enemy came.

To fight the American colonies was to fight England. The colonies on the main-land, assisted by England, were comparatively safe against the French invaders. But it was impossible to keep the ships of France from lighting, like harpies, on this well stored Island.

In July, 1689, "a large bark, a barge, a large sloop, and a lesser one"—three men of war with their transport stood towards the bay on the east side of Block Island. The inhabitants were greatly alarmed, and doubtful whether the vessels were French or English, hostile or friendly. The vessels anchored, while on the shore were standing brave men filled with anxiety. A boat was lowered and a few approached the shore. One, when near enough, left the boat and stepped from rock to rock until he addressed, in English, with friendly words, those upon the shore. His name was *William Trimming.* They questioned him closely, as they stood holding their arms for defense. He made them believe his vessels were under the command of George Astin, a noted English privateer to whom they were friendly, that they were in need of wood, water, and a pilot to conduct them safely into Newport harbor. Having gained the confidence of the Islanders he returned to his vessel, and soon made signal for a pilot. Several, "in hopes of some great reward," at once went aboard, and were immediately clapped under the hatches, and there under threats were compelled to tell what they knew of the means of defense on the Island. Upon this information the French, still supposed to be English, lowered three boats, and with about fifty men in each, having their guns concealed, approached the deceived and amused spectators who directed the enemy how to shun the hidden rocks in the Bay until they came to the wharf where the said guns were suddenly seized and leveled at the Islanders with horrid threats from the invaders. The soldiers thus overpowered and taken prisoners, the Island became a prey to the perfidious Trimming, whose men broke the guns of the Islanders in pieces upon the rocks and confined the owners in the stone house of Captain James Sands. The French pillaged the Island, killing all kinds of cattle for food, and what they did not need they killed for spoil to impoverish the people. Our informant, Rev. Samuel Niles, says,—"they continued about a week on the Island, plundering houses, stripping the people of their clothing, ripping up beds, throwing out the feathers, and carrying away the ticking." Their abuses to the venerable Simon

7*

Ray are related in our biographical sketch of him. They entered the house of Dr. John Rodman, a skillful physician and devoted Quaker and insulted his wife, "a very desirable gentlewoman," between whom and the insolent Frenchman the Doctor sprang, as the ruffian cocked his pistol at Rodman who bared his bosom and said,—"Thee mayest do it if thou pleasest, but thou shalt not abuse my wife." During the week of plundering on the Island the French in the vessels captured two English vessels bound ·up the Sound, sinking the one laden with steel, and preserving the other for her cargo of liquors.

News of this invasion in some way reached the mainland while the French were upon the Island, and quickly, at night, a ribbon of bonfires was seen along the shore from Pawcatuck Point (south of Westerly, R. I.) to Seconet Point. This alarmed the privateers and they left with the intention of taking New London, but the fire upon them there in the harbor was so hot that they retreated. Meanwhile two vessels of war were fitted out at Newport for the defense of Block Island, under the command of Commodore Paine, and Captain John Godfrey. On their arrival here, and learning of the sacking of the Island, they pursued the enemy. On Fisher's Island they surprised seventeen Frenchmen and killed the deceitful Trimming through whose perfidy Block Island had been captured.

The French, on their way from New London to continue their plundering of Block Island, met our men-of-war under Commodore Paine to the westward of Sandy Hill. There, perhaps, it was that our informant, the Rev. Mr. Niles, was stationed while viewing the naval battle, the first, probably, fought within the waters of Block Island. As Mr. Niles was an eye-witness, his description is most reliable, and we quote it here in full.

"Our English vessels stretched off to the southward,

and soon made a discovery of a small fleet standing eastward. Supposing them to be the French they were in
quest of, they tacked and came as near the shore as they
could with safety, carrying one anchor to wear and
another to seaboard, to prevent the French boarding them
on each side at once, and to bring their guns and men all
on one side the better to defend themselves and annoy the
enemy. The French probably discovered them also, and
made all the sail they could, expecting to make prizes of
them. Accordingly they sent a periauger before them,
full of men, with design to pour in their small arms on
them, and take them, as their manner was, supposing they
were unarmed vessels, and only bound upon trade. Captain Paine's gunner urged to fire on them. The Captain
denied, alleging it more advisable to let the enemy come
nearer under their command. But the gunner still urging
it, being certain (as he said) he should rake fore and aft,
thus with much importunity, at length the Captain gave
him liberty. He fired on them, but the bullet went wide
of them, and I saw it skip on the surface of the water
several times, and finally lodged in a bank, as they were
not very far distant from the shore. This brought them
to a stand, and to row off as fast as they could and wait
until their vessels came up. When they came they bore
down on the English, and there ensued a very hot sea-
fight for several hours, though under the land, the great
bark foremost, pouring in a broadside with small arms.
Ours bravely answered them in the same manner, with
their huzzas and shouting. Then followed the larger
sloop, the captain whereof was a very violent, resolute
fellow. He took a glass of wine to drink, and wished it
might be his damnation if he did not board them immediately. But as he was drinking a bullet struck him in the
neck, with which he instantly fell down dead, as the
prisoners (before spoken of) afterwards reported. How-

ever, the large sloop proceeded, as the foremost vessel had done, and the lesser sloop likewise. Thus they passed by in course, and then tacked and brought their other broadside to bear. In this manner they continued the fight until the night came on and prevented their further conflict. Our men as valiantly paid them back in their own coin, and bravely repulsed them, and killed several of them.

"In this action the continued fire was so sharp and violent, that the echo in the woods made a noise as though the limbs of the trees were rent and tore off from their bodies ; yet they killed but one man, an Indian of the English party, and wounded six white men who after recovered. They overshot our men, so that many of their bullets, both great. and small, were picked up on the adjacent shore.

"During the next night our vessels were replenished with ammunition from the Island, but in the morning it was discovered that the enemy had taken [*French*] *leave*. Our vessels pursued them so closely that they were obliged to scuttle the prize vessels before mentioned—the one laden with liquors, and she was overtaken while sinking."

This first invasion of Block Island by French privateers aroused the country to such a degree that men-of-war from Boston, and from New York were dispatched to the rescue and for the pursuit of the enemy.

The next act of hostilities on the Island was by a part of the former invaders, before the close of the same year 1689. This second attack was in the night, and, though brief, was very alarming and destructive of property in a manner similar to that previously described. No one was killed. Mr. Niles, our informant, was the chief sufferer, as seen in our sketch of him. But as the war between France and England continued, the depredations of the enemy were repeated. Of the next alarm and plundering of the Island Mr. Niles says :

"The French came a third time while I was on the Island, and came to anchor in the bay on Saturday, some time before night ; and acquainted us who they were and what they intended, by hoisting up their white colors. None of the people appearing to oppose them, and having at this time, my aged grandparents, Mr. James Sands and his wife, to take care of, with whom I then dwelt ; knowing also, that if they landed they would make his house the chief seat of their rendezvous, as they had done twice before, and not knowing what insults or outrage they might commit on them, I advised to the leaving of their house, and betaking themselves to the woods for shelter, till they might return under prospects of safety ; which they consented to. Accordingly we took our flight into the woods, which were at a considerable distance, where we encamped that night as well as the place and circumstances would allow, with some others, that for the like reasons fell into our company. The next morning being Lord's day morning, I expressed my desire to go occultly and see the conduct of the French, and their proceedings. (See on Capt. James Sands.)

"Having had but little sleep the night before, I proposed to Mr. Thomas Mitchell to keep a good look-out, and watch their motions, till I endeavored to sleep a little, and thus to proceed interchangeably ; when I made the hard ground my lodging for the time, which was long. Upon my awaking he lay down, and as he lay and slept, the French fired many guns at the house, and I heard several bullets whistling over my head. Suspecting they had made some discovery of us, I awakened him, telling him what I had observed, therefore that it was advisable to shift our quarters. Accordingly, as we were moving from the place we espied a large ship about a league to leeward of the township, riding at anchor (the fog at sea had been very thick till then), which happened to be Captain Dobbins, in the Nonesuch man-of-war, stationed in those seas, which we at first sight supposed. This ship appearing put the Frenchmen into a great surprise, by their motions, by running up to their standard on the hill, then down again, and others doing the like. The man-of-war still making all sail possible, there being but a small breeze of wind at southwest, and right ahead, according to the sailors' phrase, they soon left the house [Capt. James Sands' stone house, then standing where Mr. Almemzo Littlefield's lawn, east of his house, is], and with all speed and seeming confusion hastened to their vessel. Upon this we went boldly to the house, and found the floor covered with geese, with blood and feathers; the quarters of the hogs they had killed hanging up in one and another part of the house—a melancholy sight to behold! Their manner of dressing hogs after they had quartered them was to singe off the hair over a flame; and their method to command the cattle was (as I saw when they took us before) to thrust their cutlasses in at their loins, and on a sudden the hind quarter would drop down, and as the poor creature strove to go forward, the blood would spout out of the hole, and fly up near or full out a yard in height."

"Soon after these privateers took to their heels," they were hotly pursued by the Nonesuch. The former steered for Noman's Land, but in the fog missed their course, ran into Buzzards Bay, where they were land-locked and captured by their pursuers. Forty of the French endeavored to escape by running ashore, but were soon seized by the people and sent as prisoners to Boston. The rest Captain Dobbins made prisoners of war, and took their ship as a prize back to Newport."

By this time it would seem that there could be but little

left on Block Island to tempt the enemy. But its fat cattle, swine, sheep. and poultry. together with the fabrics of household industry. for many years, were scented from afar by the freebooters of the sea. Hither they continued to come for plunder, and from 1698 until after 1706 it was in a condition like that of a continued siege, for in 1706, the Governor and Council of Rhode Island reported as follows : "We have been also this summer as well as the last obliged to maintain a quota of men at Block Island for the defence of Her Majesty's interest there."

Meanwhile a *fourth* hostile demonstration was made upon this little "Isle of the sea," whether by the French, or by pirates, is a matter of uncertainty, as the latter were then numerous. At that time Capt. Robert Kidd with his piratical crew was roaming the seas and striking terror to many an island and seacoast city. But at this fourth and last attack during the long wars between France and England, the Islanders met the enemy "in an open pitched battle, and drove them off from the shore," no one in return receiving any injury, "except one man slightly wounded in his finger." Where that bloodless battle-field, on the part of the Islanders is, we are not informed. Probably it was in the vicinity of the old Pier.

During the above period of hostilities on Block Island, its inhabitants were not only plundered by privateers, and burdened with the expenses of self defence, but heavy taxes came upon them from abroad. In response to their remonstrances the Rhode Island Assembly, in 1696, remitted to them "one penny on the pound," of the levy on the Islanders. This was "penny wise." In 1700 the proportion of the colony tax of £800 allotted Block Island was £22, and this was remitted on the ground of the great expense they had borne in maintaining their soldiers. So great was the danger from deceitful visitors then, that the town passed the stringent law of fining a man five pounds for bringing ashore any man or woman from abroad without reporting the same to the town authorities immediately. Judge of the anxious days and sleepless nights during a period of twenty years, while threatened with a neighboring host of savages, while repeatedly invaded by privateers and pirates; while constantly watching the surrounding waters, and maintaining laws that disarmed their superior numbers at sunset, and punished them for walking abroad after nine o'clock at night; while burdened with the expense of maintaining their own little standing army, and also that upon the main-land; and while, for their own support the fields must be cultivated, and material raised upon their farms for the distaff, the big spinning-wheel, and the loom. It was in reference to the above manifold burdens that in 1697 the following memorial was indicted, probably by Simon Ray:

"SEPTEMBER the 5th, 1697.

"To the Honoured Governor, Deputy Governor and the Rest of the Members of the General Assembly of Rhode Island and Providence Plantations:

"The humble petition of the poor distressed Inhabitants of Block Island which expect daily No other than to be Invaded, our houses demolished, our persons and Estates become a prey to the enemy If no other assistance can be had than what we can Raise within ourselves. We both think and find it very hard that we should be forced to hire and pay men's wages at our own charge since we are or should be a member of a Colony that in our opinion ought to protect us who as yet have Not any from as a Colony we do suppose a thing not to be paralleled with In the King's Dominion that one part of a province or Colony that think themselves most secure should rather Reject than protect that part that Is In imminent danger. We your humble petitioners humbly consider the charge will be easier for a whole Colony to bare than a poor handful of distressed people which are always in fears, horrors, and troubles. We do suppose that one hundred and sixty pounds a year would supply with men and ammunition which is but a little for a Colony to raise. We do suppose that as Justly as submission may be expected from us we may expect Relief in time of distress. We find that if we have money enough we may have men enough. If they cannot be spared in our own Colony we can be supplied otherwheres. Thus your distressed petitioners wait for your favorable and speedy result."

(Signed by 30 freeholders.)

To the foregoing piratical period in the history of Block Island the following case of kidnapping in 1717 properly belongs. It is still involved in mystery. The occurrence is authenticated by the depositions of reliable witnesses, and by the town record of the same, still preserved, of which we give here a copy:

" BLOCK ISLAND ales NEW SHORAM
Aprell ye 18th 1717.

We the subscribers testifie and say that as we went on board of a large Sloop, Baulsgrave Williams Commander, as by some of his men's Report, and he Likewise being on shore to get some refreshment in order as he said to go to Boston on s^d day aforementioned, we and severall others went on bord with him. after that we had been on bord of him about an houre or two (being then in our Harbour Bay) we all came out of s^d Sloop into our Boat without any molestation ; but after that we were put off from the Sloop Some distance Rowing to make the Harbour we were imediatly Comanded on bord again, not knowing what their business was with us ; as soon as we came along side of the Sloop three of our men that were in our Boat with us were forcibly taken from us and commanded to come on bord of them, one of which was

pulled out of the boat into the Sloop by violence and the
other two commanded to go on boarde of them. After
this manner were those men taken from us (viz.) George
Mitchell, William Toesh, and Doctur James Sweete ; and
forthere Deponents say not.

THOMAS DANIELS,
JOHN RATHBUN,
THOMAS PAIN.

The three persons within personally apeared before me
one of his majesty's Wardins or Justices of the peace
of Block Island and took their Sollem Ingagements to
the contents within mentioned as attest pr. me

JOHN SANDS, *Dep. Warden.*

MAY ye 19th, 1717.

my Self being present on bord the boat when the men
were taken out as within mentioned."

The last-mentioned act of hostility justifies the preceding and subsequent measures of defense adopted by
the Islanders and assisted by the Colony of Rhode Island.
In 1708 the Assembly, on condition the Islanders had
truly laid out their due proportion of money for arms and
ammunition, enacted that they should have a quota of
fifteen soldiers for their defense, and that " The Honored
Governor, Assistant, and Major of the Island shall order
said quota from time to time as they shall see cause, and
to abate the number as they shall see cause for, and the
men of Block Island to use said quota kindly, and find
them with provisions (at their own charge), as is convenient for soldiers." In May 1711, a quota of twelve soldiers was furnished the Island, they finding their own
arms and ammunition, and receiving thirty shillings a
month. In November of the same year their pay was
increased to forty shillings a month. But at this time
they were, perhaps, less needful, as the notes of war
began to die away. and soon after were only heard faintly
echoing like far distant thunder from foreign shores.
Nations hostile to England found it easier to fight her

elsewhere than among the American Colonies. If the war of King George in 1744, and the conquest of the Canadas ten years after affected Block Island at all it was only as the spent shock of a far-off earthquake, leaving the inhabitants to pursue their peaceful avocations with very little interruption until the sad day arrived when the Colonists, by civil oppression, were compelled to turn their guns upon the government from which they had sought and obtained protection. Meanwhile, however, lessons of self-government and of timely preparations for defense had been learned, and, in the year 1740, we find the same put in practice by an act of the General Assembly of R. I., authorizing the field officers of Providence, and Kings counties to impress from each ten able-bodied men to be sent to Block Island. by the 20th of April of that year, to serve there six months, to be under the care and command of the Captain of the Island [Capt. Edward Sands], and by him "billeted out at the charge of the inhabitants of said Island," receiving £3 per month each from the general treasury. A battery, it seems by the following act of 1740, had been planted here previously upon Harbor Hill, nearly back of the gothic cottage of Mr. Darius Dodge, a suitable place for protecting the bay and harbor. This act was, "That the six great guns at New Shoreham be mounted on carriages, in the most convenient manner, as shall be judged by the inhabitants ; and that they, at their own charge, procure two barrels of gunpowder, one hundred and twenty great shot and forty pounds weight of musket-balls ; and that Captain Edward Sands, and Mr. Nathaniel Littlefield procure carriages for said guns, and draw money out of the general treasury to pay for the same." This was done with special reference to the war between Spain and England.

In 1745 the Islanders petitioned the General Assembly for increased protection, and in response it was " Voted and resolved that twenty-one soldiers be sent to New Shoreham, seven out of each county * * and there to remain * * until the return of the Colony sloop from the expedition against Cape Breton, or till further order from the General Assembly."

THE REVOLUTION.

That Block Island, a little speck out in the sea, should take any active part in so great a struggle as that which began its premonitions in 1774 could hardly be expected. But as the pulse of the smallest artery beats in harmony with the greater—all being one organic system—so the energetic, public-spirited men of this Island in the latter part of the eighteenth century were ready to move in any direction with the organic body of American Colonies for the maintenance of their most cherished rights and privi-leges. The leading men here then, too, were known abroad, and esteemed for their personal excellences, and their patriotism and sacrifices in the hostilities of the Revolution were an honor to the Island. While the storm of war between the Colonies and the Mother Country was gathering, the inhabitants of Block Island, after having enjoyed the sweets of civil and religious freedom for more than a century, and being in themselves a little model democracy, joined heart and hand with all American patriots, as they put upon record the following sentiments relative to

BRITISH DUTIES ON TEA.

" Proceedings of the People of New Shoreham, in Town Meeting."

" At a town meeting held at New Shoreham, March 2, 1774, John Sands, Esq., moderator.

WHEREAS, there has been sent to this town a copy of the resolves entered into by the town of Newport, and a request to lay the same before this town, with a design that said town would unite with the other towns in this Colony in supporting their just rights and liberties :

1. Therefore we the inhabitants of this town, being legally convened in town meeting, do firmly resolve, as the opinion of said town, that the Americans have as good a right to be as free a people as any upon the earth; and to enjoy at all times an uninterrupted possession of their rights and properties.

2. That the act of the British Parliament, claiming the right to make laws binding upon the Colonies, in all cases whatsoever, is inconsistent with the natural, constitutional, and charter rights and privileges of the inhabitants of this Colony.

3. That the express purpose for which the tax is levied on the Americans, namely, for the support of government, administration of justice, and defense of His Majesty's dominions in America, has a direct tendency to render Assemblies useless, and to introduce arbitrary government and slavery.

4. That a tax on the inhabitants of America, without their consent, is a measure absolutely destructive of their freedom, tending to enslave and impoverish all who tamely submit to it.

5. That the act allowing the East India Company to export tea to America, subject to a duty payable here, and the actual sending tea into the Colonies, by said Company, is an open attempt to enforce the ministerial plan, and a violent attack upon the liberties of America.

6. That it is the duty of every American to oppose this attempt.

7. That whosoever shall, directly, or indirectly, countenance this attempt, or in anywise aid or assist in running, receiving, or unloading any such tea, or in piloting any vessel, having any such tea on board, while it remains

8*

subject to the payment of a duty here, is an enemy to his country.

8.   That we will heartily unite with our American brethren, in supporting the inhabitants of this Continent in all their just rights and privileges.

9.   That Joshua Sands, Caleb Littlefield, and John Sands, Esqs., and Messrs. Walter Rathbone, and Edward Sands, Jr., or the major part of them, be appointed a committee for this town, to correspond with all other committees appointed by any town in this Colony ; and said committee is requested to give the closest attention to everything which concerns the liberties of America ; and if any tea, subject to a duty here, should be landed in this town, the committee is directed and empowered to call a town meeting, forthwith, that such measures may be taken as the public safety may require.

10.   And we return our hearty thanks to the town of Newport for their patriotic resolutions to maintain the liberties of their country ; and the prudent measures they have taken to induce the other towns in this Colony to come into the same generous resolutions.

WALTER RATHBONE,
Town Clerk."

This was a bold measure for a little island, so far from adequate protection, to take. Without fortresses on the land ; without a man-of-war of their own ; without a certainty that a single war sloop could be spared from the American navy for their protection ; with shores on which privateers could land their crews at any point ; and with a fresh recollection of the repeated pillaging of their homes by an enemy less formidable than the one now provoked, the brave Islanders, in the above resolutions, as nobly laid their property, their lives, and their sacred honor upon their country's altar as did the men whose names were appended to the Declaration of Independence.

As the gathering storm-cloud darkened over the colonies active measures were taken to remove from Block Island such resources as might tempt the enemy to assault the inhabitants ; as also might aid and comfort the enemy by falling into their hands, and as might by timely removal be saved, in value, to the Islanders, and also help the American army. Accordingly the General Assembly, in August, 1775, passed the following act :

"It is voted and resolved that all the neat cattle and sheep upon New Shoreham, excepting a sufficiency for the inhabitants, be brought off as soon as possible, and landed upon the continent ; that two hundred and fifty men be sent upon that Island to secure the stock until it can be taken off." Thus military law was enforced. Active measures were at once taken to enlist one hundred and ninety men to assist in executing this transportation. James Rhodes was appointed commander of these men, and Gideon Hoxie, assistant. They, with George Sheffield, were empowered, at the expense of the colony, to remove, in the most prudent and effectual way, said stock to some place on the continent, the committee of safety supplying all necessary arms and provisions. The above-named Rhodes, Hoxie, and Sheffield were appointed to appraise the stock, which was transported at the expense and risk of the colony. Such stock as was suitable was to be sent immediately to the army. Such as was not fit for market was to be sold at public or private sale, unless the owners should choose to keep the same at their own risk.

The following account of stock taken from Block Island at the beginning of the Revolution is here given in full, for several reasons, chiefly to show who were here then, what stock they had, how great were their sacrifices for

their country, and to indicate their feelings as they parted
with their favorite cows, their working oxen, their cloth-
producing sheep, and the lambs which in the preceding
spring the children had tenderly nursed by their firesides,
the familiar lowing and bleating of which stock were to
be heard no longer.

*Sheep and Lambs taken by the colony from Block Island,
September 2, 1775.*

		£	s.	d.
Giles Pierce, 241 fat sheep and lambs, . .		78	6	6
John Paine, 78 sheep, . . .		25	3	0
Walter Rathbone, 17 " . .		5	10	6
Abel Franklin, 32 " . . .		10	18	0
John Littlefield, 62 " . .		20	3	0
Capt. John Sands, 150 " . . .		34	02	6
Edward Sands, Jr., 20 " . . .		6	10	0
Joshua Sands, Esq., 5 " . .		1	12	6
Henry Willis, Jr., 15 " . . .		5	7	6
Samuel Rathbone, 4 " . . .		1	6	0
John Barber, 96 " . . .		34	4	0
Thomas Dickens, 11 " . . .		3	11	6
John Mott, 2 lambs, . . .		0	13	0
Hezekiah Dodge, 3 " . . .		0	17	6
Benjamin Sheffield, 6 " . . .		1	19	0
Henry Littlefield, 2 " . .		0	13	0
John Mitchell, 5 " . . .		1	12	6
Thomas Mitchell, 9 " . . .		2	18	6
Jeremiah Mitchell, 1 " . .		0	6	6
John Littlefield, 43 " . . .		13	19	6
Capt. John Sands, 169 store sheep and lambs,		42	05	0
John Littlefield, 148 sheep, . . .		37	0	0
John Barber, 175 " . . .		43	15	0
Thomas Mitchell, 27 " . . .		6	15	0
John Mitchell, 10 " . . .		2	10	0

			£	s.	d.
Jonathan Mitchell,	10	sheep,	2	10	0
Joseph Mitchell,	3	"	0	15	0
George Franklin,	8	"	2	0	0
Henry Littlefield,	5	"	1	5	0
Nath'l Littlefield,	12	"	3	0	0
Edward Sands, Jr.,	29	"	7	5	0
Joshua Sands,	4	"	1	0	0
Ezekiel Sheffield,	14	"	3	10	0
Henry Willis,	2	"	0	10	0
John Mott,	1	"	0	5	0
Giles Pierce,	441	"	110	5	0
Abel Franklin,	28	"	7	0	0
John Paine,	23	"	5	15	0
Walter Rathbone.	9	"	2	5	0
Nath'l Littlefield, Jr.,	6	"	1	10	0
Henry Willis, Jr.,	10	"	2	10	0
Tormut Rose,	6	"	1	10	0
Daniel Mott,	4	"	1	0	0
Jeremiah Mitchell,	3	"	0	15	0
Ezeziel Rose,	4	"	1	0	0

Total sheep and lambs, 1,908 ; the Rhode Island colony allowed for them £534 9s. 6d.

We find no complete account of cows and oxen taken off.

In February, 1776, the General Assembly took measures to completely strip Block Island of every thing that was not absolutely necessary for the existence of the people there, who were urged to use their utmost diligence to comply with the decisions of Capt. John Sands, Joshua Sands, and William Littlefield, who were an authorized committee to determine what number of neat cattle and sheep should be left upon the Island, and to remove to the main all the stock "not absolutely necessary for the use and consumption" of the Islanders. This committee were also authorized to collect the fire-arms on the Island and agree with the owners for the payment for the same, and also that all the warlike stores then on the Island be immediately removed thence and delivered to the Rhode Island Committee of Safety.

Was not that a solemn time, when this lonely, isolated little spot was so completely divested of its former competence? The policy adopted was much like that of befriending a banker by taking away his money to save him from being robbed. There was this compensating feature, however, in this case—there was a promise to pay the Islanders on the condition of victory and independence, and this condition was the talisman that revealed to the world the unsurpassed faith and patriotism of this miniature, insular democracy that had already without ostentation celebrated its centennial of freedom. Doubtless, however, there was much lamentation over the desolate condition of the Island, as it now appeared tenfold more impoverished than it did after the repeated invasions of the French privateers. After the cattle and sheep were nearly all removed for the sustenance of the army, Edward Sands, Jr. was seen on the Island going from house to house numbering the people suggesting the thought that as the stock had gone to be slaughtered, so the able-bodied men would soon be chosen for the battlefield. Their condition was pitiable in the extreme. Indeed, what other portion of the colonies so remote from protection, or in any condition was required in the outset to give up so much for freedom? Had they not retained their fish-lines and nets they might have been almost justified in saying to Liberty, "Lo, we have left all, and have followed thee."

That the colony of Rhode Island meant to act wisely in stripping the Island, and felt tenderly towards its inhabitants, there can be no doubt, in view of all the circumstances. Not many months after, the Assembly put upon record expressions of sympathy and honest purpose. For doing so they had abundant reason. Every movement, almost, on the Island, was one of alarm. In August 1775, Andrew Waterman raised twenty-nine minute men who, with him, were hastily dispatched to the Island. About the same time, while Joseph Dennison 2d and his company were transporting from there stock to the main, in the schooner Polly, all were taken by the enemy, making a bill of loss and service against the colony of £374, which was promptly paid. Soon, too, the soldiers enlisted in the spring for six months' service on the Island would finish the term specified, and the Governor was requested by the Assembly to consult with General Washington as to his wishes concerning the forces on Block Island. At about the same time, also, charges of treachery were pre-ferred against one of the citizens, and for his reported betrayal and delivering up two seamen to a British man-of-war, Jonathan Hazard, Esq., was dispatched to Block Island with a sufficient military force to arrest one John Wright, and to look after "some other inhabitants of suspected political character," and to confine them in jail to be tried at the next session of the Assembly. To give the climax to this alarming movement Mr. Hazard was also instructed to "earnestly exhort the inhabitants of New Shoreham to remove off from the Island." This exhortation the Assembly seasoned in the following manner. In May, 1776, it apportioned to the various towns of the colony a quantity of salt—thirty bushels for Block Island ; but in the September ensuing the Assembly " Voted and resolved that no part of the salt ordered to be distributed within this State, be delivered to the town of New Shoreham; but their proportion thereof be reserved for said inhabitants to salt any provisions that may be brought from the said town to the main, there to be disposed of." There was one fable which, if the Block Islanders had ever read 'it, they then remembered—the fable of the *Vulture and the Lamb.* The lamb's bones were spared for the jaws of the lion. Such was the evening of the darkest day on Block Island. To the foregoing was added the following :

"WHEREAS, the inhabitants of New Shoreham, from their peculiar situation, are entirely in the power of the enemy, and very pernicious consequences may attend the intercourse of the said inhabitants with the continent, by means of the intelligence and supplies which the enemy may procure thereby:

"It is therefore voted and resolved, that the said inhabitants be, and they are hereby prohibited from coming from said Island into any other part of this State, upon pain of being considered as enemies to the State, and of being imprisoned in the jail in the county where they may be found, there to remain until they shall be discharged by the General Assembly. And all officers, both civil and military, and every other person being an inhabitant of this State, is hereby directed and empowered to apprehend all persons so offending, and to commit them, as aforesaid.

"Provided, nevertheless, that this act shall not extend to any inhabitant of the said Island who shall remove from thence with his or her family, with an intention to settle in any other part of the United States.

"It is further voted and resolved, that in case any person in this State shall be convicted of having any intercourse or correspondence with the persons so offending, he or she shall forfeit and pay as a fine, to the use of this State, £30, lawful money, to be recovered by the general treasurer, at the inferior court of common pleas, in the county where the offense shall be committed.

"It is further resolved, that a copy of this act be inserted in the Newport Mercury and Providence Gazette."

When the Islanders gathered around their evening firesides, and men, and women, and children read, or heard read this last act which virtually made them prisoners of war, like Napoleon on St. Helena, and that, too, by their friends, leaving them in a worse condition than his, wholly unprotected, and dependent upon their own hands for food and clothing, with pastures and stables left vacant, it is not surprising if many a tear coursed the furrowed cheeks of age, if many a wrathful speech was uttered by younger men, if many a maiden's heart trembled for fear, and if all expressions of the Islanders settled down together into wailing notes kindred to those heard in the wilderness from those who mourned that they had not died in Egypt. But, as in the wilderness there were a few whose faith and heroism looked beyond the smoke and thunders of Sinai to the grapes of Eschol and to the land of milk and honey, and choose to go on, fearless of the sons of Anak, rather than go back to feed upon the leeks and garlics of bondage ; so on Block Island, when the heavy guns of war were booming near, and the clouds of God's providence thickened into darkness that could be felt, the faith and patriotism of the Sands, the Rays, the Rathbones, the Littlefields, the Dodges, and others of the Islanders saw the end from the beginning, and that end was FREEDOM, civil, and religious, and many *lived* to see the sight in reality, and to leave a posterity ever to be proud of their noble sires.

The last act of the General Assembly, above-mentioned, prohibiting the Block Islanders from intercourse with the main-land, was too much—too stringent, and was amended soon after its enactment, and it is due to the Assembly to repeat the amendment in full, here :

" This Assembly, deploring the unhappy situation of the

9

inhabitants of New Shoreham, and willing to give them every relief in their power, and being also necessitated to provide for the general safety,

"Do resolve, in addition to, and amendment of, the act passed at the last session, respecting the said Island, that the committee appointed in the said act may permit such of the inhabitants of the said Island as they can confide in, to go to Pawcatuck river, to procure at the mills there, such a quantity of meal as shall be necessary for the inhabitants of the said Island ; they taking the same and other necessaries on board, under the direction and with the written permission of George Sheffield and Phineas Clarke, or either of them, who are hereby directed to transmit to the said committee an account of all the articles so taken on board for the said Island.

"That the said committee be empowered to permit such inhabitants of the said Island as they can confide in, to proceed to any part of the colony, to transact the necessary business of the Island ; and that no other person belonging to the said Island, besides the deputies, shall go to any other part of the colony, excepting to Goat Island, in the township of Newport, upon the penalty of being committed to jail, as in the aforesaid act is directed."

This was a great relief to the Islanders. It opened a few rents in the dark cloud, and let them see avenues, though narrow, to traffic and attainment of things needful for support and happiness. Before the close of 1776, by an act of the assembly Messrs. John Sands, Edward Sands, Jr., and Simon Ray Littlefield were given "liberty to bring any provisions, hides, or other articles" from the Island, to any part of the state of Rhode Island, and to carry back to the Island leather, cloth, and necessaries in general for their own use, but their boatmen were specified and restricted to be Godfrey Trim, and John Rose, Jr. In March, of the next year, 1777, an act was passed permitting the Islanders then on the main, who chose to do so, to return home under the inspection of the commanding officer of the district ; and those on the Island had the permit to go off, but all this going and coming was to close by the 10th of the next month, April. Stephen Franklin, Jr., however, and his parents, after the 10th were allowed to return to the Island, having been unable, for good reasons to return before the 17th. In September, of 1777, the Islanders who had removed to the main, in consideration of the property they had sacrificed at home, "in the beginning of this unnatural, cruel war ; " and of the service they had rendered against the enemy ; and in consideration of their having been "excluded their proportions of flour and iron," were exempted from paying taxes.

During the year 1778 things seem to have held about the even tenor of their way as through the year preceding. But in 1779 a thunderbolt fell upon Block Island with an alarming crash.

The General Assembly, on information of illicit trade between the Island and the main ordered on the last Monday in February. 1779. the sheriff of King's County to "apprehend Waite Saunders, Thomas Carpenter, and Peleg Hoxie charged with having carried on an illicit commerce with the inhabitants of New Shoreham." He was also ordered to summon " Wm. Gorton, Robert Champlin, John Cross, Samuel Taylor, Simon Littlefield, John Sands, John Paine, Stephen Franklin, Edward Sands, and Robert Congdon to appear immediately before this assembly, upon the penalty of £150, lawful money each, for non-appearance." What the result of this action was we are not informed. Passing to and fro between the Island and the main continued under close inspection, as in the cases of William Robinson, and Benjamin Sheffield, of Charlestown, going to Block Island to collect rents ; and of Edward Sands and his wife, John Sands, Simon Ray Littlefield, George Franklin, John Paine, John Littlefield, and Stephen Franklin, (probably returning home from the trial for illicit commerce) taking with them in their own boat, " plow-irons," " cart-wheels, two setts of cart-tire, three iron bars, a parcel of wooden household furniture ; " and of Thomas Dickens, bringing with him necessaries in general. In the meantime a vigilance committee were watchful of all intercourse to and from the Island. In May, of 1779, the town council of Westerly were ordered to seize a quantity of grain that Stephen Franklin, Jr., of Block Island, had left in the hands of Phinehas Clarke, of Westerly. By the return of Ray Sands, Edward Hull, and Nathan Gardner, Jr., to the Island to collect rents, in June, 1779, we learn that they were among the number who left the Island during the war. In August of this year the General Assembly passed an act from which it is most clearly seen how completely the Islanders were abandoned to the cruel mercies of the enemy, cut off, as they then were, from the resources of the main-land. We quote the preamble, and epitomize the act :

" WHEREAS, many evil minded persons, not regarding the ties of their allegiance to the United States in general, and this state in particular ; but influenced by the sordid principles of avarice, continue illicitly to correspond with and supply the inhabitants of New Shoreham, in the county of Newport, with provisions, and other articles, to the great detriment and distress of the virtuous inhabitants of this state.

"And whereas, the said town of New Shoreham hath been for a long time, and still is, within the power and jurisdiction of the enemies of the United States, whereby they obtain, in consequence of the evil practices aforesaid, supplies for themselves, and intelligence from time to time of the situation of our troops, posts, and shores ; by which means they are enabled to make frequent incursions, and thereby commit devastations upon, and rob the innocent inhabitants of their property, and deprive them of their subsistence ; wherefore,

"Be it enacted, &c." This act prohibited all trade with the Islanders of every description, except by special permits, upon the penalty of the confiscation to the state of all the property, personal and real, of the offender, and to this might be added the compulsory service in a continental battalion, or vessel of war, until peace should be declared ; or, if the offender were a female, or unfit for a soldier or a sailor, he or she was to be punished corporeally.

In September, 1779, John Rose, and Frederick Wyllis, of Block Island, were taken by an American privateer, on board a British vessel, were delivered to the sheriff ; he delivered them over to Col. Christopher Greene, and he passed them over to Maj. Gen. Gates to be treated as prisoners of war, or dismissed. In May, of the same year, the above-mentioned Stephen Franklin, Jr., of Block Island, was under arrest to be tried before the General Assembly, but instead of trying him at a civil tribunal he was handed over to Maj. Gen. Gates to be tried by him as a spy, the result of which we do not know. For the grain which he left in care of Phinehas Clarke, of Westerly, in the preceding May, which was confiscated, the Assembly paid to his father, in Dec., 1779, £145 16s. 0d. The grain probably belonged to the father. In the latter part of this year much of the stringency was removed from the Islanders. The acts prohibiting their passing to and fro between the Island and the main were repealed, but all restrictions on transportation of provisions and merchandise were continued. This repeal was a source of much joy, for previously even Mrs. Lucy Sands was

9*

obliged to appear before Maj. Gen. Gates to obtain a permit to visit her family on the Island. Acts of courtesy were interchanged. But even Governor William Greene, in Feb., 1780, had to comply with the rule requiring a permit to transport articles of exchange, as in the case of sending then six barrels of cider to Block Island for his brother-in-law, John Littlefield, Esq., and his family. That was more welcome than the messengers from the colony, in the July following, who landed upon the Island with authority to take all the horses, cattle, grain, fish, and cheese as in their opinion could be spared by the inhabitants, and for the same to give certificates to the owners for future adjustment. These certificates, however, were no better than receipts for a levy on the Island for supporting the war, unless the amount taken should prove to be more than a just proportion of a state tax, in which the surplus was to be credited on the next tax to be assessed. Thus the Islanders, besides the depredations from the British, denied traffic on the main, unrepresented in the General Assembly of Rhode Island, unprotected by the colony from the enemy, was burdened with a heavy tax. This was taxation without representation; nay more, it was the imposition of a heavy burden upon those cut off from the common privileges on the main and abandoned to the cruel mercies of the enemy. But even this their faith and patriotism could endure while patiently waiting for the dawn of freedom.

In 1781, several permits to pass and repass between the Island and the main were granted, and occasional seizures of contraband articles and sales of the same by the sheriff occurred. Goods, also, were transported to and fro, but under close inspection.

In 1782, the " Refugees " were making considerable disturbance here. They threatened to destroy the property of Henry Champlin, seize his person, and carry him off to New York, and therefore he was permitted to leave the Island and take his goods with him. For some misdemeanor, during the war, the estate of Ackurs Sisson here was confiscated to the State, and taken possession of by Mr. John Sands in behalf of the colony.

At last the bright day seen by faith in 1776 was realized in May of 1783. The tempestuous, long night of the Revolution was over. The thunder of artillery died away, and the hail of musketry was felt no more by the heroes of freedom, and the rainbow of peace upon the receding cloud again arched the little " Isle of the sea." Of what account to its patriotic inhabitants were the vexations and losses of the seven years of hostilities, since now they were under the banners of independent American colonies ? There were glad hearts, music and dancing, psalms of praise to the God of freedom, and thanksgiving for victory and peace once more, as the messengers of the General Assembly read the good news to the Islanders, " That all the rights, liberties, and privileges of the other citizens of this State be restored " to them, and that all restrictions of travel and traffic were removed.

Of the personal experiences on the Island during the Revolution we can gain but little knowledge besides what is traditional. A few incidents from the memories of bright, aged people here who remember distinctly how, when they were young, their parents told what they had seen, and heard, and experienced, are here given.

THE REFUGEES.

Deserters and criminals, during the Revolution, found Block Island to be a convenient refuge. Once here, as communication with the main was so much restricted, they were not easily detected by the officers of justice. They were desperate characters from both armies, but mostly from the American, or from some nest of tories. They were a scourge to the Island, unprincipled and cruel in their demands.

At a house a little east of Mr. Wm. P. Ball's residence, on his land where a beautiful spring is still flo.wing, and old quince and ornamental trees are yet standing, in the latter part of the war, one of those desperate refugees made his appearance. He was seen approaching at some distance by the watchful inmates, and the terrified husband, by the aid of his wife, took refuge up stairs in a large pile of flax, where, at the risk of smothering, he was quickly concealed. The intruder made many saucy demands, one of which was : "Where is your husband ?" The woman answered sharply, "I hav'nt any !" She had divorced him five minutes previous. One or two more inquiries aroused her indignation above all fear. He then demanded of her a knowledge of what she had in that chest in the corner, and threatened to break it open, whereupon she defied him to touch it, and springing for her scissors. with the pointed blade made ready to stab, she made for him exclaiming, "Get out of this house, you infernal villain, or I'll kill you with these scissors !" Perhaps she was emboldened by Shakespeare's "quietus with a bodkin." The refugee considered retreat to be, in that case, the better part of valor, as no *man* can fight a woman.

The substance of the above was told to Mrs. Margaret Dodge, now eighty-six years old, by her mother who remembered well the incidents of the Revolution as they occurred on the Island.

Mrs. John Sands, during the same period, while alone in her house, with her babe, saw a band of refugees coming to her door, and knowing their desperate character, laid down her babe, seized a gun and stood with it at the door ready to shoot the first that might attempt to enter and thus drove them away.

They sometimes came from the main to the Island in sufficient force to row their light boats, called "Shaving Mills," with great rapidity, and thus they could capture a weaker craft, or escape one stronger. A galley with nine oarsmen, with such a boat, tradition says, came to the Island in a rough sea, for plunder. It approached the Old Harbor Point Landing, where the water has always been deep, and the rocks dangerous. The surf was dashing fearfully and the galley of refugees attempted to land, but were swamped and all drowned in the evening. It is said that while they were straining every muscle upon their oars, the Islanders on the beach heard a powerful voice among them saying : "Pull ! boys, pull for your lives !" followed by the cries—"Help ! help !" and for many years afterwards persons in that vicinity claimed to have heard the same command at night when no boatmen were there, and within the memory of the living, scores of men at a time have thus been deceived, and hence originated the "Harbor Boys," or ghosts of the Old Harbor Landing—ghosts of the struggling refugees rowing for the shore. The frightful call of the Harbor Boys died away about the time the Palatine ship of fire sailed off to return no more to Block Island. The ghosts of the Harbor Boys were a fit crew for a phantom ship of fire.

The despicable character of the refugees of the Revolution is seen in the following statement of Mrs. Raymond Dickens of what she used to hear her grandmother, wife of Thomas Dickens, relate.

The latter was a widow, and they came to her house and demanded her money. She told them she had none. They threatened to break open a chest to see. She opened it for them and let them see its contents. Satisfied that she had no money, one seized her red silk handkerchief and carried it off. They seem to have been the offscouring of both armies and of the vilest inhabitants of the main-land.

While here at one time, in a tavern, they stacked their guns in a room opposite the bar-room in which they were drinking, while one John Mitchell was asleep—supposed to be drunk—in the room with the guns. Unbeknown to the refugees he took the best one of their guns and put it up the old-fashioned chimney, and continued to be drunk, apparently, until after their searching was over, and they had left. Then the gun came down chimney and did good service for the Islanders many years since the memory of Seneca Sprague whose father for a long time was its owner.

As a protection the Islanders kept a barrel of tar, or oil, on Harbor Hill (nearly back of the Beach House), and another on Beacon Hill, ready to be burned at night as a signal of approaching refugees. As soon as these were seen the shores of the Island were picketed, and doubtless in more than one instance the marauders got more than they came for. They generally came in the night.

THE WAR OF 1812.

During our last war with England, Block Island in the outset was proclaimed neutral. This proclamation was well known by the English commanders, and it was so constantly respected by them and their officers that the inhabitants can hardly be said to have suffered on their account. Indeed, in some respects, they were a pecuniary benefit, for their men-of-war, frequently anchored in the bay, were a home-market for cattle, sheep, poultry, and supplies in general, and for these an adequate sum of specie was promptly paid. Not a murmur of complaint against English plunder, like that of the French here in 1689–90, lingers upon the Island. It even makes one feel proud of his "mother country" to hear, sixty years after that war, so many speak of the honorable bearing of the British officers on Block Island and in its surrounding waters. It is true the officers and soldiers took things with which the owners were unwilling to part, but the invariable testimony is that an equivalent was always paid in gold or silver. Meanwhile, too, the Island was exempt from the taxes and service in the army to which those upon the main were subjected. They were at liberty also, as neutrals, to carry on trade with our own people in any of our ports, submitting, of course, to the inconvenience of being searched and examined in reference to English goods in their possession, and likewise of having their vessels hailed by the English ships.

Captain Thomas Rose, the father of Mrs. Margaret Dodge, while coming towards the harbor, from the fishing-grounds, was about to pass an English man-of-war of seventy-four guns, when suddenly he heard the report of a cannon and saw a ball skipping on the water before his bow. He at once tacked, sailed up to her frowning broad-side and there held this little dialogue : " Who are you? " " Thomas Rose of Block Island." " What is your business ? " " I'm a fisherman." " What have you in your boat ? " " Necessaries for my family." " That's all—go on and good luck to you," and he bore away homeward again thankful for the honors maintained in war.

One vessel of the enemy captured Nathaniel Dodge in a friendly way and resorted to various means to induce him to act as pilot for them in the Sound, but he evaded the service by feigning idiocy and insanity.

Commodore Hardy, of the British navy, during the War of 1812, anchored in the bay his seventy-four gun ship, and was so friendly with the Islanders as to give them a dinner-party aboard his vessel, and many accepted his invitation.

One principal object which the British vessels had in

coming here was to obtain a supply of water. This they got mainly at Middle Pond, Chagum Pond, at the north end of the Island, and at Simmon's Pond, a small basin of fresh water then nearly in front of the harbor black-smith shop, but now filled up and nearly forgotten.

A few relics of that war are still remaining upon the Island, such as a book of valuable reading in the possession of Mr. William Dodge, thrown overboard from an English vessel between Block Island and Watch Hill, while hastily clearing itself for action. It floated, and was picked up by Mr. Dodge's father. A few old-fashioned horse-pistols were left by the soldiers, and are now occasionally used by the boys for shooting rats.

Deacon Richard Steadman, an aged citizen, relates, in substance, the following incident of the War of 1812 : While a British man-of-war was lying near the Island several marines came ashore, went to the house (now owned and occupied by Mr. George Sheffield) of Mr. Ray Thomas Sands, and wanted to buy his pigs and turkeys. He refused to sell them on any conditions. They threatened to take them *nolens volens* ; but he declared to them *they should not have them*. They told him if he said much more they would seize and carry him to Halifax! He dared them to do it. They then marched him to the shore, took him aboard the frigate, and handed him over to the commander, whereupon he was asked what he had to say for himself, and he replied : " Give me a bottle of liquor, and good keeping, for I am a neutral Block Islander." His demand was complied with for two or three days with good nature, and then he was returned to the shore and to his family.

Mr. Samuel Ball remembers the following incidents : His father, in 1812, occupied the house now owned and occupied by the said Samuel. Then, during the war, two English vessels, the *Poictiers*, a seventy-four gun ship, and the *Medstone*, a war-sloop came to Block Island, and the commanders and their officers came ashore. While viewing the land they stopped at Mr. Ball's and called for dinner, courteously. The present Mr. Samuel Ball, then a little boy. went into the yard and picked them some flowers. His father, Samuel Ball, Sen., superintended dinner preparations, but the one commander and his officers so much outranked the other and his officers that two tables had to be set. and in different rooms, and the two parties did not converse with each other. One of the commanders was probably a man of great distinction.

Mr. Ball also says that the Island boys caught many little pond turtles and sold them to the British who took them on board their vessels for amusement, trimming them up in red ribbons, and marching them about their decks. Not even one of these turtles was taken by the English without payment.

It is pleasant to hear the old people, without an exception, now speak of the gentlemanly bearing of these British soldiers towards the men, women, and children of the Island in the War of 1812, and also to record the incidents, however simple, that commemorate such humane behavior in times of hostility. "Small things discover great," says Bacon, which agrees well with what Aristotle said long before : "The nature of every thing is best seen in its smallest portions."

The aged Benjamin Sprague, now in his 89th year, well remembers the following incidents of the War of 1812. The first of the British vessels that then came to Block Island appeared on the fishing-grounds at the southward of the Island, and there hove to near the fishermen. They took John Clark aboard to pilot them to the Middle Pond. About a dozen boats well-filled with fish weighed anchor and followed the English vessels, which signaled the fishing boats to keep at a proper distance, until the heavy anchors were dropped opposite the Middle Pond. Then, as said Benjamin Sprague's boat was nearest, the English signaled him to come up, but to the rest to stay back. His little pole masts then came alongside the man-of-war and a few heads looked down, and one said, "How do you sell your fish?" "Twenty cents apiece," replied Mr. Sprague, and an order quickly came back for a num-ber. "Please pass us down a bunch of yarn to tie them up," said Mr. Sprague. It was quickly furnished, and the first fish sold to the English by the Islanders was soon on deck of the man-of-war. "Please pass your money down as soon as you get your fish," said Mr. Sprague. This was done until the boat was emptied, and a second one signaled to come up as Mr. Sprague went away, reporting to the one he met, and the rest of his craft. the price established. They all sold out, and returned home, with cash in hand, to their families.

During the War of 1812 the Island, in a measure, was subject to martial law. The inhabitants, as neutrals. were restrained by both American and English laws from favoring, in a hostile sense, either nation. Certain goods were contraband, and certain information might be fatal to the informant. The sale of rum to the English was punishable by them. Such sales were made, however, at considerable risk, and much profit. Mr. Sprague, the octogenarian, tells the following story: "I lived at the Harbor, and the English ships were by the Middle Pond. I said to my wife,—I am going to try my chances. So I got some chickens, ducks, beans, and a jug, and started for the ships. When I got down by the minister's lot, with my hands full, and things under my arms, all at once several English officers hove in sight on horseback, by George Sheffield's, with their bright gilded uniforms. My heart jumped right up into my throat, for I knew they would ask what I had in that jug. and they were soon up to me. They touched their hats, bowed, and halted. I nodded my head, for my hands were full. Said one. 'What have you to sell?' I answered, 'ducks, chickens, and beans.' Said he, 'What's in that jug?' I looked up in his face, and did not answer. He laughed, and said, 'I'll buy your ducks, chickens, and beans, and go on and let my steward have them, and let my men have a drink apiece, but don't let any of them get drunk." They went on and so did I. Now, said I, there's good sailing and I'll make a good voyage. So when I arrived at the Middle Pond the marines were on its east shore washing the ship's clothing. The steward paid me for my ducks, &c., and I told him about the rum, and he nodded assent. I then went near the marines, put up two fingers, and beckoned them to follow me. I went down by the bank, behind some willows, and two came. The rum was half water, and I sold each a pint for a dollar a pint; after they went back, two more came, and so on until I sold all out to them at a dollar a pint. As it was then about noon they urged me to dine with them, and I did, and they had their English rum with their rations. They asked me to drink some, and I did. Then they asked me if I did not think their rum was better than mine. I told them yes, but did not tell them how much of mine was water."

To those unacquainted with the origin of the name Block Island it might seem to have been derived from its position as a *stumbling-block* in the pathway of vessels, and from the multitude of them wrecked upon its shores. All the facts concerning them would fill a volume full of interest. The few here given may be taken as an index to many other wrecks not mentioned. The one to which we give the most attention has received more notoriety, perhaps, than all others, and yet but very little direct knowledge of it is attainable, and that knowledge is based *only upon tradition*, and that tradition has been the nucleus of so much speculation, poetic fancy, and superstition that the following is presented with some timidity, anticipating as we do, quite opposite opinions from some things here said concerning

THE PALATINE.

This was the vessel whose supposed wreck upon Block Island Whittier has made the subject of a fine little poem entitled *"The Palatine."* That a vessel of this name was cast away upon this Island, or anchored here not long after its settlement, there is considerable circumstantial evidence. But this statement is contrary to the speculative theory that said vessel did not bear that name, but some other, the name *Palatine* originating from the Palatinates, or emigrants on her at the time she came ashore. But did ever a ship go to sea without a name? Were sailors, as were the Islanders, ever known to call her by any name except *her own?* Were a vessel from Turkey, laden with Turkish emigrants, to be wrecked on any New England island, if her name were Palatine, would the inhabitants call her *Turkey?* And that too simply because she was from that country, while they could read her name which she carried? No, *Palatine* was the name of the *vessel.* This is not only reasonable, but is also in harmony with traditional fact. Mr. Raymond Dickens, now aged seventy-five years, hale, and of clear memory, born on the Island, said only a few days since that when he was a boy he frequently heard his grandfather, Thomas Dickens, at about the age of eighty, speak of the *ship* (not passengers) *Palatine.* These two had memories that carry us back to about 1736, and Simon Ray, one of the first settlers of the Island, was then living. He might have told Thomas Dickens about the *Palatine,* or others in the prime of life, from whom Thomas Dickens got the information that he gave to his grandson, Raymond Dickens, who now communicates the same to us. By these, and similar links of tradition, we are enabled to authenticate the beginning of the chain of facts here presented. There was, then, a vessel by the name of Palatine, that came, many years ago, to the shores of Block Island.

Poetic fiction has given to the public a very wrong view of this occurrence, and thus a wrong impression of the Islanders has been obtained. This criticism is not applicable to Mr. R. H. Dana's poem entitled the *Buccaneer,* for *he had no reference in it to the Palatine.*

It is due to Mr. J. G. Whittier to give here his own explanation concerning his poem:

"21st 10 mo. 1876.

"Dear Friend:

"In regard to the poem *Palatine,* I can only say that I did not intend to misrepresent the facts of history. I wrote it after receiving a letter from Mr. Hazard, of

Rhode Island, from which I certainly inferred that the ship was pillaged by the Islanders. He mentioned that one of the crew to save himself clung to the boat of the wreckers, who cut his hand off with a sword. It is very possible that my correspondent followed the current tradition on the main-land. * * *

"Mr. Hazard is a gentleman of character and veracity, and I have no doubt he gave the version of the story as he had heard it."

"Very Truly Thy Friend,
John G. Whittier."

Whittier's poem has these stanzas :

> " The ship that a hundred years before,
> Freighted deep with its goodly store,
> In the gales of the equinox went ashore.

> " The eager Islanders one by one
> Counted the shots of her signal-gun,
> And heard the crash as she drove right on.

> " Into the teeth of death she sped ;
> (May God forgive the hands that fed
> The false lights over the Rocky Head !)"

> " O men and brothers ! What sights were there !
> White upturned faces, hands stretched in prayer !
> Where waves had pity, could ye not spare ?

> Down swooped the wreckers like birds of prey,
> Tearing the heart of the ship away,
> And the dead had never a word to say.

> " And there with a ghastly shimmer and shine,
> Over the rocks and the seething brine,
> They burned the wreck of the Palatine.

> " In their cruel hearts as they homeward sped,
> ' The sea and the rocks are dumb,' they said,
> ' There'll be no reckoning with the dead.' "

All of this barbarous work is here charged upon a little population of as pure morals as ever adorned any part of Puritan New England. Let no one suppose that the poet

was aware of misrepresentation and injustice to the
Islanders. He, like others, doubtless supposed that the
piracy once common about Block Island was carried on
by the inhabitants. But that was not the case. Pirates
from abroad, near the beginning of the eighteenth century, infested the Island, and as they sallied forth from
this point upon our own and foreign vessels they gave a
reputation, probably, to the Island which in nowise
belonged to the descendants of the Pilgrims.

See the account of the capture of pirates from Block
Island, and recovery of their money, in the case of the
Bradish pirates, Colonial Hist. of N. Y., Vol. IV, p. 512.
Also the account of the pirate vessels Ranger and Fortune
headed for Block Island when captured by the Greyhound,
1723, twenty-six of whose pirates were executed at Newport, on Gravelly Point, July 19, 1723.—R. I. Col. Rec.,
Vol. IV, p. 329 and 331. As late as 1740, the Rhode
Island General Assembly voted an appropriation of £13
13s. "for victuals and drink to the pirates at Block Island,
and their guards;" and from the fact of keeping pirates
as prisoners on the Island, many abroad doubtless heard
frequent mention of "Block Island pirates," without distinguishing them from the native citizens of the Island.
But in all of these cases the pirates were foreigners to the
Island, lodging there only temporarily.

There is ample evidence of the strict laws of the
Islanders, and of their rigid observance concerning
wrecks, and of the voluntary humanity from them
towards unfortunate sailors. It was probably according
to the directions of the venerable Simon Ray, Chief Warden, as he was, and preacher of the gospel, or according
to the wishes of his son, Simon Ray, Jr., that the deceased
passengers of the Palatine were taken the long distance
from Sandy Point to his house, and afterward buried in
a pleasant spot near his dwelling, in a decent manner, an

example subsequently imitated within the memory of the oldest inhabitant now on the Island.

The tender feelings entertained here for the sailor is indicated by the town authorities in 1704. Then Capt. Edward Ball was Crown Officer on the Island. A sailor's body came ashore. Capt. Ball, by the authority of the Crown of England ordered Constable John Banning to summon a jury of inquest. After "solemn" examination their verdict was: "We find no wounds that occasioned his death, but we conclude that the water hath been his end, or cause of his death." People who do thus are not such as set false lights, and murder shipwrecked sailors.

So, in August 1755, about the supposed time of the wreck of the Palatine, the sloop *Martha and Hannah*, Capt. William Griffin, from Halifax to New York, was stranded on Block Island, and the captain was drowned while the crew, four in number, came ashore. At once a coroner's jury was summoned, the corpse was viewed, testimony was taken, and all was done that the best of civilized society could require of the Islanders. They were not pirates, poetic fiction "to the contrary notwithstanding," any more than the rats of the old stone mill and the characters of Cooper's Red Rover were realities belonging to Newport.

By request, Mr. Charles E. Perry, an Islander and a gentleman whose scholarship and extensive research concerning the Palatine entitle him to a high degree of confidence, has prepared the following:

"*Memoranda of Facts and Traditions connected with*
THE PALATINE."

"She came ashore on Sandy Point, the northern extremity of Block Island, striking on the *hummuck*, at that time a little peninsula connected with the Island by a narrow neck of land. As the tide rose she floated off, and was towed into Breach Cove, near the Point, by the Islanders in their boats. The passengers were all landed, except one woman who refused to leave the wreck, and most of them were carried to the house of Edward Sands (who built and lived in the house now owned by John Revoe Paine, Esq.), and Simon Ray who owned a large part of the " West Side," and lived in a house near the one now owned and occupied by Raymond Dickens, Esq., a part of the timbers of the former being used in building the latter. Many of these passengers, weakened by starvation and disease, soon died and were buried on a little spot west of the house of Wm. P. Lewis, Esq., and their graves, without a fence, or a name, though of late too closely approached by the plowshare, still remind us of the ship Palatine.

" Some of the passengers, however, lived and left the Island, and one of them gave to the little daughter of Edward Sands, then twelve years old, a dress of India calico or chintz patches as the material was then called. This little girl was my grandmother's grandmother, and my grandmother has often heard her relate this incident. My grandmother's grandmother died in 1836 at the age of ninety-six, from which data (she being twelve years old when the ship came ashore), I conclude that she was wrecked about the year 1752.

" One of these passengers, a woman, married a colored slave belonging to a Mr. Littlefield. Her name was Kate, and was commonly called *Kattern*. She was known as Long Kate to distinguish her from another who was then called Short Kate. The former had three children, *Cradle*, whose descendants have died or moved away; *Mary*, from whose descendants *Jack*, a colored man now in the employment of Hon. Nicholas Ball, and remembered by many who have stopped at the Ocean View Hotel, has descended; and *Jenny*, whose posterity have died and left the Island.

"*Letter from Charles Mueller, U. S. Consul at Amsterdam*, dated July 4, 1870, states that the Custom House archives there have been searched, from the year 1602 to the year 1799, and the records of the Dutch Trading Society from 1700 to 1786, but no information was gained, although the record was found of a ship *Palatine* which was wrecked in the Bay of Bengal, July 14, 1784.

"*Frederick Shutz, U. S. Consul at Rotterdam*, in a letter dated Nov. 8, 1870, is also unable to give information, though the Custom House Records there were searched for a period embraced between 1736 and 1766; those from 1738 to 1743 were missing.

"*A Letter from R. H. Dana, Jr.*, states that his father's poem—THE BUCCANEER, was simply a work of imagination, founded on no fact, and having no reference to the Palatine.

"*A Letter from J. G. Whittier* states that his first hint of the story of its wreck came from James Hazard of Newport, that his knowledge on the subject is very limited, and that he has a plate said to have come from the Palatine.

"The gist of the traditional accounts of her seems to be, that she sailed from some German port, laden with well-to-do emigrants, bound to Philadelphia, that the captain died or was killed on the passage, that the officers and crew starved and plundered the helpless emigrants, and finally, in their boats, abandoned the vessel which drifted ashore, as previously stated, during the week between Christmas and New Year's."

"The ship was undoubtedly burned, with the woman left on board."—CHARLES E. PERRY.

In what manner, or why she was set on fire we can hardly conjecture. Her timbers and irons were too valuable to the Islanders to be wasted. Where were the laws then for piracy ? Certain it is that the strict laws of the Island would have duly punished the known incendiary, had he been a citizen.

Mr. Benjamin Sprague's Recollections about the Palatine.

Although eighty-eight years old, Mr. Sprague does not seem to have any disease preying upon his constitution, and he talks of the scenes of his childhood and youth as though they were present, visible realities. He says he heard his parents say much about "Dutch Kattern," as she was called, and that it was well understood by them that she came from the ship Palatine. He well knew Kattern's daughter Cradle, a mulatto, as Kattern married a negro, soon after she came upon the Island. Mr. Sprague, by remembering the character commonly ascribed to "Dutch Kattern," enables us to gain some insight into the character of the traditions of the Palatine. He says she reported that the crew starved the passengers to get their money. He says she was a noted fortune-teller; that she would hide away behind a wall, or in a thicket of bushes, and there lie in a trance for hours. On returning to the house much exhausted, and being asked where she had been, she would reply that she had been home across the sea, to Holland, and then would give an account of the condition of her kindred there as she had just seen them. She lived on the Neck, and was believed to be a witch. The Islanders were afraid of her. Mr. Sprague has no recollection of ever having heard any account of the *burning* of the Palatine, nor do the other old people of the Island know any account of any such burning of the wreck. All they pretend that is known about a burning Palatine is contained in their notions of the *Palatine Light*.

After more than two years of the best of opportunities to inquire into the legend of the Palatine, being on intimate and friendly terms with all of the most aged and reliable inhabitants of the Island, the writer is prepared to make a note of the following observations:

That a ship named *Palatine*, about 130 years ago, came to Block Island, and left a considerable number of her passengers, who were in a diseased and dying condition: *That* these passengers received no treatment but kindness from the Islanders: *That* the Palatine was never burned by the Islanders, since to them every stick of its timbers, and every bolt were valuable; and especially since none can give any of the details of her burning: *That* she was *never burned at all*, but was wrecked in the Bay of Bengal, in July, 1784, according to the account in the records of the Dutch Trading Society, and reported by the American Consul, *Charles Mueller*, at Amsterdam in 1870: *That Dutch Kattern*, one of the passengers, who was landed on Block Island, who married a negro slave, who got her living in part by fortune-telling, in those days of superstition, and who was feared as a *witch* by the Islanders, has received far too much credit for truthfulness in reference to the Palatine legend: *That* neither the silence nor the words of the maniac, Mark Dodge, who, by good authority, is said to have burned the only windmill on the Island, is entitled to much weight in reference to this legend: *That* the *Palatine Light* in reality had no more relation to the ship Palatine than it had to Bunker Hill Monument, and that the superstitions, and fictitious relations of said ship and light originated in the days of the witch, "Dutch Kattern," and of the "old opium-eater," as he was called, who occupied the house previously owned and occupied by Simon Ray, Jr., the house so famous for ghosts and the dancing mortar, in the days of Dutch Kattern: *That* the fortune-teller and witch,

Dutch Kattern; the inveterate "opium-eater," of the haunted house; and the maniac, Mark Dodge, are poor authority for authenticating a legend that criminates a civil, Christianized community, and reduces them to a level with barbarians and pirates: *That*, as widely as the report has been circulated that Mr. R. H. Dana referred to the Palatine, in his "Buccaneer;" and that as far as Mr. J. G. Whittier, in his "Palatine," has made the false impression that the Islanders, by false lights, wrecked said ship, murdered its passengers and crew, robbed and burned it, so far and wide said report and impression should be contradicted. For the prince of showmen to "humbug" the lovers of deception; or for a poet to clothe up an ordinary fact in startling garbs of fiction; or to call an ancient fur-trader's castle a "stone mill," may be tolerated; but the representing of an entire community of law-abiding Christian people as barbarians and pirates, and that too, on the testimony of a *witch*, an *opium-eater*, and a *maniac*, is intolerable.

Take, then, from the legend of the Palatine, *witchcraft*, *opium reveries*, *insanity*, and *superstition*, and we have left a Dutch trading ship, stopping at Block Island to leave diseased passengers, among whom was the low-bred "Dutch Kattern;" we find also at that time the same minds that invested the Ray house with ghosts and a dancing mortar, amply furnished with the materials for rigging the light off Sandy Point with masts, ropes, and sails, and for giving it a cargo of lies to feed the fancies of poets, and the phantom-chasers of posterity. Dutch Kattern had her revenge on the ship that put her ashore by imagining it on fire, and telling others, probably, that the light on the sound was the wicked ship Palatine, cursed for leaving her on Block Island.

There is some evidence that the Dutch trading-ship, Palatine, was on her way from the West Indies, homeward, at the time of leaving her diseased passengers on Block Island; for she left *Lignum-vitæ*, which still remains among the inhabitants. It was left in the rough, in logs, and in the absence of mills the Islanders made mortars of sections of that tough, hard wood. The octogenarian, B. Sprague, says they were made by boring the top of the block full of auger holes, over which a heated cannon ball was placed to burn out the desired cavity. A few of these mortars still on the Island are all known as *from the Palatine*. They have done good service in furnishing meal for the primitive inhabitants, and if Block Island should, in future, produce an abundant crop of relics from the Palatine to compete with the thousands of spokes from the wheels of Washington's wagon, the crop would probably be inadequate to the hungry demand.

THE PALATINE LIGHT.

To this superstition, poetry, and speculation have given notoriety. This light, whatever it may be, whether a superstitious figment of the imagination, or an unaccountable reality, as a legend handed down from generation to generation, and always believed by many to be true, is certainly a phenomenon. Those whom we hear speak of having seen it at the present day have been persons more competent to believe in the marvelous than to read and write. Not many months since such an Islander was heard to speak very solemnly of having seen the Palatine Light off on the Sound. His more intelligent neighbors, though knowing him to be a man of candor and veracity, expressed their opinions by a smile of incredulity. And yet, the concurrent testimony of so many, not only upon the Island, but also upon the opposite main-land, is so strong that a strange light off Sandy Point, in different parts of the Sound, has been seen from time to time, resembling a burning ship, that no one feels quite ready to pronounce it all a myth. The convictions of many concerning it are so truthfully expressed by Whittier that his stanzas are here inserted:

> " Nor looks nor tones a doubt betray,
> ' It is known to us all,' they quietly say;
> ' We too have seen it in our day.'
>
> " For still, on many a moonless night,
> From Kingston Head and from Montauk Light,
> The specter kindles and burns in sight.
>
> " Now low and dim, now clear and higher,
> Leaps up the terrible Ghost of Fire;
> Then slowly sinking the flames expire.
>
> " And the wise Sound skippers, though skies be fine,
> Reef their sails when they see the sign
> Of the blazing wreck of the Palatine."

That a phenomenal light at different times and places in the Sound in sight of the Island has appeared during the last century is quite certain, and superstition has associated it with the Palatine. That an inflammable gas should rise through the water and burn upon its surface is not impossible, as in the case of burning springs and brooks. This light. as long ago as 1811, attracted the attention of men of standing. Dr. Aaron C. Willey, for a number of years an inhabitant of the Island, and well-known abroad, addressed the following letter to Dr. Samuel Mitchell then living in New York City :

"BLOCK ISLAND, Dec. 10, 1811.

" DEAR SIR : In a former letter I promised to give you an account of the singular light which is sometimes seen from this place. I now hasten to fulfill my agreement. I should long since have communicated the fact to the literary world. but was unwilling to depend wholly upon the information of others. when by a little delay there was a probability of my receiving ocular demonstration. I have not, however, been fortunate in this respect, as I

could wish, having had only two opportunities of witness-
ing this phenomenon.   My residing nearly six miles from
the shore which lies next to the region of its exhibition,
and behind elevated ground, has prevented me from seeing it so frequently, perhaps, as I might otherwise have
done.   The people who have always lived here are so
familiarized to the sight that they never think of giving
notice to those who do not happen to be present, or even
of mentioning it afterwards, unless they hear some particular inquiries made.

"This curious irradiative rises from the ocean near the
northern point of the Island.   Its appearance is nothing
different from a blaze of fire.   Whether it actually
touches the water, or merely hovers over it, is uncertain,
for I am informed that no person has been near enough
to decide accurately.   It beams with various magnitudes,
and appears to bear no more analogy to the *ignis fatuus*
than it does to the aurora borealis.   Sometimes it is small,
resembling the light through a distant window, at others
expanding to the highness of a ship with all her canvas
spread.   When large it displays a pyramidical form, or
three constant streams.   In the latter case the streams
are somewhat blended together at the bottom, but separate and distinct at the top, while the middle one rises
higher than the other two.   It may have the same appearance when small, but owing to distance and surrounding
vapors cannot be clearly perceived.   The light often seems
to be in a constant state of insulation, descending by
degrees until it becomes invisible, or resembles a lurid
point, then shining anew, sometimes with a sudden blaze,
at others by a gradual increasement to its former size.
Often the instability regards the luster only, becoming
less and less bright until it disappears, or nothing but a
pale outline can be discerned of its full size, then returning its former splendor in the manner before related.

The duration of its greatest and least state of illumination is not commonly more than two or three minutes. This inconstancy, however. does not appear in every instance.

"After the radiance seems to be totally extinct it does not always return in the same place, but is not unfrequently seen shining at some considerable distance from where it disappeared. In this transfer of locality it seems to have no certain line of direction. When most expanded this blaze is generally wavering like the flame of a torch; at one time it appears stationary, at another progressive. It is seen at all seasons of the year, and for the most part in the calm weather which precedes an easterly or southerly storm. It has, however, been noticed during a severe northwestern gale, and when no storm immediately followed. Its continuance is sometimes but transient, at others throughout the night, and it has been known to appear several nights in succession.

"This blaze actually emits luminous rays. A gentleman whose house is situated near the sea, informs me that he has known it to illuminate considerably the walls of his room through the windows. This happens only when the light is within a half a mile of the shore, for it is often seen blazing at six or seven miles distant, and strangers suppose it to be a vessel on fire."

Dr. Willey, in the same letter, states that when he saw it in the evening of February, 1810, and in the evening of December 20th following, the appearances were essentially those above described Of the notion of its connection with the Palatine, he adds : "From this time, it is said, the Palatine light appeared, and there are many who firmly believe it to be a ship of fire, to which their fantastic and distempered imaginations figure masts, ropes, and flowing sails.

"I have stated facts to you, but feel a reluctance to

11*

hazard any speculations.   These I leave to you and other acute researchers of created things.   Your opinion I would be much pleased with.

"With the highest feelings of respect,

(Signed)   AARON C. WILLEY."

Hon. S. L. MITCHELL.

MODERN WRECKS.

THE MARS.

An English Merchantman, in 1781, was pursued by our war vessel, in the Revolution, was stranded on Block Island, and captured as a prize, and her goods were seized to be sold by the sheriff of Kent County, R. I., to pay for keeping in prison "Dennis Byrne and his woman-servant. who were taken in the said ship, unless the owners or captors discharge the said debt."

THE ANN HOPE.

A large East Indiaman, laden with spices and merchandise, came ashore in the night, in a snow-storm, on the south end of the Island, about the year 1806.   Her captain's name was Lang.   Several of the crew were drowned, and their bodies were found and buried in view of the wreck.   When she was discovered in the morning by the Islanders her upper deck, on which were several cannon, then used to fight pirates, had floated away a quarter of a mile.   One man's body came ashore and the citizens were endeavoring to resuscitate him when another was seen struggling in the surf, and one of those working over the apparently drowned man mentioned, said : "Let us try to save that one out there in the water, for this man is as good as dead," whereupon the latter exclaimed, "Na ! indade, I'm as good as a half a dozen dead men !"   Several of the crew were saved, but the ship and cargo were a

total loss.   The Islanders saved a few bags of coffee, and
some other things before all was carried away by the tide.

Wreck of The Warrior.

She was a large two-mast schooner. distinctly remembered by several of the oldest Islanders.   She carried
goods and passengers between Boston and New York.
The wind was blowing a heavy gale, the sound was white,
and two seas were meeting on the bar at Sandy Point,
and there dashing their waves against each other in such
fearful conflict as no pen can describe.   Upon that bar by
the fury of that gale she was driven.   The Islanders
hastened to the shore to render assistance to the perishing.
The following account of the scene is from an eye-witness,
Mr. Benjamin T. Coe, then the Inspector of Customs at
New Shoreham.   His letter was addressed to John C.
Morrison, Esq., of New York.

"New Shoreham, April 27, 1831.

"Dear Sir:—Yours of the 19th has come to hand
this day.   There were no goods saved from the *Warrior*,
of the description you mentioned.   .

"It is impossible to describe the awful situation of that
vessel when she first came on shore, the sea breaking over
her masts, and seven souls hanging to the rigging, not
more than one hundred and fifty yards from us, and completely out of the power of man to render them any
assistance—the vessel striking so hard as to drive her
bottom up, both masts unstepped, and fell, at the same
time ripped up her main deck and the goods immediately
washed out of her and drove away to the eastward.   Some
cotton and calico drove ashore here, one sack of hides,
something like forty dozen carpenters rules, &c.   What
goods were saved I delivered to Mr. Charles Brown, the
agent from Boston. and Mr. Charles M. Thurston, of
Newport, to whom I must refer you.

"I am informed there were thirty tons of iron in the bottom of the vessel, which is, I think, now buried up with sand, as there has been no part of said bottom seen about the Island. When the weather grows warmer I intend to make an examination for the bottom of the vessel. It may be the case that some heavy articles can be found. If any thing of the kind you mention should be found I will give you the earliest information in my power. Our insulated situation renders it very difficult— we have no chance of writing, only when our boats go off. and that is not frequent.

Your Ob't Servant,

Benjamin T. Coe."

Other witnesses tell essentially the same story, with some additional particulars. One describes the bar from the shore to the ship as sometimes nearly naked between the heavy seas passing over it from the westward. He says that one of the sailors, larger and more resolute than the rest, used great exertion to keep them from becoming benumbed by the cold, by keeping them active. As he saw no hope of assistance from the hundreds on the shore he made the desperate effort of running on the sand bar to the land between seas, but when a little more than half way he saw a high wave driven with great violence coming upon him, he bravely turned and met it head foremost, and soon after was picked up dead upon the beach. Others on the wreck lashed themselves to the deck. and, after the storm, were taken off by the Islanders, all dead and blackened by the bruises received from débris. That was a solemn day when the citizens looked upon the seven corpses laid upon the green bank, not far from the wreck. Captain Scudder, all of his crew, and passengers finished life's journey together in that worst of places for a vessel, in a gale.

Mr. Amhad Dodge, who well remembers the awful scene, says his father helped to make such coffins for those unfortunate sailors as were made for respectable citizens, and the bodies were decently laid out, and religious services were held at their burial. Their seven graves may now be seen in the northwest corner of the Island cemetery. Capt. Scudder and his mate, it is said, have been removed by their friends, who expressed a happy surprise in finding the dead so decently buried by the hands of strangers.

The total number of lives lost on the Warrior was probably twenty-one. The bodies of seven men and a colored woman were rescued, while the rest floated away as did the goods and pieces of the wreck into the ocean. Mr. Anthony Littlefield, whose house was near the disaster, says that not long after the wreck he was in Boston and heard a man say that he was on board the *Warrior* just before she sailed, and that she then had in all twenty-one—eighteen men, two women, and a colored servant. Mrs. Anthony Littlefield laid out the body of the colored woman, who was buried near Sandy Point, and all the other bodies were taken to the house of her husband.

This fearful wreck was the result of carelessness, as is supposed, on the part of the watch. She, with two others, becalmed the previous evening, anchored at the westward of Sandy Point, upon which she was driven in the morning. The other two vessels, one of them being the smack *Luna*, escaped from their dangerous position.

Mr. Weeden Gorton says he saw men jump overboard like sheep while the Warrior was going to pieces.

The Jasper

Was a schooner bound from Boston to New York, laden with cut stone, in 1839. She came ashore on the east side of the Island, and was got off, considerably damaged, throwing her cargo overboard. Some of the stones were rescued from the deep by the Islanders, and may now be seen at their houses, used as steps. One at the Spring House, and another at the residence of Mr. Lorenzo Littlefield, and others at the Central House, have attracted attention by their size and beauty. Another vessel, laden with cut stone, was wrecked on the east beach.

THE PALMETTO, *Capt. Baker*,

Was a large steamer, the only one totally wrecked near, or on the Island. In the year 1857, bound from Philadelphia to Boston, she came near enough to strike a concealed rock, known as Black Rock. The Captain attempted, then, to run her ashore in the dense rain and fog, but she filled so rapidly that he took the crew and passengers into life boats and piloted them around from the south end of the Island to the harbor, while she and a valuable cargo sank to the bottom, in seven fathoms of water. She soon went to pieces, and her merchandise for weeks was seen floating in fragments about the shore. One citizen still has some of the sole leather which he rescued, more than he is likely to wear out.

THE MOLUNCUS,

A brig, came ashore on *Grace's Point*, west side of the Island, in the year 1855, laden with molasses. At that time a Wrecking Company here was in readiness to do good service. A very severe storm drove her ashore. She was soon boarded, in the evening, for a contract to get her off. As she was so fast aground, the Captain, crew, and Islanders all left her, and came ashore to the house of Robert C. Dunn, where they were more comfortable. There they bantered considerable time about the price of getting her off, and into port. At last the agreement was made. the condition being $2.500. The con-

tract was drawn and signed by both parties, each taking
a copy. By this time it was quite dark, and the wind
was blowing a gale. But the Island wreckers undertook
to examine the brig as far as possible to decide upon the
gear necessary to get her off, and accordingly went out to
see her, when, to their great astonishment, they could see
nothing of her—*she was gone!* Here was a case to try
their metal, as sailors and wreckers. The furious waves
were coming towards them and madly breaking at their
feet. These were accompanied with winds howling fearfully, and over all brooded thick darkness. Rain was
falling in torrents, and the wind moved an Island barn
from its foundations. They had neither light nor compass, and only a frail surf-boat with which to venture
upon such a sea. Yet, without parley, with a reckless
daring unexcelled, the more venturesome of the wreckers
seized their boat, shoved it into the water, and one after
another leaped in and pushed off, until Capt. N. L. Willis,
Frank Willis, Sylvanus Willis, (brothers,) Simon Ball,
Wm. P. Ball, Silas Mott, S. R. Allen. Luther Dickins,
and Thomas Rathbone, were fairly launched, and out at
sea looking in almost pitch-black darkness for the lost
brig. Soon they were far from the Island, tossed here
and there, not knowing to what point they might be
driven by the wind and tide. The direction of the wind
was their only guide. All eyes were strained for the
faintest outlines of a vessel, but none could be seen. An
occasional thought of their own danger would now and
then flash across their minds and intensify their anxiety.
Were they not earning their money, in case they should
find her, and should ever come ashore again ? Were there
not anxious hearts then upon the Island ? At last, through
the spray and darkness something like a shadow of a ship
was seen. "Steady, boys ! haul steady to the wind'ard
for your lives!" said the Captain, in an old "sea-dog"

tone that meant what sailors alone can fully understand. Soon all hearts grew light, and the oars were pulled with such a force as they had never felt from human hands before. Words were few, as all approached the brig, miles away from the Island, rocking in the deep troughs, with her tall masts almost lying flat upon the sea first on one side and then on the other.

How could she then be boarded? Her lee side was carefully approached, and as it came to the water's edge, the little boat was there, a sailor leaped upon the brig's gunnel, and hove a line back to his comrades, who then came astern, went aboard, hoisted sail, and next morning were in Newport, where their well-earned $2,500 in gold were laid before them, but by unfortunate advice they declined to accept it, claimed salvage, spent about $1,000 in a law suit, and at last took the money stipulated in the contract.

MARY AUGUSTA.

A schooner, Capt. J. W. Holt, of Ellsworth, Me., laden with two hundred and seventy-three tons of coal for Somerset, Mass., in a severe storm on the 4th of April, 1876, was driven upon the shore near Sandy Hill, at nine o'clock P. M. "As she struck she inclined slightly seaward, so that the waves broke over her deck. The men sprung aloft, and there for seven hours clung to the rigging, a storm of snow and rain beating upon them, and the cold waves sweeping white below. They were seen in the morning, and a boat manned by Messrs. Edward Hayes, John Dunn, Augustine Dunn, and Edward Sprague succeeded in bringing them ashore in safety. There were four men and the captain. They had not slept for two nights, and were almost exhausted. They went to the house of Edward Champlin near by where they found the comforts of home." Her cargo was taken out, and she was got off, and taken to Newport.

The "Mays."

The singular coincidences occurred on this Island of two schooners of the same name, "May," in the month of May, 1876, from the same port at the same date, of the same destination, coming ashore on the same day, the 21st, and at nearly the same point, the southwest part of the Island, one at 7.30 P. M., and the other at 8.00 P. M. The first, the *Catherine May*, a two-mast schooner, Capt. Davis, was got off on the 24th by the Old Wrecking Company of the Island, and taken to Newport for $2,000 ; and the second, the *Henry J. May*, a three-mast schooner, Capt E. E. Blackman, was got off on the 22d, by the same company, badly damaged, and taken to Fall River by two steamers, for $3,000. These, like many others, would have been a total loss had it not been for the immediate action of the Island wreckers.

The multitude of wrecks upon the Island is indicated by the following facts : In about the year 1850, in September, six vessels came ashore in one day. About the year 1846, the same number came ashore the same day in June. A catalogue of all grounded here during the past century, would doubtless approach, or perhaps, exceed a thousand in number. Many of these were got off uninjured, or but little damaged. Steamers have grounded here many times without serious disaster.

It is ascertained that during fourteen years, from 1854 to 1868, the loss of property by wrecks on the Island amounted to the sum of $378,000. A visitor here can hardly turn his eyes without having in sight pieces of wrecked vessels, used for posts in fences, gates, and for hitching horses, and in buildings. Nearly all the harrows of the Island have teeth made of ship-bolts. The posts of a long piece of fence near Sandy Point are from the timbers of vessels.

WRECKING.

Wm. P. Lewis, Esq., Secretary of the "Old Protection Wrecking Company of Block Island," furnishes the following facts. During the last seventeen years it got off from the shores of said Island and Point Judith, twenty-one schooners, five barks, and three brigs. The amount of property thus saved has been equal to about one million and two hundred thousand dollars, besides those vessels saved by the New Wrecking Company. During these seventeen years five schooners were lost on the Island, valued at $120,000. Previous to the organization of said Old Company the vessels lost and stranded on the Island far exceeded, during the preceding seventeen years, those saved during the last seventeen years.

The wreckers take all the risk of losing their property, their lives, and failing to get their wreck into port, in which case they receive no pay. Once the Old Company raised a wreck, put all pumps to work, and raised water through the hold by pulleys, and started for New London, towing the hulk with a little tug. A short distance from the Island they were struck by a sudden, fearful storm, and the seas rolled and pitched wreck and tug so that all on board expected to perish. They weathered the gale by keeping the fire of the tug from extinction.

The Old and the New Wrecking Companies here have done much to save life and property. The Old Company existed several years without a competitor, and while they received none too much for the risk and expense they incurred, their receipts were considerable. The New Company was organized a few years ago with a desire to share more largely in those receipts. The two Companies, however, "threw together," and shared equally for the removal of wrecks until the spring of 1876, when it was found best to separate entirely. Each company is amply furnished with empty casks for raising, and "gear" for hauling off; but their dangerous work is likely to be greatly diminished in future by the additional light-house recently erected, by the fog-signal here. and also by the greater familiarity with the Island obtained by vessels that now come here for the protection of the new government harbor.

The following account is given as a specimen of Block Island wrecking.

The Laura E. Messer.

The Laura E. Messer. a three-masted schooner, of 700 tons burthen. Capt. J. F. Gregory. from Newport to Baltimore, in the early part of the winter of 1874–5. ran upon Sandy Point in a fair wind and not very dark night. She had a light cargo, a few hundred barrels of apples, and the delay in getting her off allowed the wind and tide to drive her high up on the bar, so that a high tide and strong wind were necessary to get her off again, making the work very dangerous, as at that point the heavy seas come up from the east and west sides of the Island and meet in fearful conflict over the bar on which she was lying. dashing each other into spray and billows in which the older Islanders have seen terrible sights of perishing men pleading for help when none could possibly be rendered.

With such danger before them two wrecking companies here, Christian men, bargained with the captain to get her off, and as many are not familiar with the skill and courage necessary in dangerous wrecking the following particulars are given.

To take this vessel from her bed in the sand required such a power as no large steamer could apply; it must be unyielding. and it was expected to be against strong wind and tide. For that power needed to be applied hourly for perhaps weeks or months in order to be constantly ready for the favorable storm and tide combined. Thus it was arranged, and the men were ready, their gear consisting of immense hawsers, smaller ropes, blocks, anchors, etc. An ingenious network of ropes over the deck, fastened to stanchions, masts, and windlass, distributed all the power to all parts of her, and also concentrated it all on two great hawsers that led from the bow to the anchors out in the ocean. one of them extending out 2,100 feet. To this were attached three heavy anchors at proper distances from each other. The other hawser ran out parallel with the first, 960 feet. and to this was added a chain 450 feet long, making a cable 1,410 feet in length, and to this were attached two heavy anchors. One of these five anchors was sufficient to hold a ship in an ordinary storm, but they all had a power applied to them that at times would move them. This was done by means of the windlass and pulleys on the deck—"The best windlass," the old captains said, "that they had ever seen."

Trim and beautiful, with her tall, perpendicular masts, there she sat upon the beach "high and dry," and every timber groaning in sympathy under the terrible strain. Moons waxed and waned, tides rose and fell, storms from the wrong direction came and went, and only a little gain was secured by wheeling her bow towards the deep. Almanacs were consulted for moons and tides, and as the highest tide came at midnight, then the wreckers were to be ready for action. On that night, amid the storm, Mr. Day and I walked four miles to see her off, and O, what a sight was around that vessel! Such a commotion where the "two sea smet!" Such a roaring of wind and waves! Some had gone aboard in the early evening. Others were asleep at the light-house close by, until twelve o'clock at night. Then the old "sea-lions" rose, lighted their pipes, and put on their oil suits with a solemn silence like that when men go into battle. They knew their danger, for if she should leave the beach and be hauled out to her anchors it was possible for her hawsers to chafe and break. and then she would be driven upon the bar again amidst breakers where every life must be lost. With lantern in hand, Mr. Day and I stood upon the shore in the howling storm and saw the wreckers one by one ascend the ladder leaning against the wreck. Soon we heard the rattle of the windlass. and we watched patiently for the "jump," as she might rise upon a swell and quickly yield to the strain from her anchors. Her masts were seen in the dim light to sway a little, but she hesitated, until the wind shifted. the tide fell. the waves were cut down. and she stayed. while Mr. Day and I walked home through falling and drifting snow, and retired at half-past four, A. M., to get a snatch of "Nature's kind restorer," fully convinced that "there is a tide in the affairs of men."

How many more moons must wax and tides flow before another favorable combination of wind and tide should occur, not one of Daboll's almanacs could tell. The number of pipes to be filled and smoked while discussing the damage likely to be done to that $5.000 gear, none could guess. At last the day came. Wreckers from all parts of the Island were there. At sunrise she "jumped" at the chance to leave the bar, as a heavy surge for an instant lifted her from the sand, and she darted for the deep water. The wind was "off shore," and she went beyond her anchors, wheeled about, as if to look back at the place of her confinement. With no cargo. light, and bow to the wind, she seemed to writhe with impatience to escape, while we on shore rejoiced that she was off and no lives lost. After waiting an hour we saw her last anchor weighed and hawser slipped, and a scene was before us so beautiful that in a quarter of a minute we were paid for all of our long. stormy walks to the wreck. It was during that instant when, like a living creature. as she was trying

12*

to get away, she was completely freed, a huge swell lifted high her noble prow, the gib was hoisted, the gale struck it, and she wheeled so hurriedly and seemed to say,— "Good-by, Block Island! You'll not catch me there again!" as her colors were run up and she proudly began her flight for Newport over the foaming billows in splendid condition.

But the best of it all is yet untold. Ordinarily, in such a wrecking job everything movable is stolen. In this, while the wreckers had access to all parts of the vessel, not a thing was molested, and the captain said he did not lose so much as a piece of rope-yarn. Why was this exception? The wreckers were Christians. More than a barrel of whiskey would have been drunk, ordinarily, during so many weeks of working in cold winds and sleet by day and by night. But here, though offered by one of the officers of the vessel, not a gill was taken, because the wreckers were Christians.' Ordinarily, among sailors, there is much profanity, but the absence of it among these one hundred wreckers was remarkable. Their few words had the firm tone of experience, softened by the friendly, Christian tone of brethren. Many of them, in years gone by, had been companions in vice. Now they were brethren together in the same Baptist church. A year before they had stood side by side in the house of God, with tears and contrite hearts asking for prayers, and there they had knelt together and plead for pardon through the crucified Redeemer. Scores of them had come into the liberty of the gospel together during the revival when, (in a population of only 1,200,) 121 were baptized into the same church. What a revival the same proportion of a large city would be!

Such are the Christian wreckers of Block Island, and the world may well thank God that there is one little spot on earth where the unfortunate mariner need not be afraid of robbery, profanity, or drunkenness.

It should also be mentioned that the hospitality at the light-house near the wreck will not soon be forgotten. The keeper, and his Baptist wife, had their table set, and their fires burning day and night for crew and wreckers, and it is believed that more than 500 meals were there furnished *gratuitously.*   That house is the successor of the one

> " Set at the mouth of the Sound to hold
> The coast light up on its turret old
> Yellow with moss and sea fog mould."

THE HARBOR.

The following facts, chronologically and briefly arranged under this subject, will doubtless be of increasing interest as one generation shall succeed another. That they are a proof of an unfaltering and commendable persistency originating on the Island none can deny, and posterity will honor those who have done most to identify by means of a permanent, public harbor this isolated point, commercially, financially, and socially with the great brotherhood abroad.

"There was no harbor." This was said, A. D. 1660, in the original memorandum of agreement to purchase and settle the Island. In 1665, Thomas Terry, one of the first purchasers, in behalf of the Islanders, presented a petition to the court of Rhode Island for assistance to build a harbor, and in response the Governor, his Deputy, and Mr. John Clarke, were appointed to visit the Island "to see and judge whether there be a possibility to make a harbor." Five years after, in 1670, the same petition was repeated by Thomas Terry and Hugh Williams, and in reply the Rhode Island Assembly appointed Caleb Carr, and Joseph Torrey, of Newport, to raise contributions "to make a convenient harbour there, to the encouradging fishing designs." It was about ten years before the results of this movement were visible.

GREAT POND HARBOR.

In 1680 the Islanders were thoroughly united in an effort which organized a Harbor Company with "liberty and license to erect and build a harbor, or harbors upon the Island in any place." The town gave the company "all the land or meadow * * gained by the making of the harbor or harbors." It also gave "two days work a year of each inhabitant," and also "the whole privilege of the harbor." Capt. James Sands was the leading man in this company, into which several new members were admitted, and acknowledged such before Chief Warden Simon Ray, Sept 14, 1686. This first harbor on Block Island was in the Great Pond, as the "land or meadow" produced by it must have come from lowering its water, and as no other water could be so reduced. This was done at a place on the west side of the Great Pond where only a narrow rim of sand separates it from the ocean, and hence that rim extending southerly and widening into arable land was subsequently known as "Harbor Neck."

In July, 1694, fourteen years after the Harbor Company was organized, it surrendered to the town its charter, evidently because the enterprise was not successful. The following ordinance was then passed : "Voted at the Town Meeting upon Capt. Sands and James Sands' terms to the town to surrender up the harbor and harbor meadows to the Island, proceeded to accept of it and take and maintain it in good repairs and enter into mutual obligations for the performance thereof." Not long after this the town leased the harbor privileges to one Robert Carr, on the condition of his making certain harbor and fishing improvements. At this time the whole enterprise was declining. Mr. Carr did not fulfill his contract, and all reverted to the town again. In 1699 the Island made another contract with Robert Carr, Jun., granting him a parcel of land "lying on the Harbor Neck," on the condition of his "binding himself for to be forward in making a harbor and promoting the fishing trade accord-

ing to the obligation of his father, Robert Carr, Sen."
Again the harbor reverted to the town, and in Sept.,
1696, was made the following record of the enterprise of
the people, and their great need of a harbor, showing
also who were voters here then :

"Wee, the inhabitants of Block Island, considering the
manyfold dangers, trobles, defucoltys and perels wee are
liable to with respect to the exporting and emporting our
goods, the chefe cause of which Is for want of the con-
venienst of a harbur ; wee therefore Eunanimusly agree
as foloeath, That is to say, leave [levy] Raise and pay one
hundred pounds In mony or the treu valu, said mony to
be levied proporsionally according to Each man's Estate
both reall and pursonall, the one thurd of which shall be
payed at or before the furst of Novembur next Inseuing
the date hereof, one third at or before the first of July
foloing and one third at or before the first of Septembr
then next Inseuing: for the Reserving In and laying out
of the same wee Intreat our loving frends and Neayth-
bours Simon Ray and Mr. Edward Ball as Trustese In the
townes behalf to take the manegment of It one them:
Wee also desier Mr. John Sands, Mr. Thomus Rathbone,
Mr. Nath'll Mott, Mr. Edward Sands to bee undertackers
of said worck. Wee also Intreat said Mr. Ray and Mr.
Ball to apointe a meeting to chuse Valuators and Rate
makers to proporsionate the above said. In conformation
as the above written wee bind our selves to each other,
the defecttive to pay all dameges to the observemante one
[on] defalte as witness our hands this third of September
1696."

John Baning,	John Daudg,
Trustrum Daudg,	John Ackers,
John Mitchell,	James Danielson,
William Rathbone,	Simon Ray,
Thomas Mitchell,	Edward Ball,

Thomas Dickens, Thomas Rathbone,
Gregory Mark, John Sands,
William Daudg, Nath'll Mott,
Joseph Mitchell, Edward Sands,
Joseph Rathbone, John Rathbone.
Samuell Rathbone,

21 Freeholders, $25 average.

This new effort was crowned with only a temporary success for in June, 1705, the enterprise was abandoned, after a continuance of twenty-five years and great expense and anxiety. The principal reason assigned by the town was that by "the providence of God that a prodidgious storm hath broken down the above said harbor and laid it waste."

THE PIER.

In 1707 mention was made of the "Old Harbor," the one at the Breach, which also may imply the existence of a new one. The new one was evidently in the bay, on the east side of the Island, for in 1707 a highway was opened, running on the west side of the Great Pond "to Sandy Point," and thence "to the Harbor," that road being the same that now runs from Sandy Point to the present Harbor. For entering this new harbor, above-mentioned, in 1709, the town taxed each foreign vessel of over four tons burthen one shilling and six pence, and the same for each period of twenty-four hours she remained in it; and those of four tons burthen and less from abroad were taxed six pence for the same harbor privileges. Said harbor was subsequently known as "*the Pier.*"

In a record of 1717, the Islanders spoke of their "Harbor Bay," and in this same year the town passed an act that foreign vessels, for entering their harbor, or fastening at their pier should be taxed as follows:

A vessel of four tons burthen, . . 0 1 0
A vessel of over four tons, and less than ten, 0 1 6
A vessel of ten tons and upward, 0 2 0

This act was repealed in 1718.

The new harbor, or pier, was serviceable about twelve years, until it, like the old one in the Great Pond at the "Breach," was destroyed by a storm. In 1723, the town petitioned the Rhode Island Assembly for assistance, and received in reply the following encouragement : "Where-as the town of New Shoreham, by petition, has laid before this Assembly the great damage they have sustained in losing their pier, in the late great storm, whereby there is scarcely any landing on said Island, to bring off any of their produce, nor no riding for vessels in a storm ; and also the great detriment, for the want of a pier at said Island, for the encouragement of the navigation of this colony, especially the fishery, which is begun to be carried on successfully, and that the inhabitants of the Island are not able of themselves to do the same.

"Upon consideration whereof, it is voted, and enacted by this Assembly, that the inhabitants of New Shoreham have liberty of gathering money by subscription, through-out this colony; and that the town of New Shoreham make a rate upon said town for completing the same."

THE NEW PIER.

This was the beginning of a new and vigorous effort which required much time and persistency to carry it on to success. The question of locating a third harbor was agitated, the first in the Great Pond, and the second in the bay, having both proved failures. Accordingly, in 1733, ten years after the commencement, the Rhode Island Assembly appointed a committee consisting of Governor William Wanton, Capt. Benjamin Ellery, Col. William Coddington, Mr. Joseph Whipple, Col. Joseph

Stanton, Capt. John Potter, Capt. Wm. Wanton, Jr., and Mr. Geo. Goulding "to go over to Block Island to view the same, and consider of a convenient place to build a pier, or harbor, and of the charge, &c., and make report to the next General Assembly." In June, 1734, the Assembly appointed as "a committee to procure materials for building a pier at Block Island. and making a harbor there," Simon Ray, Peter Ball, Henry Bull, Wm. Brown, and Wm. Wanton, Jr., the first two being from the Island, and then Representatives, or "Deputies." in the General Assembly. This committee were authorized also "to go on with the work and perfect the same as soon as conveniently may be," and accordingly they began the work of "cutting a passage through the beach." Where this was, except at the old pond harbor or near, it is not easy to imagine. In February, 1835, however. this project was stopped by an act of the General Assembly, which at the same time appropriated £1,200 for "making an addition to the old pier, or building a new one." In August of the same year Capt. Simon Ray and Capt. Peter Ball were appointed by the Assembly "a committee to improve the £1,200 allowed to build a pier at Block Island, or repair the old one." In February. 1736, nothing had been done to the pier. The work was soon after begun. The old pier was preserved, and a new one built near it. Frequent storms were damaging both while the work was going on, and the money appropriated to build was spent to a considerable extent in repairing both piers. In 1742 the town petitioned the Assembly again for another appropriation, saying : "As your petitioners have been at great charges to repair the same, and their endeavors have hitherto been fruitless, by the frequent storms that have happened, before the same could be completed." In response £200 were appropriated, and drawn from the treasury by Capt. Edward Sands. In June, 1743, £400

13

were also appropriated by the State; to be paid only when the work was completed. In May, 1745, Messrs. Samuel Rodman, Teddeman Hull, and Abel Franklin, a State committee to view the pier, reported to the Assembly that they "found it to be completely finished."

This work was quite inadequate and was not of long endurance, and the town, in 1762, through a petition presented by Messrs. Edmund Sheffield and Joseph Spencer, applied to the Assembly for a lottery charter, the avails of which were to be appropriated in making a harbor of the Great Pond, and in improving its fisheries. The lottery was granted, but was unsuccessful. In 1773, a similar petition, very ably drawn up, was presented in behalf of the town by John Littlefield and John Sands, asking for an appropriation of money, and hoping to raise all additional funds needed "by lotteries." The great need of a harbor then was set forth by the following facts : The necessity of swimming their horses, cattle, and sheep to the vessels and hoisting them aboard; high frieght on account of difficult landing; dangers of life, and damage to goods and animals ; value of a harbor to fisheries; the convenience of the Great Pond for a harbor, and its fish; and the benefits to the Island, doubling the value of it by a good harbor; advantages to the colony, "and to the neighboring governments." The petition made the following record: "The most effectual remedy for all these evils may be provided by cutting a channel from the sea into the aforementioned pond, which is large enough to contain the whole British navy, and deep enough for any vessels in this colony. Between the sea and the pond there is a sand-bank about twenty rods wide, and on the pond side, ten feet of water within two rods of the bank, which soon increases to thirty feet; and on the side of the sea there is also a very ·fine bold shore; that a channel was formerly cut through the said bank, and became so navigable, that vessels of seventy and eighty tons burthen have actually sailed into the pond, but the place where the said channel was formed not being properly defended on the sea-side, it filled up with sand.

"The place now proposed for opening a communication with the sea is about a quarter of a mile southward from the old channel, where the water is much deeper, and the channel will be secured by a point of rocks that lies to the southward. which affords the greatest prospect of obtaining an effectual and lasting harbor." (See R. I. Col Rec., VIII., 209.)

In August, 1773, Stephen Hopkins, Eseck Hopkins, and Joseph Wanton, Jr., a committee of examination of the Great Pond and the adjacent beach, reported back to the Assembly feebly in favor of the above project, which was never carried out. The Revolution soon began to absorb the attention of the colonies, and Block Island was prompt in passing a resolution to co-operate with all American citizens in opposing the aggressions of England. The long struggle for independence which followed, and the general exhaustion of the country put a long-continued obstacle in the way of further effort to secure a harbor for Block Island.

POLE HARBOR.

The Pole Harbor. as it may be designated, was begun about the year 1816. A single individual, at low tide, near the shore end of the present breakwater, sunk a few spiles close to each other, about six feet deep, the upper parts of them rising above the water from ten to fifteen feet. To these he could tie up his boat in ordinary weather. Others followed his example, until long rows of such poles extended out into a considerable depth of water at high tide. Between two parallel rows, stones were placed, and little piers were thus built up. This construction was carried on for many years by so many

Islanders that a forest of oak poles became the principal harbor into which twenty or more boats could enter at a time for lading or unlading, except in a storm. Then the boats were drawn up on the shore out of reach of the water. Well do the older inhabitants now remember the many stormy nights when in the cold wind and rain they were obliged to leave their comfortable beds and yoke their oxen, and go to the harbor and assist one another in hauling up their boats. Thus matters went on for half a century, the pole harbor being far better than none, with little improvements here and there, until the poles were over one thousand in number. After many have been removed for the present harbor, seven hundred and fifty are now standing in 1876, and are still of considerable service, in fair weather, to the fishermen. Some of them, like the stumps of the old pier still visible, will doubtless long remain after they are useless, and after those who set them have all passed away, many of them to enjoy "A Home Beyond the Tide," "Safe Within the Vail," of which we have heard them sing so heartily since the great religious awakening in 1873.

GOVERNMENT HARBOR.

The Government Harbor, at Block Island, next and lastly claims our attention. "In 1838 the two Houses of Congress passed resolutions directing the attention of the departments to this subject, and authorizing a favorable report." (*Cong. Globe*, Feb. 16, 1867.) In 1867 it was again agitated, after the long lapse of nearly thirty years, and after an able speech in its favor by Senator Sprague, of Rhode Island, Congress took action in favor of constructing a breakwater at Block Island. But this national movement did not begin at Washington. What was done there was, in a measure, the effect of preceding causes. By coming back from effect to cause we shall find that this Government Harbor, already affording so much profit and pleasure to the public, originated on Block Island. In Jan., 1867, previous to the action of Congress in Feb. of that year, the Rhode Island Assembly instructed the Senators and Representatives in Congress from this State, "to use their best exertions to procure an appropriation from Congress for the purpose of building a breakwater, or of securing a safe harbor for vessels at said Island." This action, too, was the result of a plan previously originated on the Island, a plan which simultaneously united the efforts of many Chambers of Commerce, the Rhode Island Legislature, and both houses of Congress. The harbor question was introduced into the U. S. Senate by Senator Sprague on the 16th of Feb., and on the 18th the Boston *Journal* said: "Hon. Nicholas Ball [of Block Island] was before the Senate Committee on Commerce this morning to advocate the appropriation for a breakwater at Block Island. The committee were so impressed by Mr. Ball's plain facts they voted to recommend an appropriation of $40,000." Gov. Padelford, in his message of Jan., 1873, also said: "Much credit is also due to the Hon. Nicholas Ball, for his unwearied exertions in behalf of the improvements on Block Island, for through his means alone the attention of the Chambers of Commerce of New York, Philadelphia, Boston, and Providence, as well as those engaged in commerce in our northern cities, was enlisted in the work."

In the second session of Congress, in 1867, the Secretary of War was directed to cause surveys to be made for a harbor at Block Island. The survey was made by Geo. W. Dresser, Assistant Engineer, under the direction of Col. D. C. Houston, and an elaborate report of the same was made Nov. 1st, 1867, to Col. Houston, who gave an abstract of it to the War Department in Jan.,

13*

1868; and in March of that year, Secretary of War E. M. Stanton reported the same to Congress.

So many have expressed opinions in reference to the Great Pond as a harbor, the following extracts from the government survey are here given:

"At the point on the west side marked *breach* the Islanders make a cut, which has to be opened several times a year for the purpose of drawing off the water from the pond into the sound sufficiently to keep the road dry, which runs along the east shore of the Island from north to south between the pond and the ocean. This *breach* is but a small ditch dug in the sand which fills up at the mouth or west end a little higher than ordinary high-water mark during the first heavy westerly blow that occurs after it is dug out.

"It has always been a favorite idea with some of the Islanders to avail of this pond as a harbor by making a *cut* on the west into it from the sound. But from all that I can learn nothing of the kind has ever been attempted, except to *open the breach* for the purpose referred to above." [Neither Mr. Dresser, nor the Islanders were then aware of the existence of the old records which we have recently discovered of the Great Pond Harbor, of which the early part of this article gives an account. S. T. L.]

"In order to make a harbor of the Great Pond at Block Island the cut should be made, if at all, at a point farther south than *the breach*, for at that point the distance from the south to the deepest water in the pond is the shortest. To make a channel available for all purposes the cut should be made at least twenty-five feet deep below mean low-water mark, and the width of which the nature of the ground will admit is not over 650 feet.

"The estimates for this excavation are made upon a basis of 25 feet deep, 633 feet average width, and an average length at the bottom of the cut of 2,425 feet, giving 996.104$\frac{46}{100}$ cubic yards of excavation.

"At fifty cents per cubic yard this excavation would be $498,052.23.

"Having made the excavation it would be necessary to protect the entrance to it from the sound by piers built out into the water. These would have to be built in the most substantial manner, of masonry, and estimated upon a basis of 20 feet wide, 900 feet long on each side, and an average depth of $17\frac{1}{2}$ feet, would require about 24,000 yards of cubic stone, and would cost from $300,000 to $500,000, making the whole cost of the channel about one million of dollars. The action of the water would bank up the sand on the outside of these piers, and eventually it would make land out to the ends of them. The pond at the time of making the survey at this point was two feet four inches higher than mean low-water in the sound. The average rise and fall of the tide on the west shore is about three feet six inches. This would cause a strong current either to or from the pond, causing sand and sediment to deposit at different points in the channel, according to the direction and stage of the tide. Bars would form at the ends of the channel, and the bottom of the sound being sand the channel would ultimately fill up on the sound end in spite of all precautions to protect it. The same causes that fill up the *breach* would fill up this, and a constant expenditure would be necessary to dredge it out.

"A glance at the soundings of the pond will show the exceedingly irregular conformation of the bottom of it, and that only a small portion of the water could be used for anchorage, without continued vexation and trouble from getting aground.

"The prevailing storms from which the most shelter is required are from the east. But this would be a head wind to beat through a narrow channel to get into the harbor or pond, and if blowing hard it would be impossible to beat in at all, while if in the pond it would be equally difficult to get out with a west wind.

"There is one point which would be of vital importance if it should become necessary to use the pond as a harbor in naval defense, viz.: it freezes completely in winter.

"Hence, I conclude that although a cut might be made and kept open at a large expense, it would *not* be available at all times either for ingress or egress, and that the advantages gained by the work would not be commensurate with the expense, particularly when compared with what might be obtained at the other point on the east side of the Island by *building a breakwater into the bay*."

In June, 1868, the bill for an appropriation for the said harbor was before Congress, asking for $74,000. It was strongly opposed by Mr. Washburn, of Illinois, in the House, and yet the vote then taken was favorable, but owing to a hurried adjournment of Congress the bill was not voted on by the Senate, and none was granted. Persistent efforts, however, were continued from Block Island and the Rhode Island Legislature and Congressional Representatives. Twelve years were thus worn away before any thing effectual was accomplished. Then the General Assembly of Rhode Island renewed its often repeated instruction to its Representatives in Congress "to use all means in their power to secure the legislation necessary to ensure the construction of the required pier on Block Island." In response to this the Hon. Henry B. Anthony, from Rhode Island, made a powerful speech in the U. S. Senate, Feb. 16, 1870, and in July, 1870, Congress made an appropriation of $30,000, for the Block Island breakwater, which already has been seen by so many who have visited the Island in fishing vessels, pleasure yachts, and steamers, that a description of it is not here needed.

Its construction was begun Oct. 22, 1870, "at 3.30 P. M., amid great rejoicing of the people." "John Beattie took the contract at $2.82 per ton, to put in granite from low-water mark, keeping the structure above tide as he proceeded, and run it so far as the allowance would permit. Under this contract the breakwater was carried some three hundred feet, and the Islanders themselves furnished about one thousand tons of stone."

In March, 1871, another appropriation was granted by Congress of $75,000. The government contracted with Messrs. Finch, Engs & Co. of Newport, for 300,000 feet of timber for the crib, or basin, as it is now called, a temporary harbor for smaller vessels until the great harbor is completed. Messrs. Place & Co., of New York, furnished 56,000 pounds of iron bolts. Messrs. Campbell & Co., of New York, agreed to place 7.000 tons of granite for the breakwater, and the Islanders laid 5,000 tons besides completing Mr. Campbell's contract. Thus the stone-work, called "riprap stone," was extended into the sea over 600 feet from the shore. It now extends out one thousand feet.

In June, 1872, another appropriation of $50,000 was made by Congress, and the contract of placing 10,000 tons of stone was awarded to Hon. John G. Sheffield, of Block Island, who did the work for $7.600 less than the lowest bid from abroad. His work was completed June 30, 1873, and by his able management saved expense to the government, and gave employment to his townsmen. Meanwhile the blasting and removing of rocks and dredging were going on and under this last appropriation the Government Harbor became a success, and soon the Islanders built boats with decks, and no longer, in storms, landed by riding the biggest of "three brothers" upon

the shore, at fearful risk, nor hauled their boats ashore
with oxen in the night, to protect them from the storm,
and fishing fleets from abroad find refuge from the dangers of the ocean.

Here it should be remarked,. to the honor of those who
have thus far done the work and received the appropriations, no complaints of embezzlement are recorded against
them. No extra appropriations over and above the engineer's estimates have been called for. On the contrary,
work, the cost of which the U. S. Board of Engineers, at
their meeting in New York, in Feb., 1868, estimated at
$372,000, has been done for $155,000. If the remaining
work can be done with equal integrity and economy, the
total cost, instead of being $2,915,016, as estimated by
said board, will be much less than one-half that sum.
This is an encouragement to the public and to Congress
to carry the harbor construction forward.

INCIDENTS.

In the construction of the harbor a few incidents have
occurred that merit a record. The removal of "Peaked
Rock" is one of them. For centuries it had been a concealed enemy to the boatmen, raising its head near
enough to the surface to sink a vessel by making a hole
in its bottom. A spindle of iron for many years had
risen from its peak to hold a keg over the danger. When
the present basin was built this formidable rock was
removed by the work of a submarine diver and the appli-
cation of dualin. Twenty-five pounds of this powerful
agency were applied to Peaked Rock, containing an ex-
plosive power of about three hundred pounds of powder.
When all was ready, and ample warning given, the elec-
tric battery produced the explosion that shook the whole
Island, threw up a high column of spray, and shattered
the rock to fragments. Other similar rocks were thus

removed from their troublesome positions. The lives of many fish, some of considerable size, were destroyed by the blasting.

While excavating for the "crib-work" of the harbor, a singular substance was thrown up in considerable quantity, of the consistency of moist blue clay. Mr. Ray S. Littlefield threw a piece into his wagon and carried it home, where it became dry and hard. After a few years he gave it to the writer, supposing it to be petrifaction. The writer proved it to be native coal, which at some future day may be an index to a mine beneath the Ocean View hill.

TOPOGRAPHY.

THE PONDS.

One of the greatest curiosities of the Island is found to be its ponds. But few inhabited and cultivated parts of the earth can be named, no larger than Block Island, with so great a number and variety of ponds as here exist. The exact number of those which do not become dry once in ten years has not been exactly ascertained, but they may be estimated at over a hundred without exaggeration. They vary in size from the duck pool to the Great Pond, which is said to cover one thousand acres. The smaller ones are so interspersed as to furnish every farmer with the benefits of from one to twenty. and as springs are not abundant, and as only one stream can approach the dignity accorded to a small brook, these little ponds are of very great convenience for watering animals and for raising fowls.

The formation of these ponds is peculiar. There is probably not one of them sustained by springs or streams. They are generally in little deep pockets formed by the surrounding steep hillocks constituting water-sheds for their respective ponds. These pockets have clay bottoms that hold the water like caldrons, and the surface-water compensates for the slow evaporation. The same surface-water for ages, before the forest was consumed, carried leaves, nuts, and bark, and decayed wood into said pockets, and hence an almost inexhaustible supply of peat has been preserved, and where there is a pond, peat, with a few exceptions. is obtained, and thus the many little farms of the Island are amply furnished with fuel for the house, and water for the animals—water not suitable for domestic purposes. These peculiarities of the ponds are found in the highest, as well as the lowest parts of the Island— on the bluffs near the steep descent to the sea, and in other places almost on a level with the ocean. The following are some of the more noted:

The Great Pond.

This name is very appropriate, given by Roger Williams in 1649, for in proportion to the land or Island, of which the pond is a part, it is an inland sea. Its length is about one-third the length of the Island, and its width is enough less to give it much of the form of an ellipse. One thousand acres are said by good authority to be embraced in its surface. Its depth is quite variable, and much like the uneven surface of the land adjacent, according to the soundings of the government surveyor who examined it, in reference to making of it a harbor. Twelve fathoms are its maximum depth, and that on the side nearest to the sea, a fact worthy of observation. It is separated from the sea on the west by a strip of land so narrow that when viewed from Beacon Hill it appears like the rim of a basin, or an arc embracing a quarter of a circle. Its easterly shore, mostly, is called the Neck, and at the southern end, Indian Head Neck. Most of that part between its southwest shore and the sea was called Charlestown a hundred years ago, and the narrow portion of said part was then known by the name of Harbor Neck, as the harbor anciently was in the Great Pond at the breach. The south end of the pond lies about midway of the Island from north to south.

By many this pond is supposed to be sustained by springs and the main water-sheds adjacent. But this is an error. From its unshaded surface more could evaporate in a day than would thus be supplied from such known sources in a week. As before seen, the surface of the whole Island is thickly indented with deep little pockets that catch nearly all the surface-water, and the clay bottoms of them prevent the formation of outlets in the from of rills and springs. All the supposed feeders of the pond combined are not equal to those that support a mill-pond on some small stream that is dry a quarter of the time in the country. Whence, then, it may be asked, does the Great Pond obtain its support? From the sea, is the simple reply. The rim between it and the sea is so narrow that the water from the latter filters through into the former. A brief examination shows this, and the principal reason why it has not been more generally admitted, seems to be that the Islanders and most of others are not acquainted with the fact that sea-water thoroughly filtered through fine sand becomes fresh. Knowing, however, that the pond is of itself fresh-water, becoming salt only as the breach lets in a little occasionally, and as the sea slops over into the pond during heavy storms, they have supposed its freshness must be the result of a fresh supply from the land, which is quite inadequate. This explanation is in harmony with the observation made by Lord Bacon that "sea-water passing or straining through the sands leaveth the saltness," and by this means he says Cæsar once saved his army. The Great Pond, therefore, is a body of fresh water, artificially, or incidentally salted enough to make it brackish most of the time ; and this is our apology, together with a preference for the shorter name, for calling it the Great Pond, instead of the "Great Salt Pond."

Formerly it contributed largely to the support of the Island. Its products of fish, oysters, clams, quahaugs, and scallops has been greatly dependent upon the salt-water admitted through the Breach, an opening into the sea that

was ample for the support of these shell-fish before, and
for a considerable time after the settlement of the Island.
The scallop shells, and others now found at the graves of
the natives show that they were common anciently; and
within the memory of the present inhabitants, oysters of
an excellent quality have been raked up there in large
quantities. Mr. Wm. P. Ball says that when a boy he
once gathered there from their native beds twenty bushels
in one day. For several years the water has been too
fresh to grow them, and hence this branch of Block
Island fisheries has "run out," a thing to be lamented, for
shell-fish are now seldom tasted on the Island. That the
Great Pond might be made the source of great profit by
opening the breach sufficiently to salt the millions of little
oysters and clams already there planted, no one can reason-
ably doubt. It is hoped that some capitalists will soon
secure this opportunity which is now in the hands of Mr.
John Thomas who well understands how to secure there
an abundance of valuable herring, shad, and shell-fish,
but lacks the means to accomplish the work necessary.
He has a fifteen-year lease of the pond from the town,
and from it has derived some revenue in his spring catch
of herrings. Besides the above transient fish the Great
Pond abounds with perch and eels, and bass have lately been
introduced.

In 1762, Block Island petitioned the Rhode Island
Assembly, through Edmund Sheffield and Joseph Spencer,
for a chartered lottery by means of which to improve the
Great Pond for fishing. In their petition it was stated
"That on the westermost side of said Island there is a
large pond, covering above one thousand acres of land,
which formerly had a communication with the sea by a
creek; that then the fishing-ground for cod was well
known, and bass was there to be caught in great plenty:
that since the creek has been stopped the fishing-ground

for cod is uncertain, they being scattered about in many places; and the bass have chiefly left the Island."

As a source of pleasure to summer visitors, the Great Pond cannot be surpassed for fishing, swimming, rowing, and sailing. Free from the swells and dangerous surf of the sea, several miles in length, and broad enough for tacking in any wind, it is evidently destined to do far more for the pleasure-seeking public than it has hitherto. Mr. Simon Ball & Sons, at the south end of it, during the summer of 1876, launched a safe and commodious yacht for the accommodation of visitors, and received a liberal patronage.

Chagum Pond.

This name is commonly pronounced *Shawgum*, and is probably taken from an Indian. We have a record of one *Samuel Chagum*, who distinguished himself here in 1711 by stealing a canoe, running away from his master, losing the canoe, and suffering the penalty from the wardens of six months added to his former period of servitude. The pond lies between the Great Pond and Sandy Point, and is about as large as a tenth part of the latter pond. It is fresh, and supported from the sea, separated from it the proper distance for filtering the sea-water. In the great gale of 1815, the sea waves were so high as to pass over into Chagum Pond, the only time of which we have an account of such an occurrence.

The Middle Pond.

This lies between Chagum Pond and the Great Pond, and is separated from the sea, west of the Island, by a narrow rim of sand, through which the salt-water is filtered and freshened. The Middle Pond is distinguished chiefly as the place where the British vessels, in the times of war, have obtained water, and where, in 1812–15, they frequently did the washing of their clothes on its green,

eastern shore. It lies west of Hon. J. G. Sheffield's residence. Chagum Pond was also a resort of the British
for water.

FRESH POND.

This is about a mile south of the Great Pond, and on
land much more elevated. The road south from the Center leads to it, and visitors in considerable numbers resort
there for the fine perch fishing. The pond itself is also
attractive, clear, and surrounded with green shores in
view of pleasant residences. It covers several acres, and
was anciently looked upon from the windows and doors
of the first school-house, and the first meeting-house on
the Island. They were located on the east shore, near the
north end. There, too, the first Island minister settled,
had his residence, and these sites were selected, probably,
with reference to the attractions of this beautiful little
sheet of water.

SANDS' POND.

The clearest, the handsomest, and the highest of all
that may be considered large enough to be noted, is this
gem in an emerald setting. It is southeast from the Fresh
Pond, and near the residence of Dea. R. T. Sands, and
his brother William C. Sands. It is remarkable for its
beauty, and for the mysterious manner in which it is supported. Located on some of the highest ground of the
Island, with no water-shed of any account, more than a
hundred feet above the sea, from which it is more than a
mile distant at the nearest point, with gravelly shores, with
but a few feet of average depth, why it never dries up is
a question that remains to be solved. No volcanic appearances are in its vicinity to justify us in classifying it with
the crater ponds on the main-land. We could imagine it
to be the terminus of a vein from a southeasterly and
higher ground were there a ledge on the Island, instead

14*

of the drift material of which it is composed.   That it is fed from some source is evident from its clearness and its fish.

HARBOR POND.

Near the old pier or harbor is a small pond, northwest from the present harbor.   This, like the Great Pond, and Chagum Pond, is fed from the sea, although separated from it perhaps twenty-five rods.   It is of a peculiar color, owing to the great quantity of iron sand through which the water from the sea filters.   At times its appearance is very rusty, and at a distance, in some reflections of the light, it has a purple tinge.   Small sail-boats and row-boats on it, owned by Mr. Negus & Sons afford much pleasure to visitors.   Its fleet of ice-boats in winter will long be remembered by the boys who have there enjoyed so many voyages, capsizings, and wrecks while accompanied by sisters, and other gentle-handed cousins and neighbors.

FORT ISLAND POND.

Only a narrow neck of land separates this from the south end of the Great Pond.   It is distinguished chiefly by the little island from which its name is taken.   It is a pretty sheet, covering several acres, of very irregular shape, bordered with green fields, and is an ornament to the landscape view from the Central House, and from Mr. Frank Willis'.   For fifteen years it has been the home of a resident whose age is not known, but his race is notorious.   He is evidently a descendant of ancestors living here while King Philip and his warriors were scalping the white people on the main-land.   He is seen only once or twice a year, and when seen a few years ago by a sturdy young man, the latter hastened to the house faint and trembling and tried to describe the "old settler."   During the summer of 1876, he was seen again, and from

the description given of him, his appropriate name seems
to be, the *Fort Island Pond Serpent.* The above facts are
easily authenticated. The serpent is evidently a large.
old, black water-snake, entirely harmless, and as shy as
the Indians who possibly worshiped his forefathers.

THE MILL POND.

We notice this, not for its size, but as the only one
here known as a mill-pond, and as a historical relic. It
was made by Capt. James Sands, and is now owned by
Mr. Almanzo Littlefield, lying south of the old mill where
corn was at first ground, and wool was subsequently
carded. Here was the first case of drowning on the
Island of which we have any account. Capt. Sands, one
of the first proprietors, then had an only child, "a girl
just able to run about and prattle a little." In an un-
guarded moment she escaped from her mother's eye, fell
into the pond near the house, and was there drowned
before she was rescued.

THE WEST SIDE.

There are three natural, or recognized divisions of
Block Island, viz.: The Corn Neck, the East Side, and the
West Side. The latter two may be distinguished as separated by the road that runs from the south end of the
Great Pond to the east shore of the Fresh Pond and
thence to the south end of the Island. The soil of the
West Side differs from that of the East Side, and the
people of the one side differ from those of the other side.
Originally, Simon Ray, and after him his son Simon, at
whose house the famous cheese was made which Benjamin
Franklin wrote about to Miss Catharine Ray, and at which
the unfortunate inmates of the Palatine were welcomed,
honored the West Side; while James Sands, and his
descendants, at the stone house and the Sands Garrison

were making the East Side famous in the vicinity of the "Sands Harbor." John Rathbone, also, was located on the West Side, little aware that the time was coming when his descendants would be reported heirs of $40,-000,000 in the Bank of England.

The natural points of interest on the West Side are not yet so well known as they will be at some future day. Nor is it easy to trace out the entangled legends concerning them. They have received but little attention from the naturalist, and perhaps less from the inhabitants. It is hoped that the few things here said may be an index, at least, to induce others to delineate more fully the peculiarities of the West Side.

Sandy Hill, there, arrests the attention of the visitor. It is near the Sound shore, with a base a quarter of a mile long from north to south, and half that distance east and west, rising about one hundred feet to a point on which half a dozen horses might stand, affording a fine view of the sea, of Montauk, and of Watch Hill, and also of the west shore of the Island. It is a pile of drift, and would be worth a fortune for sand and gravel if properly located. It is almost wholly destitute of vegetation, except the tuft of grass on the top which makes the *tout-ensemble* look somewhat like a Chinese head. Its base rests upon a bed of peat, which shows that it was thrown up *after* the Island had produced vegetation. At its eastern foot is a famous deposit of "firing," "tug," or peat, as it is called.

Grace's Cove is near Sandy Hill, and the place it occupies is sometimes call Grace's Point, and has been distinguished somewhat as a place for landing small boats. It was there, probably, that the Mohegan Indians landed when they came by moonlight from Stonington, or Watch Hill, in force, to fight the Manisseans, and were so barbarously destroyed at Mohegan Bluff.

Dorry's Cove is at the terminus of the road that runs

from the Center to the west beach. It seems to have taken its name from an ancient owner by the name of Tormot Rose, whose name was sometimes written Dormut. or Dormud. He owned the land adjacent, and gave the cove, now partially filled up with sand, some notoriety by a little incident of dumping a cart-load of stone into the cove, and accidentally losing an ox by so doing—the team going back with the falling load. Mr. Rose mourned bitterly the loss of his ox, and was chided for it by a neighbor, who said to him. "Why, Mr. Rose, you mourn for your ox more than Job did for the loss of all of his;" whereupon the afflicted man replied that "Job never had so likely an ox!" The cove is now distinguished as a landing for fishermen, where they draw up their boats above the tide and seas, and where they have a few fish-houses.

Cooneymus is the name of the place where the West Side Life Station is located. It seems to be an Indian name. It is here spelled according to pronunciation, as the writer has never seen it written or printed, and in answer to inquiries how to spell it, he is informed that probably "it never was spelled." It is a very convenient shore for hauling up the boats of fishermen, as at Dorry's Cove, and is a well selected spot for the station from which men patrol the shores in each direction.

The Palatine graves are on the West Side. They are on the land owned by Mr. Jeremiah C. Rose, and are found by strangers most readily by going south from the Center until the first right-hand road is reached, thence by that to the gate of Samuel Allen, Esq., and thence to the house of Mr. Raymond Dickens. From his house it is but a few steps to said graves, and the old foundations of the ancient Simon Ray house, and Mr. Ray's deep old well are also near the house of Mr. Dickens. Indeed native timbers that were once in Mr. Ray's house are now doing good service in the house of Mr. Dickens. who, during fifty years had an eye frequently upon the old dancing mortar mentioned in another place.

The Bluff scenery of the West Side, in some respects excels, especially that at the southern extremity. From it the vessels of the Sound, those "outside," Montauk, Long Island, and the Connecticut shore are conspicuous. Sites for summer residences, in time, will be selected, no doubt, upon the sightly points of the West Side, roads to which could be made with but little expense. The land is cheap.

Beacon Hill is the most conspicuous point on the West Side. It is the highest land upon the Island, and is nearly west from the Center. Its name originated from the beacon placed upon it in the Revolution, to warn the Islanders of the approach of the refugees. In making coast surveys, a beacon on this hill has been of service. It is visited by many strangers in the summer for the splendid view there obtained. From its summit the encircling waters are seen except at one small point at the southeast, and the whole Island is spread out into a beautiful landscape of a thousand hills and hundreds of ponds, most of which are hid from the spectator, as they are in the little indentations between the hills. Beacon Hill is visited both on foot, and in carriages, by ladies and gentlemen. From it, in a clear atmosphere, distant views over Long Island, into Connecticut and Rhode Island, and in the direction of Cape Cod are obtained with a good glass. Access to it heretofore has always been free, by the kindness of the owner, Mr. William Dodge, but the increased number of visitors, and the trouble they have made him by opening his fence, and the damage to his field will justify him in future in making a small charge for admission. The hill is about three hundred feet high.

Mohegan Bluff, proper, belongs to the West Side according to tradition. It is the high point next to the sea

where the Mohegan warriors were penned up and starved
by the Manisseans. The former in coming to the Island
would naturally land on the West Side, at Grace's Cove,
Dorry's Cove, or Cooneymus, as the "Moheague country"
was lying to the northwest of the Island. Soon after
they landed, Niles says, the Manisseans "drove them to
the *opposite part* of the Island, where, I suppose, the cliffs
next the sea are near, if not more than two hundred feet
high." This account seems to locate Mohegan Bluff near
the new light-house. But as a compromise the name may
well apply to the entire bluff range across the south end
of the Island. "Bluff" is more appropriate than "Cliff,"
as there are no rocks.

THE EAST SIDE.

East and West are correlative terms, designating points
that may be the farthest possible from, or the nearest possible to each other. Indeed, in respect of direction they
contradict the philosophical dogma that no two objects
can occupy the same space at the same time. To this fine
point, however, it is not our intention to reduce the two
sides of Block Island. They differ, and yet are parts of
a unit.

On the East Side the natural attractions are varied.
The Bathing Beach is not only a place of pleasure, but also
of study. The mineralogist may there find a field for
thinking. Anciently that beach was more bold. Banks
twenty-five feet high covered with grass, and unbroken,
save in one or two narrow gullies, stretched from Clay
Head nearly to the Old Pier. The foot of that low bluff
was bathed winter and summer by the rising and falling
tides, and by the dashing spray of the storms from the
east. Mrs. Margaret Dodge, now eighty-six years old,
recollects well her sports in childhood with other children
along that steep bank next to the sea, up which it was

difficult for them to climb, it was so steep and sandy. When they could not leave the beach and climb up the bank, they reached the latter place by going to the little deep cut in the bank through which they ascended. Now that bank has all disappeared, and a few sand-hills in the back-ground remain as relics and monuments of a former period. That bank has been carried away principally by the strong winds of winter, which have moved its sand as though it were snow. The millions of tons thus moved in twenty-four hours, if stated, would be incredible. Imagine a thin sheet of sand drifting past your feet like water gliding over a smooth surface, and then look upon a surface a mile in length and a quarter of a mile in breadth, thus moving to the sea whose receding waves and surf carry off the sand as fast as it is deposited. Such has been nature's process of making the bathing beach from the fine sand of the once beautiful bank that bordered the bay of Block Island.

The Black Sand of the bathing beach has attracted considerable attention. It was once a part of the boulders which nature ground up to sand in some of her great mills or mortars long ago. After that it was commingled with the common sand of the Island. It is iron, too heavy to be blown off into the sea and drifted about, and hence it remains forsaken by its old comrades of "little grains of sand." Several acres of this, very fine, and containing a large percentage of iron, are covered by a lease in the hands of a New York party who contemplated shipping it to some foundry. Much of the northerly part of the bed has sand very beautiful under the microscope, which reveals particles resembling jasper, amber, and diamond. Before the invention of blotting-paper this sand was sold quite extensively for sand-boxes, and one of the Islanders made quite a business of it.

The bathing beach thus beautifully constructed by

nature is one of the chief attractions of Block Island. The sand is fine, clean, and compact, and unless disturbed by some unusual storm, its descent into the sea is gentle, and the surf is moderate, yet sufficient to produce the desired excitement for the bathers. There the words are verified :

> " On smoother beaches no sea birds light,
>   No blue waves shatter to foam more white."

It is near enough to all of the hotels of the Island, for while it is a source of health and pleasure its scenery of little houses, queer dresses, and unusual positions and movements should be somewhat retired from the more refined associations of the piazza, the dining-room, and the parlor. A little walk, or a longer ride before and after bathing adds to its enjoyment, and carriages are readily obtained when desired. The ox-team of two yokes attached to the great wagon from the Ocean View, with the colored man Jack, a descendant from the Palatine, for driver, will not soon be forgotten by the ladies and gentle-men who thus rode to the beach, all attired for a bath so grotesquely that one hardly knew the other.

The Harbor, a historical sketch of which is given else-where, is the most important place on the East Side. There, after an effort of centuries, a safe and permanent protection to vessels has recently been secured. There the first steamboat wharf of the Island was established. There the treasures of the deep have been landed for the support of many generations. There the old fishermen see to-day relics of the past, in the shape of large casks, that remind him of remote ancestors. There, from child-hood, he has gone up and down the bank in the steps of his forefathers, has counted and dressed his fish as they did, has carried them to the fish-house and salted them as they did, and thence has wended his weary way home-ward to eat and sleep under the roofs and by the firesides

15

which they erected. When an old man now can no longer "go to the Harbor," his earthly enjoyments are considered very limited, and his work about finished, When they could go there, they needed not the excitement of the theater, the saloon, the club-room, and the rat-pits of cities, nor of the American race-course, nor of the bull-fights of Spain; for at the Harbor, each fall and spring, and occasionally in winter and summer, scenes a hundred-fold more exciting than the gay regatta sailing fancifully for a cup of gold, were witnessed by the Block Islanders, as fathers and brothers repeatedly stood there and watched their dearest kindred far out on the sea struggling in the tempest against wind and tide, to gain the shore in their little open boats. Not cups of gold, but *lives* were there at stake, when the tumbling billows tossed those boats here and there with the white foam until by wonderful skill the harbor was gained, and that, too, sometimes anciently by selecting the biggest of the "three brothers," and coming ashore high and dry on his back. To do this is one of the most dangerous and skillful tricks of the seaman, for to get in advance, or to be too far back of this highest wave, would almost surely swamp his boat in the surf and drowning would follow. Such exciting scenes, where so many hearts have been pained with anxiety, and then thrilled with rejoicing over kindred safely landed, have made the Harbor a place of dearest associations in the memories of the Islanders. The hotels at the Harbor are mentioned in another place.

The Shores of the East Side do not differ materially from those on the West Side. They have sightly points, ravines, and coves, and bowlders suitably distributed to make a border of pleasing variety.

The Old Harbor Landing, about midway from the Ocean View to the Mohegan Bluffs, is one of the old landmarks of Block Island passing into oblivion. It was once a place of similar note to that of Cooneymus on the West Side. It obtained some distinction from a wreck which occurred there many years ago, and also for the drowning there of a galley of refugees, nine in number. It is adjacent to Old Harbor Point.

The land rises gradually from the National Harbor to the south end of the Island where the highest and most picturesque bluffs are to be seen. They can hardly be called *grand* by one who has sailed from St. Paul down the Mississippi to Prairie du Chien, or has stood at Omaha and looked across the plain to Council Bluffs, or has looked from the dizzy heights of the Yosemite, but they will justify many of the eulogies which they have received. To gain a full impression of their power the visitor must stand on their brows and gaze far out upon the sea, and also at their feet by the water's edge and look up to those frowning brows, a wink from which might be more dangerous to the spectator than was the nod of Jupiter's head on high Olympus.

The New Light-House is one of the noted objects of the East Side, of which special mention is made elsewhere. The greater advantage of its having been located on the West Side on a high bluff at the south end, will be discussed as long as the greater number of wrecks continue to occur at this latter place. Vessels coming from the south, after passing Montauk, fall into a dangerous current that passes between Montauk and Block Island, and are thus carried from their course and wrecked on the latter for want of light and a fog-signal on the southwesterly part of the Island. Three valuable vessels have been wrecked there since the new light-house was erected, but wrecks have hardly ever occurred near said light-house.

THE CORN NECK.

This is the northerly part of Block Island, and contains about one thousand acres. The soil is naturally productive, with more clay at bottom than elsewhere on the Island. No doubt it took its name from the great amount of corn which it produced, both for the natives and for the subsequent settlers. For many years after the settlers came they designated it by the above name, which is now shortened by dropping the "Corn," and calling it simply "The Neck." But the original name seems the more appropriate, distinguishing that part more clearly from the Harbor Neck, and Indian Head Neck. It is naturally separated from the main part of the Island by the small pond that nearly connects the ocean on the east with the south end of the Great Pond, or by a line running nearly east and west, and passing across the south end of the Great Pond a little north of Samuel Mott's residence.

In 1689 the town, as a body, occupied and controlled the Corn Neck, as seen by an act then passed as follows: "That all the cattle shall be brought out of the 'Corne Neck' yearly, at or before the first of May, only working oxen to remain until the 10th." In a still older record, dated Nov., 1676, the town council ordered all the swine to be removed from the Corn Neck by the 10th of Dec., and any man had liberty to kill those not "fetched out" by that date specified. This also indicates that this part of the Island was not inhabited.

In October, 1692, a similar ordinance was passed, requiring their removal by the 21st of that month on a penalty of "two shillings and sixpence for the first defecte, and for the second defecte five shillings." At that time there was probably a town fence separating the Corn Neck from the main part of the Island, as such a fence certainly existed in 1705. It was about ninety-six rods long, was maintained by all who owned land on said Neck, and was spoken of as "against the Corne Neck." This fence was so nicely apportioned for maintenance by the proprietors of the Island that it was divided off to each man interested by rods, feet, and inches.

It seems quite certain from the above facts that there were no inhabitants on the Corn Neck for the first forty or fifty years after Block Island was settled. Thomas Terry, some time after the settlement, lived on Indian Head Neck, and he was there "remote from the other English inhabitants," who, in 1756, with the exception of two or three families, were all within two and a half miles of the meeting-house at the Fresh Pond. The first indications which we have of settlers on the Neck is the record of the laying out of a road there in April, 1707. As that record is instructive on several points it is here given verbatim.

"For the convenience and privilege of the Queen's Majesties subjects.

" Therefore we, the authority and town council on this instant have ordered and determined that there shall be forthwith a highway of forty feet in breadth laid out through the undivided lands, beginning at the old high-way from Charlestown fence holding the breadth of forty feet and so running to Sandy Point and from Sandy Point to Captain Edward Sands' bars, and from the pond by the end of the land of Nathaniel Dickins, deceased, from thence to the harbor, which highway to remain and continue a public highway free and clear from fence, bars, or gates, being made across said highway, only the fence by the harbor to stand, and also the fence at Charlestown likewise to stand."

In 1812, during the war with England, there were prominent families on the Neck, such as Ray Thomas Sands, who lived where Mr. George Sheffield now resides,

15*

and Mr. John Gorton, commonly known as "Governor Gorton," who lived where Mr. John G. Sheffield's residence stands. It is now thickly populated by an intelligent, enterprising, and moral class of citizens, who have a good school-house, in which they hold religious meetings a considerable portion of each year. They carry on farming successfully, and secure considerable income from their pound fisheries.

Clay Head, is the most prominent part of the Neck, and is conspicuous for its high bluffs as seen by the spectator approaching the Island from Newport. On those bluffs are sightly and beautiful locations for summer residences. Its clay is of three qualities, mainly blue, other red, and some white, and it seems a pity that such beautiful material is not utilized.

A note should here be made of a phenomenon at Clay Head in the winter of 1876–7. Its first appearance was in Sept., 1876, soon after a smart shock of an earthquake in the night. Near the edge of the high bluff on Mr. John Hayes' land was a cart road where sea-weed had been carted many years. Soon after said shock a fissure an inch wide, about one hundred feet long, ten feet from the edge of said high bluff, was seen, and instead of an avalanche, that earth outside of the fissure, including the cart track, began to settle down perpendicularly, settling some days nearly a foot, and this settling has continued until the broken-off mass 100 feet long and 10 feet wide has gone down 15 feet, leaving a perpendicular bank mostly of sand intermingled with clay. That mass is settling daily, March 16, 1877. Why, or how it can settle perpendicularly is mysterious. Is there a portion of the Island sinking? Has a cavern been forming there by the escape of clay or quicksand? A larger portion of Mohegan Bluff has settled similarly. Has there been a 'crushing of coral beneath the Island? Native coral has been found on the east, and on the west shores. The diminution of the Island is rapid in some places.

Sandy Point is the extreme north end of the Neck. On the extremity of the Point was anciently a peninsula called the *Hummuck*. It was an elevation of land on which small trees and bushes grew, and at low-tide was reached on foot. The old inhabitants now speak of having gathered wild plums there. It was washed away long ago. The Point as a sand-bar, extends several miles from the Island, and is a waymark for sailors.

Chagum Pond is a part of the Neck, and is distinguished as the place where the English vessels in times of war got their fresh water. It is supplied from the sound, and by filtering through the sand, from the sound to the pond, the water becomes fresh.

THE CENTER.

Here the people from all parts of the Island frequently come for various purposes. Here the greater part of the local trading is done, at the three stores, two of which are at the four corners, and the other but a little distance north. Hither most of the sea-moss is brought from the west shores, and here the West Side fishermen market their fish, and here the greater part of the poultry, butter and cheese, eggs, and much of the oil find a market. Here the town council meet and the town elections are held at the town hall. Here, too, the Baptist church is located, which can seat three hundred, leaving over one hundred of its members outside, were all to assemble there at one time. At the Center the first high school of the Island has been conducted successfully over a year by Mr. A. W. Brown.

The Center is the least bleak in appearance of any part of the Island. Mr. Lorenzo Littlefield's fine residence, adorned with ornamental trees, walks, shrubs and flowers, and productive fruit trees, is an ornament to the Island, which it is hoped others will imitate. His pond of full-blooded wild geese should be seen by visitors. Hon. Ray S. Littlefield's new two-story, French-roof house also adds to the improving appearance of the Center. Mr. Alvin Sprague's enlarged and modernized store, accommodating a family in the upper part, adds much to the improved appearance of the Center. The wall about the Church lot, and the grading of the Church grounds in 1875, materially changed the pasture-like appearance in front of the house where, during seventeen winters, so many slipped and fell after meeting. Nor should the new blacksmith shop at the Center, built in 1875, be overlooked—built by Mr. R. B. Negus, and used for a paint shop by Mr. Andrew Dodge, in the summer of 1876— the first paint shop on the Island. There many old carriages were made new in appearance. One of the best of common schools is also kept at the Center, lacking only a new house, soon to be had, doubtless.

The Block Island Cemetery is near the Center, at the north of it, and on an elevation that overlooks much of the East Side, the Corn Neck, and the waters at the north and east. Its centenary graves, the multitude of others with their brown-stone, slate, and marble monuments, and its perfect destitution of tree or shrub, in an enclosure of about ten acres, render it an object of interest to strangers. An imposing monument, in the highest part where are the remains of the ancient Rays, and Sandses, and others should be erected in honor of the first settlers whose record there is now hardly legible.

MISCELLANEOUS.

THE POUND.

This important keeper of the peace as well as of stray cattle claims a brief notice, for it has doubtless prevented many a feud between neighbors by keeping their animals from trespassing. The following is a record of the first pound upon Block Island.

"At a meeting at the hous of Mr. Simon Ray, Sr., October 14, 1701, the being greatly sensible of the greate want of a common pound, wee the wardin and town counsell with the rest of the free inhabitants of New Shorum have concluded and agreed upon that there shall be a comon pound erected of thurty futs square sefesiant of seven futs high with a good sefesiant gate fit to pas and Repas out and in with a sefesiant lock and kee, and to be erected and fenced by the last of November next insuing the date hereof and to be placed neere to William Daudge's new dwelling house, and the charge to be leved by proporshon of a rate by the hole estate. of said Island."

"Entered according to Ordur pr

NATH'LL MOTT,

Town Clerk."

Its location was near the north end of Fresh Pond. It was in bad proportion, its walls being nearly one-fourth as high as they were long, and it was found to be too small, and consequently, in 1707, another was erected, in place of the former, forty feet square, six feet high, at a cost of £7. In 1708, the keeper received two pence " pr head for turning the key." The same fee was continued in 1709.

The pound regulations in 1714 were very strict and minute. The keeper's fees were sixpence for the admission of a horse or cow. About the year 1860 the present pound was built at the Center, near the church, where it is too likely to remain. Mr. Rathbone Littlefield made it useful in the summer of 1876.

CROWS AND BLACKBIRDS.

In 1693, at a town meeting, an act was passed by which a bounty on crows was established. They were designated as "crows or ravens," and were doubtless then here, as they have been elsewhere, very destructive to the corn crop as it sprang up soon after planting. The bounty was sixpence each for the heads exhibited to the town treasurer between the first of January and the middle of June following. Very respectable names appear among the sportsmen and claimants of bounties. Over ninety crows were killed that season.

From their abundance on the Island at the season of nesting, those acquainted with their habits could safely infer the existence here then of forest timber, for they nest only in forests of large trees.

In 1717, a bounty on blackbirds was established. Either because their heads were less destructive, or because they were more numerous and easily obtained, it required twelve of their heads to draw as much from the treasury as did one crow's head, the bounty on them being only half a penny each. No crows trouble the corn fields here now, since no trees for nesting remain. Blackbirds are abundant still.

POULTRY.

It is doubtful whether another territory can be named in our country, of equal size with Block Island, where so much poultry is produced, and so many eggs are first marketed, as here. No better facilities for raising geese, ducks, hens, and turkeys could be desired. Hardly a farm is so small as to be destitute of one or more little ponds. The fields furnish ample range for all, and the women and children excel in raising the young for the early market, and for the Thanksgiving and Christmas demands. Hardly a family is so over-nice as to exclude from its firesides in the chilly days of March and April the tender brood in the comfortable basket. There the visitor may hear notes quite as musical to the Islander as are the sharp warblings of the canary to others whose pets only please the eye and the ear.

The Eggs that are exported from the Island may be estimated at an amount not less than twenty-five thousand dozen annually.

The dressed and live poultry exported and consumed at the Island hotels amounts to more that twenty-five tons annually. Mr. Lorenzo Littlefield has had on hand at a time 1,000 geese; at another 1,000 turkeys.

MARKING SHEEP.

An Island law requiring sheep to be marked, and the owner's mark to be registered in the town clerk's office was enforced in 1680; e. g., "*John Niles his Mark.* A cropp off ye right ear and a hapenny under (ye cropp to be high upon ye eare): a slitt in ye left ear and hapenny under."

SHEEP-FOLD.

In 1696, many sheep ran at large on the Island a part of the year, and an act was passed by the town requiring them to be folded, or to be put into the "common pen," each night, probably for safety, on account of the Indians, and this rule was enforced by a penalty of £5. *Goats* were then kept upon Block Island.

The Island is well adapted to the raising of sheep, and in 1776, as well as at the present time' some farms were well stocked with them. They are mostly of the larger kind, with wool not the finest. The January and February lambs become very large for early market. The sheep are remarkable for the number of lambs which they raise. In the spring of 1875, five ewes belonging to Edward Mott raised ten lambs, three having twins, one having a triplet, and another having one. About the year 1700 many sheep and lambs were taken from here to New York.

HIDDEN TREASURE.

About eighty years ago a small vessel anchored in Cow Cove, and from it three men came ashore. They entered the carriage road that leads from Sandy Point to the Harbor, and after proceeding some distance, stopped and commenced digging in the middle of the road. This was towards evening, and as they were strangers the Islanders viewed them only at a distance. During the night they disappeared. The next morning Mr. Isaiah Ball went to the place named in the road, and there discovered that they had dug up an earthen pot that held about eight quarts. Suspecting that it had contained money, Mr. Ball moved the fresh earth about with his hands until he found a piece of silver of the value of ten cents. This coin has been examined by one skilled in numismatics, and by him is described as "Spanish Cob Money, issued by a Bourbon family of Spain, previous to 1753, in the eighteenth century." Its date seems to be given in the Roman and Arabic numerals, thus : M 94. This coin is in the possession of Mr. Lorenzo Littlefield, and was presented to him by Mr. John S. Ball, the son of the said Isaiah Ball who related the above circumstances to the said donor.

There has been considerable effort by the Islanders to find hidden treasures on their shores. Marvelous stories have been told of sights seen, and of sounds heard while prospecting for the imagined pots of gold and silver. These stories have served well as scape-goats for the follies of those who have wasted time and strength in searching at random for what is only imaginary, while the legitimate pursuits of gain have been neglected.

CHRISTMAS TREE.

Christmas had visited the Christian people of Block Island more than two hundred times before its children were cheered with the presence of a Christmas tree. The first one ever seen here was in the winter of 1875, brought by the pastor of the First Baptist Church from his home in Bridgewater, Mass. It was a beautiful fir, one of his ornamental trees, at the roots of which he laid his axe for the sake of the pleasure and good it might afford the children of Block Island. It was placed in front of the pulpit, and rose to the wall above. The ladies adorned it finely with stars, tapers, and presents. The burning tapers on its branches, the glittering stars in the evening, and the gifts on it and under it, produced a fine effect, and gave a happy expression to many bright young faces. That tree was well planted in the memory of the children, most of whom had never seen a fir tree before. It also attached them to the Sabbath-school to which it was given.

THE HOUSES.

The houses of Block Island have their peculiarities. Those built by the inhabitants are all wood, with one exception; that is stone. They are of convenient size on the ground, but why they are so low it is not easy to

16

ascertain.   But a very few are over one and a half stories high, and the one story is much lower than usual in such houses.   Perhaps there has been a precaution against their being blown over by the strong winds.   They are mostly shingled on the sides, as this covering endures the storms best.   They are nearly all white, and newspaper and magazine writers have reported them *painted*, when in truth not one in twenty was painted.   They were *whitewashed*, and this is done annually, in the spring, and thus the houses are well preserved.

The inside structures indicate economy.   The rooms are so numerous that they are necessarily small.   They are plastered, mainly, and papered with bright colors and showy figures.   Almost every family has more or less of papering and inside whitewashing each spring.   The doors, cupboards, and what ceilings there are have uniform colors, either blue or green, with few exceptions. They are generally comfortable.

The location of the houses arrests the attention of the observing.   They are scattered so much that at no place can there properly be said to be a village on the Island. Nearly all are connected with farms ranging from one acre up to three hundred.   They are most densely located at the Harbor, but not more numerous, perhaps, than in the vicinity of the Center.   Nearly all, too, are so located as to have an extensive view of the sea, and from their windows and doors, the departure and arrival of vessels are studiously observed, and generally with telescopes that cost about ten dollars each.   It might be well for some visitors to remember these far-seeing instruments, especially at the bathing beach.

A few dwelling-houses of good taste have been erected during the past few years on the Island.   Mr. Darius Dodge's Gothic cottage near the Harbor, Mr. Aaron Mitchell's, and others, and Mr. Noah Dodge's soon to be completed, and the best, are an improvement on the older houses, and these will soon be excelled by others, probably.

Flower-gardens are a recent ornament to the grounds about the houses. Mrs. Lorenzo Littlefield's at the Center, is very attractive in summer, and silently reminds the Islanders of the fact that God makes flowers to be seen as well as fish and vegetables to be eaten, and that Adam and Eve were first placed in a garden and commanded to "dress it and to keep it."

THE STORES.

It would be difficult to tell how many stores there are upon the Island if we were to enumerate all the places where a little tea, tobacco, and candy are sold, and a few eggs and fowls are bought. But there are five dealers who have stores, properly so called. At the Harbor where the post-office is kept, the firm of Ball & Willis has done a thriving business; on Paine street, Mr. J. T. Dodge is doing likewise, while Messrs. Lorenzo Littlefield, Alvin Sprague, and Wm. P. Ball are buying and selling largely at the Center, each in his own store. If any doubt that all of these five merchants are models of patience and business tact, they have only to observe the endless routine of barter to which they are subjected in order to realize any profits in money. A boy with a hen under each arm; a woman with a bag of sea-moss; a farmer with a cart-load of dressed turkeys; a one-horse wagon with cheese and butter; another with jugs of fish-oil; tons of cod-fish; bundles of paper-rags; old junk; potatoes and oats; and frequently a child with an egg in each hand; these are daily customers and commodities that keep up a large mercantile business in dry-goods and groceries and a few fancy articles, amounting in all to about one hundred thousand dollars annually.

THE CARRIAGES.

The improved roads of Block Island naturally became an inducement for better carriages. The need of any better than the cart for oxen has been felt here but recently. The distances were short, and easily walked by the active men and vigorous women. It is within the memory of the older inhabitants that the first wagon was owned upon the Island. Mr. Ray Thomas Sands is said to have introduced that improvement, an article then new to the eyes of many, for people did not travel abroad then as now. Indeed, there are those now upon the Island who were never beyond its shores, and one of them told the writer that she was "just as well off as if she had been on the main, and now she was so old she never wanted to go away." In the year 1875, there was but one span of horses frequently driven here, that of Mr. Hamilton Ball, Mr. Lorenzo Littlefield having driven a span previous to 1875. Single carriages, however, had then become quite numerous, and about sixty were counted at the funeral of Mrs. Frederick Rose in the summer of 1875. At the present time fashionable buggies are quite common, and there are a few good carryalls. That of Mr. John G. Sheffield will be remembered by the children as one of the first of their knowledge. In the summer of 1876, covered carriages were frequently seen going to noted points of the Island, and the visitors at the hotels for the first time here had ample accommodations of carriages. Mr. Howard Mott then opened the first livery stable of Block Island, kept at the Ocean View. Many who are now in childhood will remember how much attention Mr. Mott's barouche attracted, as part of its occupants rode backwards so indifferent to the horses and driver. They will remember, too, how odd it looked, on "steamboat days," to see one seat, two seat, open and covered buggies, and two-horse carriages thickly stationed around the Harbor, with "To Let," pasted on some of them, and all waiting for passengers to the various hotels and to different parts of the Island. All of this took place, for the first time, two hundred and fourteen years after the first settlers landed and saw no other houses than the wigwams of the Manisseans.

The ox-cart is still the principal vehicle for business. One man is making his mark in the memories of the rising generation, not only by his singing, but by the one animal, which became an *ox* when he was several years old, and which the owner prides, or humbles himself in driving in thills attached to a short wooden yoke on the animal's neck. He is tolerably well represented in Harper's Magazine for July, 1876, except as his horns there are a little too upright and delicate.

The olden time for horse-back parties is gone for ever. Nice buggies and carriages have superseded the saddle, except as it is used occasionally by men and boys. The old side-saddles may now be seen in barns and sheds gathering dust and rust. These are steamboat times; no fears of the railroad on Block Island.

THE ROADS.

For two hundred years the inhabitants of Block Island enjoyed the principal luxuries, or perhaps it should be said *necessaries* of life without having the trouble and expense of making one mile of turnpike, or graded carriage track. There was hardly any use for them—no market, no factories, no commerce to require any amount of teaming, and no special desire to ride in carriages, not enough certainly to stimulate the people to the construction of roads. As a cart and an ox-team could go anywhere, and as no wagons were in use, lanes here and there, and cart tracks across the meadows and pastures answered every purpose. If there were gates to open, and bars,

16*

and fences to be taken down, what mattered? Nobody was in a hurry. "Time enough," the last words said now, as one leaves his neighbor's house, where he is urged to stay longer, seems to have been then the motto on the cart and oxen, on the rough roads, on the hand-cards, and spinning-wheels—yes "*time enough*" was one of the . rich possessions of those days too soon forgotten.

The roads, such as they were, the lanes, the bridle and foot-paths of the Island, until within a few years, may be illustrated by the threads of a large, circular spider's web. As such, especially in winter, they may be seen to-day. Fifty years ago the only mode of riding faster than the slow pace of oxen was on horseback. The principal roads then, and previously, were those that cross each other at the Center, at right angles; the one extending from the Harbor to the west beach, and the other from the south end of the Great Pond to the Fresh Pond, and thence to the southerly and southwesterly parts of the Island; and also the road from Sandy Point to the Harbor, and the one thence to the vicinity of the new light-house. Many houses are still inaccessible, except by lanes and gates. There is no public road to said light-house, while one is greatly needed for the accommodation of citizens, and for the pleasure of summer visitors who desire so much to see the bluffs on which the light house is located.

During the two years of 1875 and 1876, more expense, and more improvements were made upon the roads of Block Island than had been made upon them during the previous two hundred years. They were widened and straightened by removing long stretches of stone wall, and were graded, sluiced, guttered, and freed from stones. They are now inviting to the carriages of visitors, and furnish beautiful drives for landscape and ocean scenery. The Islanders, too, have, for the first time, learned the value of good roads in time-saving, in the greater loads drawn, saving the wear and tear of wheels, and in the comfort of riding. There is still room for improvement. No one can imagine how much better the roads are now than they were three years ago, unless he then saw them so narrow in places that teams could not pass each other, with numerous hills as sharp as house roofs, and with mud and water that had to be forded, while the wheels were jolting over little bowlders almost constantly.

HORSEBACK RIDING.

For two hundred years this has been one of the pleasures and necessities of this Island. Twenty years ago Mr. Henry T. Beckwith, in his excellent historical sketch of Block Island, said: "The people are fond of horsemanship, and raise excellent saddle-horses for the purpose. I saw one afternoon at the close of the day a party of a dozen of them, young men and women, starting out for a moonlight ride. The women also go a-shopping and visiting in this way, though not so absurdly arrayed as ours are with dresses which almost reach the ground when they are upon the horse, and impede them when they get off so that they cannot walk. Twenty years ago [in 1830] this was the only mode of riding, and some of the roads are now better adapted for it than for any vehicle, but open wagons have been introduced to a considerable extent. There is but one covered vehicle on the Island, a chaise owned by the doctor." On horseback was the only riding for speed or pleasure until recently.

In this manner the Islanders in olden times enjoyed as merry hearts as ever graced the costliest vehicle. Riding parties were frequently had when the young men and maidens vied with each other in horsemanship. Fine horses, good saddles for both sexes, and winding roads and paths animated by fifty horses and riders, some with continental light breeches and stockings adorned with bright knee-buckles, others in gracefully flowing riding dresses of home manufacture, and all with health, vigor, and cheerful spirits galoping around the hills, through the ravines, sometimes two abreast and racing, then trailing in single file, jumping fences and leaping ditches, with merry laughs and shouts that no one was afraid to utter, and at last all coming to a halt and dismounting at the house designated, where the well-furnished table and the fiddler were in waiting for a pleasant evening in November, were some of the enjoyments over the ancient highways of Block Island. If a horse for each of the party was not convenient, there were saddles with "pillions," and on one of these the fair one rode while her reinsman rode in front, and although their faces were not then *vis a vis* as ladies and gentlemen are now seen in their fine carriages, yet their voices and feelings were none the less happy, except when, in the time of haunted houses, frightful ghosts gave them a race in the night like that of *Tam O'Shanter's* gray mare.

POPULATION.

The following may be considered a nearly accurate statement of the population of the Island from its settlement, at different periods, to the present year, 1876.

Year.	White.	Colored.		
1662	30	400	Indians.	
1700	200	350	"	
1730	290	200	"	Negroes 20
1748	300	150	"	" 30
1755	378	115	"	" 40
1774	575	51	"	" 42
1776	478	50	"	" 43
1782	478	30	"	" 45
1790	682	20	"	" 47
1800	714	16	"	" 45

Year.	White.		Colored.		
1810	722	13 Indians.		Negroes	43
1820	955	10	"	"	46
1830	1,185	5	"	"	47
1840	1,069	6	"	"	45
1850	1,262	3	"	"	44
1860	1,320	1	"	"	28
1865	1,308	1	"	"	30
1870	1,113	1	"	"	
1875	1,147	1	"	"	39

OFFICERS FOR 1876-7.

Hon. Ray S. Littlefield, Senator.

Hon. J. T. Dodge, Assemblyman.

William P. Lewis, First Warden.

Almanzo Littlefield, Second Warden.

George Jelly, Third Warden.

Ambrose N. Rose, Town Clerk.

Jeremiah C. Rose, Town Sergeant.

ASSESSORS.

Marcus M. Day, Ambrose N. Rose, Edward H. Champlin, William P. Lewis, George J. Sheffield.

William P. Lewis, Chairman of all the town, and Town Council meetings.

MASONIC LODGE.

The *Atlantic Lodge of Free and Accepted Masons*, of Block Island, was constituted July 12, 1876, with a new and commodious hall at that time first occupied.

ODD FELLOWS.

In August, 1872, Messrs. Nicholas Ball, George Jelly, Horatio N. Milikin, Frederick A. Rose, George A. Rose, John G. Sheffield, Joseph H. Willis, Lorenzo Littlefield, Ray S. Littlefield, and Aaron Mitchell, withdrew from

Rhode Island Lodge No. 12, and were organized into the *Neptune Lodge*, No. 26, of Block Island, and duly received its charter from the Grand Lodge. It now has forty members, and its hall is at the Center.

PHYSICIANS.

The first, and, perhaps, the most noted physician of Block Island was *Mrs. Sarah Sands*, the wife of Capt. James Sands. An account of her is given in connection with the biographical sketch of her husband. Her skill in medicine and surgery, in 1680, and also in years previous and subsequent, was extraordinary.

Dr. John Rodman was a physician of the Island in 1689, and is described by an intimate acquaintance, Rev. Samuel Niles, as being "a gentleman of great ingenuity, and of an affable, engaging behavior, of the profession of them called Quakers. He also kept a meeting in his house on the Sabbaths, with exhortations unto good works, after the manner of the teachers in that society, but more agreeably than I suppose is common with them, whose meetings I had attended in my younger time."

Dr. James Sweete was a resident, and successor of Dr. Rodman, in 1717. Our knowledge of him is very limited. He was kidnapped in the Bay, on the 18th of April, 1717, together with Thomas Daniels, and William Tosh, mysteriously by a foreign vessel, as described in the article on *Hostilities*.

Dr. Aaron C. Willey was the Island physician in 1811, and a literary correspondent of some distinction. His relatives are still here, and are highly esteemed citizens. He was much respected at home and abroad for his medical skill and general knowledge. His account of the "Palatine Light" is the most sensible one given of that once attractive but now extinct phenomenon. His description of it is given under the head of Wrecks and Wreckers.

Drs. Philips, Bowen, Angell, Woodruff, Buttrick, Maryott, Mann, and Tucker belong to the medical succession on Block Island. As a physician, Dr. J. T. Mann ob tained an enviable distinction for skill in the treatment of fevers especially, and for his light charges. It was with much regret that many of the Islanders parted with him and his genial family for any one that might become his successor. The writer has but a slight acquaintance with either of his predecessors, or his successors.

LAWYERS.

Gentlemen of the legal profession can safely file the plea of an *alibi* to all the peace and discord of Block Island. Only as foreigners to the Island have they had any thing to do with its affairs. This is strange enough. Where else can a population be found equal to this that has never had a resident lawyer? A population more than two hundred years old! The present Chief Warden, Wm. P. Lewis, has rendered eighty civil, and twenty criminal judgments, and in but *one* of these hundred trials was a lawyer, or "pettifoger," a participant.

CENSUS OF NEW SHOREHAM, ALIAS BLOCK ISLAND FOR 1875.

POPULATION, males, 612; females, 535; total, 1,147. Born on Block Island, 1,032; born in United States, 1,138; foreign births, 9; colored inhabitants, 40. Of each 100 population 97 are American born, the largest percentage of such of any town in the State. Between the ages of 60 and 70, living, 61 persons; between 70 and 80, 36; between 80 and 90, 13. Married persons, male and female, 477; widowed, male and female, 67; divorced, 2. Total, attending school, 299; Number over

15 years who can neither read nor write, 45; all between 10 and 15 years of age read and write. Deaf, 2; deaf and blind, 1; blind, 3; idiotic, 10. Voters born on Block Island, 300; foreign born, 3; born off the Island, and in United States, 12; total voters, 315. Number of farms, 159; acres in them, 4,817; their cash value, $357,100. Number of horses, 137; cows, 261; oxen, 274; sheep and lambs, 2,437; swine, 462; value of cattle sold in 1875, $16,007. Acres of corn, in 1874, 316; bushels raised, 13,791. Pounds of butter, 20,395; of cheese, 4,580. Bushels of potatoes, 12,784; of onions, 383. Value of eggs and poultry in 1875, $23,394. Pounds of wool, 4,883. Cords of peat dug, 544. Total value of farm products, in 1875, $102,615. Farms of between 3 and 10 acres, 23; of 10 to 20 acres, 52; of 20 to 50, 64; of 50 to 100 acres, 14; of 100 to 200 acres, 4; of 200 to 300 acres, 2. Sea drift, 6,444 cords. valued at $12,838. Fish caught, 1,067,810 pounds, valued at $42,026, in 1875.

BOAT BUILDING.

This has been carried on here only for the accommodation of the Islanders. *John Rose*, of Revolutionary times, was the first boat-builder upon the Island, of whom we can obtain any account. He is probably the one mentioned in the Colonial Records of Rhode Island, as having been captured with another, by an American privateer and delivered over to the "Honorable Major General Gates to be treated as prisoners of war, or dismissed." Each nail put in the boats which he built was driven into a hole first bored with a gimlet. *Lemuel B. Rose* was the next boat-builder.

Dea. Sylvester D. Mitchell, now living, has been the principal builder during the past twenty-five years, having built ten new ones, and re-built ten others, averaging in cost from $250 to $800. The deacon goes upon the

main, cuts his timber in the woods, directs the sawing at
the mill, imports the same, lays his own keel, finishes
and warrants every piece of wood, and every nail from
stem to stern, and "all have been successful."

MECHANICAL.

BLACKSMITHING.   For about twenty years the early settlers were obliged to go to Newport to patronize a blacksmith.   We find none of the "sons of Vulcan" on the
Island until March 20, 1683, when the town gave a hearty
reception to a *Mr. William Harris*, making him a donation
of four acres of land on the east shore of the Great Pond.
From that date the smoke of the forge and the ring of
the anvil have continued to be the principal signs of
mechanism here.

In 1758, the blacksmith shop and tools were an institution belonging to the town, and were then leased to *Mr.
Joseph Briggs* for smithing.   At present two shops are
sustained, and have monopolizing prices.   One is occupied
by *Mr. John Hooper*, and the other by *Mr. Richmond Negus*,
the former at the Harbor, and the latter by the Harbor
Pond.   *Mr. Simeon Ball* also carries on the business in a
modest way, where, besides other work, he is willing to
shoe horses on the condition of the owners cutting off
said animals' legs and bringing only them to his shop.
He has no intention of exposing his precious life around
the heels of fractious horses.   It may become a question
whether his terms are not the cheapest, unless his competitors reduce their prices.

CARPENTERS AND JOINERS, upon the Island, have been in
good demand during the past few years of rapid improvement in buildings, both public and private.   Messrs.
Almanzo Littlefield, John Thomas & Sons, and John Rose,
of the West Side, have held their grounds well as builders, although some houses have been erected here by

17

workmen from abroad. Mr. Thomas claims the " inside track " of all his competitors, because he is master of the trowel and stone-hammer as well as of the mallet, chisel, and plane. Mr. Leander Ball is carpenter, joiner, and lumber dealer.

WATCH REPAIRING, and mending of all kinds of fine metals are done by Mr. Marcus M. Day. However unpretentious his shop and jewelry store may be, none who know him will distrust his ingenuity or his honesty.

BOOT AND SHOE-MAKING, as well as mending, is done by Mr. Nathaniel Hall, and by Mr. ———— Harrison, the latter having hung out the first *sign* for such work, it is said, ever known on Block Island, a thing needed here about as much, in former days, as it would be in a large family where each expects to know all about the other's business.

DRESS-MAKING is done *professionally*, for the first time here, by *Miss Ann Maria Rose*, whose natural accomplishments and education on the main fit her well for making " good fits " for others. *Miss Hattie Littlefield* has also taken a course of instruction in a fashionable shop and has entered upon the work of improving the fashions and figures of the Island ladies. If these two young ladies will omit the *belittling* extremes of fashionable fitting they may do much to increase the pleasures of the eye without diminishing the comforts of the body, an evil that has brought a dark shadow to many American households.

THE MILLINERY of the Island, to one, at least, is quite a mystery. That neat, becoming hats are worn by ladies, young and old, and by the little girls is certain. But where they come from is as mysterious as the *whence* of the swallows or the wind. Certainly there are no windows on Block Island where the jaunty hat, the ostrich plume, and the bright ribbon catch the passer's eye. An enormous trunk, however, not quite large enough for a shop, and very easily handled, has been seen several times at the Harbor, and at the Center. One or two ladies are supposed to be umpires for the spring and fall styles suitable for the Island.

PAINTING, house, sign, and fresco, is done by Mr. William Greene.

MASONRY, in a professional manner, is done by Mr. Alonzo Mitchell.

THE MILLS.

INDIAN MORTARS.

The various grades of these upon Block Island correspond with other things in the different times in which
they were used. The writer has one of that grade used
when the Island was called Manisses, and when only Indians were here to do the grinding. It was discovered
by Mr. Isaiah Ball, father of the present Mr. John Ball,
buried in the ground, and by its sides were a pestle, and
an Indian stone ax. The three articles, mortar, pestle,
and ax, were the main furniture of the wigwam, which
doubtless stood a little south of Mr. John Ball's house,
where they were found, and near them was a large quantity of shells also, near enough to the Great Pond to be
carried to said wigwam conveniently.

This primitive mill is simply a rude stone mortar. The
stone of which it is made, externally, resembles one just
taken from the field wall. It weighs about seventy-five
pounds, and shows no marks of man, except the bowl that
was excavated by other and harder stones. It is unlike
the most of the granite of the Island, and is more like a
gray sandstone. The excavation in it will hold less than
two quarts. Into this the squaws put the corn by the
handful, and there pounded, and ground it to meal. The
pestle with which this was done, is a harder species of
stone, such as are found upon the beach. It is about five
and a half inches long, and three inches through from
side to side in the middle, rounded at the ends like an egg,
both ends being of nearly equal size. It is smooth, and

nicely fitted to the hand, and of convenient weight for the purpose of pounding in the mortar. On it are still remaining Indian characters, made, it seems, by some thickened juice or sap, of dark brown, and of such a nature as to whiten the stone beneath the ink, or juice, so that when the latter has worn away and disappeared, the hieroglyphic beneath still remains. Two characters are well defined; the one representing a stalk of corn half grown, and the other resembling a full-grown stalk. Such was the simple structure of a Manissean mill ages ago.

WOODEN MORTARS.

These were an improvement upon those used by the Indians. They were introduced by the early settlers, and though rude in structure, were far more serviceable. According to the sample now before me, and the tradition of the oldest inhabitants now living on the Island, the wooden mortars were made of lignum-vitæ. They were mere sections of the body of a tree, about sixteen or twenty inches long, and ten inches in diameter. At one end they were hollowed out sufficiently to hold several quarts of corn. Their pestles were of stone, and were longer and heavier than the Indian pestle above described. The wood was so hard, and so tough, as well as exceedingly cross-grained, that no amount of pounding could split them or wear them out, as is evident from what is known of the one now in the possession of the writer, and of which the following is a history.

The Dancing.

There is good reason for giving it this name, as will be seen presently. It is lignum-vitæ, fourteen inches high, about ten inches in diameter, and is nearly as heavy as would be the same bulk of stone. Its capacity is about four quarts. The grains are diagonal, for the most part,

17*

and hence it is not cracked by use or age.   It is weather worn, gray, and shabby outside, with a very uneven surface, occasioned in part by an ax while it was used as a splitting-block, and in part by the storms of half a century with which it is well known to have been beaten in winter and summer.

This mortar is an intimate acquaintance of the oldest inhabitants of the Island, the following of whom, consulted separately, agree in stating its origin.   Mrs. Margaret Dodge, eighty-six years old, of remarkably clear memory; Mr. Anthony Littlefield, and his wife, each eighty-four years old; Mr. and Mrs. John Ball, over seventy; Mrs. Caroline Willis, eighty-one; and others all agree in stating that this mortar was brought to the Island in the ship *Palatine.*   As an item of possibly corroborative testimony, it was owned for a long time, and used in the family of the venerable Simon Ray, at whose house several of the unfortunate inmates of the Palatine were received and cared for.   There it remained until he and his family passed away, and the house was occupied by those of another name.

During a considerable period after this change the old Ray house was said to be haunted.   Sights and sounds were there witnessed, it is said, which our nerves protest against repeating in an attempted description.   In comparison with them the present fabrications of spirit-rapping and table-dancing are puerile.   This mortar, according to tradition, was then an inmate of said haunted house, and fell into line with the performances of the other surroundings.   The abovenamed persons say that among its strange antics were those of dancing around the room, untouched, throwing itself on its side and rolling to and fro, and then righting itself again, and hopping up the chamber floor several times in succession.   Hence it took its name as the *dancing mortar.*   The writer vouches for the truthfulness of this ancient performance no further than the statement here given corresponds with the account given to him. His own private opinion of the matter is that all the dancing that mortar ever did was in the imagination of one who was then known as the "old opium-eater," and who was a near neighbor to the old mortar.

It surely does not dance now. This, however, is no proof that it did not dance then. The wonder is that it is still in existence, when we consider its treatment. More than fifty years ago its old home, the Simon Ray house, was taken down, and a part of it put into the new house then built and now owned by Mr. Raymond Dickens. But the old mortar had a questionable reputation, and was refused a place in the new house, perhaps, because it was old and less needed than formerly. Fifty years, Mr. Dickens says, he has seen it about his premises, and nearly all of that time it has occupied the humiliating place of a stone in a fence wall. There the writer recently found it, placed well-nigh the bottom of the wall, on its side, with big and little stones above it, as though there were danger of its having another dancing fit. But no, it will not dance again. Its youth is gone. Fifty years of pestle pounding, and fifty years more of storms and sunshine, wet and dry, have given it a gray appearance unbecoming the dance. Its place is now upon the retired list of the antiquarian, where its rosettes of gray and yellow moss within shall never be disturbed by hands that banish hunger with pounded corn.

Mortars of a similar description, the best mills then upon the Island, were also used for chairs or stools, by turning them bottom end up and sitting on them.

THE HAND MILLS.

A great improvement on the mortars were those little stone mills which seem to have been made very much after the pattern of those mentioned in the Bible. They were constructed of the upper and nether stones, about two feet in diameter, and were similar in construction to those now driven by water or steam-power. They were worked by means of an upright shaft, like a broom-stick, the upper end of which was stationary, while the lower end was connected with the top of the upper stone about half way from its center to its circumference. This stone, resting upon a pivot in its center—a pivot that could be raised or lowered, was turned by taking hold of the said shaft and moving it round and round with one hand while the other hand would feed in the corn as needed. Two persons at a time could grasp the shaft and make the stone revolve quite rapidly. Even at the present time there are persons who occasionally use these mills, still kept as relics, for grinding samp.

WINDMILLS.

The First Windmill.

This was of short life and little value. It stood upon the elevated ground now known as the Colored Burying Ground, and was built about sixty-five years ago. It was a little affair, not over twelve feet high, with board wings made in sections to be taken off or put on according to the force of the wind. The whole mill was turned around to bring the vanes into the wind, and when brought to the right point its frame work was wedged up to keep the mill from revolving while the vanes were going.

Honeywell's Mill.

In the early part of the present century this mill was erected upon the elevated ground east of the north end of

Fresh Pond. It was a rudely constructed affair, although an improvement on its predecessors. It was mainly like the windmills now in use, but its cap was turned by means of a long lever, made of a ship spar, descending from the cap obliquely to a cart-wheel on the ground, the end of which, like an axle, entering the hub of said wheel, and resting there. When the cap needed to be turned to bring the vanes into the wind the cart-wheel was rolled around, and by its carrying the lower end of the long lever along, the cap was turned and the vanes were thus adjusted.

The Harbor Mill.

It is not easy to decide where this mill was first built. That it was brought to the Island from some other locality is certain. Three localities are mentioned, Fall River, Swansey, and Long Island. It was brought here about the year 1810, by Capt. Thomas Rose, in the schooner *Greyhound*, and was set up and owned by Mr. Samuel Ward. It was located about a hundred feet northwest of the Providence House, and was forty years old at that time, making it now more than a centenary. While there, about forty-five years, it did good service. An inferior wood-cut of it may be seen in Harper's Monthly for July, 1876. A child was killed by one of its vanes, at the Harbor. About the year 1856, Capt. E. P. Littlefield sold it to Mr. Jonathan Ball, its present owner, who moved it to its present location, not far from the Center. Its weight of a hundred years, and the strong winds necessary to keep it going, make a trembling that would frighten the Red Rover rats of the Stone Mill at Newport if any of them were in and about its old crannies.

The Littlefield Mill.

About fifty rods north of the town house, at the Center, stands a windmill that was erected in 1815, and began its career in the great September gale of that year. Completed on the twenty-second, and accepted as the fulfillment of the builders' contract, on the twenty-third its sails were put on, and grinding begun, when, to the consternation of all beholders, the fearful gale blew off its four arms, thirty feet long each, which came down tumbling and crashing near the house of the owner. Its next casualty worthy of mention was in a gale less violent, not many years ago. The wind was so strong that the break did not check its too great velocity. It stands on the top of a sharp little hill, and while men were plying the break with all their might, but ineffectual, a Mr. Roberts, just then, for a particular reason, feeling himself to be much stronger than he really was, grasped one of the long vanes by its lower end as it was sweeping past him with great velocity, and about one second from that instant he was high in the air, some think forty feet, and that was the last he knew of himself until an hour or so had elapsed from the time his friends picked him up for dead near the bottom of the steep little hill. The fall nearly killed him.

This mill, owned by Hon. Ray S. Littlefield, is capable of grinding one hundred bushels of excellent corn-meal in a day when the wind is favorable. The quantity ground in it annually may be estimated at from nine to ten thousand bushels. A large amount of grain is brought from abroad and ground here, in addition to the corn raised on the Island.

THE SANDS MILL.

While Capt. James Sands, one of the first settlers, and a carpenter, was alive he had a mill-pond, and a mill which was used for grinding corn, as such a mill is known to have been there anciently. It stood where the old mill now stands that belongs to Mr. Almanzo Littlefield, near the old Sands Garrison.   Many years ago it was made over into a mill for carding wool, but did not give satisfaction to its patrons, and for this reason, as well as for a scarcity of water, ran out, and is a mill now only in name, the back side of which is represented in the number of Harper above mentioned.

Such have been the mills of Block Island, and none, perhaps, have ever furnished better meal, as multitudes of summer visitors prove by their demands for corn-cakes. Many will remember with pleasure the Littlefield mill, so near the Central House, and in and around which the children have played in summer, and within whose dusty walls some of them have been gathered for an hour's Sabbath-school, where they have sung their familiar hymns and recited their lessons to the lady visitor, who faithfully directed their minds to things above this world of dust and ashes.

This mill, on the street through which most of the funeral processions of the Island pass, has always been stopped while they have been passing.

PUBLIC BUILDINGS.

Although the public buildings of Block Island are of humble proportions when compared with some in other places, yet they are commendable in themselves, and indicate the moving of new life and increased enterprise on the part of the inhabitants, who are daily learning the import of the old classic maxim that "*the gods help those who help themselves.*" The Islanders have seen this illustrated in the government appropriations which have followed the persistent efforts to secure the harbor, the new light-house, and the life-saving stations. They are learning, too, that good public houses are necessary *first* to bring public patronage, and that the greater the patronage secured by one house, the more are attracted to others. Two first-class, high-price hotels here are of great advantage to those of less pretension, for the multitude follow the few in fashionable life, and the great luxuries of the Island are as abundant at the cottage as at the palace. The refreshing sea-breezes, the bathing-beach, the splendid scenery, the sports upon the water, and the palatable denizens of the deep are as accessible to the day-laborer as to the millionaire.

LIGHT-HOUSES.

The *first* light-house on Block Island was erected on Sandy Point, the northerly extremity, in the year 1829. Its keeper was William A. Weeden, formerly of Jamestown, R. I., who also kept its successor during its first two years.

The *second* one was built on said Point in 1837, and

was more durable than the first, but was succeeded by another, after an existence of about twenty years.

This second house was a substantial building, located, not on the extremity of the Point, as was its predecessor, but farther from the encroachments of the sea. It had two towers, and its lights were shown from them by means of parabolic reflectors. (Gen. J. C. Woodruff, Eng'r 3d Light-House Dist.)

In 1839 Mr. Weeden resigned, and in his place Mr. Simeon Babcock was appointed, and held his position until 1841, when Mr. Edward Mott was appointed keeper under President Harrison.

The *third* light-house was erected on the same Point in 1857, and was kept by Mr. Mott until 1865, when Mr. Simeon Babcock was replaced as keeper under President Polk's administration. This last house did service only about ten years. These three houses on Sandy Point, all built within twenty-eight years, were rendered unstable by the shifting of the sand of the Point on which they were located.

The *fourth*, on Sandy Point—the well-built, stone structure now standing, was erected in 1867, and is likely to be serviceable to navigators of the sound for many years to come. During this succession of light-houses on said Point the keepers have held their positions according to the successive changes of politics. Mr. Babcock, above-mentioned, held his appointment from 1845 to 1849, when Mr. Edward Mott was replaced under President Taylor. In 1850 Mr. Enoch Rose, Jr., was appointed keeper under President Filmore, and held his position under President Pierce, until he died, and was succeeded by Mr. Nicholas Littlefield, who continued as keeper through Mr. Buchanan's presidency. In 1861 Mr. Hiram D. Ball was appointed keeper of the Sandy Point light-house, under President Lincoln, and still retains his position, one of far more responsibility, and strictness of attendance than those are aware of who are not familiar with light-house regulations.

This last-named house is a favorite resort for visitors, both on account of the natural scenery, and the agreeableness of the respectable family of Mr. Ball, the keeper, whose ample means could furnish him a far more pleasant home, especially in winter.

The New Light-House.

The *fifth* is the new light-house. This is situated on the southeast end of the Island, on a bluff one hundred and fifty-two feet above mean low-water. The lantern is fifty-two feet above the ground, making a total height above water of two hundred and four feet. It was built in the summer of 1874 by Mr. L. H. Tynan, of Staten Island. It is a two-story brick dwelling, attic, with octagonal tower, accommodating two families, and cost the government $75,000. .The glass of the lantern cost $10,000, and consists mainly of prismatic pieces too pure to be touched by the visitor's fingers, for the greater the perfection the more perceptible and injurious the soiling. Six persons can stand at the same time within this lantern, which is of the first order of lights. It has been seen thirty-five miles, and is examined with interest by multitudes of summer visitors, who are courteously waited upon by the keeper, although he is not required to do this by the government. It was first lighted Feb. 1, 1875. It consumes from nine hundred to one thousand gallons of lard oil annually, burning four wicks at the same time, one within another. The largest is about $3\frac{1}{2}$ inches in diameter; the next, 3 inches; the next, $2\frac{1}{2}$ inches, and the inmost $\frac{7}{8}$ of an inch in diameter.

Mr. H. W. Clark, keeper of the light-house, has held that position from the first, on the moderate salary of

$600. Mr. Nathaniel Dodge, first assistant, has a salary of $450, and Charles E. Dodge, second assistant, has $400.

The *fog-signal* is one hundred feet southeast of the new light-house, and is under the superintendence of the keepers of said light-house. It is blown by the steam of a four-horse power engine, there being two such that one may be used while the other is under repairs. The sound is made in immense trumpets directed towards the sea, seventeen feet long, of cast metal. These do not *make*, but direct the sound which is made by a *siren*, near the small end of the trumpet, inside, made of brass, like the buzz in the striking part of a clock, and is ten inches in diameter. Upon this siren the steam strikes and causes it to revolve with so great velocity as to produce the warning sound which is heard from two to ten miles, according to the condition of the atmosphere.

LIFE-SAVING STATIONS.

These are houses built by government for men, and the necessary apparatus for saving the lives and property of shipwrecked vessels. There are two such on Block Island, one on the West Side, at Cooneymus, and the other at the Harbor. The former was established in 1872, at an expense of $1,400 for the building. The latter, at greater expense, was built in 1874. Each accommodates seven expert sailors, one being captain, and they patrol the shores each night through the winter, on the watch for wrecks. They have cooking-stoves, tables, closets, dormitories, beds, boats, ropes, life-preservers, rubber suits for inflation and floating, &c., &c., all that is needful for their business. The two stations employ fifteen men, one of them being paymaster, and they draw pay to the amount of $2,700 yearly.

Had these stations been here in 1831 when the *War-*

rior was wrecked on Sandy Point and all lives lost, twenty-one, many might have been saved by the use of the mortar which throws a line far out over seas in which no boat can be managed. The Cooneymus station has such a mortar, and one is expected for the Harbor station. These. with the two light-houses, and the two wrecking companies, and the fog-signal, are a great protection to commerce. They lack the supplementary signal station.

MEETING-HOUSES.

The first of these erected upon the Island was located near the north end of the Fresh Pond, and easterly of it. That was then a central point for the inhabitants. There, too, the only Island school-house was then located, also a pound, and a windmill. At that time, according to a memorandum made by the Rev. Dr. Stiles, the houses were located, " all but two or three, within two and a half miles of the meeting-house." This was said of them in 1756.

The second meeting-house, after the first had done good service about half a century, was built in 1814, and was located on Cemetery Hill, and was described by Mr. Henry T. Beckwith, of Providence, in 1857, as being "similar and equal in appearance to those of others of the country towns of the state," and as containing "the old square pews and sounding board." This house was built by the town, as was its predecessor at the Fresh Pond by the First Baptist church of New Shoreham. Subsequently the town appropriated the house for a town house, exclusively, and moved and fashioned it into the town hall, now located at the Center.

The third meeting-house was located on " Graves Hill," east of the Center, and near the road thence to the Harbor, and by the lane leading from said road to the house of Mr. Joshua Dodge. It was built " on shares," and was occupied by the First Baptist church until the year 1857.

The fourth house of worship on Block Island was erected by the Free-Will Baptists, on the West Side, in the year 1853, and was burned in 1863.

The fifth house of worship was the one at present occupied by the said First Baptist church, and was dedicated on the 25th of August, 1857. Its erection was chiefly due to the Rev. Mr. Gladwin's untiring devotion to the enterprise, encouraged by the liberality of Mr. John G. Sheffield and other active citizens, who set an example of Christian sacrifice which the rising generation will do well to imitate. To some who still speak tenderly of Mr. Gladwin, who has gone to his reward, and who labored for the present house against much bitter and blind opposition, his success seems almost superhuman.

When this house was dedicated the steamer Canonicus brought from Providence and Newport eleven hundred passengers, then said to be "one of the largest and most agreeable steamboat excursions ever known." The house cost $2,500, and was paid for promptly. Since then it has been improved, and its grounds graded and walled; the latter was done in 1875. During the same year a furnace was placed in it, the first furnace ever brought upon the Island, and hence it was a novelty to many that elicited sailor phrases quite novel to the pastor, as those phrases were applied to the furnace.

In this house was placed the first and only bell ever hung upon Block Island. Though small, it is far better than none, and its clear notes are undisturbed by car wheels, whistles, and tramping on pavements.

Here it should be added that the present good condition of this house is due in a great measure to the good care it has received from its first and almost only sexton, *Mr. Samuel Ball.* This good care has been equaled also

18*

by his promptness for nearly a score of years to his post, and that, too, when business cares and domestic duties have pressed their claims upon his attention. But few boys are now upon the Island who, when they are old, will fail to remember some of the wholesome talks of " Uncle S. Ball."

The sixth meeting-house of the Island was built on the West Side, in the year 1869, by the Free-Will Baptist church. Before it was completed it was demolished by the great "September gale" of that year. It was intended to be similar in size and finish to the one at the Center. Its loss was a sad calamity.

The seventh house of worship is the one at present occupied by the Free Will-Baptist church, and is located on the West Side of the Island, from which the landscape and ocean scenery is very beautiful.

HOTELS.

Previous to 1842, no public houses for boarders were kept upon Block Island. If any persons came from the main on business they stopped among the inhabitants wherever they could find accommodations.

In 1842, *Mr. Alfred Card* opened his house at the Harbor, where the Adrian House is now located, for boarders or excursionists. He says: "There I set the first excursion table for boarders of pleasure," ever furnished on the Island. The first party consisted of seven men "from Newport," one of whom was Mr. Van Buren. They stayed two days, and "they were the first party that ever employed, at Block Island, a boat and boatmen to carry them a fishing." "John L. Mitchell and Samuel W. Rose carried them out." For twenty years Mr. Card's popularity was increasing, and with it his patrons increased in numbers, and his accommodations were greatly improved. During this period two other houses for visitors were opened, and another was needed.

The Spring House.

This was opened to the public in 1852. Though at that time only an unpretentious cottage it was an improvement on its predecessors in location and conveniences. Of the hotels in 1857, a competent judge and writer said:

"The hotel accommodations at the Island consist of three small houses, lodging altogether about one hundred persons, and situated near the landing. Of these the Spring House, as it is called, is the most desirable, as it possesses much the finest situation upon the hill, over-looking the other two. The view of the ocean from it is very fine; the house being situated some sixty or seventy feet above the sea, a very little back from it, and with the land sloping down so as to give an uninterrupted view, the prospect is one upon which the visitor dwells with never-failing pleasure."

After having been kept twelve years by Mr. Card, the Spring House, in 1870, was sold to Mr. B. B. Mitchell, the present proprietor. It has received many improvements in size and otherwise. In the early part of 1877 its elegant addition fronting the north was erected, indicating an enterprise that anticipates the wants of many and first-class boarders. Its name is taken from its boiling springs one of which has mineral qualities.

The Ocean View Hotel.

The proprietor of this large and beautiful structure had no sooner witnessed the success of the Harbor enterprise, in which he had taken the deepest interest for several years, than his large plans were laid to meet the demands of visitors to the Island. The beauty of its location, and the elegance of its architecture are too well known by its many patrons to need description. The building was erected in 1873, opened in 1874, and enlarged in 1875. The proprietor, Hon. Nicholas Ball, by his activity in securing a harbor, formed acquaintances with many persons of distinction, and thus has done much to attract first-class patrons, whom he endeavors to retain by ample accommodations now existing and planned for the future. The name of the house—*Ocean View*—indicates one of its chief attractions, as well as its spacious and beautiful grounds.

In addition to those already mentioned, which have been pioneers in hotel enterprise, there are several others that have done a fair business; some have been recently completed, and still others are in process of construction. The *Adrian House*, kept by Mr. Charles Willis, near the Harbor; the *Beach House*, M. M. Day, proprietor; the *Woonsocket House*, kept by Mr. Alanson Rose; the *Rose Cottage*, a boarding-house, kept by Mrs. Matilda Rose; the *Sea-Side House*, Frank Willis, proprietor, recently enlarged; the *Central House*, kept by Hon. Ray S. Littlefield, new and commodious; the *Littlefield House*, kept by Halsey Littlefield, and nearly completed; the *Providence House*, A. D. Mitchell, proprietor, and Samuel Mott's residence at the south end of the Great Pond, have all been proved by their many respectable patrons to be comfortable and pleasantly located homes for summer visitors to Block Island. Besides these still others are soon to be built and opened.

The High-Land House, Mr. Alonzo Mitchell, proprietor, a new and beautiful structure, located on a high point south of the Harbor, to be opened in the summer of 1877, has its attractions.

The Shore Saloon, opened in the summer of 1875, located near the steamboat landing, kept by Mr. Ellery Barber of Westerly, accommodates many who come to the Island to remain only a few hours. Its tables seat about one hundred and twenty-five.

RAPID IMPROVEMENT.

Those who visited Block Island ten years ago now see in it a marked change from its condition then to that of the present. Now, instead of throwing out tons of ballast, unstepping masts, packing away sails, and hauling up boats at midnight, in cold storms, with oxen, and a score of men to steady the boats, and instead of the slow work of getting said boats back, rigged for fishing, consuming time, they pass into a safe harbor, and as soon as desired, hoist sail, and go direct to the fishing grounds. This and other improvements are well represented by the following extract from an address of Hon. Nicholas Ball, delivered in November, 1876. He says:

"Let us see what has been done for us within the last seven years, for surely our memory ought to carry us back over that short space of time. Government has appropriated the sum of $265,000, for a harbor at Block Island, and all but $62,000 or $63,000 has been expended here, and well and economically expended, too. I have not time to enumerate the benefits afforded by the works thus paid for, not to any one person or family alone, but to every family upon the Island. Without fear of contradiction, I will say that it saves to every consumer of a ton of coal, one dollar per ton; to every consumer of a cord of wood, one dollar and fifty cents per cord; to every purchaser of a thousand feet of lumber, one dollar and fifty cents per thousand; for every sack of salt used, fifteen cents; for every barrel of flour brought here, fifty cents per barrel, considering the former risk in bringing it in open boats, liable to get wet on the passage; and on all our imports, the gain is in proportion to the above. Our exports are large and various, and in former days when we could use only open boats, were exposed to great risk from water and frost. I have known many a boat-load to be sold at a great sacrifice to escape a coming storm. We were thus frequently placed at the mercy of foreign purchasers, who might make almost any bargain with us, well knowing that we could not wait and run the risk of our freight getting damaged by rain. Now, we can safely trust our merchandise in the hold of our schooners, and wait until a good market is found. . Add to the above that the fishermen get more fishing days each year, than they did under the old system of hauling up the boats every storm, and you may safely say, where the fishermen formerly caught three quintals of codfish, they get five quintals now, the fish, of course, to be as plenty in one case as in the other. Our mail comes to us now three times per week instead of once, as formerly. Then it came in a small, open boat; now it is brought in a commodious schooner, with deck and cabin. During July and August of the past summer, the mail came five days out of the seven, and on three of those days in each week, we received two mails.

Are the results of these appropriations of any advantage to the Block Island people? Who can be so ungrateful as to say "No, we did not want them?"

During the same space of time the government has appropriated money for two Life-Saving stations, in which are employed fourteen men, drawing pay to the amount of $2,700 per year. There has also been built, at a cost of $75,000, a new light-house, wherein are employed three men, who together receive $1,250 per year, besides some $150 expended yearly for hauling supplies to the building.

In 1854, this town then, had the following persons

employed by government; one light-house keeper, one postmaster, and one inspector of customs. Government positions were not increased in number until within seven years. Now we have four light-house keepers, one post-master, one inspector of customs, one man in charge of the government breakwater, and fifteen men employed in the life-saving service. The pay of the three men in 1854 amounted to about $840 per year; the pay of the twenty-two men now employed amounts to $6,145 per annum."

Nor are the above financial improvements all that have recently been made on Block Island. The great achieve-ment of obtaining a harbor has given a grand, living impulse to everything else. Since then, of necessity, the roads of the Island have been straightened, widened, graded, cleared of stones, at an expense that would have startled the people ten years ago. Buggies and fine car-riages have superseded the ox-cart, the saddle and pillion. Beautiful and staunch yachts and smacks with decks and comfortable cabins, as the "Dixon," the "Anthony," and the "Hattie Rebecca," are owned by the Islanders, and used for carrying mail, passengers, freight, and for fishing instead of the open boats, many of which are still in use. Within the past five years, more new, modern buildings have been erected here than were built during the fifty years preceding, and at a greater cost than all the houses here of the two hundred years previous. The frequent arrival of steamers in the summer has infused new life and enterprise into all kinds of business, and into all grades of society. Even deaf and dumb "Blind Henry" has felt the impulse, and with his cane picks his way from the West Side to the Harbor, at the risk of his life, to hold out his hat for a pittance from the passing stranger. For the accommodation of the multitude of visitors brought here by means of the Government Harbor, large and beautiful hotels have been multiplied, market increased for the delicious fish direct from the sea, and employment furnished for many who would otherwise be absent from the Island, and still more new and beautiful hotels and private residences are under contemplation. Mr. Noah Dodge's residence, just completed, so sightly, large, and convenient, will incite others to imitate his example. The schools, also, are receiving increased attention. The new and commodious school-house on the West Side, the new ones contemplated at the Center, at the Harbor, and at the Gulley, together with the establishment of the High School, the first of the kind on the Island, and the rapid increase in number and variety of newspapers and periodicals, and the *infusion* of intelligence and refinement from visitors, are all evidences that the Islanders have no intention of being rated as "degenerate sons of noble sires." Nor is the least of this rapid improvement here the newly realized luxury of having friends abroad, as well as at home. The Island is no longer, socially, a cart-wheel with some one leading man for a hub, around which the rest of the inhabitants, like spokes, revolve. The rim is broken: the spokes are out. No one moves with others unless he chooses to do so. Many have been to the Centennial. Many have formed pleasant acquaintances with boarders, living abroad, and have learned that if one does not receive merited honor "in his own country, and in his own house," he may obtain it elsewhere. This advantage, formerly denied, in a great measure, to the Island so remote from the main, is now enjoyed by means of safe and ready transit to near and distant towns and cities. Nor should the rapid improvement in the churches of the Island be passed without notice. Instead of the stove, there is the furnace; instead of the smoke of *tug* commingled with that of kerosene to stifle the preacher, in winter, now the fresh air from the furnace warms the main auditorium; instead of the church grounds lying as left by the farmer, uneven, steep, where for successive winters there were many ungraceful slips and falls, now the lot is graded, walled, and suitably furnished with steps; instead of the short-lived Sabbath-school in summer, nipped by the first frost of autumn, now it continues the year round, with *such* concerts, monthly, and Christmas festivals as the children will not soon forget; and instead of the $750 salary paid a few years ago, now one of $1,200 is paid promptly, and the church is abundantly able to pay more. While the most of this is said of one of the churches, the same ratio of improvement has been in the other, whose numbers have been less and means more limited, but their zeal and improvement, perhaps, none the less commendable.

The greatest of all material improvements on Block Island, indeed, the mother of all others, has been the convenience of landing secured here by the construction of the Government Harbor. As evidence of this, consider the following contrast. Previous to the Harbor, behold that cloud coming swiftly, darkening, and accompanied by a sudden roughness of the sea that puts the fisherman's boat into great peril. He hastens from the Bank homeward, but before he reaches the Bay his frail masts can hardly weather the gale. By the most skillful exertions he skims over the enormous waves until he has neared the old landing-place, but there he sees the waters leaping upon the shore and gliding back in such fury as to threaten his open boat with sinking. He dares not attempt to land. His kindred stand upon the shore in dismay. The boat is tacked this way, and that way, while its inmates are pumping and bailing for their lives, and liable to be sunk any instant, while the gale increases in fury and the waves toss, dash against, and into the boat so as to make death by drowning seem inevitable. Then, in the moment of desperation hear the captain say: " Boys,

19

we shall be drowned if we stay here, and we may as well take our chances going ashore!" The vessel is now seen headed for the landing. Rapidly she glides either to safety or to destruction. Eyes upon the shore fill with tears, lips quiver, and in agony friends interpret the fearful crisis. There is just one way, and *only* one in which it is possible for that boat and crew to land in safety, or in other words to escape immediate destruction. She must ride upon the shoulders of the largest of "three brothers"—the wave that will carry her so high upon the shore that the next wave will not reach her, and thus afford the crew a moment in which to escape. "Steady! Steady! Not too fast," says an old sailor on the shore. For if the boat gets too far upon said "brother's" shoulders she will pitch over and be buried in an instant. Neither must the boat lag behind his shoulders, for if she does the receding wave will swamp her. Her sail is raised or lowered, by the inch, to keep balanced on that giant wave. "She rides! She rides!" says another, while others stand in breathless silence, and the critical instant of life or death hastens—the great wave breaks upon the shore amid the howling winds—the fisherman's boat is left there, and the crew are saved, while the "big brother" retires to the deep, like the whale that landed Jonah.

Such, for scores of years, had been the perilous landing, at many times, on Block Island. But now how changed! The boats are more safe in going to a distance, for if a storm arises they fly to the Harbor like doves to their windows, and such joyful expressions as have been seen there no pen can describe, as the frail boats have reached the quiet water and anchored, or tied up in safety. There, too, the steamboat moors at the wharf, and tens of thousands visit the Island now, instead of the occasional stranger in years previous to the Harbor.

Not the least improvement on the Island is one of the latest—the removal of the old fish houses, in the winter of 1877. For nearly a century they had stood on the bank in front of the Pole Harbor, and had done too good service to be despised. In them, generations now gone did much to rear the present inhabitants, as well as to feed millions abroad. But they were no better than their occupants who grew old, retired, and disappeared from the places afterwards occupied by those more youthful. So the modern spirit of improvement has freed the bank from what was latterly deemed an eye-sore and a nuisance by visitors, to whom the first impression on visiting the Island hereafter will be much more pleasing than formerly. The new houses erected under the bank west of that Basin will be more convenient for the fishermen, and far less offensive to strangers. It is hoped that Mr. Nicholas Ball may live many years to continue his improvements.

THE FIRST STEAMBOAT EXCURSION.

The Rev. George Wheeler, present pastor of the Free-Will Baptist Church of Block Island, claims the merit of originating the first steamboat excursion to this place. He was then a grocer in Providence, in 1853, and chartered the steamer *Argo* for the purpose. She brought two hundred and fifty excursionists, and by her trip cleared eighty dollars for the benefit of the first meeting-house, then in process of erection, built by said church. The steamer anchored in the Bay, and the passengers were landed by row boats.

SCHOOLS.

In 1857 there were five district schools on the Island, and at that time the School Commissioner reported them to be "as good schools as those in any of the country towns in the State." The same schools are still maintained.　Since the former date two new, modern school-houses have taken the places of the old ones.　The one on the Neck is large and well-furnished, and was built but a few years ago.　The new one on the West Side was built in the fall of 1876, and is a great improvement on its predecessor.　The building of other school-houses soon is contemplated, and needful.

A new stimulus for improvement has been given to the district schools by the establishment of a school of a higher grade, thus gratifying the natural love of promotion, by higher attainments.

ISLAND HIGH SCHOOLS.

A school of advanced grade has long been talked of as greatly needed in New Shoreham.　The first step towards establishing one was a vote of the town in 1874, giving the free use of the town hall to any one who would take the responsibility of the enterprise.

In the summer of 1875, Prof. S. A. Snow, principal of the high school at Oxford, Mass., canvassed Block Island. with the intention of opening a school; but decided that, without aid from the town, the undertaking would be impracticable.　In town meeting, October, 1875, a motion to appropriate money for the above-named purpose was lost, and the project was accordingly abandoned.

During the same October, the town was again canvassed, this time by A. W. Brown, of Middletown, R. I., who offered to open the school at a tuition-rate of ten dollars per pupil, provided that twenty-five pupils should be assured, or a part of that number, and pecuniary aid to supply the deficiency.　Nineteen pupils were promised for one year.　The amount wanting was divided into six shares, the total not to exceed two hundred and forty dollars, and to be diminished by the amount paid by any additional pupils obtained.

Messrs. Lorenzo Littlefield, Nicholas Ball, William P. Lewis, Hiram Ball, and Arthur W. Brown took the responsibility of one share to each; the remaining sixth was assumed by Messrs. Alvin H. Sprague and Thomas H. Mann, M. D.

On Monday, Nov. 29, 1875, the Island High School was opened at the town hall, which had been fitted up for the purpose. Edith Ball, Adrietta P. Ball, Annie I. Mitchell, Annie Payne, Addie Smith, Ray G. Lewis, Schuyler C. Ball, Erwin Ball, Hamilton Mott, and William T. Dodge, entered at the beginning of the first term, during which the number increased to sixteen.

The second term opened, on Feb. 14, 1876, with increased advantages. Rough pine tables had been used before; but now these gave place to handsome tables of ash, well made, and convenient. A first class orchestral organ was procured for the use of the school. Miss Kate L. Backus, of Ashford, Conn., was employed to assist in the work of the school, to teach instrumental and vocal music. The school increased rapidly in efficiency, and gave, at the close of the term, a successful exhibition, and has continued with varying but ever-improving fortunes to the end of the sixth term (Feb. 3, 1877).

Reports have been given to the pupils at the end of each five weeks of term time. In these, the amount of previous training received by each pupil is taken into consideration. The abilities of pupils are not compared, but account is taken of the manner in which their powers are exerted, and of deportment. The following are the names of those who have ranked first, second, or third in either of the reports issued: Addie Smith, Annie Payne, William T. Dodge, Annie I. Mitchell, Clarence Littlefield, Ray G. Lewis, Fanny Payne, and Frank Littlefield.

The following-named pupils have been noted, while attending the school, for unexceptionally good behavior:

19*

Addie Smith, Ray G. Lewis, Annie Payne, C. Ellie Champlin, Fanny Payne, Grace E. Jelly, and Isaac S. Hooper.

Most of the old pupils are still in attendance, and other names have been added to the roll. The name of one beloved of all is now graven on one of the stones that dot the neighboring burial hill. Thomas J. Rose left Block Island, at the close of the summer term of 1876, to pass the long vacation with relatives in Newport. Returning to attend school at the beginning of the fall term, he was stricken by diphtheria, and died Sept. 12th. The members of the school stood by the grave as the body of their playmate was committed to the earth. He rests well, within view of the ocean which he always loved, and which soothed him in his sickness by the solemn slow song of its waves.

In closing this sketch, it is only necessary to add that the Island High School, now firmly established, is in good working condition; and there is every prospect that it will grow in numbers and in usefulness. Thus the zeal and competency of its principal, Mr. Arthur W. Brown, joined with the enterprise of the Islanders, have raised a standard of education on Block Island which fulfills the wish and the prophecy of an able writer and visitor here in 1860, who said, "One further improvement seems to be demanded, and as this necessity is felt by the most intelligent Islanders, I trust it may soon be made; and that is, *the permanent establishment of one school of a higher grade,* so located that each district can contribute its quota of advanced scholars annually. There is the material here, the demand for it, and, I trust, the *will*." (W. H. Potter.) Large universities have had smaller beginnings, and it is hoped that this High School may be a perennial fountain of pure learning to the rising generations.

ISLAND LIBRARY.

On Saturday evening, March 6, 1875, at a meeting of ladies and gentlemen who were interested in obtaining better advantages for intellectual improvement than were then enjoyed upon Block Island, and who believed that a public library would furnish larger privileges to that end, an organization was formed, under the name of "The Island Library Association." At this meeting. held at the office of Dr. T. H. Mann, a constitution was adopted, creating the various offices of the association, specifying the duties of each officer, and providing for his proper election, and the election of successors. By-laws were passed, providing for the proper care of the library; and for an annual tax of one dollar for each gentleman, and of fifty cents for each lady.

The following are the names of the members who assisted in the organization : Mrs. Wm. P. Ball, Mrs. Nicholas Ball, Miss Effie Ball, Mrs. Herman A. Mitchell, Mrs. Charles Willis, Mrs. John Hayes, Jr., Misses Alice Lewis, Charity Ball, and Mary T. Rose; Messrs. T. H. Mann, Daniel Mott, James Hammond, Ralph E. Dodge, Amos D. Mitchell, J. W. Smith, Burton Dodge, James E. Mitchell, Howard Millikin, Robinson Lewis, Marcus M. Day, Nicholas Ball, Orlando Willis, Aaron W. Mitchell, John W. Millikin, Chester E. Rose, Edwin A. Dodge, William C. Card, William M. Rose, Everett Millikin, and Leander A. Ball.

At the first meeting, the following officers were elected:

President—Thomas H. Mann, M. D.

Vice-President—Marcus M. Day.

Secretary—Orlando Willis.

Librarian and Treasurer—Halsey C. Littlefield.

Board of Trustees—Thomas H. Mann, Orlando Willis, William C. Card, Mrs. William P. Ball, and Mrs. John Hayes, Jr.

Some fifty dollars were subscribed; the constitution and by-laws were printed; but during the summer, the matter received no attention.

The next winter, the subject was again agitated, and, in January an attempt was made to procure funds. This time the efforts made were more successful. His Excellency, Gov. Henry Lippitt, and Mr. Rowland Rose, both of Providence, gave twenty-five dollars each. Subscriptions of ten dollars were received from Prof. Eben Tourjée of Boston University; from Messrs. Whitford, Aldrich & Co., Hartwell & Richards, and Congdon & Aylesworth of Providence; and from Mr. Lorenzo Littlefield of New Shoreham. Messrs. William P. Lewis, Alvin H. Sprague, William P. Ball, John G. Sheffield, and Arthur W. Brown, gave five dollars apiece. Fifty-eight others subscribed sums varying from fifty cents to three dollars, Hon. Nicholas Ball gave seventy-eight books, and a donation of fifty standard English works was received from Mr. Amos D. Mitchell, proprietor of the Providence House. Prof. Eben Tourjée, of Boston University, promised one hundred volumes; Hon. Wm. P. Sheffield of Newport, promised one hundred volumes as soon as the library should number four hundred volumes.

On the evening of Friday, February 24, 1876, the association met and elected as

President—T. H. Mann, M. D.

Vice-President—Nicholas Ball.

Secretary—Charles E. Perry.

Librarian and Treasurer—Arthur W. Brown.

Board of Trustees—T. H. Mann, C. E. Perry, Alvin H. Sprague, Mrs. L. Littlefield, and Miss Alice Lewis.

The library, numbering two hundred and fifty volumes, had been arranged in a neat case made by Leander A. Ball and located at the town hall. After the abovementioned election of officers, some forty volumes were distributed. Since that time the library has been in constant use, and has grown rapidly. Hon. William P. Sheffield has given one hundred and thirty-four volumes, thus more than making good his promise. Other donations have been received from Messrs. T. W. Higginson, D. C. Den-ham, and Jas. E. Hammond of Newport; from Messrs. Samuel Austin, T. B. Stockwell, and J. C. Greenough of Providence; and from Mr. C. E. Perry of New Shore-ham. Large additions have also been made by purchase.

The library now contains more than five hundred volumes ; it is doing a good work, and it is hoped will long continue to grow. Donations of books from the friends of learning may be of great service in this iso-lated community.

It is due to Mr. Arthur W. Brown, Principal of the Island High School, the first of that grade ever opened on the Island, to say here that he originated the plan of this first public library on the Island, and that chiefly by his enterprise it has become a valuable institution.

MUSIC.

Although we have no evidence that Block Island was anciently one of the isles of the sirens where ships were charmed ashore by the sweetness of music, yet here is found more than an ordinary natural talent for the art most captivating. Voices full and rich in melody here are in need of nothing but culture to make them distin-guished. Not a native of the Island can sing by note independently, and yet the church singing is truly musical and devotional, inflenced more by the movements of the sea than by the songs of the birds. Nor is this undulating movement of the good old tunes disagreeable. It is simply natural, and not artistic.

Instrumental music, until recently, was limited to the fife, flute, drum, and violin, the latter being in demand in the time of horseback rides, pillions, and private house dancing after a husking. We have no knowledge of any Islander who has excelled in music or poetry. Indeed, we know of but one who ever attempted poetry, and he died over a hundred years ago. His poetry was adapted to his music, as one might judge of the accounts of both.

Rev. Samuel Niles, a native of the Island, while pastor of the church in Braintree, Mass., had a contest with his church about singing by note. His church made arrange. ments to do so. The Sabbath came; the church assembled; but no minister appeared. He was informed that "they were all present before God to hear all things which were commanded him of God." His reply was that "he would not preach in the meeting-house unless they would sing *by rote.*" There is some of his sentiment on the Island, which it would be well to overcome by a few good singing-schools in winter after the boats are hauled up. The poetry of Mr. Niles indicates his musical culture; for example:

> " A cannon splitting slew brave Captain Hale,
> Worthy esteem, whose death all do bewail ;
> Brigadier Dwight here stands in honor high,
> Colonel o'er train of the artillery."

Music by *note* is what the Islanders need to give scope to their rich, melodious voices. Then they will have an independence and harmony which they cannot otherwise obtain. Towards this point they are evidently aiming, for there are now among their families six pianos, and eighteen organs, and the young are learning with commendable progress.

TREES.

While Block Island is destitute of forest groves of large and small trees, it is erroneous to report, as some have, that it is entirely destitute of them. Many houses and yards are adorned with them, and instead of there being none, the ornamental and fruit trees of the Island, though small, may be counted by thousands. During the past few years the nursery-men from abroad have been here repeatedly, and have driven quite a lively business. Those who come here only in the mild zephyrs of summer have not the faintest idea of the severity of the wintry winds upon the trees, even stripping them, sometimes, of their green leaves, in the early autumn, and literally whipping the limbs to death before spring. But little, if any, more beautiful apples were seen at the Centennial than grew in the same year on a tree in Mr. Lorenzo Littlefield's orchard—several barrels on the same tree. A greatly increased interest is taken in the culture of fruit, and with proper patience and energy the best of apples, pears, and quinces, and cherries might be produced, as well as the smaller fruits. The hardier fir trees might be made to enclose a plat that would thus be protected from the bleak winds, and within the enclosure luxuries of fruit could be obtained to which the children of the Island are too great strangers.

SUMMER VISITORS.

It is comparatively but a short time since the attractions of Block Island have been made public. The little open boats from here, occasionally seen mooring at the wharves of Newport, Stonington, New London, and Norwich, laden with fish and produce, and sometimes with oxen, cows, calves, sheep, fowls, and men and women, some lowing, some bleating, some crowing and cackling, and others talking and laughing while on their voyage, were not the best advertisement for strangers accustomed to palace cars and the elegant saloons of steamers. From what they saw they greatly misjudged the Island and its inhabitants. This, it may safely be said, thousands have since acknowledged. Nor was it for the interest of neighboring places of resort to speak of the attractions of Block Island, but rather to point out what of it was repulsive. The very sight of the Island, as seen by those passing Sandy Point, repelled, for many scores of years, rather than attracted strangers. Its destitution of trees, its unpretentious buildings, its shores unfrequented by shipping, with here and there its little pinnaces fishing, and these lying bottom up, in the winter, on the land, while there were no public works during the cold season to indicate life and enterprise—these gave the impression to strangers which the poet has expressed in the triplet:

> "Lonely and wind-shorn, wood-forsaken,
>   With never a tree for spring to waken,
>   For tryst of lovers or farewells taken."

But occasionally health and pleasure-seekers who cared less for the gaudy shows of fashionable resorts than for the pleasures of Nature's walks, halls, and parlors—fields under the great blue dome, where none breathe the unhealthy odors of gas and kerosene lights, where none require fans in the heated days and evenings of summer, and where all experience the truth that exercise along the sea shore, in the pure sea breeze, gives a relish to food which all the sweets and spices of the Indies cannot afford, and a refreshing to sleep that makes one feel like saying in the morning from his very heart, "So He giveth his beloved sleep," a few such, not many years ago, looked across the waters to Block Island and imagined that here was a desirable place for rest and recuperation. One such seeker, a distinguished resident of one of the cities of New York, stopping at a large hotel on the main, occasionally looked through his glass towards Block Island, apparently a speck away out at sea, and inquired of the proprietor: "What is that away there?" "O, that is nothing but Block Island—a little sandy place," was the reply. The inquirer decided that he would see that

" little sandy place," and improved the first opportunity, and instead of sand, found beautiful fertile fields; instead of a land breeze much of the time, he found a pure salt-air sea breeze refreshing, and cooling night and day; instead of fish that had been caught several days and kept on ice, his table was furnished with the best direct from the ocean, and from that time he has been an annual visitor, bringing with him his many excellent friends each summer. Thus others have come, and induced their acquaintances to follow, until one steamer, the Canonicus, in 1875, brought to the Island over 10,000 passengers. Add to these the visitors by the steamer Ella, from Norwich, Connecticut; those by Capt. Card's Yacht, and others on excursions from various cities, loading their steamers down to the water's edge, and also the elegant pleasure yachts from abroad, and some estimate can be made of the visitors to Block Island.

The character of these visitors is an item of interest. From the glimpses which the writer has had of fashionable resorts, he is certain that the Block Island visitors are *sui generis*. If they have airs at home they lose them before landing here, and while remaining breathe an air of health and freedom. If they are wealthy there, they make but a modest show of it here. If they are cramped and fettered there by the conventionalities of societies, as an English orator said of slaves and England, their fetters fall from them as soon as they step foot upon these shores. That they are well bred is evident to a competent observer. They are the solid men and women of the most moral circles of the country. The faster sort, if they come at all, tarry but briefly. For such the social atmosphere is not congenial either from the great majority of visitors, or from the Islanders. Intemperance is not tolerated. A few with plenty of money, desirous of a plenty of liquor, have tried the Block Island hotels, and very

20

soon have been asked to settle their bills.   And yet, innocent, healthful amusements are common here.   Some of
the best families in the country are annual visitors to the
Island, from many different cities and villages.   It is a
favorite resort for many from Norwich and Hartford,
Conn.; Troy, N. Y.; Philadelphia; Washington, D. C.;
and New York city.   Professor JOSEPH HENRY of the
Smithsonian Institute, Judge INGALLS of Troy, N. Y., and
others of like distinction have spent so many summers,
or parts of them, at Block Island that they seem here
almost like citizens.

PRESIDENT GRANT's visit formed an item of history.
This occurred on the 18th of August, 1875.   Such swelling accounts of it have been read in the newspapers that
a truthful one can hardly expect to be credited.   He was
on a brief tour in New England; stopped at Bristol, R. I.
and through Senators H. B. Anthony and Major General
Burnside was invited by Hon. Nicholas Ball to visit Block
Island.   On the 18th the revenue cutter *Grant* appeared
in the offing, and soon anchored in the Bay.   Two boats
were lowered into which the President with his escort,
Secretary Bristow, Attorney-General Pierrepont, Senators
Anthony and Burnside, and others entered and were
rowed into the Harbor by the well trained mariners, while
all the available flags were flying.   The presidential party
were all obliged to climb over the decks of two vessels
before reaching the wharf, where the President was welcomed by Hon. N. Ball, and escorted to the Ocean View
Hotel.   Never, probably, was there less excitement on
the arrival of so distinguished a visitor.   Had it not been
for the visitors present not a single hurrah would have
been raised.   It was singular as it was.   Far more of the
Islanders, a few days from that, were at the funeral of a
pious young mother on the Neck.   It is a pity that more
of the children were not induced to meet the President,

for their future gratification. He dined, shook hands
with those introduced to him, affectionately beckoned to a
bright little girl to come to him, visited the new light-
house, and took leave for Cape May about 3 P. M.

Never before did the writer so fully understand the
meaning of Peter's saying: "Lo, we have left all," as
when he saw fishermen—good men too, mending their
nets by the way-side, while the President was passing,
without stopping to see him. Hon. Nicholas Ball, Hon.
J. G. Sheffield, and others of the Islanders exerted themselves commendably to show proper respect for national
"dignities."

CIVIL POLITY OF BLOCK ISLAND.

A MINIATURE DEMOCRACY.

From its settlement in 1662, until the present, it has been essentially that of a miniature democracy. Its sixteen proprietors owned equal shares of the soil. Those of them who did not move to the Island with the settling party transferred their privileges here to their tenants. All were equals in civil rights, except as they conferred them temporarily upon one or more of their number. As Massachusetts had relinquished her claim upon the Island in favor of John Endicott, Richard Bellingham, Daniel Dennison, and William Hawthorne, it became private property, and when, as such, it was sold to the settlers, they entered upon it as a private corporation, or compact of their own construction. Their civil and religious views were doubtless well known to Clarke and Williams, the founders of the Rhode Island colony, and therefore they had Block Island included in the charter which they and others obtained from CHARLES II, in 1663. This charter secured for the Island the same polity granted to the said colony. In the first year's enjoyment of this charter James Sands and Joseph Kent, in behalf of the inhabitants of Block Island, petitioned the General Assembly of Rhode Island for civil protection and order, and were responded to by a committee, the chairman of which was Roger Williams, who most cordially conceded to the Islanders the boon which he had so anxiously sought for himself, namely, a civil freedom that should exercise no authority over the religious convictions of any so long as those convictions did not disturb the peace of community. Hence in his report to the Assembly it is said: "At present this General Assembly judgeth it their duty to signify His Majesty's pleasure vouchsafed in these words to us, verbatim, viz.: That no person within the said colony at any time hereafter, shall be in any ways molested, punished, disquieted, or called in question for any difference of opinion in matters of religion, and do not actually disturb the civil peace of the said colony." This was so harmonious with the Islanders that they sought a union with the whole colony which greeted them in the language of the Assembly thus: "Our well beloved friends and countrymen, the inhabitants of Block Island."

In May, 1664, the Assembly appointed James Sands and Thomas Terry, and impowered them to call a meeting of the Islanders who were to choose a third man as their assistant in the local government of the Island. These three were authorized to call public meetings from time to time for mutual regulations and safety; to engage a constable, and clerk; to grant warrants. and try cases in which was involved not more than the value of " forty shillings," and also to grant appeals to the General Court of the colony. In 1665, the inhabitants elected their first representatives, James Sands and Thomas Terry. In 1672 they also petitioned for their incorporation as a town, and received their charter as such. From that time until the present they have elected their representatives and town officers by the vote of the majority of their freemen. That charter required two wardens, first, and deputy wardens, and to these, "three wise, honest men " were to be added, by a majority vote, to constitute the Town Council. Thus, up to the Revolution, with a voice in the General Assembly, and with the privilege of self-government at home, during a period of one hundred years, Block Island enjoyed all the freedom and inde-

20*

pendence that it desired, bearing its proportion of State taxes, paying £29 in the year 1700, and relying upon the same protection from the colony accorded to other towns. In this respect it was sadly disappointed during the War of the Revolution. Though abandoned to the cruelties of the enemy it ever maintained its principles of civil and religious freedom, and of self-government, and was none the less loyal at the close of that struggle than were other towns of the colony more highly favored. Its civil polity of exercising its own freedom in choice of its rulers; of maintaining religious freedom; and of unity with the colony, and the Republic at large, has remained kindred and cotemporary with the fundamental principles of the colony founded by Roger Williams. In 1783 it was granted the special privilege of choosing Ray Sands, a citizen of South Kingston, to represent the Island in the General Assembly, and also of subsequently choosing "any person, being a freeman in any town in the State, who is seized in his own right of a freehold estate in the said town of New Shoreham, to represent them in General Assembly." This was granted on account of the inconvenience of passing from the Island to the mainland.

The following extracts from the ancient records of the Island are here given as illustrations of the foregoing, and as historical facts interesting also as items of antiquity.

TOWN OFFICERS.

Town Officers in 1676.

Peter George, Head Warden.
Simon Ray, Deputy Warden.
James Sands, Assistant Warden.
Robert Guthrig,   "   "
Turmot Rose,   "   "
Robert Guthrig, Town Clerk.

William Tosh, Constable.
— Trustom Dodge, Sen. Sergeant.

Quarterly meetings that year were held at the house of the head warden, Peter George; and a special court was called by John Williams. In 1674 there were thirty freeholders.

TOWN OFFICERS IN 1700.

Simon Ray, Head Warden.
Joshua Raymond, Deputy Warden.
Nathaniel Mott, Town Clerk.
James Danielson, Sergeant.
Edward Mott, Constable.
Thomas Rathbone, First Townsman.
Job Card, Second Townsman.

In the year 1700 the freemen of the Island were between thirty and forty in number, and the population varied but little from 200.

The freedom and independence of the Island were so great in 1692 that its inhabitants regulated the standard of their own currency. A parcel of land was then sold, and the following articles in payment were called *specie*. The amount to be paid was £175, and to be "In spetia hereafter mentioned, viz.: In pork at three pounds per barrel, in beef at thirty-five shillings per barrel; all such as shall pass the packer at Boston. Wheat at four shillings per bushel; barley at three shillings per bushel, all merchantable and clean; butter at sixpence per pound; tallow at fivepence per pound ; all new milk cheese at fivepence per pound." All of these articles were legal tender, at some price, and hence were called "spetia."

During the same year the authorities of the Island summoned a jury of inquest on the body of *Tepague*, an Indian from Long Island.

In the year 1701 the inhabitants banished from the

Island one *William Preshur* and his wife for their immorality, or poverty.

In 1708 the freedom of the ballot-box was *enforced* by the following act: "That all the freeholders and freemen of Shorum shall personally appear at each respective quarter meeting, and there to attend to business of the day according to the charter or privilege of Shorum, upon the penalty of five shillings for every officer's not appearing, and 2*s.* 6*d.* per day for each freeman's not appearing according to warrant."

During that year a poor tax of £24 was levied and raised by the town.

In 1721 the town, in the following act, is seen to have been in a measure its own legislature: "That if any person or persons shall go through any man's land and shall leave open either bars or gate, or shall go through any man's fence without leave of the owner thereof, the person so offending shall pay ten shillings and moiety to the informer and the other moiety to the town."

In March, 1683, the town donated four acres of land to a blacksmith, the first on the Island, by the name of William Harris. That year, too, it recognized the name "Great Salt Pond," in 1636 mentioned by Roger Williams as the "Great Pond."

At the commencement of the Revolution the Island was virtually banished from the colonies, and left a prey for the enemy. The inhabitants foresaw the tempest gathering and sure to break upon them and made provision to bear it manfully, and to retain their chartered rights which they had faith to assure them would be enjoyed by them again after the storm of war had passed over. Accordingly, on the 9th of January, 1776, they put upon record the following: "Voted and resolved that all the town records, and all the other papers in the Clerk's Office that relate to the town be immediately sent by the

Town Clerk to Paul Niles, in Charlestown, requesting him by a letter to have care of them.

JOHN SANDS, Esq., Moderator.
WALTER RATHBONE, Town Clerk."

REVOLUTIONARY PERIOD.

Charlestown lies directly north of Block Island, and is the nearest land to the latter.

During the long struggle for independence, the inhabitants of Block Island, with no earthly ally, amenable to no higher civil authority than its own, except as claimed by Great Britain to belong to its crown, enjoyed and exhibited all the fundamental principles of a pure democracy. Whether familiar with any treatises of jurisprudence, like those of Justinian, Vattel, or Blackstone—whether they had ever seen a civil code or not, they certainly had a knowledge of human rights and duties, and they put that knowledge into practice in a manner that would have been a model for the sages of Athens and for the writer of our Declaration of Independence. The town records of this little, forsaken, war-pillaged Island in sight and hearing of the wrathful guns booming on the main, show a love of freedom and a faith in its attainment that were marvelous. The following may be taken as an index of the same, and also as an illustration of the clear and just views here entertained of the true civil polity for the attainment and maintenance of which they mutually, man by man, laid their lives upon freedom's altar. They said,—

"At a Town Meeting held in New Shoreham, Aug. 14, 1779.

JOHN SANDS, *Moderator.*

" *Whereas* the safety and well-being of society depend entirely under God upon the legal and strict administration of justice, and the execution of good order and wholesome laws; and

"*Whereas* the critical situation of this Island is such, and. in all probability will continue during the present contest between Great Britain and the United American States, as to render it impossible to have the same protection and security from the laws of our country and the courts of justice established in this colony or State, as before the commencement of the present war which must in its consequences render the persons and properties of the inhabitants very insecure:

"We have therefore thought proper for the preservation, protection, and security of our persons and properties, to adopt the regulations. contained in the following resolutions which we conceive to be warrantable upon the principles of self-preservation and the good of society."

The above preamble was followed by a series of resolutions of which the following is an abstract:

"*First:* That two assistant wardens be elected, and to have the same power as the head warden formerly had—the three to transcend the town charter, in judging of actions involving more than '*forty shillings.*' and also in deciding upon criminal actions.

"*Second:* That said wardens be a civil court to determine all civil and criminal actions *without appeal;* and in trials for life said wardens to summon to sit with them six freeholders, making a court of nine, a majority of whom made the decision final, *without appeal.*

"*Third:* Said freeholders to be finable £20 each for absence.

"*Fourth:* That said court be guided by State laws as far as possible, *except in trial for life*, in which case proceedings were to be 'according to law and evidence.'

"*Fifth:* When there were no laws to guide the wardens they were to act according to the best of their knowledge of the laws of the land."

To the above was added the following:

"We do further resolve in the most solemn manner that we will at the hazard of our lives and fortunes give every assistance, aid, and support to the wardens, assistant wardens. and other civil officers, in the execution of their offices in the legal administration of justice, and in the execution of the laws of the land, and in the execution of whatever regulations have been or may be adopted by this town for the preservation, protection, and support of the persons and properties of the good people of this Island."

During the same meeting at which the above was adopted by the citizens of Block Island, they proceeded to act upon town matters with as little apparent trepidation as though they were wielding the power of a nation, although they were trampling upon the crown of England, transcending greatly their colonial charter, and were liable any day to be invaded by a British fleet. On that day they said in their records:

" Whereas the native Indians being extinct in the town of New Shoreham that had claims in and to the land commonly called and known by the name of Indian Land, situate. lying, and being on the West Side, &c." This land was sold for town purposes.

All through the Revolution, town meetings were held, officers elected, good order maintained, real estate transactions occurred, marriages and deaths and births recorded, wills were made, the poor cared for, taxes assessed and collected. estates-inventoried and recorded, and not a complaint of hardships, nor a word of doubt of ultimate triumph of our armies in the struggle for independence. After the war, families that had fled to the main returned, the old paths of civil order were resumed, the above rules of *necessity* were abrogated, the charter of 1672, and its subordinate laws have been followed, and Block Island to-day bids fair to compete in good order, enterprise, and prosperity, successfully with her sister towns of the State.

THE MINISTER'S LOT OR LAND.

This is the name commonly applied to a portion of Block Island which was set apart, by the suggestion of Simon Ray, at the time of surveying the land for settlement, as a means of supporting the gospel on the Island. In the original compact of the first purchasers were included these words:

"*That there should a quantity or portion of land be laid out for the help and maintenance of a minister, and so continue for that use forever.*"

In that original survey made by the proprietors of the Island, in 1661, the portion above-mentioned was surveyed or laid out, and named, on the plot designating the various divisions, "Minister's Land," and it was also designated as "Lot 15." This land is located on the northerly part of the Island, and extends from the east shore of the Island to the east shore of the Great Pond, and contains about fifty acres. Mr. Simon Ray Sands has in his possession a copy of the original plotting of the Island for its sixteen proprietors, and said copy shows the boundaries of the Minister's Land.

In the year 1691, thus early, the town began to reap the avails of this land. In that year was made the following town record, as a lease to Mr. John Dodge, leasing to him "the whole use of all the minister's share of uplands and meadow upon this Island, excepting the five acre meadow lott in Edward Ball's improvement; and he hath promised to pay to the town council for the use and benefit of this Island, the sum of forty shillings to be pay in current pay equivalent to money by the middle of next December ensuing."

At the same town meeting it was voted, "That John

Dodge shall have the four-acre lott that belonged to the Minister's part, at five shillings per year for two years— or any other person. John Dodge refusing, William Rathbone to succeed him in it and to have said land two years, to pay five shillings per year, and to lay it plain, fit for mowing—to pay equivalent to money."

From the above we learn that nearly one hundred and ninety years ago the town recognized certain lots as the " Minister's Land," and that this land was in three divisions, one *large lot*, one of *five acres*, and another of *four acres*. The distinction also of "uplands," has reference to the large lot lying between the Neck road and the east beach.

In 1756, according to an old "memorandum of Block Island," in the 10th Vol. of the Mass. Hist. Col., this land for the support of the gospel received considerable attention. It says: " There is a ministry lot on Block Island which rents for 400*l.*, old tenor per annum. Mr. Maxfield received part of it A. D. 1756." The four hundred pounds were equal to $50.00. Indeed, over a hundred years ago, this appropriation of land for the support of a minister on Block Island was so well known abroad that it gave character and name to the whole Island which was called by some, then, the "Ministerial Lands."

As there was no organized church to take the supervision of this land, at the time of the settlement, the town assumed its supervision. And here, be it remembered, the *first settlers were not all proprietors*, the proprietors who donated said land. By a comparison of the names of the original *donators* of this land with the *first settlers*, it will be seen that one-half of the latter may have come as tenants, or as second purchasers, and these latter, by no subsequent act could change that first compact which appropriated the land and its avails. In other words, that appropriation was a grant for a specified purpose, and to

21

"continue for that use forever."   This grant was like those made in England about one thousand years ago, and have been known as church property which may be rented, but not deeded away; nor can the avails of such land be lawfully appropriated to town or individual purposes instead of the one specified in the original grant.

It may be an interesting task, at some future day, to examine the Block Island town records to see what the town has done with the Minister's Land, and to ascertain how large a sum of principal and interest may have accummulated in the town's treasury as moneys received from the said land, moneys *not used* for the "maintenance of a minister." Under the town management parcels of said land have passed into the continued occupancy of individuals, and the income from the part still designated as the " Minister's Lot," has dwindled to the sum of about fifty dollars a year. This sum is divided between the two churches of the Island. No other so good land, and so beautifully located, on the Island produced so little income, or could be hired for the same money. Lands each side of it, of the same quantity, probably could not be rented for five times the sum of fifty dollars.

That a better use of this land could and should be made, is certain. According to the value of other lands, the Minister's Land ought to be worth $4,000, yes, much more than this, if that deeded away be included. This price, by those who would like to obtain the land, of course, be spoken of in the old words: "It is naught! It is naught!" (Prov. 20: 14.) But when the price of land just over the fence is considered, the above statement will not appear extravagant. This land, like similar lands in other places, both in America and in England, can be leased for a term of centuries, although it cannot be deeded away, and most men would pay as much for a lease to run 999 years as for a deed.

An effort was made in the year 1875 to secure a larger income from the Minister's Land. A meeting, on the 4th of May, 1875, was held at the First Baptist Church of Block Island, at which a historical sketch of the said land was presented by the pastor. and there thirty-six of its members signed the following: " We the undersigned, members of the First Baptist Church of New Shoreham, believe that the avails of the 'Minister's Lot,' originally numbered ' 15,' should be used for building a parsonage for said church, and for such other purpose as may be in harmony with the original grant of said lot No. '15,' and we therefore mutually request a full attendance at a church meeting to be held on the 29th inst. at 7.30 o'clock, at our house of worship. then and there to take such action in the matter as may be deemed best for the cause of our Lord and Master."

Accordingly, on the 29th mentioned the church passed certain resolutions, and appointed a committee to carry them into action, an account of which may be seen on the church record.

No report has been made from said committee, and no parsonage is yet built, although two are greatly needed, and many persons desire to be free from any course that shall look like that of Ananias and Sapphira who " kept back part of the price."

CHURCHES OF BLOCK ISLAND.

Pious families were among the first settlers of Block Island. Before they saw it they assigned a portion of its soil for a perpetual support of the gospel. The instructions to the surveyor to set bounds to their homes also authorized him to bound the "Minister's Land." They were evidently kindred spirits of Roger Williams, with whom they associated freely. The historian Niles, a native of Block Island,. personally acquainted with the first settlers, speaks in highest terms of the piety of four of the most influential of the earliest inhabitants. Of his grandfather, James Sands, he says: "He was the leading man among them." "He also was a promoter of religion in his benefactions to the minister they had there in his day, though not altogether so agreeable to him as might be desired, as being inclined to the Anabaptist persuasion. He devoted his house for the worship of God where it was attended every Lord's day or Sabbath." The "minister" here mentioned was the writer himself, Rev. Samuel Niles who was a Congregationalist, ordained at Braintree, Mass., in 1711. He preached on Block Island only as a licentiate. James Sands is above spoken of as an *Anabaptist*, which meant then what the term *Baptist* does now, "and he did not differ in religious belief from the other settlers."—(Sheffield.) Mr. Sands, as the "leading man" of the Island, evidently had more influence as a Baptist than his grandson Niles had as a Congregationalist. Like Roger Williams, Mr. Sands defended the religious freedom of those opposed to him in doctrine, as seen in his support of Mr. Niles. There were also others who planted the same seeds of freedom on the Island in the infancy of its society. They evidently believed that the doctrines and forms of religion were from God, and not from men, and that all Christians have a divine right to tell what they know of God's revelation to men without hinderance or permit from human orders.

The *Rays, Simon,* and *Simon Jr.,* also exerted a power-ful religious influence on the early Islanders. Mr. Niles, their cotemporary, says of them: "He and his son, as there was no minister in the place, were wont, in succes-sion, in a truly Christian, laudable manner, to keep a meeting in their own house on Lord's days, to pray, sing a suitable portion of the Psalms, and read in good sermon books, and, as they found occasion, to let drop some words of exhortation in a religious manner on such as attended their meeting." They were both what we now call "lay preachers," and continued to exert their salutary influence more than ninety years, the father until his death in 1737, and the son until he died in 1755, up to which period we find no record of an organized church on the Island. It was probably visited by missionaries occasionally.

The first invitation of a minister to settle on Block Island was given to Mr. Samuel Niles in March 1700, who was then a young man and graduate from Harvard College. The invitation was not from a church, but from the town, and is here presented as a mirror of the society here then.

FIRST MINISTER CALLED.

"NEW SHOREHAM, March the 7th, 1700.

"We, the inhabitants of said Island, being deeply sensi-ble of the great love of God in Christ Jesus in laying

21*

down his daily call to us to be providing for our souls to be fed with his heavenly manna, and for that end to be instructed by his word and to have our souls instructed and edified by him in his promises, that the word of God be preached and sounded forth in the purity of holiness according to the Scriptures. We, underwritten, being sensible that where we partake of the spiritual gifts bestowed upon a teacher and minister of his word, so we ought to be liberal givers in our temporal, and for that end we have hereunto subscribed, do allot, and freely give up our right and interest in a certain piece of land being five or six acres more or less, as it shall hereafter be laid out by such men appointed for that end who are Simon Ray, Esqr., Joshua Raymond, Esqr., and Edward Ball, who after the laying out of the said land are appointed to appraise the said land what it may be in value per acre, which said land we do freely give and bequeath the right and disposition thereof unto Samuel Niles and his heirs forever, for the use to build and erect a dwelling-house for him that he reside amongst us as a faithful minister and preacher of the gospel amongst us as God shall enable him, desiring God to endow him with the most great and largest gifts of His Spirit which may prove to the drawing of our souls and the souls of such as may come under the power of his ministry to God, and for that end and furtherance in souls, a work for his sustenance, we do acquit all claim to him said Niles and his heirs forever from any claim from us and our heirs forever to said land, and this said act to be a record of our gift as witness our hands. It is also to be understood that there is always and forever a drift-way through said land for egress and ingress to pass through by him said Niles and his heirs at all times forever, hanging of gates for that end that there may be a passing through as the way runs, or by the layers-out of said land may be set out for the use of the inhabitants of said Island."

This was signed by twenty-eight freemen, ten by "his mark."

On the following day Messrs. Ray, Ball, and Raymond, the committee appointed by the town, surveyed, or staked out the lot designated, lying east of the northerly part of the Fresh Pond, and Mr. Niles accepted a deed of the same, about seven acres in all. This land he retained several years after he left the Island, and sold it in 1716 for £105. He wrote his history of the Indian and French wars in 1760, and died in 1762. In that history he frequently speaks of Block Island, of its religious leaders up to the year 1755, but says nothing of a church on the Island. There probably was none during his life-time, although for more than a century the leading men here were truly Christian, some of whom were lay preachers, and meanwhile there were temporary preachers from abroad. Mr. Niles preached about two years on the Island, and with reference to the remarkable escape from injury of the three Sands families coming from their homes on Sands Point, L. I., to Block Island, as their vessel was fearfully shattered by lightning, and no one hurt, on the following Sabbath he preached from the text: "*Were there not ten cleansed, but where are the nine?*" This was in the year 1702.

According to a memorandum of the Rev. Dr. Stiles, Mr. Maxwell received part of the rents of the "Ministry Lot," in the year 1756. In Sept., 1758, the Islanders "Resolved that Capt. Edward Sands, present town treasurer, forthwith hire one hundred and twenty-four pounds in old tenor, and pay the same unto Mr. Samuel Maxwell for his serving as a minister in said town the last four months." We have learned of him but little.

There was a meeting-house on Block Island in 1756.

In 1758 the town voted to board up the broken windows, which shows that it was unoccupied, and perhaps a mark for missiles.

In 1759, June 25th, the town voted a proposal to Rev. David Sprague to become their minister, offering him the use of the three ministerial lots, and also the use of the "proprietors' land thereto adjoining, running southerly as far as the south end of the Great Fresh Pond," during his service.

On the 28th of August, 1759, an amendment was made to a former vote, and it read thus: "So long as said David Sprague shall serve the inhabitants of the town by preaching to them the gospel of Christ according to the Scriptures of truth, making them and them only the rules of his faith, doctrine, and practice." This indicates clearly the persuasion of the people before they had an organized church.

There was a town vote to repair the meeting-house in August, 1764, and another in April, 1766, and at the time of passing the latter it was voted that one acre of land be leased to Rev. David Sprague, M. D., "Ninety nine years for one barley-corn a year." His house was built upon this "acre," near the Precious Spring, on the east shore of Fresh Pond. This seems to have been about the time of commencing his pastoral labors on the Island, although in August, 1759, the town had

"*Resolved*, that Capt. Robert Hull and Samuel Rathbone are chosen a committee to write to the Rev. David Sprague and give him with his wife and family an invitation to come and settle among us."

On the 19th of April, 1775, the town repealed all the previous acts concerning the use of ministerial and town lands granted to "Dr. David Sprague." On the 29th of May following a similar vote was passed, appended to which was the statement that "Dr. David Sprague was about to remove from the Island." This left the sheep without a shepherd during the remainder of the Revolution, except as they were ministered to by the abiding "Good Shepherd," and the faithful deacon, Thomas Dodge.

Under the call given to Mr. Sprague by the town he and a few baptized, believing members organized themselves into a regular Baptist church, October 3, 1772, as seen in the records of the First Baptist church of New Shoreham.

In 1772 a little band of Christians on the Island associated themselves in covenant relation for mutual watchfulness and spiritual improvement. They were not formerly organized as a church, and yet they were pledged to God and to each other to live "according to the rule and order of the gospel." They recognized no bishop, nor ecclesiastical body as their superior. They had a house of worship, made their own appointments, chose their own moderator and clerk, and exercised all that religious freedom in worship for which they well knew Roger Williams had contended so bravely, and which the Islanders had enjoyed for more than a century. How long previous to 1772 they had been accustomed to maintain covenant meetings, we are not able to say. From their record, commencing Sept. 3d, of that year, it is evident that such meetings had been customary. At that meeting their record says, "Bro. T. Dodge owned his covenant to God and hath renewed his fellowship with his brethren." The same was said of three other brethren, viz.: Trustom Dodge, Ezekiel Rose, and James Rose. To this it was added: "The following sisters, Catharine Adams, Mary Woodley, and Experience Sprague each owned their covenants and renewed their fellowship." Rev. David Sprague was present at this meeting, and also at adjourned meetings of Sept. 10th and 17th. At the latter he "read a copy of his ordination, which was solemnized July 12, 1739."

FIRST ORGANIZATION.

At an adjourned meeting, October 3, 1772, they "Then read the articles of fellowship with one another, and then the church gave Elder Sprague the right hand of fellowship to administer the ordinances of God as an evangelist." Here we have the first mention of a "church," on Block Island. We see it self-organized, taking the Scriptures as their guide and rule of action, choosing their own minister, and by their act of giving him the "right hand of fellowship," exhibited their sense of equality with him in regard to religious freedom and ecclesiastical authority.

The following names are included in the first church of Block Island, at the time of its organization, October 3, 1772.

REV. DAVID SPRAGUE, Pastor.

Lay Members.

Thomas Dodge, Ezekiel Rose, James Rose, Henry Willis, Mercy Willis his wife, Hannah Dodge, and Margaret Franklin; eight in all. James Rose was the first church clerk.

On the 2d of January, 1773, the pastor of this church "preached to show and prove by reason and the sacred Scriptures what a gospel church is, and when capable of discipline according to all the laws of Jesus Christ the King and Head of the church, and then proved by Scripture that we are such a church."

At this last-named meeting the pastor called upon each brother "to pass single before the Lord to see whether there was one in the church that was called of God to the office of a deacon." Thomas Dodge, in doing so, confessed his conviction that he was called of God to give himself up to the Lord for that service. Then the pastor,

Mr. Sprague, "met him in a covenant way and declared that he believed that his dedication was of God, and gave him fellowship in the office of deacon." This office he held until 1784, and so well "used the office of a deacon" as to purchase for himself "a good degree," for he was then ordained pastor of the church. Rev. David Sprague was the first pastor of it, and continued as such until 1775.

Rev. Thomas Dodge, the second pastor, was a cotemporary and intimate associate with the Baptist pastors who organized the Groton Union Conference soon after his ordination, at which one of them officiated, Isaiah Wilcox, who preached the ordination sermon, gave the charge, and the right hand of fellowship, the deacons of the church, Oliver Dodge making the first prayer, and Dea. Trustom Dodge making the second. This occurred Aug. 19, 1784, and on the first Sabbath in September following, Mr. Dodge administered the Lord's Supper. During his ministry of twenty years this church was one of the churches that composed the Groton Baptist Association, and continued such until 1834 when it was transferred from that association to the Warren Baptist Association.

Rev. Thomas Dodge, above mentioned, was a man of sterling worth, and is still remembered by some of the oldest inhabitants of the Island, where he was born in 1737. He preached in the house of worship that stood near the Fresh Pond, and in that beautiful mirror reflecting the heavens he was wont to follow the example of his Lord. There, on the 13th day of November, 1784, he immersed his first candidate, Mercy Littlefield. He labored with his hands for his support, and while in apparent health and vigor suddenly died on the beach at the Harbor, November 11, 1804, in his sixty-seventh year. His grave in the Island cemetery is distinguished by an appropriate marble slab. He was doubtless one of the main pillars of the church while deacon, during which time the Island was so fearfully scourged by the War of the Revolution. During that period the church was greatly scattered, and Mr. Dodge probably followed the example of his excellent predecessor, the venerable Simon Ray, doing all the essential work of a pastor except the administering of the ordinances.

On the day of Mr. Dodge's ordination the church adopted a series of articles of faith, eleven in all, and a solemn covenant to keep them in practice, and in fellowship with each other. A written copy of these articles is still in the possession of the same church. A few of them are here quoted as unequivocal evidence of the character of the first church of Block Island.

First Article. "We believe that the Scriptures of the Old and New Testaments are the words of God and the only rule of faith and practice."

Fifth Article. "We believe that the justification of God's children or Believers, is only by the Righteousness of Christ imputed to them without the consideration of any works of Righteousness done by them, and that the full and free pardon of all their sins and transgressions past, present, and to come is only through the blood of Christ according to the riches of his grace."

Sixth Article. "We believe the work of Faith, concerning regeneration, and sanctification, is not an act of man's free will and power, but of the mighty efficatious and attractive grace and power of God."

Eighth Article. "We believe that all those who are chosen by the Father, redeemed by the Son, and sanctified by the Spirit shall certainly and finally persevere and hold out to the end, so that not one of them shall ever perish, but shall have everlasting life."

Ninth Article. "We believe that Baptism and the Lord's Supper are ordinances of Christ to be continued in his church and practiced by Believers after his own example and in obedience to his commands until his second coming, and that the former is requisite to the latter."

Tenth Article. "We believe that the first day of the week ought to be kept as a Sabbath day of rest, &c."

No one familiar with the faith and practice of the regular Baptists will be at all doubtful of the character of the first church of Block Island as he examines the above articles. They recognize no authority in the church but the Scriptures; no justifying merits in good works; no power of free will to effect, or produce faith, conversion, regeneration, and sanctification; no final perishing of the saints; no baptism of unbelievers, as infants; no communion with persons before their immersion, and no Sabbath but the first day of the week. These articles adopted on the 19th of August, 1784, were doubtless expressions of views that had been entertained from the earliest settlement of the Island. Thirty-one names were put upon record at the time of adopting said articles, in 1784.

In 1815, thirty-one years thereafter, the same articles were copied from the old manuscripts and were adopted as the standard of faith and practice, and were subscribed to by Enoch Rose and the other members of the church present at the time of their adoption. The committee appointed for the examination and copying said articles were "Enoch Rose, Samuel Mott, and Edward Dodge, together with Elder E. Stedman," January 6, 1815.

Enoch Rose was chairman also of the meeting when appointed chairman of the committee for examining and copying the old articles of faith, and as chairman he presented them to the church for acceptance, February 4, 1815. He probably took an active part in church affairs during the interval between the death of Rev. Thomas

22

Dodge, in 1804, and the settlement of the next pastor, Rev. Enoch Stedman. Mr. Rose was baptized by Rev. Thomas Dodge, on the 4th of September, 1785, and although a troublesome member, several times, during his thirty-four years of standing in the church, the members bore with him until the early part of the year 1818. Then, on the 21st of February, the church put upon its record the following: "Taking up the matter that so highly concerns as we trust for Christ and his cause sake, as it respects our brethren Enoch and John Rose who have gone out from us and fellowshipped such as deny the Divinity of Christ our God and Saviour, and also refused to be admonished by us, and deny the government of the church; therefore we withdraw the hand of fellowship from them, and all that hold them in communion." This case of discipline clearly illustrates the mode of church government in this church. Mr. Rose had been deacon for twenty years, but in excluding him the church exercised its own independent authority.

In 1817 *Rev. Enoch Steadman* became pastor of the first church of New Shoreham, and held that office during a very troublesome period in the church, much of the trouble originating from Enoch Rose's defection, and from various vices. He was highly esteemed in the Groton Union Baptist association, which met about the time of his death, and put on record the following: "Our beloved father and brother, Enoch Steadman, pastor of the church of New Shoreham, has left this world, to receive, we hope, the everlasting reward of the righteous in the mansions of the blessed. By this stroke another is added to the list of the destitute churches." Rev. Mr. Steadman was buried on the 19th of June, 1833, in his seventy-fourth year, after a pastorate of sixteen years. He is also remembered as having been a soldier in the war of 1812, previous to his ministry.

The *Rev. John S. Dill*, March 29, 1834, was called to the pastorate of the first church of Block Island, and accepted. At the same time the church voted to ask assistance from the convention. He had troublesome members. In June, 1836, the church voted him and his wife letters of dismission. During that month they were visited by Rev. Arthur A. Ross. Things were sadly mixed during the year following—troublesome members defaming the character of Rev. Mr. Dill. In July, 1837, a council was "held in the Baptist meeting-house at New Shoreham;" letters and records were examined; the troublesome members confessed their wrongs, as well as Mr. Dill, and mutual forgiveness was expressed. On the following day, at an adjourned meeting, all the members agreed to "bury all their difficulties with each other, and in future live together according to their covenant obligations, and strive together for the faith of the gospel." It was also voted unanimously that nothing had been brought before the council to impeach the character of Rev. Mr. Dill. Rev. Arthur A. Ross, and Robert Dennis were committee from the convention at this council. On the 26th of August, 1837, the church voted Mr. Dill a dismission from the pastorate of said church, after a settlement of three years and a half.

Rev. Elijah Maccomber was Mr. Dill's successor. His pastorate began Jan. 1, 1838, and his first year's salary was $250, "and also the appropriation from the convention." In April of that year Wm. A. Weeden was appointed a "tidingsman, to keep order in the meeting-house." On the same day a committee of five were appointed to raise funds to secure a parsonage. In September, 1841, measures were taken for the incorporation of the church under the name of the *First Baptist Society of New Shoreham*. It seems to have had no pastor during the summer of 1841. In June a pulpit committee of five were appointed. In September it was voted to raise a subscription to induce Rev. Mr. Maccomber to return to the Island. He was in a church-meeting, Feb. 11, 1842, and again became pastor of said church. On the 4th of March, 1843, one hundred and ninety-seven members renewed their covenant with each other. Then followed a continuation of former discords, Millerism excitement, and exclusions which sadly characterized Mr. Maccomber's entire connection with this church. Many, doubtless, were unjustly excluded, and some unwisely admitted. His chief error seems to have been in fixing the precise time of the second Advent, of denouncing the Bible in case of failure, and of severity towards those who did not adopt his Millerism. His pastorate closed in 1844, and in October of that year a pulpit committee was appointed to consider the character of candidates for the pulpit.

Rev. Silas Hall, from the Baptist church in South Kingston, R. I., was received as a member of the First Baptist church of New Shoreham, Apr. 26, 1845. In June of that year the articles of faith and practice were read before the church, and approved. In July a slashing vote was passed in reference to those who had embraced the Miller doctrine, and for several months afterwards similar votes were repeated, until it was evident that those who sowed the wind under Mr. Maccomber's pastorate reaped the whirlwind while Mr. Hall served the church. In August, 1846, the church was so badly divided that at a meeting on the 29th, it was voted to lay their records before the Warren association which met at Pawtucket, Sept. 9th and 10th, following. The association put upon record this statement: "A persevering adherence to the errors of Millerism is an offense meriting exclusion from a Christian church," but omitted action upon the particular acts of said church, and appointed a committee to visit and advise with its members. On the 28th of September said committee came to the Island and read to the church a most conciliatory and wise address, in which they justified the exclusion of "those persons who had embraced Millerism and denounced the church," but reproved the church as acting in a "language and spirit unnecessarily hasty and severe," and advised the church to relinquish the services of both ministers upon the Island, Messrs. Maccomber and Hall, as soon as possible and to unite in the support of another.

In May, 1848, the church called the *Rev. Joseph P. Burbank*, and he entered heartily upon the labors of reconciling former discords and restoring excluded members. His salary the first year was $200, keeping of his horse, "separate from grain," and assistance from the convention. During his pastorate of about two years a better spirit pervaded the church.

Rev. C. C. Lewis was called by said church, Jan. 18, 1852, and continued his pastorate up to the spring of 1856. He suffered much from taking an active part in politics.

Rev. Albert Gladwin, during the summer of 1856, then a licentiate, served the church faithfully, and distinguished his labors by raising funds to build the present house of worship. It September of said year Rev. Dr. Jackson, and Rev. S. Adlam, of Newport, visited and counseled the church. The new house was formally delivered to the church by Mr. Gladwin, at a meeting held Dec. 31, 1857, at which time a vote of thanks was given to Mr. Gladwin for his services, together with $244.99 of unpaid subscriptions "as a remuneration for his services in collecting funds for the purpose of building and furnishing this house, and also as building committee to get the same built and furnished. and for his services with us as a minister of the gospel."

Rev. Cummins Bray, in September, 1858, was called to

22*

the pastorate of said church, on a salary of $350.00. He was a faithful minister of the gospel of *peace*. During his ministry old wounds were healed, and a new and healthy spiritual life became apparent. A judicious observer, and visitor to the Island, in 1860, wrote: "In this work of charity and reconciliation much credit is due and is freely accorded to their present pastor, Rev. C. Bray, whose judicious labors in the cause of temperance, and his kindness of heart which is patent to all have made him a general favorite over the Island." His pastorate closed Oct. 1, 1865.

Rev. J. H. Baker, Oct. 19, 1866, became pastor of said church, and continued such until Jan. 19, 1867. He was about that time taken with a paralytic shock in the pulpit, and never recovered.

His paralysis was first discovered while he was praying, as he repeated several times his last words in the pulpit, *"being not a forgetful hearer, but a doer of the work."*

The church treated him with great kindness thereafter, until his removal from the Island. During his pastorate Rev. Wm. Taplin was his assistant much of the time, after which the church was supplied by the latter, and by Rev. Mr. Harris until March, 1867.

Rev. I. B. Maryott, April 1, 1867, began his pastorate with said church, and continued his faithful labors until April 1, 1872, during which time the church was blessed with a good degree of peace and prosperity. *Rev. Solomon Gale*, as pastor, served the church from April 1, 1872, to February, 1873.

Rev. R. Russell was called to the pastorate of this church, April 1, 1873, and continued his services until September 30, 1874. He will long be remembered as the aged minister with the elastic step and cheerful spirit of youth, under whose ministry occurred the great revival of the winter of 1873–4, during which he baptized 121 members. Salary, $750.00.

Rev. S. T. Livermore of Bridgewater, Mass., was called to the service of this church, in the fall of 1874, and began his labors November 1st. Salary, $1,200.00. Members in 1876, four hundred and six.

In the history of the First Baptist Church of New Shoreham we find ample evidence of the stability of a religious society that governs itself independently of bishops, or of bodies clothed with higher grades of ecclesiastical authority. There is also seen evidence of the truthfulness as well as the irony of the saying of a prelate that "There must be a divinity in the government of the Baptist churches or they would ruin themselves by their follies." We own this with a degree of glory, in that we have only Christ for our Head and Ruler; and of shame, in that we so poorly exemplify his rules of church order. Yet with his Word as our only law of faith and practice, in spite of all our follies, we feel safer than we should by recognizing any intermediate authority between us and Him. Thus this church, from a germ planted in the days of Roger Williams, and by his kindred spirits who gladly left the places of persecution on the main-land, took up their abode on a lonely island far out at sea, to dwell among savages, unprotected by a strong force, has become a large and fruitful vine, sending out its branches to the sea all around. Many a time has the writer been asked by visitors at the Island, on learning the circumstances of its settlement: "Why did they come here, so far from the main, and settle amid so many Indians?" The most reasonable answer that he has yet been able to give has been: "They came to Block Island for the same reason that Roger Williams went to Providence." They, however, did not wait to be banished. But they did immediately put in practice the sentiments for which he had been banished, and have continued doing so until the present. In no part of the world, perhaps, has religious freedom been maintained so purely for two hundred years as on Block Island. Here it has never been disturbed by any civil enactments. Here no ecclesiastical authority has ever infringed upon private opinions of religious faith and practice. Here the church has never felt the overruling power of bishops or synod. Here no religious duties have been enforced upon helpless infants. Here the ordinances have ever been administered in their primitive simplicity. Here the acts of sprinkling, pouring, and signing with the cross have never been witnessed. Here the minister has no more ruling authority in the church than the youngest member. No authority is recognized in it except that which comes from the Scriptures. Thus amid the severest trials, this church, depending upon its Head for life and protection, has stood and prospered while the great hierarchy of Rome has ceased to trample upon the necks of kings and to slaughter the saints with racks and guillotines to subdue the world to its ecclesiastical authority, and politically has faded away. While civil and religious freedom has stood on Block Island two hundred years, how many kingdoms have fallen!

Its most remarkable revival occurred during the pastorate of Rev. R. Russell. It began with a few in a prayer-meeting, in a time of coldness, and resulted like the "handful of corn in the earth upon the top of the mountains," amid ice and snow where a divine power made "the fruit thereof shake like Lebanon." The pastor was then absent considerable of the time on account of his son's sickness, but the meetings continued with increasing power until human instrumentalities were almost invisible amid the manifestations of God's power. The places of intemperance were deserted; profanity

ceased; enemies became friends: one hundred and twenty-
one were baptized; the aged minister with whitened
locks flowing in the wind. nerved with superhuman
strength, with his frail body warmed by a divine fire
within, from Sabbath to Sabbath, surrounded with ice,
stood in his chosen Jordan and immersed score after
score of rejoicing converts, verifying the simple old
couplet,

> " Brethren, if your hearts are warm,
>   Snow and ice will do no harm."

The baptismal scenes, for many years, have been at the
south end of the Great Pond. a short distance northwest
from the house of Mr. Samuel Mott, and have been very
impressive.   While many witnesses assembled on the
slightly elevated shore, the candidates met at Mr. Mott's
house for preparation where many rooms were warmed
and opened for their convenience.   When all were ready,
the pastor with the senior deacon, followed by a choir of
male singers chanting a recitation of all the circumstances
of Christ's baptism, followed by the candidates, and these
by their friends, marched in a procession to the water.
There, after prayer, the ordinance was administered.
There many have felt the deep conviction that the ordinance was not of man, nor to please man.   In the winter
of 1876 three young ladies were thus baptized.   The
wind was blowing strongly; the waves came a long distance on the Great Pond; the shore was bordered with
ice and snow, as one after another, in the presence of a
multitude, walked calmly down into the water. and on
returning to the shore exchanged kisses with her companion going down to the liquid grave in obedience to a
divine command.   Many a heart was cheered with the
strong conviction that the power sustaining these delicate
females in such a Jordan would be ample support in

approaching and fording the river at the end of life's journey.

The present officers of the church are, Deacons Richard Steadman, Robert T. Sands, and Samuel P. Dodge; Clerk, Edward Mott, and Mrs. Alma Hayes, wife of John Hayes, Jr., organist.

Order of religious services: Sabbath-school at 10 o'clock A. M.; preaching at 11 A. M.; short discourse and conference-meeting in the evening. Covenant-meetings on the Saturday before the first Sunday of each month, and prayer-meetings Thursday evenings.

In all of the meetings of the church a competent observer sees that the emotional element exceeds the intellectual, a preponderance far preferable to that of the reverse. During the sermon the best of attention is given by the congregation, nearly all of whom seem to be hungering and thirsting for the bread and water of life, regardless of the baskets and pitchers in which their spiritual food is presented. Scripture *matter*, not scholastic *manner*, is their desideratum. To them a few sailor phrases properly used for communicating the gospel are far more valuable than flowers of rhetoric and syllogisms of logic, and the inimitable force and beauty of their use of such phrases must be heard by appreciating minds in order to be properly understood. "Shipped for the voyage;" "fair winds for a while;" "shipped to work, not simply as a passenger;" "the old ship has never foundered;" "to have good sailing, we must launch out into deep waters;" "when troubles would sink me, religion buoys me up;" "I have sailed most happily while on my watch, keeping the star, King Jesus, in view;" "my course is laid for the heavenly harbor;" "the Bible is my chart and compass;" "in storms and fogs I have sailed safely, while following the chart;" "I expected storms as well as fair weather when I went aboard for the voyage;"

"the old ship has never lost a true sailor overboard;" "poor steerage;" "going astern;" "in too shallow water;" "out of the course;" "sailing by false lights;" "meeting head-winds and back-flaws;" "slept off prayer, and was grounded—am on a new tack headed off shore for deep water;" "I saw the rocks and breakers ahead, and went about;" "our ship has a safe Captain;" "the dying brother was aked—how about that anchor? He answered—*she holds!* "—these are some of the phrases which are frequently heard in the covenant and conference meetings, and none can appreciate their force unless they are familiar with sailing. Occasionally a few are so happily combined, and filled with such ardent and sacred emotion as to make some of the refined and pet terms seem very tame. Such an utterance enforced by a corresponding character of its author, and this utterance instantly followed by a hearty *Amen* from the audience, have often produced more apparent good than an entire discourse of cold and dry speculations, or of word paintings.

This church insists upon having unwritten sermons. The present pastor, once questioned by a member as to the extent of the notes which he used in the pulpit, satisisfied the inquirer by saying, "my notes are about like your lobster buoys."

FREE-WILL BAPTIST CHURCH.

We are not able to give the precise date of the origin, or organization of this church. According to McClintoc's Cyclopædia there were no Free-Will Baptist churches in North America previous to 1780. A disinterested writer who gave an account of the churches of the Island in 1860, did not mention the date of the organization of this church, although he had free access to its records, and speaks of them as the "records in the hands of Mr. Allen, which I perused with care."

Rev. Enoch Rose, the principal originator of this church, was a member of the First Baptist church of New Shoreham until February, 1818. Not long after that date the Free-Will Baptist church originated, previous to which there had been but one church on the Island. Mr. Rose became the first pastor of the new church, and continued such until the year 1835.

Rev. Elijah R. Rose, was the second Free-Will pastor, and was ordained April 3, 1835, and continued his pastorate about ten years, during which the church joined the Rhode Island association of Free Baptist churches.

Rev. Ezekiel R. Littlefield, the third pastor, was ordained June 17, 1845, and continued as such only a few years.

Rev. Jacob Harvey, the fourth pastor, was ordained in June, 1849, and closed his pastorate in 1852. For some time thereafter the church was supplied by Rev. Wm. Taplin. For several years, previous to 1874, it was in a declining condition, weakened by division and want of a pastor. In 1860, Mr. Potter wrote: "I am informed that the attendance of the Free-Will Baptists on Sundays is small, and that the church has very much declined from its former prosperity."

Rev. George Wheeler, of Providence, was called to the pastorate of this church, Oct. 25, 1874. Its members then were fifty-four. His labors were blessed, in the winter of 1875–6, with a precious revival, in which he baptized forty-two. The church now numbers one hundred and twenty-four, and is in a peaceful, prosperous condition. Its house has been repaired, and refurnished, and its Sabbath-school is full of life and progress. Nothing is clearer than the good evidence that this church was fortunate in obtaining the services of its present pastor. Its first house of worship was built in 1853, and burned in 1863. ,

SEVENTH-DAY BAPTISTS.

Seventh-Day Advent Baptists, on Block Island, were self-organized into a worshiping body in April, 1864. Although not generally known as a church, having had no house of worship, there are devoted Christians among the few now remaining. There were about twenty-six of them in 1874.

23

THE INHABITANTS.

It is a difficult and delicate task to describe an individual, and much more so to give an accurate representation of a community. A gentleman once remarked, "Islanders are always peculiar." It was much easier for him to say this than to point out their peculiarities. For as Islands differ from each other in products, climate, and employment, so do their inhabitants. Their present characters are also modified by the original stock from which they have descended.

The Block Islanders are almost wholly descendants from genuine, primitive New Englanders. No other part of the United States, probably, has so light a sprinkling of foreign elements as has Block Island. Here, in a population of 1,147, one Portugee, one Irishman, one Swede, and a few English, *nine in all*, constitute the foreigners. 1,138 American born, out of 1,147. Of this number 1,032 were born on Block Island.

Physically, the men are uncommonly vigorous. With their industrious habits, healthy air, freedom from the anxieties of speculation, excessive strife for display, and the fears of want while fish traverse the ocean, they can hardly be otherwise than healthy, and of long life. By deducting from the population three-fifths as children we have left about six hundred and ninety adults. Sixty-one of these are between the ages of 60 and 70; thirty-six between 70 and 80; thirteen between 80 and 90; and of the six hundred and ninety adults, one hundred and ten are over sixty years old, or nearly one-sixth of the adults are of this age; and ninety-seven out of a hundred of the whole population are American born. The good health and vigor of the men are the result of good living as well as of a good climate. No tables are furnished with a healthier diet. If salt pork has been more common than in other places, an abundance of fresh fish has greatly prevented its evil consequences.

Intellectually, the men of Block Island are in advance of country towns on the main. Their frequent visits to ports along the coast from Portland to New York, and the longer voyages that some have taken to foreign countries, have given them a good practical knowledge of men and things which makes them persons of better judgments than many who are more extensive readers, and more highly refined. They know how to drive a good bargain as well as to steer a vessel, and they have the excellent faculty of keeping what they have gained. and of living within their means. A more independent community can hardly be found. Their courage, however, is mainly exhibited in battling with the sea, which requires all that can be cultivated. One writer has said of them: "They are a clanish race; think themselves as good as any others (in which they are quite right); their ambition is to obtain a good plain support from their own exertions, in which they are successful to a man; they are simple in their habits, and therefore command respect; they are honest, and neither need, nor support any jails; they are naturally intelligent." The Island has never had a lawyer for a citizen.

The women of Block Island, like mother Eve, seem to be made from the ribs of their husbands. The wives are true, genuine "help-meets," in every sense of the word. With no thoughts of menial inferiority, but with a consciousness of their legitimate sphere of coöperation. they respect themselves and "reverence their husbands." Not

one of them evinces the notion that she was made to be
an idler or to busy herself in devising ways and means to
spend the earnings of others. They are vigorous, industrious, virtuous, dignified, and genial. They are tidy, but
not gaudy; frank, but never simpering; if lacking in
refined education, this is compensated for by a large
supply of common sense and native genius. There has
never been a milliner's shop, nor a dress-maker's, nor a
tailor's on the Island, and although there are ladies here
able to keep three servants, these ladies can do their own
cooking and chamber-work, their own dress-making, and
keep their children well clothed by their own personal
efforts. Neither do they seem to feel any more degraded
by doing this than did Eve whose husband owned the
whole world. Another has well said of them: "The
women are healthy with bright eyes and clear complex-
ions, virtuous and true, and as yet without the pale of the
blandishments and corruptions of fashion." It is refreshing to find the women of an entire community so happy
in the enjoyment of true independence, and in coming so
near to filling the pattern: "In her tongue is the law of
kindness. She looketh well to the ways of her household, and eateth not the bread of idleness. Her children
arise up and call her blessed; her husband also, and he
praiseth her." A newspaper correspondent, who seems to
be a very competent judge, says: "The women are generally good-looking, with here and there a beauty." What
more can be said of the women of any locality? The
greatest numbers of the Island "beauties," are described
in the saying:

"Pretty is that pretty does."

CAPTAIN JAMES SANDS.

The Sands family is traceable back into English history
seven or eight centuries, and at various times some of that

name acted conspicuous parts in national affairs, especially in the reigns of Henry VII and Henry VIII. Sir
William Sands, at that time, had much to do in securing
the downfall of Cardinal Wolsey, and in sustaining
charges against Pope Clement the VII. The American
family of this name probably sprang from that of a Mr.
James Sands of Staffordshire, England, who died in 1670,
aged 140 years, and his wife lived to the age of 120.
Forty-eight years previous to his death the subject of this
sketch, Capt. James Sands, was born in Reading, England, and his father, Henry Sands, the first of the name
in New England, was admitted freeman of Boston in the
year 1640, thirty years before the death of the elder
James Sands. Thus we may infer, if not demonstrate.
the line of relationship between the English and American families of Sands.

Capt. James Sands, born in 1622, was a young man at
the time the noted Ann Hutchinson made so much disturbance among the good people of Massachusetts, who·
banished her from the colony on account of Antinomian
preaching. She went to East Chester, N. Y., there settled,
and employed Mr. Sands to build her a house, the following account of which is given by the Rev. Samuel Niles,
who was the grandson of Mr. Sands.

"In order to pursue her purpose she agreed with Captain James Sands, then a young man, to build her a
house, and he took a partner with him in the business.
When they had near spent their provisions, he sent his
partner for more which was to be fetched at a considerable distance. While his partner was gone there came a
company of Indians to the frame where he was at work,
and made a great shout, and sat down. After some time
they gathered up his tools, put his broad-ax on his
shoulder, and his other tools into his hands, and made
signs to him to go away. But he seemed to take no

23*

notice of them, but continued in his work.   At length
one of them said, *Ye-hah Mumuneketock*, the English of
which is, 'Come, let us go,' and they all went away to the
water-side for clams or oysters.   [They were near the
Hudson river.]   After some time they came back, and
found him still at work as before.   They again gathered
up his tools, put them into his hands as before they had
done, with the like signs moving him to go away.   He
still seemed to take no notice of them, but kept on his
business, and when they had stayed some time, they said
as before, *Ye-hah Mumuneketock*.   Accordingly they all
went away, and left him there at his work—a remarkable
instance of the restraining power of God on the hearts of
these furious and merciless infidels, who otherwise would
doubtless in their rage have split out his brains with his
own ax.   However, the Indians being gone, he gathered
up his tools and drew off, and in his way met his partner
bringing provisions, to whom he declared the narrow
escape he had made for his life.   Resolving not to return.
and run a further risk of the like kind, they both went
from the business."   Mrs. Hutchinson hired others to
finish her house.   Soon after she with her whole family,
sixteen in all, was murdered by the Indians.

It was in 1658 that Mr. Sands with his wife came from
England and landed at Plymouth, and soon after this he
undertook the building of the house for Mrs. Hutchinson.

A short time after his return from that undertaking to
Massachusetts, he became identified with the enterprise of
settling Block Island, three years after his arrival from
England.   In what year he came to the Island we are not
certain, for his name does not appear among the sixteen
who came here in April, 1661, nor is it in the list of those
who met August 17, 1660, at the house of Dr. John
Alcock of Roxbury to buy the Island; and yet, in the
memorandum of the survey, his name is mentioned, and

also the numbers of the lots that constituted his sixteenth part of the Island. This is sufficient to identify him with the first purchasers and settlers thereof. His lots were numbered 12, and 14, and 15, the latter two owned by him and John Glover. He came from Taunton to the Island, and was soon distinguished as a prominent citizen.

In March, 1664, the General Assembly of Rhode Island notified the inhabitants of Block Island that they were under the care of the Rhode Island government, and at the same time informed James Sands, then a freeman of Rhode Island, to come "in to the Governor or deputy Governor, to take his engagement as Constable or Conservator of the peace there."

In May, 1664, Mr. Sands with Mr. Joseph Kent, presented to the General Assembly of Rhode Island, a petition in behalf of the Islanders that Joseph Kent, Thomas Terry, Peter George, Simon Ray, William Harris, Samuel Dearing, John Rathbone, John Davies, Samuel Staples, Hugh Williams, Robert Guthrig. William Tosh, Tollman Rose, William Carboone, Tristrome Dodge, John Clark, and William Barker might be admitted as freemen of the Colony of Rhode Island. The Assembly referred the petition to a committee consisting of Roger Williams, Thomas Olney, and Joseph Torrey, who reported favorably upon all the above names except Hugh Williams. against whom was a rumor of his having said some words reproachful of the colony. After further examination as to his loyalty, however, he was admitted freeman. Mr. Sands had been previously admitted, and he is probably the James Sands mentioned as a freeman in 1655, and as a representative of the General Court of Commissioners, held at Newport, May the 19th, 1657. (Col. Rec., I, p. 300, 355.) Capt. James Sands, with Thomas Terry, was the first representative from Block Island to sit in the General Court of Commissioners of Rhode Island, admitted

such in 1665. In 1672, he was foremost in presenting
the petition to have the Island incorporated under the
name of New Shoreham, and the General Assembly
granted the request, but in so doing preserved the old
name *Block Island*, the chartered name being "New
Shoreham, otherwise Block Island."

He understood the carpenter's trade, as is evident from
what has been said of his undertaking to build a house
for Ann Hutchinson. This knowledge helped him in
erecting his own house on Block Island. He located it a
few feet east of the house now occupied by Mr. Almanzo
Littlefield, close to the mill and bridge on the road from
the Harbor to the Center, or Baptist church. He built it
of stone, and Rev. Samuel Niles, his grandson, frequently
speaks of it in his history of the Indian and French
Wars. Our evidence of its location is circumstantial, but
conclusive.

There is not an individual on the Island, besides the
writer, probably, who can say with any degree of certainty
where the "garrisoned" house stood.

Mr. Sands was brave, humane, and a devoted Christian
as well as an enterprising citizen. There was difference
of opinion between him and his grandson, Mr. Niles, to
preclude the suspicion that might arise in the minds of
some that the latter overpraised the former. Moreover,
the latter wrote at too advanced an age to be prejudiced,
or biased from the truth by personal considerations. Mr.
Sands' courage is seen in the following extract concerning
the Indians here and the few settlers: "The English,
fearing what might be their [the Indians'] design, as they
were drinking, dancing, and reveling after their usual
customs at such times, * * went to parley with them,
and to know what their intentions were. James Sands,
who was the leading man among them, entered into a
wigwam where he saw a very fine brass gun standing, and

an Indian fellow lying on a bench in the wigwam, probably to guard and keep it. Mr. Sands' curiosity led him to take and view it, as it made a curious and uncommon appearance. Upon which the Indian fellow rises up hastily and snatches the gun out of his hand, and withal gave him such a violent thrust with the butt end of it as occasioned him to stagger backward. But feeling something under his feet, he espied it to be a hoe, which he took up and improved, and with it fell upon the Indian."

In another connection Mr. Niles says of him: "He was a benefactor to the poor: for as his house was garrisoned, in the time of their fears of the Indians, many poor people resorted to it, and were supported mostly from his liberality. He also was a promoter of religion in his benefactions to the minister they had there in his day, though not altogether so agreeable to him as might be desired, as being inclined to the Anabaptist persuasion. He devoted his house for the worship of God, where it was attended every Lord's day or Sabbath."

"*Anabaptist*" was then a term used to designate such as are now called Baptists, and Mr. Sands' powerful influence did much to establish Baptist sentiments on the Island.

That he was an enterprising citizen is evident from the simple statement: "Mr. Sands had a plentiful estate, and gave free entertainment to all gentlemen that came to the Island." To this it is added: "When his house was garrisoned it became a hospital, for several poor people resorted thither."

Such are the facts that furnish the outlines of one of the noblest characters of New England. An intimate friend of Roger Williams, the first freeman on the Island, the first representative from it in the Rhode Island Assembly, the one who procured the citizenships to the Islanders as freemen and presented to the State the petition for the chartered rights of a township; making his house the hospitable home of visitors from abroad, the garrison, and the place of worship for the Islanders, and a hospital for the poor and suffering. "He died in the 72d year of his age," (Niles) and instead of the humble slab, from which the letters and figures are so worn by time, in the Block Island cemetery, lying over his grave, there should be erected a monument more expressive of his great excellences. His simple epitaph reads:

HRE LYES INTVRRED THE
BODY OF MR JAMES SANDS SENIOVR
AGED 73 YEARS WHO DEPARTED THIS
LIFE MARCH 13 A. D. 1695.

He represented Block Island in the Rhode Island General Assembly in the years 1678, 1680, and 1690. His descendants are very numerous, and some of them distinguished. Three of his four sons, during the French privateering on the Island removed to Cow Neck, now Sands Point, on Long Island. At the same time they retained their farms and cattle on Block Island, to which they annually returned in the summer. Their kinsman and intimate acquaintance, Rev. Samuel Niles, says of them: "Captain John Sands, Mr. James, and Samuel Sands, each of them leaving a farm at Block Island, which they stocked with sheep, were wont to come once a year at their shearing-time on the Island, to carry off their wool and what fat sheep there were at that time and market at New York." One of them, it seems, returned to remain permanently after the French had ceased their depredations, and of him we give the following items.

HIS DESCENDANTS.

CAPT. JOHN SANDS.

Mr. Niles describes him as "a gentleman of great port and superior powers," as the eldest son, and successor of his father, the original settler of Block Island. He was admitted freeman here in 1709, and in the years 1713 and 1714 was representative of the Island in the Rhode Island General Assembly. His brothers, James and Samuel, removed to Cow Neck, now Sands Point, Long Island, and there remained permanently, while the youngest of the four brothers continued with his father on Block Island. His. name was EDWARD, was born in 1672, admitted freeman in 1696, died in 1715, aged forty-three years. He probably left a child bearing his name, for another

EDWARD SANDS

Came upon the stage of public life in 1734, being then admitted freeman from Block Island. He was its representative in the General Assembly from the year 1740 to the year 1760. In the meantime he had a son born who was named

EDWARD SANDS, JR.

Of him we have a brief record in a ponderous old tome now in the possession of Mr. Simon Ray Sands of Block Island. It is an immense quarto, heavily bound in boards, richly ornamented with heavy corner pieces and clasps of brass, printed in 1715, the year the senior Edward died, and by him was presented to the younger Edward. Its title is "The Book of Common Prayer, and Psalter." It is carefully kept as a precious heir-loom, and has been visited by persons of distinction in latter years. In it is the following record of the subject of this sketch: "Edward Sands Born ye 2 Day of April A. D. 1748. Also: "Edward Sands, Jr. was Married to Deborah Niles and eldest Daughter of Paul Niles, Esq. the 14th Day of December 1769 by John Littlefield, Warden."

During the stormy time of the Revolution he was well known by his patriotism, and in 1774 was appointed by his townsmen on the committee of resistance to the English tea-tax in favor of the East India Company. In 1776, he with others protested against the bill passed by the Assembly of Rhode Island for the establishment of small-pox hospitals in the various towns. In the same year he was appointed by the Rhode Island Assembly to take the census of Block Island, and by a special act was allowed to carry on trade with the colony. By the same authority in 1777, he was "surgeon of the regiment of artillery;" in 1779, by an act of the Assembly, was permitted to return to the Island, showing the vigilance kept upon all movements in those times of military rule; and in 1785, represented his town in the General Assembly.

RAY SANDS.

Of him, in the old book above described, is this record: "Ray Sands, Borne January ye Fifth at Eleven o'Clock in the Morning, A. D. 1736." He was a cotemporary of Edward, Jr., and was a man of great energy and influence. Made a freeman in 1759, at the early age of twenty-four, he began his public career as representative in the Rhode Island Assembly, in 1761, and held it also in 1767. At the time post-offices were first established in Rhode Island, Mr. Ray Sands was appointed post-master at Tower Hill, in 1775. When the muster-rolls were filling up for the Revolution, Ray Sands, by both Houses of the Rhode Island Legislature, was appointed captain of a military company of South Kingstown. In 1776, his was the third company of that town. During that year he was appointed to the office of Major, and before its close was promoted to that of Colonel, and was brought into active service, as seen by the following act: "It is voted and resolved, that Col. Joseph Noyes and Col. Ray Sands be directed forthwith to accompany the troops of horse stationed at Boston Neck and Point Judith; and that they procure convenient quarters for said troops as nigh said places as possible." In 1776, his regiment captured a ferry-boat from the enemy near "North Ferry." In 1777 it was discovered that he had received his colonelcy by an error of entry by the Clerk of the Assembly, whereas it should have been lieutenant-colonel. The mistake was rectified to his honor, as he continued none the less patri-otic, and received a vote of thanks from the General Assembly, "for his vigilant and spirited conduct as colo-nel." After a considerable time had elapsed since he left Block Island, and as he had a farm here, an act was passed, subject to Major-General Gates, then commanding the United States forces in Rhode Island, permitting him to return again to the scenes of his childhood. Mean-time he made South Kingston his home, as we learn from the following act of 1783, viz.: "It is voted and resolved that the said Ray Sands have liberty to go upon the said Island and bring off his negroes, household furniture and provisions, with any other articles of the produce or growth of the said Island; provided that he go from the port of Newport, under the inspection of the intendant of trade there, and upon his return enter in the said intendant's office all the articles he shall bring, taking care that no British goods or prohibited articles be brought in his boat, under penalty of forfeiture of his said boat, and all the articles therein, and being also liable to a pros-ecution therefor." In the same year of this removal his townsmen and kindred on the Island chose him, an inhab-itant of South Kingston, to represent them in the Gene-ral Assembly, which soon after made this record: "It is therefore voted and resolved, that the choice of the said

24

Ray Sands as aforesaid, be, and the same is hereby approved." In 1787, he was also representative from Block Island, and according to the family record, in the old book, died March 11, 1820, aged eighty-four years.

JOHN SANDS.

Cotemporary with the above Col. Ray Sands was a relative by the name of John who was also distinguished as a prominent citizen. His town made him representative in 1773. In the same year he was active in efforts to secure a harbor for Block Island, to which allusion is made under the head "The Harbor." In 1774, he was appointed by the colony to take the census of the Island, and was also, in 1774, on the committee of resistance to the tea-tax. In 1775 he was chosen captain of a company of which Samuel Rathbone, Jr., was lieutenant, and Wm. Littlefield, ensign. That year he was authorized "to take an account of the powder, arms, and ammunition" of Block ˙Island. That year was distinguished by the removal of goods from the Island to the main-land by military authority to prevent them from falling into the hands of the English. Mr. Sands parted with 105 sheep for £32 2s. 6d., and "169 store sheep and lambs" for £42 5s. 0d. In 1776 he, as captain, was in command of the Block Island company of militia to serve in the Revolution, with Simon Littlefield for lieutenant, and John Pain for ensign. That year he, with Joshua Sands and William Littlefield was authorized by the Rhode Island Assembly and "appointed a committee to determine what number of neat cattle and sheep" should "be left upon said Block Island for the necessary use of the inhabitants." He had then state license to carry on trade with the colony on the main-land. In 1777, Adjutant Stelle, who came to the Island in the sloop Diamond, "to manage an exchange of prisoners" with England, boarded at the house of Capt. John Sands, as did also the. prisoners, for which he was allowed by the Government £12 14s. 08d. In 1783, he was representative in the Rhode Island Legis-lature, and by that body was appointed to take possession of the confiscated estate of one Ackurs Sisson on Block Island. In 1790, he was also representative in the state councils.

Mr. John Sands was chairman of the town meeting of Block Island, August 14, 1779, when that extraordinary document was adopted, of which he was probably the author, in which the citizens assumed rights so far tran-scending the charters of England and the colony to said Island as virtually to erect it into a self-constituted, inde-pendent democracy, wielding the power of life and death. He was the great man of the Island during the Revolu-tion.

Joshua Sands was in active life in 1774, and was one of the anti-tea-tax committee in that year.

Robert Sands, son of Col. Ray Sands of South Kings-ton, in 1781, in reply to a petition presented to the Assem-bly "that his father is possessed of a large real estate on Block Island, which he has committed to his care," was "permitted to go upon the said Island, under the inspection of Gideon Hoxie, Esq." to which was added, to show the rigor of the times, "that he do not return without the order of this Assembly."

Mrs. Lucy Sands, in 1779, by permission of the Gene-ral Assembly and Major Gen. Gates, visited her family on Block Island.

But we must draw to a close this imperfect sketch of the Sands family of Block Island whose public spirit, patriotism, wealth, and high tone would be an honor to any part of the world. Their descendants have made a record in America, in the various professions and walks of life, that will compare favorably with their ancient

English record dating back to 1041. But few, however, are now upon Block Island. Those in the direct line from James Sands, the first settler here, now living upon the Island are Mr. Simon Ray Sands, his brother Edward Sands, Dea. Robert Treadwell Sands and his brother Wm. C. Sands, who are highly esteemed, and well-to-do citizens.

The first-named, commonly called "Col. Sands," as well as the others, bears much of the air and high tone of his ancestors. He was Representative in the Rhode Island Legislature eight years, 1840–1848, five years in the Senate, and three years in the House. His father's name was William Pitt Sands, whose father's name was Edward Sands, Jr., whose father was Edward Sands, whose father was Capt. James Sands, the first settler.

The present Col. Sands had two grandfathers of the name of Sands who were brothers, viz., John Sands, and Edward Sands, Jr. John's daughter, Catharine, married Edward's son Wm. Pitt, the father of Col. Simon Ray Sands.

Mr. Nathaniel Sands, who formerly owned the real estate where the Adrian House is now located, is still remembered with esteem by many of the Islanders. He removed to East Greenwich, Rhode Island, where he died. His widow and daughter there still survive.

MRS. SARAH SANDS.

This lady had virtues and culture which entitle her to more than a passing notice. Although at this distant day we can give but a few outlines of her character, yet these may indicate to some the beauty of the portrait had it been properly delineated in due season. There is also incidental, collateral information obtained from the biographical fragments of her now presented. In speaking of Captain James Sands, one of the first settlers, his grandson, Rev. Samuel Niles, says:

" His wife was a gentlewoman of remarkable sobriety and piety, given also to hospitality. She was the only midwife and doctress on the Island, or rather a doctor, all her days, with very little, and with some and mostly, no reward at all. Her skill in surgery was doubtless very great, from some instances I remember she told me of. One was the cure of an Indian, that under disgust, as was said, he had taken at his wife or squaw, shot himself. putting the muzzle of his gun to the pit of his stomach, and pushing the trigger. The bullet went through him, out and opposite at his back. He instantly fell, and one of the spectators who happened to be in the field at the time, and heard the report of the gun, told me, after he was fallen and wallowing in the blood, he saw the blood and froth issue out of his back and breast as often as he drew his breath. He was perfectly healed, and lived a hearty, strong man even to old age ; whom I afterward knew, and often saw the scar at the pit of his stomach, as large or larger in circumference than our ordinary dollars passing among us."

"Another signal cure she told me God made her an instrument of making, was on a young woman that was struck with lightning through her shoulder, so that when she administered to her by syringing, the liquid matter would fly through from the fore part to the hinder, and from the hinder part to the foremost, having a free and open passage both ways, yet was cured, and had several children, and lived to old age. I also knew her long before her death. She had also skill, and cured the bites and venomous poison of rattlesnakes."

Her husband, in his last will, made her the sole executrix of his estate which, after his death, was inventoried as follows:

24*

James Sands' Estate, March 13, 1694:

"About 400 acres of land.

Fifty-six head of cattle, small and great:

Three horses—mare, colt, one horse:

Thirty swine, old and young:

About 300 sheep:

A Negro woman—house and barn, and mill.

Sundry household goods not appraised."

Mr. Sands died in March, 1695, and in March, 1699, Mrs. Sarah Sands, his widow, had a lawful record made of the following emancipation of her slaves:

"Know all men by these presents that I, Sarah Sands, of Block Island, *alias* New Shoreham, in the Colony of Rhode Island, Providence Plantations, in New England. Wife to Mr. James Sands, of Block Island, and made sole executrix by my said husband, James Sands, at his death, and having three Negro children born under my roof and in my custody, being left to my disposing by my above said husband:

"Know ye therefore that I, the above Sarah Sands, do hereby and voluntarily give and bestow of them as fol-loweth, that is to say:

"First: I give to my granddaughter, Sarah Sands, daughter to my son, Edward Sands, one of the Negro girls named Hannah: The other Negro girl I give and bequeath unto my granddaughter, Catharine Niles, daugh-ter to my son-in-law, Nathaniel Niles, of Point Judith in the colony above said—the two Negro girls I freely and voluntarily give to my two grandchildren above named until the said Negroes come to the age of thirty years, and then I do by these presents declare that they shall be free from any service, and be at their own disposal—the Negro girl given to my granddaughter, Catharine Niles, is named Sarah.   The other negro above said being a boy named *Mingo*, I freely give and bequeath to my grandson, Sands Raymond, son to my son-in-law, Joshua Raymond, of Block Island above named, which I give freely until that he the said Negro boy comes to the age of thirty-three years, and then to be free and his own man and at his own disposal forever after that he shall arrive to the age of 33 years; for I Sarah Sands do by these presents freely declare that I have made a promise that no child whatsoever born under my service and care shall be made a slave of any longer than is above specified, and for the confirmation and ratification of this my free and voluntary act, I have under set my hand, and affixed my seal this ninth day of March, in the year of our Lord one thousand six hundred and ninety-nine."

Signed in presence of

SAMUEL NILES. SARAH SANDS.

Two years and a half passed away and Mrs. Sands, conscious of her approaching end, in her last will, left a preamble to it that speaks well for her character, revealing a faith which was her brightest ornament through her long and eventful life mostly spent among her fellow-Islanders, many of whom she had seen in their barbarous state, and all of whom, with her devoted companion, she had labored to improve both socially and religiously.

HER WILL.

"In the name of God, Amen. I Sarah Sands of Block Island, *alias* New Shoreham, in the colony of Rhode Island, and Providence Plantations, in New England, being aged and weak in body, but of sound and perfect memory—Praise be given to Almighty God for the same—and knowing the uncertainty of this life on earth, and being desirous to see that things in order be done before my death, Do make this my last will and Testament in manner and form following :

"I being wife to Mr. James Sands deceased, and made sole executrix by my said husband, as by will bearing date June the 18th, 1694, may plainly appear, That is to say, First, and Principally; I commend my soul to Almighty God my Creator, assuredly believing that I shall receive full pardon and free remission of all my sins, and be saved by the precious death and merits of my blessed Saviour and Redeemer Christ Jesus; and my body to the earth from whence it was first taken, to be buried in such decent and Christian manner as to my executor hereafter named shall be thought most meet and convenient: And as touching such worldly estate as the Lord in mercy hath lent me, my will and meaning in the same shall be implied. . . .

[Things specified for each.] That they shall be equally divided amongst my five children, viz.: John Sands, James Sands, Samuel Sands, Sarah Niles, and Mercy Raymond. . . . . .

Signed in presence of   SARAH SANDS.
　　　Samuel Niles, and
　　　Hannah Rose, Oct. 17th, 1703."

In Sept., 1704, she gave her negro woman to her grandson, Rev. Samuel Niles, to be kept by him ten years, at the expiration of which time she was to be free for ever thereafter.

MR. SANDS' STONE HOUSE, AND THE SANDS' GARRISON.

Their location is established, in the writer's mind beyond a doubt, by the following circumstantial evidence, to have been nearly where Mr. Almanzo Littlefield's residence is now standing.

THE HOUSE.

That Captain James Sands had a stone house, used as a garrison and hospital, in times of necessity, is admitted, and shown by Mr. Niles' History.

1.   His sixteenth of the Island—nearly all of it, as seen in the original plat, a copy of which is in the possession of Col. S. Ray Sands, embraces the house lot, and mill-pond now owned by Mr. A. Littlefield.

2.   Rev. Mr. Niles, grandson of Capt. J. Sands, lived some years with his grandparents in the stone house, and he says the mill-pond was "near the house." He speaks of that pond as having a "flume."

3.   He says that house was "*not far from the Harbor*," which then was the "Old Pier."

4.   The house was within *musket shot* of a French privateer lying at the Pier. After the French had plundered it and returned to their vessel they "*fired many guns at the house*," says Mr. Niles, and adds: "I heard several bullets whistling over my head."

5.   When the French took the stone house they "set up their standard on a hill *on the back side of it*" [the *house*]. After it had stood there some hours an English vessel hove in sight, which "put the Frenchmen into a great surprise," whereupon:

6.   They were seen "running up to their standard on the hill, then down again, and others doing the like."

7.   Mr. Niles, when the French landed, was "in fair sight of the house," and at the same time "saw them coming from the water-side," while just behind him was a "*large swamp*."

8.   The outlines of *a cellar still visible* between the present old water-mill and Mr. Almanzo Littlefield's house, and he states that part of a cellar-wall is there covered up.

9.   No other mill-pond on the Island could have had a "flume," and a flume implies the presence of a mill.

10.   The mill-pond now there *has been there from the most ancient traditions.*

11.   Mrs. Sarah Sands, widow of the above James Sands, in her will transmitted to her son the "mill," and the "mill" was in the inventory of her husband's estate soon after his death.

12.   The stone house of Mr. Sands was "garrisoned." This implies the presence of a body of soldiers.

13.   That garrison existed when the men of the Island were only "*sixteen and a boy.*"

14.   The mill-pond and mill were near the house and garrison when Mrs. Sands had "but *one little child*, a girl, just able to run about and prattle a little" when she was drowned in said mill-pond.

15.   Said garrison was established in the time of "*Philip's War*," as a protection against the Block Island *Indians.*

16.   The *earth work* of an ancient garrison that commanded said stone house on *three sides, is now seen*, directly east of the spot where said house stood, and within pistol-shot of it, with a sharp hill back of it or east of it, and adjacent from which the whole region around was visible to a sentinel.

17.   The "upland in a great swamp" to which Mr. Niles fled the first time the French came to Mr. Sands' house, was a convenient place of concealment, lying a short distance northwest of the location of said house. The upland and swamp remain, and are easily pointed out, lying a little distance west of Erastus Rose's house.

SIMON RAY.

It is much to be regretted that we have so little information of this good man.   From what we have, however, it will be seen that he devoted his fortune, his talents, and even his life to the welfare of Block Island. His father, Simon Ray, came from England, and died in 1641, leaving a large estate in Braintree, Mass., and hence the younger Simon had ample means to pay for his sixteenth part of the Island, to move here in comfortable circumstances, and also to assist others in its settlement.

He was born in 1635. Six years after, his father, Simon Ray, Sen., died. Nineteen years after said death, the son, at the age of twenty-five, met his fellow-townsmen, "Thomas Faxun, Peter George, Thomas Terry, Richard Ellis, Samuel Dering, all of Braintree," at the house of "Mr. John Alcock, Physician, in the town of Roxbury, in the colony of Massachusetts," "August the seventeenth, 1660, then and there to confer about" the settlement of Block Island. At that meeting Mr. Ray not only pledged himself to pay a sixteenth of the purchase-money for the Island, and to bear his proportionate part of the expense of moving the colony of sixteen families there, but he also with Mr. Samuel Dering, for the greater convenience of transporting the passengers," built a shallop upon their own cost and charge for the promoting and settling of said Island." At Braintree, in April, 1661, he, with his fifteen colleagues embarked, in said shallop, for Taunton, and thence came to Block Island. Here, for seventy-seven years, he witnessed the vicissitudes of the Islanders with an interest that may well be regarded as paternal. It is a pity that he kept no more of a record of his experience for the benefit of posterity.

Mr. Ray seems to have been a man of great physical endurance, of an even temper and mild disposition, of sound judgment, kind feelings for all classes, even the Indians, and of deep religious convictions, manifested in works of faith and charity. In September, 1704, at the age of sixty-nine, he left us the following index of his character, at a time when the inhabitants of New England probably hated no other objects in existence so much as they did the Indians. Mr. Edward Ball was the " crowner," or the king's attorney or sheriff, on the Island, and is therefore mentioned first, as a mark of respect, in the following address:

" To Mr. Edward Ball, and the rest of the town council: Whereof, Penewess the late sachem being dead to whom the land reserved for him belonged, and now belongeth to his countrymen whereof Ninicraft being willing for to assist them in the putting of the land to rent so as for to be at a certainty of receiving rent yearly' for it, I pray you let there be no bar nor hindrance towards that proceeding, but rather be helpful to them in the matter, for it is fit that they should make the best improvement they can of what belongs to them; which is all I have to trouble you with at present, remaining yours to serve in any thing that I am capable.

SIMON RAY, Warden."

His recommendation was adopted by the town, October 6, 1704. By it we learn that the Indians were allowed to hold land on the Island, to collect rent for the same, and that instead of confiscating to themselves the land left unclaimed after the petty sachem's death, the Islanders humanely put in practice the kind feelings of their chief warden. Ninicraft, then, was the chief of the Narragansetts, and of the Block Island Indians.

The old records of the Island show plainly that Mr. Ray was ever watchful and laborious for the welfare of his townsmen pecuniarily, socially, and religiously. While others fled to escape from invading pirates and French privateers he firmly and patiently submitted to the worst that might come. As evidence of this the following incident is here given: " When the French came into the house they found only the old gentleman and his wife;

all the rest of the family were fled. The French demanded his money. He told them he had none at his
command. They, observing by the signs on the floor,
that chests and other things were lately removed, and the
money, which they principally aimed at, asked him where
they were. He told them he did not know, for his people had carried them out, and he could not tell where
they put them. They bid him call his folks, that they
might bring them again; which he did, but had no answer,
for they were all fled out of hearing. They being thus
disappointed, one of them, in a violent rage, got a piece
of a rail, and struck him on his head therewith, and in
such fury that the blood instantly gushed out and ran on
the floor. Upon which his wife took courage, and sharply
reprehended them for killing her husband, which she
then supposed they had done. Upon which they went off
without the game they expected., After the flow of blood
was over, he recovered his health, and lived many years
in his former religious usefulness." (Niles.)

That he was a man of great religious influence upon
the Islanders is evident from the above writer, Rev. Samuel Niles, an intimate acquaintance and admirer of Mr.
Ray. He says: "He and his son, who was of the same
name, and after bore the like distinguishing characters of
honor and usefulness that his father had done before who
is now lately deceased, as there was no minister in the
place, were wont, in succession, in a truly Christian, laudable manner, to keep a meeting in their own house on
Lord's days, to pray, sing a suitable portion of the Psalms,
and read in good sermon books, and, as they found occasion, to let drop some words of exhortation in a religious
manner on such as attended their meeting." Thus, here
on this little "isle of the sea," beyond the sound of any
church-going bell, without permit by imposition of human
hands, but in accordance with a higher commission, the

25

chief warden of the Island, by preaching and practice inculcated or planted the seeds of piety which in after generations have borne most ample harvests.

His residence was on the west side of the Island, but a short distance northerly from the house now owned and occupied by Mr. Raymond Dickens, whose house is built in part of the one anciently occupied by Mr. Ray. His dwelling was unpretentious, and his home had an air much less popular than the more stately mansion of the more public and enterprising Capt. James Sands. At Mr. Ray's house a part of the unfortunate inmates of the Palatine were cared for while their diseased and emaciated bodies lingered in life. From his house they were borne to their last resting place, a hillock about seventy-five rods southeast from the hospitable home of Mr. Ray.

What more perfect pattern of a good citizen can be drawn than we find in the life and character of Simon Ray, of Block Island? From the age of twenty-five to that of nearly one hundred and two we see his fortune, his time, and talents devoted to the temporal and spiritual interests of his fellow townsmen. He penned the preamble and resolution to which he called their attention, in his eighty-fifth year, for the preservation of the forest timber, then becoming scarce on the Island. There is evidence also that his hand drew up that first call of the Island to a minister of the gospel—a copy of which call we have given in another place. In harmony with the outlines of his character in the foregoing statements, are the facts inscribed upon his humble monument by those who knew him well. A gray stone slab lying over his grave in the highest part of the Block Island cemetery contains these words: "This monument is erected to the memory of Simon Ray, Esq., one of the original proprietors of this Island. He was largely concerned in settling the Township, and was one of the chief magistrates, and

such was his benevolence that besides the care he took of
their civil interests, he frequently instructed them in the
more important concerns of our Holy religion.

"He was deprived of his eyesight many years, cheerfully submitting to the will of God. His life being in
this a living instance, as in all others, of a lovely example
of Christian virtue."

For many years. probably on account of his blindness,
the town meetings were held at his house, though remote
from most of the other houses, and such was the venera-
tion of the people for him that they continued to elect
him as chief warden almost continuously for about half
a century, and for about thirty years he was their representative in the Rhode Island General Assembly. His
name is still a common household word, even where all
knowledge of him has faded away, and "Ray" seems to
be destined to continue here as long as names for infants
shall be needed. The outlines of his cellar, and the deep
old well still mark the place of his dwelling. His blood
relatives, however, are nearly, if not entirely, extinct from
the Island.

Simon Ray, Jr., succeeded his father in local offices,
and in distinction for personal excellences. His daughters were greatly admired, and married eminent persons;
his estate was large, and he is entitled to an honorable
remembrance. His son-in-law, Samuel Ward, known as
Gov. Ward, of Revolutionary fame, was Mr. Ray's ad-
ministrator. After his death the following inventory of
a part of his "movable estate" was recorded in 1757:

"24 Cows, [probably old tenor] .	£1246
4 Oxen,	340
4 Heifers,	225
1 pr. of Steers, .	116
10 2-year olds, .	540
14 Cattle 1 year old.	110

200 Sheep,	.	.	. £900
10 Hogs,	.		72
2 Chains and 2 yokes,	.	.	8
1 Plough,	.		6
1 pair shod wheels,	.	.	. 12
Dick's time for 10½ months,		.	. 100

THOMAS DICKENS, }
ABEL FRANKLIN, } Appraisers."

The following letter from the Hon. William Greene, Ex-Lieut. Gov. of Rhode Island, of East Greenwich, is here inserted with great pleasure, and will doubtless be read with much interest.

EX-LIEUT. GOV. GREENE'S LETTER.

"EAST GREENWICH, Nov. 8th, 1876.

"REV. S. T. LIVERMORE.

"*Dear Sir:*—A painful attack of rheumatism prevented my sending you the enclosed paper last week, as promised. I have compiled it from family records in my possession and believe it to be correct. I am the grandson of Catharine, daughter of Simon Ray, Jun', whose widow —a granddaughter of Roger Williams—died in this house, and was buried in my grandfather's family burial ground, from which her remains have never been removed.

"In April, A. D. 1661, Simon Ray, with fifteen others, emigrated to Block Island. At his suggestion the property was divided into seventeen parts, and one was set apart for the support of the gospel. He was an excellent and highly useful man. The records of the Island bear ample testimony to his activity and importance in its settlement, and show him to be chief and leader of the company. His life was prolonged far beyond the usual span, and it was not until he was nearly ninety years of age that he ceased to hold the principal office in the community to which he had for sixty years been a father.

Meantime he had reared a son to fill his place; and in outward darkness—for he had become blind—he waited for long years for his summons home. Ten years before his death he made his will, in which he gave freedom to his negroes, for the respect he held for them, they having been brought up with him from their infancy; giving them also whatever they had been able to produce for themselves by their own labor during his life.

"Some of the ancient records of Block Island are apparently in the handwriting of Simon Ray, or Raye, as his name was sometimes spelled. He died in March, 1737, in the one hundred and second year of his age. He was buried in the cemetery on the Island, and a monument, now almost illegible, was erected over his grave. He left four children, viz.: Sybil, Mary, Dorothy, Simon.

SIMON RAY, JR.

"Simon Ray, Jr., or Captain Simon Ray, as he was commonly called, was born April 9, 1672, and was a worthy assistant and successor of his father, though he attained not the same great age. He passed the allotted term of three score years and ten, and filled with credit to himself, and usefulness to others, the most important offices in his native Island. He was twice married, and outlived his father only eighteen years, dying at the age of eighty-six years. He, too, sleeps in the rough sea Isle where he first saw the light, dying on the 19th of March, 1755. His name stands on the book of records, at first, Simon Raye. or afterwards, Simon Ray the second.

" His children were, Judith Ray, born October 4, 1726; Anna Ray, born September 27, 1728; Catharine Ray, born July 10, 1731; and Phebe Ray, born September 10, 1733. Judith married Thomas Hubbard of Boston; Anna married Governor Samuel Ward of Rhode Island; Catharine married Governor William Greene of Rhode Island;

25*

and Phebe married William Littlefield of Block Island. Catharine, daughter of Phebe and William Littlefield, was early left an orphan, and was adopted by her aunt Catharine, wife of Gov. Wm. Greene; and while a resident in that family, was married to Major-General Nathaniel Greene of the Revolution. After the death of Gen. Greene she married Phineas Miller and resided in Georgia until her death.

Very respectfully,

W. GREENE."

CATHARINE RAY.

In reference to the last-named lady, and native of Block Island, the following extract from the Life of Major-General Nathaniel Greene, written by George Washington Greene, is here added.   He says of her:

"The maiden's name was Catharine Littlefield, and she was a niece of the Governor's wife, the Catharine Ray of Franklin's letters.   The courtship sped swiftly and smoothly, and more than once in the course of it he followed her to Block Island, where, as long after her sister told me, the time passed gleefully in merry-makings, of which dancing always formed a principal part.   She was an intimate acquaintance of General Washington's wife, Martha, meeting her many times at Army Headquarters, whenever the army rested long enough to permit the officers' wives to join them.   An intimacy sprang up between her and Mrs. Washington which, like that between their husbands, ripened into friendship, and continued unimpaired through life.   His first child, still in the cradle, was named ,George Washington, and the second, who was born the ensuing year, Martha Washington."

As the daughter of the honored Simon Ray, Jr's, daughter Phebe, as the wife of the famous General Greene,

and as an intimate friend of the wife of Washington, she
has reflected honor upon the little Island of her childhood and ancestors. Her aunt Catharine has an equal
claim upon the kind remembrance of the Islanders.

FRANKLIN'S CORRESPONDENCE.

Catharine Ray, mentioned in the above extract from the
Life of General Greene, was the granddaughter of the
venerable Simon Ray, and the third daughter of Hon.
Simon Ray, Jr. She was born on Block Island, July 10
1731, and married Governor William Greene, famous for
a long period as the chief magistrate of Rhode Island.
She was also much admired by Dr. Franklin, who wrote
some pleasant things to her, and about her; and she cor-
responded freely with Mrs. Franklin. This friendship
between the Doctor and the Block Island maiden was
strengthened by the pleasantry that originated from the
gift which she made him of some cheese from her father's
farm, concerning which the distinguished philosopher and
statesman wrote:

"Mrs. Franklin was very proud that a young lady
should have so much regard for her old husband as to
send him such a present. We talk of you every time it
comes to the table. She is sure you are a sensible girl,
and a notable housewife, and talks of bequeathing me to
you as a legacy; but I ought to wish you a better, and
hope she will live these hundred years; for we are grown
old together, and if she has any faults, I am so used to
them that I don't perceive them. As the song says:

> " Some faults we have all, and so has my Joan,
> But then, they are exceptingly small;
> And now I'm grown used to them, so like my own,
> I scarcely can see them at all."

"Indeed, I begin to think she has none, as I think of
you. And since she is willing I should love you as much

as you are willing to be loved by me, let us join in wishing the old lady a long life and a happy, etc."

Subsequent to this Dr. Franklin wrote to his wife in a more serious tone concerning his young friend on Block Island, dating his letter, London, Dec. 3, 1757, and saying: "I am glad that Miss Ray is well, and that you correspond. It is not convenient to be forward in giving advice in such cases. She has prudence enough to judge and act for the best."

In January. 1763, the Doctor wrote to her from Philadelphia, saying: "Mrs. Franklin admits your apology for dropping the correspondence with her, and allows your reasons to be good; but hopes when you have more leisure it may be resumed."

It is also complimentary to Block Island that Mr. John Bigelow, one of Franklin's biographers, says of one of its daughters: "Franklin had a remarkable affinity for superior people," and "it is pleasant to follow the growth and loyalty of his friendship for Miss Ray."

The same friendship and intimacy continued after Miss Ray's marriage to Governor William Greene, and surely it is not a little remarkable that the first families of this little Island have held rank with the first families of America; for we find the descendants of Simon Ray intimately associated with the families of Franklin, of Washington, of Roger Williams, of Gov. Wm. Greene, of Gov. Samuel Ward of Revolutionary fame, and of Major-General Nathaniel Greene of military renown.

THOMAS TERRY.

No one, perhaps, took a more active part than Thomas Terry in the settlement and improving of Block Island during his short residence here. He seems to have been a man of very different bearing from the high-toned statesman-like Capt. James Sands, and the more quiet, even-tempered, moral Simon Ray. Mr. Terry had great self-possession, shrewdness, and withal a daring unexcelled by the bravest. Thus in these three men we find the little Block Island colony of sixteen families favored with the three important characters of statesmen, moralist, and hero. That Thomas Terry was the latter none can doubt who properly estimate the few incidents of his life that we are able to gather.

He was present at the house of Dr. John Alcock in Roxbury, Mass., the 17th of August, 1660, "then and there to confer about" the purchase of Block Island. He was from Braintree, Mass., and was one of the six who built a "barque for the transporting of cattle to said Island for the settlement thereof," and in April, 1661, left Braintree with others for Block Island, stopping on their way at Taunton.

In May, 1664, he, with James Sands, petitioned the Court of Rhode Island for the admission of the Islanders as freemen of the colony, and in response was appointed by said court to proceed with Mr. Sands to inaugurate the first steps of civil government on the Island, and they did accordingly. At the same time Mr. Terry was admitted 'freeman of the colony. In 1665, as representative from Block Island in the Rhode Island General Assembly, he was intimately associated with Roger Williams, John Clark, and other distinguished persons. During that year he petitioned the Assembly for assistance in building a harbor on the Island, and thus secured a visit of inspection from a committee consisting of Governor Benedict Arnold, Deputy-Governor William Brenton, and Mr. John Clark. In 1670, Mr. Terry presented a similar petition. In 1672, he was one of the foremost in obtaining a charter for the Island to become a township.

His one-sixteenth of the land here purchased was

located in different parcels, the largest two of which were the extreme south end of the Island, extending from the east to the west shore, and the narrowest part of the Neck, embracing Indian Head Neck. On the northerly part of the latter his house was located. He seems to have been quite forward in making slaves of the Indians, for as early as 1669, six of his Indian slaves escaped from him and caused considerable trouble in the colony. Mr. Terry wrote to Francis Lovelace, then governor of New York, concerning these six Indians, and said governor wrote to Governor Arnold, of Rhode Island, about the matter as follows: " Mr. Thomas Terry, of Block Island, informs mee that hee hath had six Indyans servants run away from him, which Ninicraft [Chief of the Narragansetts] protects and keepes, though none of his Indians. I think you may do well to admonish him of it, and that hee ought not to doe the least injury to the English under whose protection he lives, without giving satisfaction for it. It may be by his answer you may judge of his intent."

The substance of the above the governor of Rhode Island, by an interpreter, communicated to Ninicraft, a very artful chief, who replied " that he had had a great deal of trouble about these servants, and that he did receive an order about them from Mr. Brenton in the winter time, when the snow was knee-deep; and that then he did send out to look, but could not find them, and that he did order them oftentimes to return to their master; but they did run away, some to Connecticott, and some to the Massachusetts. That Thomas Terry had done very badly with him in the business, and caused him a great deal of trouble; that once an old man, one of his Indians, did complain to him that Thomas Terry had taken two children out of his house by force, which were now grown young men, and were two of the six that Thomas Terry did now demand; and that he did advise the said Indian to complain to the Governor against him; that he might hear them both; further, he saith that yesterday he met one of the four Indians that were brought to Thomas Terry upon Quononicutt, and did intend to have brought him over with him, and did bring him some part of the way; but he run from him, and that he would have had the English there to have got on horseback and rid after him, but they said it was no matter. He also said if Thomas Terry had not intended to have taken away my life, he might as well have informed you that I, being at a dance on Block Island about three or four years since, I seeing a servant of his there, sent him home to him, to his house; but the next morning the said servant came again, and I sent him to his house again; and he returning, I sent him back again the third time. This I believe he did not acquaint you with, although there are several witnesses that can testify to the truth thereof."

The above transactions not only give us a glimpse of personal characters, and of those peculiar times, but they also point to the cause and mode of exterminating the Indians of Block Island. Slavery was the cause, and running away was the mode, evidently. Mr. Terry seems to have been more familiar than any others of his fellow-citizens with the language and habits of the Indians. He conversed with them in their own tongue, and knew well how to take advantage of their ignorance, and how to manage their passions. Amidst the greatest perils he was master of the situation. The following incident given by his friend Rev. Samuel Niles is in point. At the time referred to, the Indians on the Island were about twenty to one of the settlers, and they had become so turbulent that the women and children of the latter were collected at the Sands' Garrison, and a close eye was kept upon the savages. Says Mr. Niles:

"They therefore kept a very watchful eye on them, especially when they had got a considerable quantity of rum among them and they got drunk, as is common with them, and then they are ready for mischief. Once when they had a large keg of rum, and it was feared by the English what might be the consequence, Mr. Thomas Terry, then an inhabitant there, the father of the present Colonel Terry, Esq., of Freetown, who had gained the Indian tongue, went to treat with them as they were gathered together on a hill that had a long descent to the bottom; [Beacon Hill ?] where he found their keg or cask of rum, with the bung out, and began to inquire of them who had supplied them with it. They told him Mr. Arnold, who was a trader on Block Island. Upon which he endeavored to undervalue him and prejudice their minds against him; and in their cups they soon pretended that they cared as little for Mr. Arnold as he did. He told them that if they spake the truth they should prove it, (which is customary among them,) and the proof he directed was, to kick their keg of rum, and say, *Tuckisha Mr. Arnold!* The English is, 'I don't care for you Mr. Arnold;' which one of them presently did, and with his kick rolled it down the hill, the bung being open, as was said, and by the time it came to the bottom the rum had all run out. By this stratagem the English were made easy for this time."

Another account of Mr. Terry's tact and bravery is given by Mr. Niles, which helps us also to understand some of the trials of the first settlers. He says:

"Another instance of the remarkable interposition of Providence in the preservation of these few English people in the midst of a great company of Indians. The attempt was strange, and not easily to be accounted for, and the event was as strange.

"The Indians renewing their insults, with threatening

speeches, and offering smaller abuses, the English, fearing the consequences, resolved, these sixteen men and one boy, to make a formal challenge to fight this great company of Indians, near, or full out three hundred, in open pitched battle, and appointed the day for this effort. Accordingly, when the day came, the fore-mentioned Mr. Terry, living on a neck of land remote from the other English inhabitants, just as he was coming out of his house in order to meet them, saw thirty Indians, with their guns, very bright, as though they were fitted for war. He inquired from whence they came. They replied, from Narragansett, and that they were Ninicraft's men. He asked their business. They said, to see their relations and friends. And for what reason they brought their guns? They replied, because they knew not what game they might meet with in their way. He told them that they must not carry their guns any farther, but deliver them to him; and when they returned, he would deliver them back to them safely. To which they consented, and he secured them in his house, and withal told them they must stay there until he had got past the fort; as he was to go by it within gunshot over a narrow beach between two ponds. The Indians accordingly all sat down very quietly, but stayed not long after him; for he had no sooner passed by the fort but the Indians made their appearance on a hill, in a small neck of land called by the English *Indian-head-neck*. And the reason of its being so called was, because when the English came there they found two Indian's heads stuck upon poles standing there. Whether they were traitors, or captives, I know not. When they at the fort saw those thirty Indians that followed Mr. Terry, they made a mighty shout; but Mr. Terry had, as I observed, but just passed by it.

"However, the English, as few as they were, resolved to pursue their design, and accordingly marched with their

26

drum beating up a challange (their drummer was Mr. Kent, after of Swansey), and advanced within gunshot of it, as far as the water would admit them, as it was on an island in a pond, near to, and in plain sight of the place of my nativity. Thither they came with utmost resolution, and warlike courage, and magnanimity, standing the Indians to answer their challenge. Their drummer being a very active and sprightly man, and skillful in the business, that drum, under the over-ruling power of Providence, was the best piece of their armor. The Indians were dispirited to that degree that they made no motions against them. The English after inquired of them the reason of their refusing to fight with them, when they had so openly and near their fort made them such a challenge; they declared that the sound of the drum terrified them to that degree that they were afraid to come against them. From this time the Indians became friendly to the English, and ever after."

The above occurrence passed entirely from the knowledge of the Islanders, so that it was news to every one of them when related by the writer in his centennial address to them on the Fourth of July, 1876. So imperfect is tradition, without a written record.

That Mr. Terry was more than an ordinary man it is easy to see from the foregoing. His coolness and nerve were exhibited in starting from his house alone to walk within arrow-shot of the enemy's fort to join his comrades. His presence of mind and wonderful courage were demonstrated in boldly, single-handed, facing thirty strange Indians armed with new guns. His daring and magic power were unexcelled by Ethan Allen at Fort Ticonderoga. See him, in an open field commanding thirty strange savages armed for battle! Behold him confronting the whole band, and disarming them one by one, and before their faces carrying their guns into his house ! Hear him then ordering them to stay just where they were until he had passed the fort and joined his comrades ! By this strategy he kept them out of the sight of the Indians in the fort until he was beyond the reach of their guns and arrows. At the same time his mind must have been upon the battle of himself and six-teen companions, with three hundred Indians now reën-forced by thirty more. His heroism that day will bear comparison with any upon the pages of history, and he and his few associates were no less tried and daring than were Leonidas and his followers. The story of Mr. Terry to his fellow-Islanders, acquainting them of his power over the thirty whom he had just disarmed, infused, doubtless, his own spirit into them. We can imagine him in consultation with Mr. Sands, Mr. Ray, Mr. Rath-bone, and others, and as he was familiar with the Indian language he understood their temper better than others, and they probably agreed with him that a show of cour-age was their greatest weapon. *Drum for your life !* was probably the only music that inspired Mr. Kent, the drum-mer, and the beating of his drum helped the little isolated band to march the more boldly within "gunshot " of the enemy whose barbarity was striking terror to the English throughout the country.

A short distance from this fort was another scene which no pen has described, and none could portray. There in the Sands' Garrison, at the foot of the hill just below the mill-pond, and on the easterly side of the outlet, were hearts of wives, mothers, and children throbbing with anxiety over the issues of that day. Prayers, sighs, tears, and crying were there sadly commingled, until they were exchanged for rejoicing over the friendly hand shaken by Thomas Terry and others with the Indians of Block Island.

It is not so probable that the Indians told a true story

when they said: "The sound of the drum terrified them to that degree that they were afraid to come against" the white men, as it is that the thirty new comers, direct from Ninicraft their chief, informed them of the punishments inflicted by the whites upon the hostile tribes on the main-land. Moreover, Ninicraft may have sent them word to be at peace with the Islanders lest he should become involved in a war with the colonies, a disaster which he studiously avoided while his neighboring tribes were being exterminated.

The locality of Thomas Terry's heroism is easily identified. The Indian fort was on Fort Island, an elevated plat of about five acres, now belonging to Mr. Samuel Mott, and in a pond a little south of the Great Pond. These two ponds are separated by a narrow neck of sand over which the road now passes, and that neck is the "narrow beach between two ponds" in Mr. Niles' account quoted above. From this "beach" the road passes up the hill upon Indian-Head-Neck, on the northerly part of which was Mr. Terry's residence, said by Mr. Niles to be "remote from the other English inhabitants," as none then lived upon the Corn Neck, but about the central and westerly parts of the Island. The place of rendezvous for the heroic sixteen and a boy, was probably in the vicinity of Mr. Samuel Mott's residence, as Mr. Terry had to go there to join his comrades. The earthworks of the fort have all been leveled down, and the writer has been able to find no relics of it except some small pieces of rude pottery, although in former years the plow frequently brought to light there various evidences of Indian warfare.

Lieutenant Terry did not remain many years upon Block Island, but removed to Freetown, Mass., near Fall River, and there spent the remainder of his days. His military abilities were there appreciated. He was elected selectman of the town in 1685-6-9-70, and 1700; "was made a deputy to the court at Plymouth in 1689, and 1690; and to the Council of War in 1690;" and in proof of the confidence in his bravery he was honored in 1686 "with the rank and commission of a Lieutenant, empowered to command all the militia of the town." (Gen. E. W. Peirce.)

It is evident from the traits of character seen in him that he was born a hero, and only needed the occasion and circumstances to have taken rank with the most successful generals. He died in Freetown about the year 1704, and was buried near his house on Bryant's Neck. As long as Block Island has descendants from the first settlers, so long will memory owe a debt of gratitude to the name of Lieut. Thomas Terry for his tactics and heroism in subduing the hostile Indians that threatened to exterminate the little pilgrim colony of early settlers.

Mr. Terry's descendants are still living in Freetown. He left there three sons, Thomas, John, and Benjamin. Thomas, like his father, became lieutenant of the town militia, in 1715; representative to the General Court in 1725; assessor, selectman more than twenty years, and in 1757 was the first justice of the peace elected in Freetown, and was known as "Justice Terry." The maiden name of his widow was Anna Williams.

Col. Abiel Terry was the son of Justice Terry, and seems to have inherited all the virtues of his father and grandfather, as well as the offices which they filled. It is said of him that after having held the office of lieutenant of the local militia, he was promoted to the post of "Lieutenant-Colonel of the Second Regiment in the local militia of Bristol County." He was an extensive owner of slaves, and died from a fall from a horse near Weir bridge. He is mentioned by Niles as the *son* of the Block Island Terry, but by mistake, for he was *grandson*

26*

instead, born in 1714, and forty-six years old at the date of Niles' mention.

Lieut. Thomas Terry of Block Island had a son John, who had a son John, who had a son Zephaniah, who had a son Silas, who was the father of the present Manasseh S. Terry, Esq., of Freetown, to whom, and to Gen. E. W. Peirce of the same place we are indebted for much of the above information.

JOHN RATHBONE.

We find his name among those who met at the house of John Alcock, M. D., in Roxbury, Mass., August 17th, 1660, there to confer about the purchase of Block Island. His father, of the same name, is said to have come from England to America in the Speedwell, a vessel accompanying the Mayflower, in 1620, and to have settled on Rhode Island. His son therefore, of whom we are speaking, was a descendant from the Pilgrims. In 1664 he was one of the number whom Capt. James Sands and Joseph Kent, in behalf of Block Island, presented to the Rhode Island General Assembly for admission as freemen. In 1683 he occupied a place in the Rhode Island General Assembly, as representative from Block Island; in 1686 was one of the petitioners to the king of Great Britain in reference to the " *Quo Warranto*," and in 1688 was one of the Grand Jury of Rhode Island.

In the year 1689, in the month of July, Mr. Rathbone had a very narrow escape from the French, who were then pillaging the Island. "They inquired of some one or more of the people, who were the likeliest among them to have money? They told them of John Rathbone who was the most likely." From this we learn that he was in good circumstances. The French proceeded to capture him, and demanded of him, as they supposed, his money. The captive denied his having any besides a trifling sum.

They endeavored to make him confess that he had more, and to deliver it to them, by tying him up and whipping him barbarously. While they were doing all this to an innocent man whom they mistook for the moneyed John Rathbone, the latter made his escape with his treasure.

He indeed then had a son by the name of John, who, by bearing his father's name, and by submitting to this terrible scourging, shielded his father and saved him from being robbed. This son probably lived in the house which stood near his father's, as the locations are still known by the descendants of the first settler.

In 1696, Thomas, William, John, and Joseph, probably sons of the original settler, together with several other Block Island names, by the same Assembly, were admitted freemen of the colony of Rhode Island.

In 1688, William Rathbone was appointed by the colony as constable for Block Island.

In 1700, Thomas Rathbone was representative in the General Assembly, from Block Island, and held that office several years.

In 1709, John Rathbone, Jr., of Block Island, was admitted freeman of the Rhode Island colony. Twenty-five years afterward another of the same name was admitted, together with Edward Sands, Samuel Dodge, Daniel Dickens, William Dodge, Jr., and John Mitchell, "all of New Shoreham."

In 1711, Capt. Thomas Rathbone represented Block Island in the General Assembly, and also in the year 1731.

In 1720, Thomas Rathbone, Jr., was admitted freeman of Block Island and the colony of Rhode Island.

In 1741, Nathaniel Rathbone, together with Robert Hull and Samuel Dunn, was admitted freeman of Rhode Island colony, from New Shoreham.

In 1759, John Rathbone, "son of John, late of New Shoreham," was admitted freeman of Exeter, R. I. He was probably the son John Rathbone, Jr., mentioned above, and in 1709 admitted freeman. It is more than possible that he bore the name of his grandfather, the first Rathbone of the Island.

This succession of Rathbones brings us within the limits of a valuable old bible record now in the possession of Mr. Walter Rathbone Mott, an aged relative of the above individuals, and a respected citizen of Block Island. This bible, printed at Oxford in 1725, was owned by Samuel Rathbone in 1743, and from him was bequeathed to his son Samuel, and after him to Walter, the son of the latter Samuel. Walter, at his death, gave it to his daughter, Mrs. Catharine R. Mott, and to his grandson, Walter R. Mott, the present owner. Unlike too many bibles at the present time which are kept to show gilt, and gather dust, it was

"The family bible that lay on the stand,"

and was used until its first binding was worn off, and many years ago was rebound; a quarto whose well-worn corners, and carefully preserved leaves, like others of the same character on Block Island, speaks well for the devoted little band of Pilgrims around whose hearth-stones, amid savages, beyond protection from the main-land, the husband, the father, the mother, and the children read and worshiped, and prayed for protection, while the war-whoop of the Indian and the "voice of many waters" commingled with the howling winds that were shaking their doors and windows.

Samuel Rathbone, born August 3, 1672, died Jan. 24, 1757, aged 85 years. He was the father of the Samuel who owned the bible above-mentioned.

In April, 1705, Samuel Rathbone, Jr., was born on Block Island, and in the year 1755, at the age of fifty, was a member of the Rhode Island Assembly, as representative of the Island. He died Jan. 24, 1780, aged 75 years. In 1775, and 1776, he was lieutenant in Capt. John Sands' company of militia here.

In June, 1734, Walter, son of Samuel Rathbone, Jr., was born, and in the year 1757, together with Oliver Ring Rose, and William Willis, was admitted freeman, and in the year 1774, he was representative of Block Island in the General Assembly, and in the same year was appointed by the Islanders, at a town meeting, as one of a committee "to give the closest attention to every thing which concerns the liberties of America." They were to resist vigorously the duty on tea, enforced by England. Walter, for sixty years, was town clerk.

In May, 1768, James and Catharine Rathbone, twins, and children of Walter, were born. Their sister Hannah married Mr. Archibald Millikin, and her granddaughter became the wife of the Hon. Nicholas Ball, proprietor of the Ocean View Hotel. Samuel Rathbone was father of Capt. Thomas Rathbone, now living upon the Island.

The above clew, leading us back more than two centuries, may be gratifying to those who would trace the living descendants' relation to the first Rathbone who settled upon the Island, and it may assist in tracing out the various branches of the Rathbone family in America, all of whom, it is supposed, originated from the Thomas Rathbone who came from England in 1620, and was the father of the John Rathbone who bought a sixteenth of Block Island in 1660, and settled here in 1662.

The outlines of the cellar (now filled) where the latter lived may be seen, about one hundred rods southwest from the residence of Mr. Amhad Dodge, and owned by Mr. Nathan Mott. A beautiful spring of water is near, and the place where the garden plat once was is greener than the adjacent meadow sward. From that point the natural scenery is charming, and it is easy to imagine the large orchard once there in bloom, the prattle of children, the herds of sheep and cattle, and sturdy men and matrons planting one of the most interesting little colonies ever known.

About sixteen years ago considerable was said in the public journals concerning "the great Rathbone estate of forty millions advertised by the Bank of England, awaiting the call of American heirs who were supposed to have settled on Block Island, in America, or in parts thereunto adjacent." In order to get, if possible, a ray of light from that *ignis-fatuus* which so many have followed through tangled and "endless genealogies," of which an ancient writer well said—"Neither give heed," (1 Tim. 4, 4,) a visitor at the Spring House here borrowed the old bible in 1876. It is an undoubted fact, however, that the Block Island Rathbones, as well as others in America, have descended from an honorable race of Saxon origin, in England, of whom one writer says they have been a distinct family there "for more than five hundred years. A wealthy branch of this family has resided in the city of Liverpool more than three hundred years."

REV. SAMUEL NILES.

He was born upon Block Island, May 1st, 1674, and was the son of Nathaniel Niles of the same place, and subsequently of Kingston, R. I.

Samuel was the grandson of John Niles, a weaver, of Braintree, Mass., and of Capt. James and Sarah Sands of Block Island. He descended from a robust ancestry, both physically and intellectually. His grandfather Niles died at the age of ninety-four, and the sturdy character of his grandparents Sands may be seen in the biographical sketch of James Sands and his wife, who was the first physician of the Island, and one of the first emancipationists of America. His own father, Capt. Nathaniel Niles, died at the age of eighty-seven.

Here, on the Island, the son spent his boyhood, and a part of his youth, making himself familiar with the habits and traditions of the Indians. He says of them, and of himself: "They were perpetually engaged in wars one with another, long before the English settled on Block Island, according to the Indians' relation, as some of the old men among them informed me, when I was young." He was a very bright and promising boy, and well improved his good opportunity for obtaining an education. His studies, however, were greatly interrupted by English and French wars, as the French committed great depredations upon the Island, of which he says: "The great spoil made on the Island by the French, in their repeated visits, and particularly on my father's interest, occasioned my staying from school six years." During this interruption he labored on the farm, and assisted in building a vessel for trade with the West Indies. Thus he spent the period from the age of sixteen to twenty-two, and then entered college at Cambridge, "the Reverend Dr. Increase Mather then being President," and Mr. John Leverett and Mr. William Brattle "were the only fellows." He graduated in 1699. An item worthy of note here is the fact that he, a native of Block Island, was the first one from the State of Rhode Island to enter college. In speaking of his teachers there he says: "The kindness of these worthy gentlemen I hope not to forget, who, I conclude, favored me the more, as I was *the first that came to college from Rhode Island government.*"

Soon after graduating he returned to the Island, where, in March, 1700, he received a most cordial invitation from the whole town to become a settled preacher of the gospel. As yet he had not been formally set apart by an ecclesiastical council to the work of the ministry. This, however, was not an insurmountable obstacle in the way

of preaching the gospel, in the estimation of the Islanders, who were deeply sensible of their need, as they expressed it, of providing for their "souls to be fed with
His heavenly manna." On the condition of his acceptance of their call, they deeded to him seven acres of land
lying between the Fresh Pond and Capt. Edward Sands'
house—the house now owned and occupied by Mr. John
R. Paine. At that time no church was organized on the
Island, and he officiated only as a licentiate, or his denom-
ination, the Congregationalist, would not have tolerated
in him then an administration of the ordinances.

Mr. Niles retained possession of said land by the Fresh
Pond until 1716, and then sold it for £105.

He was ordained and settled at Braintree May 23,
1711. He wrote, in 1760, a history of the Indian and
French wars. From the French he suffered much,
pecuniarily and bodily, while he was on Block Island
taking care of his grandparents, Capt. James Sands and
his wife. He wrote somewhat extensively on theological
subjects. In 1818, President John Adams spoke of him
thus respectfully: "Almost sixty years ago I was an
humble acquaintance of this venerable clergyman, then,
as I believe, more than four score years of age, * * *
I then revered, and still revere, the honest, virtuous, and
pious man." He died May 1, 1762, just eighty-eight
years old.

The following record which he left of himself is instructive in several respects, as exhibiting not only his own
character, but that of the invaders, and the indignities to
which the Islanders, about the year 1689, were subjected.
He says: "Before the year was expired some of the same
company with others, landed in the night and surprised
the people in their beds, and proceeded in like manner as
before, plundering houses, stripping the people of their
clothing, killing creatures and making great waste and

spoil, but killed no person. I suppose I was the greatest sufferer of any under their hands at that time; for before I had dressed myself, one of their company rushed into the chamber where I lodged. After some free and seemingly familiar questions he asked me, which I answered with like freedom: but being alone, without any of his company. not knowing what dangers might befall him (as I after apprehended), on a sudden, and with a different air, he says to me, 'Go down. you dog.' To which I replied, ' Presently, as soon as I have put on my stockings and shoes.' At which, with the muzzle of his gun he gave me a violent thrust at the pit of my stomach, that it threw me backward on the bed, as I was sitting on the bed-side, so that it was some time before I could recover my breath. As soon as I could, I gathered them up. He drew his cutlass and beat me, smiting me with all his power, to the head of the stairs, and it was a very large chamber. He followed me down the stairs, and then bound my hands behind me with a sharp, small line which soon made my hands swell and become painful. How I managed after with my stockings and shoes I have now forgotten. However, after this I met with no abuse from them the whole time of their stay on the Island." This was during the second invasion.

For the above, and similar accounts of occurrences on Block Island, the name of their author, who knew them to be truthful. ought to be cherished in grateful remembrance by all subsequent generations. And as we are now grateful to him for the historical facts which he has preserved from oblivion, so we may learn our own obligations to keep a record of the present for the benefit of others hereafter. How gladly would we learn of Mr. Niles some of the simplest things of his day on this Island! Such as where the different houses were located, how certain names originated. and where certain things

27

occurred, etc.   Were it not from circumstantial evidence from Mr. Niles, combined with similar evidence from original surveys and deeds, it would seem impossible to identify the spot where Capt. James Sands' house of stone was erected, and where the location was of the "garrison," sustained on Block Island, previous to 1700, partly by the colony, and chiefly by the Islanders for their protection against Indians and invaders.   Even now there are public houses here which may be as little known two hundred years hence, unless a knowledge of them shall be preserved by a written record.   To-day not an inhabitant can tell where the most noted spot of the Island was in 1690. That spot was where Capt. James Sands' house, and the garrison close by it, were erected.   We regret that Mr. Niles has told us no more.

In rapidly tracing the steps of Mr. Niles from his youth on Block Island to his grave in Braintree we shall be much indebted to Professor Park, of Andover.   All the germs of the sturdy character of Mr. Niles were seen in his youth upon this Island.   Here he toiled for a support; here he tenderly cared for his grandparents; here he firmly resisted the Roger Williams' spirit of the Islanders, even in the persons of his venerated grandparents; here he exhibited his unwillingness to yield a point, as when he leisurely drew on his stockings in the night while under the flourishing weapons of a robber; here he displayed his financial ability, as when he accepted that part of the call to the ministry of Block Island—that part which consisted of a deed of seven acres of land which, after he settled at Braintree, he sold for £105; and here he exhibited that lack of appreciation of an ardent zeal in religion which subsequently characterized a pastorate of half a century without a revival.   "Mr. Niles exhibited here a specimen of that irrational conservatism which loses the greater good in order to avoid the lesser evil."

Had he been more flexible and ardent perhaps his long pastorate would have been upon Block Island, instead of that at Braintree, and it is possible that the Islanders might have become Congregationalists instead of being Baptists.

Mr. Niles had more than an ordinary scholarship for his time. He was a very good linguist, and most proficient in the Latin language. He seems to have been cold and logical, like Emmons, and as far in practice from Whitefield as is the North Pole from the Equator. Of the five works of which he was the author, the only one now of public interest is that for which he could not get a publisher—his history of the Indian and French Wars. Professor Park says: "Mr. Niles was a remarkably independent man. He did not countenance the revivalists whom Edwards befriended. He refused to admit Whitefield into his pulpit. In the early years of Braintree the town had been disturbed and the church injured by the fanaticism of Mrs. Anne Hutchinson. Mr. Niles, remembering the troubles caused by her new measures, resisted the new measures of Whitefield and his associates." The professor quotes from Mr. Niles, as saying: "Mr. Whitefield is now (1745) making a second visit to us, in pompous progress, from town to town, followed with the loud acclamations of many people, while some from whom more manly things might be expected, seem to lay their necks at his feet, to trample on at pleasure, as if his word was not only his own, but their law also, according to that, '*Stat pro ratione voluntas.*' "

"It is obvious from the writings of Mr. Niles, that he confined his attention to the *evils* of revivalism in his day, and did not look through them to the real *good* which overbalanced the evils. His church was not distracted by the wild enthusiasm of the times; this was a blessing;

but the church was favored with no revival for sixty years; this was a calamity far outweighing the blessing."

The Block Islanders to-day may rejoice that in the infancy of their society they had such men as James Sands and Simon Ray, fired by the spirit of Roger Williams, to resist the influence of the cramping, cold formalism of a leader of Mr. Niles' temperament. "He preached his own ordination sermon." "Stern in his doctrine, he was also strong in his will. He was severe in the discipline of himself and of his household. He was the bishop and ruler of his people. He trained his parishioners, as his children, in the way they should go."

His tact in business affairs, seen on Block Island, as he accepted the deed for the land without rendering for it the service expected, in 1700, was subsequently exhibited at Braintree. Whether he inherited, or learned his shrewdness of the Islanders, or acquired it after he "entered into the College at Cambridge, the Rev. Dr. Increase Mather then being President," and became a citizen of Massachusetts, it is not easy to determine.

"Randolph, Quincy, and Braintree, were formerly one town. When Randolph was separated from Braintree it seemed needful to run the dividing line in a certain direction, which would give to Braintree a comely shape, and promote the convenience of Randolph. But if the line had been drawn in that most suitable course, it would cut off a large farm of Mr. Niles; and for that farm, being then in Randolph, and not in his own town, he would be compelled to pay taxes. The pastor was roused; he petitioned the great and General Court, and caused the dividing line to be run so as to include his own farm in his own parish, and thus to save his taxes, although this process gave to the Braintree township a singularly uncouth form, and disturbed the comfort of Randolph. This was done before he wrote his treatise on original sin.

What minister, at the present day, could spoil the configuration of two townships, in order to accommodate his own agricultural interests ?

"An inditer of rhymes, an historian, a metaphysical and biblical divine, an exact disciplinarian, having an iron will and an indomitable perseverance, this many-sided pastor was noted far and wide as a *man of affairs*. He was, for example, an expert horseman. He drove a charger that no other man in his parish could ride. When the pastor mounted him, the animal moved along at a slow, stately pace, but when a layman ventured upon the back of the animal, he became very soon, in a physical as well as ecclesiastical aspect, a *lay-man*. If a farmer in the region owned a vicious colt, intractable to the yeomanry of the town, he led the unruly beast to the bishop, who was a kind of Rarey; and the dignified elder subdued the colt, almost as easily as he would put the bit and bridle upon a wayward parishioner who undertook to leap over the parish fence and run away from his taxes."

Mr. Niles, in spite of his original sin, and manifest follies, was a man of more than ordinary excellences. Like others who have gone from Block Island, he has reflected honor back upon the place of his nativity, both in his life and in his posterity. He had a son Samuel, who graduated at Harvard in 1731, and was subsequently known as the Hon. Samuel Niles, of Braintree. The latter had two sons who became distinguished, viz.: Rev. Samuel Niles, of Abington, Mass., and Judge Nathaniel Niles, of Fairlee, Vermont. Both of these grandsons of the Block Islander, and Braintree Divine, "inherited his sharpness of insight; and in consequence of their skill in perplexing an adversary, each was called *Botheration Niles*. Each received this *sobriquet* while he was a member of Princeton college, the pastor of Abington being then designated, *Botheration primus,* and the judge at Fairlee being then called, *Botheration secundus.*"

The Block Island records contain many items of interest concerning the Niles family; none of the name, however, are living there now, but many relatives by marriage. The following indicates the line of descent.

John Niles, of Braintree, 1639–1696; his son, Capt. Nathaniel Niles, of Braintree and Block Island, 1640–1727; his son, Rev. Samuel Niles, Block Island and Braintree, 1674–1762; his sons, Rev. Samuel, and Judge Nathaniel. From this line, those who desire, can trace out various branches. See address of R. S. Storrs, D. D., at Braintree, 1861; Rhode Island colonial records, and Hon. Wm. P. Sheffield's historical sketch of Block Island.

ANGELL.

This name early appeared upon the records of Block Island, but of late years it has not been numbered among its citizens.

Mr. William Angell, in the latter part of the Revolution hired a farm on the Island, and by permit from the General Assembly moved here his family and furniture. This was in the year 1782.

Hon. William G. Angell, born on Block Island, moved to Burlington, Otsego County, N. Y., and there, in 1825, was elected a representative in Congress, reëlected in 1829, and was a member of the committee on Indian affairs and on the territories. *Dr. Angell* of Providence has lived here and is a summer visitor, professionally, and for pleasure.

BALL.

The first inhabitant here of this name seems to have been one *Mr. Edward Ball* who was deputy warden to the town in 1702, and was also entitled "Crowner," as representing in authority the Crown of England, and held the relation of sheriff to the constable and people.

Mr. John Ball appears next in time on the records, and was admitted freeman on Block Island in 1709. Whether, or how related to Edward we cannot state.

Hon. Peter Ball was admitted freeman in 1709. and in 1734 represented the Island in the General Assembly together with Simon Ray. In 1735. he was among the foremost in building the new pier—in obtaining for it an appropriation from the State of £1,200. He with Simon Ray was appointed by the Assembly to appropriate said money for its legitimate purpose, in 1735.

Mr. Isaiah Ball, one of the old landmarks, passed away about the beginning of the present century, known as a hardy, industrious farmer.

Mr. John S. Ball, son of Isaiah, is now between seventy and eighty years old, living where his father lived, doing as he did, with a plenty of life's necessaries, free from its ostentations, and with a feeling of independence known to but few whose fortunes are top-heavy. He glories in having lived so long "without a doctor," and in a defiance of the medical profession. He is bound to die, he says, a "*natral death.*"

Mr. Samuel Ball, a cotemporary of Isaiah, is well remembered as a man of energy, straightforward dealing. and extraordinary memory. He seems to have been the oracle of the Island in regard to its ancient traditions. Of him it was frequently said: "He is as good as the records."

Mr. Samuel Ball, son of the former. still survives, occupying the old mansion left by his father, and in his old age is carrying out the good principles which he inherited. While his strong will exhibited in stirring habits and in a life of rigid honesty, will long be remembered, his decided expressions of love for the right and disapproval of the wrong, so often heard, in all places, will not easily slip from the memory.

The numerous branches of the Ball family now on the Island are not easily traced to their respective origins. The following is a brief sketch of one of them, who has taken rank among the first men of the Island, and of the State.

Hon. Nicholas Ball, born in December, 1828, inherited a fondness for the sea, and when a young boy shipped as cook for $6.00 a month, and during the next summer had $7.00 a month. Subsequent to this. a few years were spent at school, and in working for farmers at ten to twenty-five cents a day, until March, 1843, when he again shipped as cook for $10.00 a month, and afterwards as seaman for $15.00 a month, and rose to the position of chief mate, on wages at $28.00 a month, visiting, meanwhile, Philadelphia, Albany, West Indies, Liverpool, Havre, and San Francisco, spending 161 days in going around Cape Horn to the last place, in 1849. After two years in California, mining, he returned to Block Island in 1851, and in October following went back to the gold mines again. In 1854. he started his mercantile business on Block Island, which he still continues, and that year was elected representative in the General Assembly, and reëlected in 1855; was elected State Senator in 1858; re-elected in 1859, '63, '64, '65, '66, '67, '68, '69, '70, '71, '72; and in 1873 declined an election to either State or home office. In 1867, assisted by his colleague, Hon. J. G. Sheffield, he began the long and laborious campaign of securing a government harbor for Block Island, for which his townsmen and the public will ever owe him a debt of gratitude. In this brief sketch only an index can be given of the time, money, and personal effort put forth by him in this national enterprise,—one which had repeatedly proved a failure under the administrations of the town alone, and the town and colony combined, as seen in the article on the *Harbor*.

Mr. Ball's good judgment, personal influence, indomitable perseverance and success in this public enterprise, furnish an example which it would be gratifying to see others endeavoring to excel. Those compliment him a little too highly, perhaps, who credit him with so much success in spite of their superior advantages claimed for the Great Pond as a National Harbor.

His personal interviews with congressmen at Washington, with the Boards of Trade at Philadelphia, at New York, at Providence, and at Boston, visiting some of these cities repeatedly: his petitions obtained by him from mercantile firms in Bangor, Boston, Newport, Providence, Stonington, New London, New York, Philadelphia, and other places directed to their respective congressmen; and his unceasing correspondence, all of which was carried on from 1867 to 1870, required an expense of time, money, and brain which but few could afford. Both approvals and complaints point to Hon. NICHOLAS BALL, as the principal founder of the government harbor at Block Island, and while accepting some of the pecuniary fruits of the enterprise, he enjoys the satisfaction of seeing his town enriched thereby thousands of dollars where he is profited hundreds. His retirement from public life, and devotion to his family, Island society, and the pleasures of the visitors, especially to those at the Ocean View Hotel, of which he is proprietor, afford him ample opportunity for reviewing the past and hoping for the future.

BRIGGS.

About the beginning of the eighteenth century two brothers of this name came from England to the United States, one of whom settled in Maine, and the other,

Joseph Briggs, settled at Kingston, R. I., and subsequently moved to Block Island where he married Margary Dodge. The old records of the Island in 1758, speak of him as leasing of the town its blacksmith shop. Here, upon the Island, he raised a family of seven children. namely, Nathaniel, Joseph, Patience, Burton, Samuel, Lydia, and Eathon.

Nathaniel, born about the year 1758, held the confidence and esteem of the whole community for his sterling worth and unblemished character in his public and domestic relations. As an active member of the Baptist church he was brought into association with many of the most prominent men of the State. The principal part of the mercantile business of the Island was transacted at his store. The residence built by him, located about south of the Woonsockett House, on the opposite side of the street, and known as "the great house," was finally taken down, and many of its timbers were put into the two-story house, near the old location, and now owned and occupied by Mr. Solomon Dodge. In the year 1802 Mr. Briggs visited New York for medical treatment, and there died, aged forty-four years. His son,

Collins G. Briggs, was born on Block Island, Sept. 30, 1798, and in the war of 1812 served his country in the United States Navy, and subsequently followed the sea in the merchants' service, until he removed to Exeter, Otsego Co., N. Y., where he married and settled in agricultural pursuits. From thence, in the spring of 1836, he removed to the town of German, Chenango Co., N. Y., and there bought and cultivated the "Bowen farm," and distinguished himself as an enterprising, moral citizen. This was in the native place, and during the boyhood of the writer, whose conscience still troubles him a little over the disturbances to which he was accessory at those good old Methodist meetings in the school-house at the "Corners"—meetings in which Mr. Briggs was a class leader.

At that place he died, Nov. 12, 1874. aged 76 years, leaving a sister, Mrs. Mary C. Eldridge, of New York city, and four children, three sons and one daughter, Luzerne J. Briggs, still residing in German; and Manasseh and Munroe A. Briggs, in Brooklyn.

Manasseh, in the firm of BRIGGS & Co., 90 Wall St., N. Y., carries on the coal and shipping business. His former wife was a Block Island lady, Mary A., daughter of Capt. Nathaniel and Lucretia Littlefield. She died in Brooklyn. June, 1862.

Joseph Briggs, brother of Nathaniel, in early life settled in Exeter, N. Y., where he followed farming until his death, in August, 1841, aged 77 years. leaving two daughters and one son.

Jeremiah Briggs, born on the Island, Dec. 30, 1792, in early life evinced a fondness for the sea, and in the War of 1812 had command of a United States gun-boat. After some years in the merchants' service at sea, he and his cousin. Capt. Nathaniel Briggs, established the firm of the "J. & N. Briggs Transportation Co.," between New York, Philadelphia, and Baltimore. Subsequently they accepted the agency of the Camden and Amboy Transportation Co., known as the inside canal line, and designated as the "Briggs Swift Sure Line." for about forty years. Captain Briggs was one of those energetic, vigorous men who by their own activity keep things around them in motion. He had not only a head for business, but also a heart for benevolence, as seen in his connection with the "Seaman's Fund and Retreat," on Staten Island, and with the "Marine Society," of the port of New York. During all his long and busy life his mind reverted to the Island of his childhood with feelings of peculiar tenderness. and in his old age frequently directed his letters to his old friends thus,—"Block Island—the holy land." His last visit to the Island was in August, 1872, and in the *Nautical Gazette* of Aug. 24, 1872, it was thus alluded to:

" Capt. Jeremiah Briggs is a veteran of the War of 1812, and now upwards of 80 years old, is well known to our readers as one of the proprietors of the Swift Sure Line of freight propellers plying daily between this city and Philadelphia. He sailed in the first privateer out of this harbor in 1812, and has spent much of his long and useful life on the sea. He is a remarkably hale, hearty, and well-preserved old gentleman, and still enjoys life with a zest that would put to shame the *blasé* fast-time of the day. The captain has a fine farm on the Jamaica turnpike, at Richmond Hill, Long Island, where he resides with his wife and family of grown-up sons and daughters —a credit to him, as well as a comfort to his declining years." He died at his residence, June 28, 1876, aged 84 years, and is still respectfully remembered on his beloved "little isle of the sea," where his name is frequently and familiarly spoken as *Uncle Jerry Briggs*.

Samuel Briggs, a native of the Island, and son of the first of that name here, spent his life in the place of his nativity. His son,

Nathaniel Briggs, born on the Island in 1802, by his fondness for the sea became master of a ship, and for several years sailed from the port of New York, and subsequently became the partner of Capt. Jeremiah, as before stated, and continued such until the death of the senior of the firm of J. & N. Briggs, since which event he has retired from active business. He has been distinguished for his benevolence in connection with several public institutions, and is an honored member in the Methodist Episcopal church in Brooklyn, where he has resided for many years.

Eathon Briggs, son of the senior Joseph, born upon Block Island, was lost at sea in early manhood. His son,

Eathon C. Briggs, born upon the Island, became master of a ship, and sailed from New York several years, and then entered the mercantile business in said city, and in 1849 removed with his family to Kinsmon, Trumbull Co., O., where he has carried on farming successfully. He and his brother, Capt. Nathaniel Briggs, are the only living male descendants of the original family of Joseph Briggs, the first above mentioned.

For nearly all of the above sketch the writer is indebted to his esteemed friend and companion in boyhood days, Manasseh Briggs, Esq., of Brooklyn, N. Y. None of the name, for thirty years, have been residents of the Island.

CHAMPLIN.

Previous to the Revolution a family of this name resided upon Block Island. In January, 1782, one *Henry Champlin*, formerly of Westerly, R. I., in a petition to the Assembly, stated that, "about two years ago he hired a farm upon New Shoreham, and went there with his family to reside; that the attachment that he had for the interest and good of his country led him, upon all occasions and opportunities, to give such information respecting the movements of the enemy, that he is considered by them as a dangerous person to their interest; and that he has had several informations lately that the refugees intend to destroy his property at New Shoreham, seize his person, and carry him off to New York." He was therefore permitted to move from the Island. His son, probably,

Nathaniel Champlin, about the year 1790, married Thankful Hull, of Block Island, daughter of Capt. Edward Hull, and here, for many years was an active. prominent citizen, distinguishing himself somewhat by his fondness for and mastery of horses. He was the *Rarey* of the Island, but in his own way, and subdued intractable

steeds by the rule,—*similia similibus curuntur.* For example, while at the Harbor on horseback, a considerable distance from home, he undertook to carry back a bushel
basket. The fiery young horse, seeing the basket handed
up to its rider, wheeled, snorted, and would not allow
Mr. Champlin to take it. " You have got to take that
basket home ! " said the rider, and dismounted; tied up
the reins, tied the basket to the horse's tail, and let him
go with basket following and heels flying. At another
time, to cure a horse that was sensitive about rattling
noises, he put a few small stones into an empty tin powder
can and tied it to the skittish horse's caudal appendage,
and let the horse loose in the pasture to enjoy all the freedom of running and kicking that the rattling can could
produce. It is said that a bundle of rye straw on fire
was sometimes a substitute for the basket and the tin
rattle.

Mr. Champlin reared an excellent family of children,
three of them now living upon the Island, *Uriah Champlin*, 81 years old, *Peleg*, and *Christopher*, younger brothers,
aged, well-to-do, and highly-esteemed citizens. *John*, son
of Christopher, and *Edward* and *Weeden*, sons of Peleg,
are excellent farmers.

DICKENS.

Roger Dickens was admitted freeman in 1709 as a resident of Block Island, and we find none here of that name
any earlier.

Thomas Dickens, in the year 1725, was likewise admitted freeman, was the grandfather of the present Raymond Dickens, and was representative for the Island at
the General Assembly in 1744, and was on the Island at
the breaking out of the Revolution, remaining on it during that conflict, going off and returning by permit of the
Assembly in 1779. He died between eighty and ninety

years old. He married Sally Franklin, Oct. 9, 1763. She was born Sept. 27, 1734, and died Feb. 4, 1792.

Caleb Dickens, son of Thomas, was born October 2, 1777, and died December 5, 1839, aged sixty-two years.

Mr. Raymond Dickens, son of Caleb, now living at the age of nearly seventy-five years, is one of the most hale, cheerful, and highly-esteemed old citizens of the Island. He well remembers hearing his grandfather Thomas tell about the " Palatine," and of the humane treatment of its unfortunate inmates by the Islanders. His sons *Anderson* and *Luther Dickens* are respectable residents.

Daniel Dickens was a resident of Block Island in 1734, and was then admitted freeman.

Amos Dickens was also admitted in 1759.

Much of the above record is obtained from the family Bible, now one hundred and thirty years old, in the possession of Raymond Dickens, Esq. It contains names and dates of the Tosh family also.

Elisha Dickens is one of the oldest inhabitants of the Island, and a respected citizen of the West Side.

DODGE.

This name appears on the first records of the Island.

Trustaram Dodge was one of the first settlers who came here in 1662. He was not one of the first purchasers of the Island; like several others who came with him to occupy lands obtained of some of the sixteen proprietors. He died in 1733; his name was sometimes written *Tristram*, and he was admitted freeman in 1664, among the first freemen of Block Island.

John Dodge occupied the Minister's Land in 1691, according to the old records, and was admitted freeman in 1709, was representative in the General Assembly in 1745 and 1751.

Nathaniel Dodge was admitted freemen in 1709, at the

same time as John's admission, and perhaps they were brothers or cousins.

David Dodge was admitted freeman in 1728, and *Alexander Dodge* in 1721. *Samuel*, and *William, Jr.*, were admitted in 1734. In 1744, *Nathaniel Dodge* was admitted, and in 1745, another by the name of *William*. *Hezekiah Dodge* was on the Island in 1775, at the beginning of the Revolution, and probably remained here through that distressing period.

Rev. Thomas Dodge, a native of the Island, was ordained to the pastorate of the First Baptist church of the Island in 1784, and continued to be its pastor until his death in 1804. See "Churches of Block Island."

The Dodges who were children at his death have grown up, and passed away, until only here and there one remains. Edmund died in 1875, and Samuel died January 2, 1877. Others of their name are more numerous than those of any other name on the Island. They are all, or a part, descendants, doubtless, from the Dodge among the first settlers, but their genealogy is so entangled and so imperfectly recorded as to discourage any attempt to trace it out. Amhad, and his brother William; Joshua, his brothers Andrew and Noah; Aaron, and his brother Edwin, may be considered as links connecting the present with the past generations. Oliver Dodge, father of Samuel, is still remembered, though he died many years ago. Robert Dodge is also mentioned as a preacher of a former generation.

"AUNT BETSEY."

It is not from any want of respect that she is here spoken of under this heading. By this name she is best known by all of her many old and young acquaintances. The multitude of strangers who have stood at her cottage window on Block Island, and have there seen her work the old-fashioned treadles, harnesses, shuttle, lathe, and

beams of her loom, and have heard her pleasant stories of
her youth, motherhood, industry, and family of children,
would consider any description of the Island incomplete
that should say nothing of "Aunt Betsey." What a
correspondent of the Scranton *Republican* said of her will
do to repeat :

"And here it must not be forgotten to mention the
name of *Aunt Betsey Dodge*, not as one of the beautiful
young ladies, but as a true representative of the olden
time. She is seventy-six years of age, straight as an
arrow, industrious to a fault, and one of the best talking
Yankee women we ever met. She spends her time in
weaving carpets, turning out piece after piece to the
astonishment of everybody; and standing by her loom,
which she has worked upwards of sixty years, the thought
arose that it was just such women as Aunt Betsey, with
her industrious economy and good sense, who gave caste
and character to the American people, and laid the foundations of their wealth. Such were the mothers in the
infancy of our republic."

The above is sustained by the following statistics: At
the age of seventy-six, during the year, she wove one
thousand yards of rag carpeting, and four hundred yards
of flannel, and spent three weeks "a visiting," besides
doing her own general housework. Almost her entire
life has been spent at the loom, and the number of yards
she has woven seems incredible. What she did the year
in which she kept a record, at seventy-six, of course was
more than equaled in younger years, and she "always had
all she could do." As she was almost constantly weaving
for sixty years, if we give her credit for only 1,000 yards
a year (including "tow cloth," kersey, flannel, and carpeting), the whole of her life-work would amount to 60,000
yards, which, if all put into one piece, would reach from
Block Island to Newport, and have enough left to encircle
28*

that city.   But her highly-esteemed children and grand-children, of whom her mention has caused so many a stranger to smile, and of whom she may well be proud, will be the best monument of "Aunt Betsey," after Time's shuttle has left its last thread in the warp of her busy life's web.   She has retired.

For industry and good sense she may be taken as a sample of many other true "help-meets" of Block Island.

GUTHRIDGE.

This is among the early names of Block Island. *John Guthridge* came to Watertown, Mass., in 1636. *William Guthridge* was there in 1642. They probably learned of the enterprise of settling the Island through *Peter Noyes*, their cotemporary and neighbor in Watertown, since he surveyed the Island for the settlers, and soon after.

Robert Guthridge settled upon the Island, and was evidently an active, promising citizen, until his death in 1692. By the inventory of his estate we learn that he was in comfortable circumstances, and besides other land owned "42 acres in the west woods," inventoried at "20 shillings pr. acre."

Henry Gardner represented the Island in the Assembly in the year 1741.

HULL.

Two men of this name a century ago were prominent on Block Island.

Captain Robert Hull, in 1741, was here admitted freeman, and in 1743 represented the Island in the General Assembly, and continued to do so until 1758, a period of fifteen years. In 1757, his tax was the highest of any in the town.

Captain Edward Hull, son of Capt. Robert, in 1766, with Ray Sands, Esq., represented the Island in the Assembly. Just previous to the Revolution he moved to

Jamestown, R. I., but still retained his farms on Block Island; in 1776 was representative from Jamestown in the Assembly; in 1779 and in 1781, obtained permits from the Assembly to visit his estate on the Island, and after the Revolution returned to Block Island, and was its representative in 1786. The farm near Sandy Point, now owned by Hon. J. G. Sheffield, and a tract including the residence and farm of Mr. Almanzo Littlefield, were formerly owned by Capt. Edward Hull, still remembered as a man of influence on the Island.

By the kindness of *Mr. Robert B. Hull*, of New York city, we are enabled here to present a genealogical line of Hulls connected with many respectable families now living on Block Island a line kindred, and parallel to that in which the distinguished General Hull and Commodore Hull are found, in reference to whom the ancient and less elegant than spirited stanza was sung as follows, tune *Yankee Doodle:*

> "Yankee Doodle, fire away,
> With cannon loud as thunder!
> The brave Decatur, *Hulls*, and Jones,
> Make Johnny Bull knock under."

Rev. Joseph Hull, with his wife *Agnes*, was minister of York, Me., and lived between the years 1594 and 1665.

Capt. Tristram Hull, his son, with his wife *Blanche*, lived in Barnstable, Mass., between the years 1623 and 1666.

Captain John Hull, his son, married *Alice Tiddeman*, daughter of Capt. Edward Tiddeman, of London. This Capt. Hull was the instructor in naval tactics of Sir Charles Wager, first Lord of the Admiralty, in 1733.— See Sheffield's Hist. Ad., Newport, 1876. John Hull was of Conanicut, and Newport, 1654–1732. His son,

Capt. Tiddeman Hull, of Conanicut, R. I., married *Sarah Sands*, the only child of Edward Sands, a son of

James Sands, one of the original proprietors of Block Island. The marriage occurred March 10, 1711. His son,

Hon. Robert Hull, of South Kingston, R. I., 1718–1768, married *Thankful Ball*, daughter of Peter Ball, of Block Island, and here became a prominent citizen, as above stated. His son,

Hon. Edward Hull, claimed as a Block Islander, married Mary, the daughter of Daniel Weeden, of Jamestown, R. I., and by marriage his descendants are numerous on the Island, though none of them bear the name of Hull. He was born at South Kingston in 1741, and died on Block Island in 1804. His children were:

Alice; born Oct. 28, 1764, and married John Gorton, of Block Island:

Weeden; born March 7, 1766, died unmarried:

Thankful; born Apr. 27, 1767; married Nathaniel Champlain, of Block Island:

Mary; born March 21, 1770, died in infancy:

Catharine; born Apr. 21, 1771:

Robert; born March 25, 1773, and married Hannah Littlefield, of Block Island:

Tiddeman, married, 1st, Lucy Hazard, and 2d, Sarah, daughter of John Andrews:

John; died unmarried:

Joanna; married Dr. Aaron C. Willey, of Block Island, the father of Mrs. Cordelia Dodge, the wife of the late Gideon Dodge, whose descendants here are numerous:

Sarah; born May 5, 1780, married Wager Weeden:

Jane; married Dr. George Hazard, of South Kingston:

Mary; died unmarried.

The children of the above Robert and Hannah (Littlefield) Hull were:

Edward; died unmarried:

Alice; married Sylvester Hazard of South Kingston,
R. I.:

Wager; married at "Babcock," of South Kingston:

William; died unmarried:

John; married ———, and had one child,—whole family
drowned in a freshet:

Sarah; married Nathaniel Chappel, of Wakefield, R. I.:

Joseph; died unmarried.

Mr. Charles E. Perry, of Block Island, has carefully
prepared genealogical branches of the Hulls, as connected
with other names by marriage, as in case of those daugh
ters who married Judge Wager Weeden, of South Kingston; Nathaniel Champlin, Esq., of Block Island; John
Gorton, Esq., and Nathaniel Sheffield, Esq., both the
latter of Block Island.

LITTLEFIELD.

The families of this name have been very numerous on
Block Island for many years, and have maintained a very
respectable position in society.

Caleb Littlefield was admitted freeman in 1721, and
Nathaniel Littlefield in 1721, and from the two the various branches now here may have originated. The latter
was representative in the Rhode Island General Assembly
in 1738, 1740, 1746, 1748, 1754.

Caleb Littlefield, Jr., was admitted freeman in 1756,
Nathaniel Littlefield, Jr., also in 1756, both on the same
day, as were their fathers. The latter was representative
from Block Island in 1758, 1762. Caleb Littlefield, Jr.,
was one of the committee of the Island to oppose the
English tea-tax, in 1774.

John Littlefield was admitted freeman in 1738, was representative in the Assembly from 1747 up to the Revolution, nearly thirty years, and in 1780 received from Gov.
Greene a present of six barrels of cider.

Samuel Littlefield was admitted freeman in 1736, *Henry, Nathaniel,* and *Simon Ray Littlefield* were on the Island in the early, and the last in the latter part of the Revolution.

William Littlefield obtained distinction by marrying the daughter of Simon Ray, Jr., Miss Phebe Ray, by his own daughter, Miss Catharine Littlefield, who married Maj.-Gen. Nathaniel Greene, by which marriage she became an intimate associate with the wife of General Washington.

Said *William Littlefield* took an active part in the Revolution, and in 1775 was appointed Ensign, and from that was promoted to the office of Lieut.-Captain. After about five years of faithful service in the American army, while on a visit to Block Island he was reported, maliciously, to the General Assembly as having assisted the Islanders in carrying on trade with the English, for which crime his name was greatly dishonored until he could get a hearing before the Assembly. He was censured, and denied his pay in 1781, but in 1784 obtained a hearing whereby the falsity of the accusation against him was admitted by the Assembly, and his pay with interest granted. In 1785, he took his seat again as a representative of Block Island in the General Assembly, and also in 1792.

Henry Littlefield, familiarly called "*Harry,*" or "old Harry," during and after the Revolution owned a large tract on the Island. He kept the only store, at the Harbor, and according to tradition, kept himself on friendly terms with the "refugees," by selling them liquor. He does not seem to have been a relative of the other Island Littlefields. It is said that in addition to his large real estate, "he had a barrel of dollars." In the height of his wealth, the tide of fortune set against him. He had unjustly taken the property of a woman whose daughter is an aged lady now living. He had taken eight of her feather beds, and she said to him, "My prayer is, that you may die so poor that you will not have a bed to die on!" Her prayer was answered.

Elias Littlefield, though a man in humble life, a resident for many years on the north end of the Island, was one of Nature's great men, and what was better, he was a most exemplary Christian, sound and clear in doctrine, familiar with the Bible, and always ready to converse upon religious topics. As we stood, one sunny day in spring, on the south side of his barn, when the winds were chilly, under the old man's farming garments, from within the old tenement of clay, shone out the bright rays of the beautiful garments of the "new man," that spoke heavenly words of his eternal youth, and of his happy home in prospect. He went there in 1875, at the age of eighty-six.

Anthony Littlefield, the brother of Elias, and Mercy, his wife, are now living, the former in his eighty-fourth year, and the latter in her eighty-fifth, both free from disease, although he has recently become blind. Their married life together, over sixty years, in comfortable circumstances, has passed away happily. They, for many years, have risen early, breakfasted by lamp-light, dined about eleven, supped about four P. M., attended to their own domestic matters without a servant or a third person in their house, with clear memories and reasoning faculties; as ready to die alone as in a crowd, and cheerful in the hope of a happy hereafter. They witnessed the fearful wreck of the *Warrior*, on Sandy Point, and received the corpses of the crew at their house for respectable preparation for the Island cemetery.

Elam Littlefield, late of Block Island, for many years was an active business man, doing a large part of the mercantile trade here, and nearly all connected with the West Side, left many friends to commemorate his excellences, and sons to emulate his business example. His large store, near his house (upon which he had no insurance), was burned. His son,

Lorenzo Littlefield, a representative in the Assembly in 1861 and 1862, commissioner of wrecks, and town treasurer, carries on an extensive mercantile business at the Center.

Hon. Ray S. Littlefield, brother of Lorenzo, and interested with him in the store, and proprietor of the popular Central House, has been representative in the Assembly since 1873 to the present, 1877.

Thomas D. Littlefield was born in 1754, and died August 30, 1829, aged seventy-five years. He was father of

Nicholas Littlefield, who was born April 8, 1783, died June 2, 1846, aged sixty-five years. His sons *Elam*, above-mentioned, *Nicholas*, and *Almanzo Littlefield*, the latter two now living, have been well-known and highly-esteemed citizens of the Island.

LEWIS.

This name is of comparatively recent origin on the Island. *Mr. Jesse Lewis*, son of Enoch Lewis, a revolutionary soldier of South Kingston, R. I., settled upon Block Island in 1806, renting a farm here of Rowland Hazard— a farm of 300 acres, for seven years. In 1810, he married Susan A. Paine, daughter of Mr. Wm. Paine, and until his death remained a worthy citizen and first-class farmer over fifty years. His son,

Hon. Wm. P. Lewis, born upon the Island April 22, 1822, in 1849 married Miss Wealthy Dodge, daughter of Capt. Gideon Dodge, and granddaughter of Dr. Aaron C. Willey, who was then the physician of the Island, and well known abroad. In 1850, Mr. Lewis was elected third warden; in 1851, deputy sheriff; in 1853, second

warden; in 1856, first warden. which office he now holds;
is licensed auctioneer, notary public, and commissioner of
wrecks. During his official services as warden (the same
as those of a justice of the peace), he has rendered judgment in one hundred cases, eighty of which were civil,
and twenty criminal. His first-class farm, and respectable family, are an ornament and an honor to the Island.

MITCHELL.

This has long been one of the familiar names on Block
Island. The more prominent among them have been the
following:

James Mitchell, admitted freeman in 1683. *Lieut.
Thomas Mitchell*, a cotemporary of the Rev. Samuel Niles,
and with him a sufferer from the French privateers in
1689. He was admitted freeman in 1696, was representative of the Island, with Simon Ray, in 1721, and held
that office in 1723, 1724, 1735, in which year he was known
as Captain Mitchell.

Thomas Mitchell, Jr., was representative of the Island
in the General Assembly in the year 1738. *George Mitchell*
was admitted freeman in 1720; *Jonathan Mitchell*, in 1728;
John Mitchell, in 1734; *Joseph Mitchell*, in 1721; *John
Mitchell, Thomas Mitchell, Jeremiah, Jonathan*, and *Joseph*,
in 1775, were on the Island and gave up their cattle to be
taken beyond the reach of the British. In 1781 *Thomas*
was a "fifer" in the Revolution. Of the generation
between the last of the above and the oldest now living
we have but little knowledge.

Barzelia B. Mitchell, father of the proprietor of the
Spring House, is one of the oldest of the name on the
Island. His father, *Jonathan Mitchell*, moved to the West
long ago.

29

MOTT.

Nathaniel Mott was one of the early residents of Block Island. As such he was admitted freeman in 1683. In 1695, he was town clerk, held his office many years thereafter, and was representative in 1710.

Edward Mott was admitted freeman in 1696; and *John Mott*, in 1721; *Edward*, in 1738; *Nathaniel*, in 1744; *John*, in 1760, and in 1775, with *Daniel Mott*, was on the Island, and parted with cattle taken by the colony. *Daniel Mott*, father of Abraham R., now living, is still remembered as a worthy citizen. *A. Rathbone Mott*, an aged citizen, and a relative of the ancient Rathbone family, will long be remembered as a golden link between the past and present. He is highly esteemed for his social and Christian virtues.

Of the Motts now living on the Island who already have, or soon will pass the meridian of life, Edward, Hamilton, Francis, Smith, and Otis, may all be mentioned as having made a good record in public estimation.

JOHN OLDHAM.

Although Mr. Oldham was neither a native nor resident of Block Island, yet his death here, and his being the first civilized trader here, entitle him to more than a passing notice. He came from England and arrived at Plymouth in the ship Ann, July, 1623, and at once took a high position as a citizen. To him was allotted more land than to any other, and that was granted to him "in continuance," a thing done then to none other. He was soon invited to a seat in Gov. Bradford's council. His promotion was less rapid, however, than his fall. In 1624, he was banished from Plymouth and forbidden to return, and by setting aside this banishment, in 1625, was expelled again "with great indignity," his offense being a strong attachment to Episcopacy. He settled at Nantasket in 1624; in 1626 was wrecked on Cape Cod and narrowly escaped, at about which time his character was greatly changed from its imperious tone to one of gentleness, and he was soon restored at Plymouth. Gov. Bradford entrusted to him a prisoner to be taken to England for trial, in 1628. In 1629 he had a claim on a large tract of land on the central part of which Charlestown, Mass., is now standing, and about that time became a resident of Watertown, Mass. That claim was contested. He was described as a " frank, high-minded man," and was admitted freeman of Watertown in 1631, where the highest trusts were conferred upon him. Mr. Oldham was one of the representatives in the first court that assembled in Massachusetts, and was chairman of the first legislative committee appointed in that State. In 1633 he went by land to Connecticut, lodging among the Indians, and probably founded the plantation at Wethersfield in 1634. His estate was the first ever settled there, Sept. 1, 1636. His death at Block Island had occurred in July, 1636, and but for that casualty the Island might have attracted little or no attention during the succeeding century. He was a man of so great enterprise and promise to the colony of Massachusetts that she could not quietly suffer the death of so distinguished a citizen to go unavenged, and hence her conquest of Block Island.

In Winthrop's History of New England we find the following circumstances of the death of Mr. Oldham, who had been out on a long trading voyage with the Indians, accompanied by two English boys, and two native men. All the sachems of the Narragansetts were in the plot to kill him, except Canonicus, and Miantonomoh. They sought his life because of his trade and peaceful acts with their enemies, the Pequots. Meantime Roger Williams was with Miantonomoh, who, through Mr. Williams, expressed great sorrow over said death, and a purpose to punish the offenders. Master John Gallop, with a twenty-ton bark, passing Block Island, discovered Mr. Oldham's vessel, with its deck full of Indians, and a canoe passing from it to the Island full of Indians and goods. "Whereupon they suspected they [the Indians] had killed John Oldham, and the rather because the Indians let slip and set up sail, being two miles from shore, and the wind and tide being off the shore of the Island, whereby they drove towards the main at Narragansett. Gallop and his men headed them, and bore up to them who stood "armed with guns, pikes, and swords." Gallop had only one man, two little boys, "two pieces, and two pistols." But he "let fly among them and so galled them that they all got under hatches." He then retired, got headway, and attempted to run them down, "and almost overset her, which so frightened the Indians that six of them leaped overboard and were drowned." He repeated the attempt, fastened to her, raked her fore and aft; stood off again, while "four or five more Indians leaped into the sea and were likewise drowned;" boarded her again, bound two Indians, threw one of them into the sea, discovered two more Indians, inaccessible, "in a little room underneath, with their swords," and then "looking about, they found John Oldham under an old seine, stark naked, his head cleft to the brains, and his hands and legs cut as if they had been cutting them off, and yet warm. So they put him into the sea." Gallop towed Oldham's vessel away, "but night coming on, and the wind rising, they were forced to turn her off, and the wind carried her to the Narragansett shore." The two Indians that were with Mr. Oldham reported similar things to Mr. Williams then with the chief sachem Canonicus. The two boys that were with Mr. Oldham were returned by the sachem Miantonomoh, with a letter from Roger Williams informing Governor Vane that said sachem had sent the sachem of Niantic to Block Island to procure said boys. Three of the Indians drowned while Gallop was capturing the Oldham vessel were sachems, and probably belonged to Block Island, as Roger Williams then wrote that there were "pettie sachems about the Great Pond." Another account of this affair is given in the article on *Indians*.

PAINE.

In the oldest records of Block Island we find this name, although not directly connected with its settlement.

Captain Thomas Paine has the honor of having commanded the expedition against the French privateers in 1690, and of having fought the first naval battle within the waters of Block Island after its settlement. Captain Gallop, in 1636, had fought with the Indians, off Sandy Point, and captured from them the vessel which they had taken from the trader, Oldham. Capt. Paine's victory is related in the article on Hostilities. When the French commander learned that he was fighting with his old acquaintance, he retreated, "stood off to sea," and remarked that "he would as soon choose to fight with the devil as with him."

Thomas Paine, perhaps a son of the former, 1736, was admitted freeman of Block Island.

John Paine, in 1745, was here as a citizen, and rose to distinction in matters of trust, representing the Island in the General Assembly in 1753, 1757, 1761, 1765, and in 1775 parted with a large stock of cattle to the government, and remained as one of the solid citizens of the Island during the Revolution.

Revoe Paine, son, or grandson of John, was born upon the Island, and here lived to a great age. He was probably the son of John, as it is said he was born about one hundred years ago.

John Revoe Paine, son of Revoe, is one of the present

residents, and is a highly esteemed citizen, both for his integrity and for his respectable family. He is one of the most extensive land owners on the Island.

Nathaniel Paine, commonly called "Uncle Nat," now a resident of Fairhaven, Mass., seems to belong to a different branch from the above. He will long be remembered among the Islanders by his zeal for religion, and by his consistent deportment, and as the father of Mrs. John G. Sheffield.

ROSE.

This has been a common name on Block Island from its first settlement, in 1662.

Tormut Rose was one of the first who came to occupy the soil, and was admitted as a freeman in 1664. His direct descendants are still upon the Island. In 1775, one of them bore the name of Tormut, which has continued to be transmitted from generation to generation, and latterly has been written *Thomas*.

Capt. William Rose came to the Island with the settling party, according to the town records, and his name has been several times repeated since then, as applied to later generations. He had command of the bark that brought the settlers, their cattle, and goods, in part, from Braintree and Taunton.

Ezekiel, and *Oliver Ring Rose, John*, and *John Rose, Jr.*, are waymarks of the Rose family here during the eighteenth century.

Rev. Enoch Rose founded the Free-Will Baptist church of the Island about the year 1820. He was a man of more than ordinary natural abilities, and exerted much good influence upon others. Persons of this name are numerous on the West Side, and on all parts of the Island they contribute largely to the population of good citizens. .

Lieut. Gov. Anderson C. Rose, late of Block Island,

obtained distinction in the political arena. Born about
the year 1826, the son of Capt. Thomas Rose, in early
years exhibited a love of learning, diligently improving
his opportunities in the common school, and during vaca-
tions. While a boy he adopted for his daily motto
"*Strive to do Right.*" He became a teacher on his native
Island, and as such is respectfully remembered by many.
In 1853, he was elected as representative to the General
Assembly without opposition and there distinguished himself by his force of character and logical powers. In
spite of strong opposition from old and influential legisla-
tors he secured a vote for the charter of a bank on Block
Island, but for some reason the bank was never established. In 1854, he was elected to the State Senate, and
also as first warden of his town, and about this time
began the study of law which he pursued successfully in
the office of Hon. B. F. Thurston of Providence. As a
senator his talents brought him prominently before the
people, and secured his nomination for lieutenant-governor
in 1855, and his election by a majority of 5,708 votes
over two other candidates. He officiated acceptably as a
presiding officer, and at the close of the term for which
he was elected turned his attention vigorously to the
legal profession, and soon after his admission to the bar
in 1857, removed to Illinois and began practice. His
slender constitution broke down, and in July, 1858, his
remains were brought back to Block Island, and in 1869
were disinterred and placed beside his mother and sister
in Cypress Hill cemetery of Brooklyn, N. Y.

Ambrose N. Rose, town clerk, Alanson Rose, proprietor of the Woonsocket House, Capt. John E. Rose,
Capt. Addison Rose, and others are well-known as descendants from ancient ancestors on the Island.

SHEFFIELD.

The first that we find of this name on Block Island was in 1758. Sheffields were here previous to this date un-doubtedly. They were numerous in other places of Rhode Island, in its earliest history, and some of them occupied honorable positions, especially Joseph and Nathaniel from 1696 to 1719.

Edmund Sheffield, in 1758, was a farmer on the Island In June, 1757, a French privateer was hovering about the coast of Rhode Island, and the State "sent out two armed vessels in quest of her, one of which touched at Block Island, where she was supplied with four sheep and a cheese by Mr. Edmund Sheffield of that place." In 1762, he was one of the representatives of the Island in a peti-tion for a lottery in order to improve the Great Pond for a harbor and fisheries.

Josiah Sheffield, in 1760, was admitted freeman of New Shoreham. At the breaking out of the Revolution there were several Sheffield families on the Island. *Benjamin* and *Ezekiel* were here then. The former left the Island during the war and lived at Charlestown, returning to his farm in New Shoreham to collect rents in February, 1779, and in October of the same year.

Nathaniel Sheffield, son of Edmund, married Mary Ann Gorton, the daughter of John Gorton and Alice Hull, daughter of Capt. Edward Hull of Block Island. His son,

Hon. John G. Sheffield, born upon Block Island, April 26, 1819, still living, has been one of the most public-spirited and respectable citizens. Most of the time from the age of twenty-three, in 1842, when he entered the General Assembly, he has occupied positions of public trust and responsibility, and at the same time has been a first-class farmer. During the rebellion, and up to the year 1873, Mr. Sheffield represented the Island in the

State Legislature, and coöperated with great vigor and personal influence with Hon. Nicholas Ball, his fellow-townsman, in securing a government harbor for the Island. Having held nearly all of the town offices, and with health somewhat impaired by a life of constant activity, for the past few years he has enjoyed the sweets of retirement at his beautiful home on one of the most sightly points of the Island—the ancient home of his grandfather John Gorton, who, on account of his personal bearing, was called "Governor Gorton," both by his townsmen and by the British soldiers of 1812, who as a mark of respect, when they visited his house, stacked their arms at a considerable distance from his residence.

In the construction of the breakwater of Block Island, Mr. Sheffield did a good work for the public and for his townsmen. In July, 1872, seconded by several prominent townsmen, he became the contractor for placing in said breakwater 10,000 tons of riprap granite for the sum of $21,900.00. His closest competitor for the contract bid $29,500.00, from which it is seen that Mr. Sheffield saved an expense of $7,600 to the government and secured employment for many of his fellow citizens. His activity for the intellectual and moral improvement of the Island-ers has kept pace with his political and pecuniary enter-prises. The records of the First Baptist Church of New Shoreham indicate his activity in building the present house of worship and in other matters.

The children of Mr. John G. and Mrs. Cordelia (Payne) Sheffield are Mary (wife of Capt. Archibald Milikin), Lucinda, John, Ella, Lila, Homer, and Arthur.

Hon. William P. Sheffield, son of Mr. George G. Shef-field, and now a resident of Newport, is a native of Block Island and a cousin of John G. Sheffield. He has ob-tained distinction in the legal profession, in financial trans-actions, in political life, and in historical research. In the

State Legislature he is at present an efficient representative, and in 1861 was elected a member of Congress from the eastern district of Rhode Island. The historical sketches of Newport and of his native Island published by him in 1876 have given great pleasure to the public. From the latter we quote the following as an index of the feelings and scenes common to the Islanders, and only wanting education or ambition to give them expression in poetry or in prose beautiful and sublime. He says : " The most attractive place to me are the high banks on the south side of the Island. Those rude, gray cliffs, which, since their creation, or possibly since the morning stars first sang together for joy, have presented their bared breasts in battle array to the sea and storm, always had a mysterious attraction to me. In my youth no neighboring dwelling or other intrusion came to interrupt the converse of the surrounding scenes with the soul of the solitary visitor. There I saw in the swelling and recession of the mighty bosom of the sea the respiration of God in nature; there in the calm and lull of the elements, I heard 'the still small voice' fall upon my ears, wooing from above all that was good within me, and in the thunder and earthquake shock of the storm, I have often stood almost paralyzed under the spell-binding influence of the warning voice thus coming from that Power which had aroused the wrath of the forces of nature, and was breaking forth in the war of the elements. There I have seen the strong ship, which had traversed every zone, crushed by the power of the ocean waves as if her sides were but wisps of straw, and been impressed with the utter powerlessness of man to contend with Him who holds the sea in the hollow of His hand, and with His will directs the storm."

Mr. George Sheffield, brother of Wm. P., is one of the

most thorough, and well-to-do farmers of the Island, and is a highly esteemed citizen.

TOSH.

William Tosh was one of the settlers who embarked for Block Island, at Taunton, in 1662. He was not one of the first proprietors, but as a citizen was admitted freeman of the colony in 1664, was constable in 1676; died in 1685, and his property then inventoried shows that he was a well-to-do citizen, having 263 acres of land and dwelling-house, estimated at £288.

Ackers Tosh, probably a son of William, born in 1684, lived until he reached his one hundred and first year, according to the stone at his grave in the Island cemetery. He was admitted freeman in 1709.

Margaret Tosh was born June 26, 1726. *William Tosh* was born in 1733.

James Tosh was born May 26, 1735. (R. S. Dickens' Bible.)

Daniel Tosh, perhaps a brother of the first settler, William, was admitted freeman in 1696, with several others of Block Island, and with James Sweet, who was then admitted, was kidnapped by a buccaneer in the bay, May 18, 1717. The fate of both of them is still a mystery on the Island.

The estate of the senior Wm. Tosh, inventoried in 1685, furnishes us with the prices of things in general then on the Island.

1 Chest and lock,	£0	5	0
1 Churn and firkins and glass bottles,	0	12	0
1 Cupboard and kneading trough,	0	3	0
1 Chest,	0	8	0
3 Bushels of salt,	0	6	0
100 Pounds of cheese,	1	5	0
1 Feather bed and bedding,	1	15	0

	£	s	d
1 Frying pan and dishes, ...	£0	2	0
1 Pot and kettle, chain trammel, . .	1	15	0
1 Hatchel, other lumber in the chamber, .	0	15	0
1 New pot and four wedges, . . .	0	18	0
Pails, hoes, and grinding stone, . .	0	14	0
2 Pitchforks and 2 old hoes, . .	0	4	0
1 Cart and wheels, ...	1	0	0
3 Chains and 2 clevises, . . .	1	10	0
3 Yokes, ...	0	6	0
Waring clothes, ...	1	6	0
13 cows and a bull, ...	30	0	0
4 Oxen, ...	16	0	0
8 Calves, last year, ...	9	0	0
6 Calves, ...	2	8	0
4 Two-year olds, vantage, ...	2	5	0
1 Heifer, 3 years old, ...	2	5	0
1 Mare and a horse colt, ...	3	10	0
30 Swine, ...	12	0	0
50 Sheep, ...	12	0	0
263 Acres and dwelling-house, . . .	288	0	0
1 Small gun, ...	0	12	0
Old iron, cabbages, and wheels, barrels, .	1	3	0
1 Qr. pot, ...	0	3	6
8 Acres of corn, ...	8	0	0
1 Indian servant for life, ...	7	0	0

WRIGHT.

John Wright was a resident of Block Island in the early part of the Revolution. In 1776 he and some of his neighbors had considerable trouble with the authorities at Newport on account of an alleged friendliness to the British.

Wm. L. Wright, a native of the Island, its first post-master, moved to Exeter, Otsego Co., N. Y., in 1837, taking children with him. His son,

George M. Wright, born in 1817, on Block Island, taught school here the winter that his friend S. Ray Sands taught; attended select school in Hartwick, N. Y., and afterward, in 1841, was employed in New York city by the firm of Jeremiah & Nathaniel Briggs, in the forwarding and transportation business. Subsequently he was superintendent of the Seaman's Friend and Retreat, on Staten Island, and in 1851, became a citizen of New Brunswick, N. J., and was there general agent of Geo. W. Aspinwall's steam towing line, in 1854. In 1855 Mr. Wright moved to Bordentown, N. J.; was there mayor three years; in 1865 was elected State Senator for three years; for many years was inspector and collector of the Delaware & Raritan Canal company—collecting millions and reporting every cent to the entire satisfaction of the company; for the last twenty years largely interested in steam boats, being a director in the Pennsylvania Steam Towing & Transportation company, and also engaged in banking. In February, 1876, he was elected State Treasurer of New Jersey for three years, and it is hoped by his old friends on Block Island that he may live long and continue to be an honor to the home of his childhood.

There are many names of excellent families on the Island not here represented. All who have desired to have their genealogy briefly sketched have had an opportunity to present the same to the writer. A whole volume, indeed, might be filled with biographical sketches of the Island families. Hereafter, it is hoped, there will be greater conveniences in ascertaining names, dates, and relations. The Milikins, the Conleys, the Peckhams, the Spragues, the Willises, the Allens, the Hayses, the Steadmans, the Coes, the Dunns, and the Gortons, and others are old and respectable names worthy of commemoration.

30

PECULIAR AND PITIABLE.

In almost every community there are persons so different from the generality of mankind, so nondescript, that without classifying them at all, each may be considered by himself as an abnormal specimen of humanity. Some can hardly be said to belong either to the sane, or to the insane; either to the civilized, or the uncivilized; either to the happy, or the miserable portions of society. Block Island has had its share of such. It has also had invalids, worthy persons, singularly afflicted.

"VARNY" was an abnormal Islander. This part of his name is all we need to perpetuate. He seems to have been a pet of "Old Harry," as he was called. The latter was very rich, and delighted in lavishing his wealth on Varny. Old Harry's pet had his own way of enjoying presents of money, one of which was to use a dollar bill for lighting his pipe. At this Harry took no offense, for he was eccentric, and was proud of his ability to furnish such a spendthrift, and even went so far as to give Varny a deed of a good farm. In process of time, however, Harry offended his protegé, and the latter, in a fit of revenge burned up the deed of said farm.

Varny's house was, for a time, one of those little stone and earth ice-houses at the Harbor, the wood-cuts of which may be seen in Harper's Monthly for July, 1876. His household companions were a dog, and a pig. For the latter he seemed to have the stronger attachment, and called him "Rig-Dug." The pig reciprocated his master's attachment, and did not seem to be embarrassed with a sense of inferiority in the family. There existed between them a uniformity of aspirations and contentment, except at certain times, when Rig-Dug would grunt good-naturedly at things which caused Varny to swear so frightfully as to make a swarm of boys run for their hiding places like rats when lightning gets into a cellar.

Those boys, though now pretty " old boys," still remember the dark nights, when the rails went down Varny's chimney, when the beach-stones made music on his door —no glass to jingle, for he had no windows,—and when they scattered for their lives to escape from the wrath of the companion of Rig-Dug and Fido.

Once Varny got the best of the joke. Some men, seeing the fun which the boys had by putting rails down said chimney, repeated the trick by putting a couple of small masts down the same. Soon after they were stepped in Varny's fire-place he kindled a brisk fire at their feet which necessitated a hasty exit. His eccentric mode of living was after he became a widower. Abnormal as he was, Varny is said to have had a son, whose name, by giving it a little touch of Latin, was

FRACUS. How he came to have this name, whether from some *fracas*, or something else, is unknown. He, too, was peculiar. His aberration from the laws of nature, living to old age in solitude; his exhibitions of rude paintings with which to interpret prophecies; and his making Gen. Washington a central figure of his interpretations; and his outdoor lectures to a passing throng; and his lonely waitings for some one to come to the place of his appointment, are evidences of his having better thoughts and feelings than did his father, and that, though he now sees with obscured vision, yet hereafter he may better understand the duties and joys of society and the glorious reality of the shadows now lingering over his mental horizon. Time and eternity may prove that Fracus is less crazy to-day than some whose elegant mansions, in view of his lonely cottage, are distinguished by guests who seek only the pleasures of the present. Some who are little here will be great in the world to come, and some who are greatest here will be among the least there.

ABNORMITY. The character to which this name is appropriate, on the Island, is as indescribable as the inside of a kaleidoscope. The rays in him are peculiarly mixed and angular. There is light in him, but of what kind, whether of nature or of revelation, or "darkness," it is not-always easy to determine. But few exhibit a greater zeal for religion, and but few are believed by some to have less than he has. He imagines himself to be one of the humblest, while evincing great pride over his imagined superiority. He has claimed the supernatural gift of praying and exhorting in what he calls the "unknown tongue." He claims that he has healed the sick in twenty minutes by his prayers of faith. He is very boastful over his obedience to all the commandments, and has embraced many opportunities to class large congregations of Christians with adulterers and thieves because they do not keep the seventh day holy as he does; and yet his behavior in seventh day meetings has been so bad as to break them up repeatedly. He repeats Scripture with great fluency, while the truths that pass from his tongue seem to have produced but a slight impression upon his mind. He goes from house to house to exhibit himself, and to talk about himself. Because David danced *before the Lord*, Abnormity glories in having a religious dance *before men*. His preaching gift is so great in his own estimation, that he begged the privilege of a dying neighbor to preach his funeral sermon on the ground that neither of the two pastors on the Island was competent for that service. He condemns persecution in strongest terms, and yet evidently seeks it. He is a great talker, and yet says but very little. He often talks about honesty, but has had the cheek to sell old hens for chickens; and when the trick was dis. covered, declared to the merchant that *they were chickens*. He is as much of a compound of contradictions as the toper's beverage in which was, ."Lemon to make it sour;

sugar to make it sweet; brandy to make it strong; water to make it weak."

Abnormity was once a little foiled. He contrived a plan for demonstrating his superiority over two ministers.

His syllogism seemed to be this: "I cured a disease, by prayer, in twenty minutes; if these two ministers cannot do as much, *then I am greater than both.*" A lame arm and shoulder, real or feigned, were a test subject. He laid his disease before one minister for trial. Then he presented himself before the other, saying: "We are commanded, if any among you are sick, to call on *the elders,* it don't say call on the doctors, but on the *elders,* to be healed by the prayer of faith. I believe in going by the Scriptures, and have come to have you cure my arm and shoulder, and you can do it, if you are a true minister— for I have cured the sick by prayer in twenty minutes— and I have tried the other minister, and he has had twenty-four hours to heal it in, and I am no better, which shows that he is not a true minister—now I want to see what you can do."

Minister No. 2, replied: "Are you willing to follow the Scriptures strictly, to be healed by the prayer of faith?" "Yes," he replied. "Then, if we go about this according to Scripture, we must follow the Scripture *order.* In the first place you must call on the "*elders,*" not one at a time, as you have done with us. In the second place, you must have *faith* in our prayers to heal you, and in the third place we must "*anoint,*" you either in part or all over, "*with oil,*" and it will be a matter for us to consider whether or not to use *kerosene.*" "Well, well," said he, " I don't know about having kerosene put on me," obtaining, perhaps, for the first time in his life, a glimpse of the necessary steps to be taken to be healed in the days of miracles. Before his visit closed, during which all was said in a serious manner, he gestured with his lame arm

30*

about as freely as he did with the other, and has not applied for healing since then.

Some of his recitations of Scriptures, some of his prayers and exhortations, and some of his exhibitions of faith, whether moved by the spirit which actuated the effeminate demoniac that followed Paul and Silas at Philippi, or by a better spirit, have certainly been extraordinary. In the sieve which Satan shakes, in spite of him, the wheat will come to the surface, occasionally. Abnormity has made a zig-zag mark which it is feared he will never straighten. He has some worthy ancestors, and many good relatives now living, and is known somewhat abroad, but should not be considered as an average, but as a peculiar representative of Block Island.

THREE DEAF, MUTE, AND BLIND BROTHERS.

They were all thus afflicted in early childhood, and all grew up to be old men. The few ideas which they obtained from partial vision in their earliest years were of great value to them in youth and manbood. Two are dead, and one is living. They were all bright boys, and by their activity and kind dispositions have secured not only sympathy from the more highly favored, but a good degree of respect from them also. Though supported mainly by the town, they have exhibited a desire to help themselves as much as possible. They were very good fishermen, by having a little assistance. Their friends conversed with them rapidly by signs made by moving their hands, and by touching various parts of their persons. They, in turn, quickly recognized and distinguished indviduals by their height, breadth of shoulders, shape, beard, faces, depth of chest, quality of dress, and by whatever their hands might touch. They were able to go to various parts of the Island, and to return alone, feeling their way with canes.   They were familiarly known as *Blind Varnum, Blind Nelson,* and *Blind Henry.*

The last one named is now living.

Blind Varnum is remembered, among other things, by his adroitness in catching lobsters that were smaller than the legal standard.   He contrived a plan by which he made the lobsters the aggresssors, and himself an actor in self-defense.   His mode of procedure was simply to have the lobsters *catch him.*   To do this, knowing well their powerful pincers, Blind Varnum would muffle his feet with stockings and rags fastened around his toes, and then, in the warm days of summer, when the tide was low, waded out into the bay, near the old pier, as deep as it was safe for him to do, and there would work his feet around the rocks, and into the sand until he felt the lobsters pinching his toes.   Thus the lobsters caught *him,* and he, in defense, mastered them, strung them, and sold or ate them.   He was drowned, while fishing.

Blind Nelson made a deep impression upon the Islanders by his religious character.   Though unable to hear or say a word, or see a thing, his religious convictions were clearly expressed, and his desire to be baptized and become a member of the church was gratified.   His faithful attendance at times of worship, was unmistakable proof of his consciousness of the fulfillment of the promise of the Saviour to be where his followers are assembled in his name.   He also gave expression to his faith and emotions in the conference meetings in a manner which others could understand.   By signs made with his hands, as he arose, the love of his heart was indicated, his hope of having his eyes opened, his ears unstopped, his tongue loosened, and of going to heaven were forcibly expressed by silent gestures, while many a tearful eye looked upon his face tinged with the radiance of faith like that which shone out from the martyr Stephen.   He died several years ago.

Blind Henry is perhaps, a little more intelligent than was either of his brothers mentioned.   During the winter he remains at home, but in summer the walk of two miles to the Harbor is frequently performed to get a few dimes from visitors, and to enjoy the many little favors conferred upon him by his well-known townsmen.   No one seems to understand better than he the times and places for meeting the new arrivals by steamer.   Many have seen him holding his hat by the way-side.   His theatrical performances, such as dancing, taking part upon the battlefield, sporting, killing his game, picking off its feathers, and eating it with a relish, using his cane for a gun, and his fingers for knife and fork—these with his jolly good nature while others are witnesses, and an occasional rap of his cane given to a perplexing boy, added to the narrow escapes from being run over by teams, keep his acquaintances mindful of his pitiful condition.

It is interesting to notice the elements of human nature in some way exhibited by Blind Henry.   His *love of money* is variously manifested.   After a year's acquaintance with a minister who always gave him a few pennies when they met, Henry, showing him great respect by removing his hat and by slapping the minister on the shoulder, instantly anticipated the little alms, and on one occasion put out his hand too soon to receive the money, and instantly withdrew it as the thought occurred to him that he was hasty in begging from a minister.   Here were evident a high respect, a strong love of money, and a quick and delicate sense of propriety, and a mortification for asking so hastily for alms, which he soon received.   Henry likes a good bargain.   When he buys pipes, tobacco, and other items, good quality and full measure are demanded, and in order that he may not be cheated, he feels of the *cheeks* of the merchants *before buying*, by gently passing his hands over their faces. Some cheeks he will trust much more readily than he will others, and some he will not trust at all.

Blind Henry gives very good evidence of having seen the Friend whom blind Bartimeus saw *before* his eyes were opened to the light of day. Two funerals had recently occurred on the Island, and Henry learned about them. Soon afterward he described them, and the characters of the deceased persons, and their destiny. The one was a devoted Christian. Without a word spoken, by the sign with his finger which indicated a curl of hair on the neck, those standing about him knew he meant a woman. With his thumbs and fore-fingers he gently pulled down his eyelids. He then laid his cane down upon the ground slowly, keeping it horizontal. Then he put one hand to one end of the cane and the other hand to the other end to represent head and foot stones. Then he stooped over the cane, and motioned with his two hands as if he were rounding up the earth over the grave. Then, after standing up a moment he stooped down, put his hands together over the imagined grave, separated them in a way that indicated the opening of the grave, repeated these motions several times, then rose up and stretched one hand high toward heaven. All understood him. He told us silently, "she is dead;" "she is buried;" "she will rise again;" "she has gone to heaven." The other funeral was similarly described, the description closing with motions indicating that the wicked man had gone down.

Blind Henry keeps the Sabbath. If he loses the day of the week he inquires for the day of rest. To rebuke a wrong, he points up.

The three deaf, mute, blind brothers were wholly mute and deaf from infancy, and all wholly blind after the

age of twenty-five.   Varnum was drowned at the age of
about sixty, Nelson, at about sixty-five, died of consumption; and Henry is now living at the age of seventy.

PAUPERS.

These are not numerous upon Block Island, for a living
is here obtained with but little exertion.   They are only
eight, in 1877, and are not sent away from home to a
county house, nor are they kept at one place.   At an annual town meeting the keeping of each pauper for the
ensuing year is given to the lowest bidder for the same.
One by one they are thus put up at auction, and distributed over the town.   They are not, however, left to the
mercy of the bidder.   If an unworthy citizen underbids
for one of the more respectable paupers, the bid is nulli-
fied by the objections of the friends of said pauper.   Thus
instead of putting the poor into the care of strangers the
Islanders keep them, at less expense, among their friends
and kindred, and the town authorities see that they receive proper attention.

SUFFERING KATY.

More than fifty years ago, in a comfortable cottage
overlooking the Sound, and Montauk, from the west side
of Block Island, a pious man looked upon the sun setting
in the western waters, to see it rise no more.   About two
months after he went to his rest his daughter Katy was
born.   While prattling upon her mother's knee, and frol-
icking about the door-yard in childhood; while strolling
over the fields and plucking wild flowers, and along the
beach gathering shells and pretty pebbles in girlhood;
and while enjoying the mirthful society of "young men
and maidens," it was well for Katy that she knew not
how long and dark a cloud was to gather over her earthly
horizon.   No youthful female with a higher, broader

brow; with more intellectual features, all most perfectly chiseled; with raven tresses, and black eyes more captivating than Katy, had walked upon the Island. But, on account of her accidental fall, suddenly the faces that were wont to meet her with smiles and gleeful words were changed, and brought her expressions of pity and words of sympathy.

Katy received an injury at the age of twenty which laid her upon a bed of great suffering. Her strength was so much reduced as to deprive her of the privilege of walking for one long year. She had previously become a member of the Free-Will Baptist church of Block Island, and bore her suffering with Christian submission. "Heaven hides the book of fate," and it was a blessing to her that she could not read in it her future. This first year of pain was only one of the ten in succession. These ten long years of painful days and "wearisome nights" were only the beginning of Katy's sorrows. One year was added to another, keeping her constantly upon her bed, until a score of them had passed by her cottage without bringing to it relief. The companions of her youth came to her bedside less frequently. Some were pressed with domestic cares, some had moved away, all had changed, and some were buried who had expected to follow Katy to her resting place. Twenty years in bed! Had she said, when first prostrated, like Job, "When shall I arise and the night be gone?" who could have supposed that the reply, "twenty long years," would have been only a partial answer to her inquiry? Yes, ten more than twenty years of pain were in store for poor Katy. She has patiently worn them away. Thirty years of her life have been spent upon a bed of pain and sorrow.

During this long period of suffering, Katy has managed much of her time to take care of herself almost entirely. No place among her kindred, however comfortable, has been able to give her such contentment as the roof beneath which she was born, and the room in which she has suffered so much. There, by means of sticks with hooks and forks on the ends of them, like those used by merchants to reach things up high, she has helped herself. There, with shelves on the wall back of her bed, and on the walls at its head, she has reached things without troubling others. There, with a small cooking-stove near her bed, with her hooks and forks that have handles five or six feet long, after the fire has been kindled, she has done the little cooking required, with some feelings of independence. There, with fuel properly placed, she has replenished her own fire without calling upon others. It would astonish many to know how much she has done to help herself during these thirty invalid years. In so doing, her will and ingenuity have been developed, as may be seen in her conversation. In the meantime her religious sensibilities have been chastened and refined as gold in the furnace. Reading the Bible has occupied much of her time when health would permit. Committing poetry to memory, and often repeating it, has also been a source of comfort. As she has considered herself, for more than twenty years, so near to death's door, the following stanzas have been repeated by her many times, as appropriate for others to remember:

> " These eyes that she seldom could close,
>   By sorrow forbidden to sleep,
>   Sealed up in the sweetest repose,
>   Have strangely forgotten to weep.

> " Her months of affliction are o'er,
>   Her days and her nights of distress,
>   We see her in anguish no more,
>   She has gained her happy release.

> " Then let us forbear to complain,
>   Since she is removed from our sight;
>   We soon shall behold her again,
>   With new and increasing delight."

After thirty years of pain and privation—of youthful hopes blasted, of social privileges denied, much of the time alone, dependent upon the kindness of a few kindred and neighbors, waiting from year to year for death to release her from sorrow, it would be better than an eloquent sermon on the text: "Godliness with contentment is great gain," for some who murmur at their lot to look into Katy's humble abode and hear her sweetly say, as she has said: "*During all my sufferings I have thanked God for my many blessings.*"

Thirty years—fifteen hundred and sixty weeks, ten thousand nine hundred and fifty days on a bed of suffering, *thanking God for many blessings!* Well, Katy has had many blessings, in comparison with one who for many more years begged for a drop of water. She has had blessings unseen by mortal vision, as well as many from the hands of friends and kindred, and while she still lingers she is blessed with a freedom from thousands of vexations common to those basking in the pride and sunshine of society. She has beautifully exemplified Shakespeare's saying:

> "There is some soul of goodness in things evil,
> Would men observingly distil it out."

Since the above was written, she died March 2, 1877, and was buried in the Island cemetery. This sketch was read, and her favorite verses sung at her funeral.

31